ACCLAIM FOR SARAH E. LADD

"The swoon-worthy romance of Jane Austen meets the suspense of Charlotte Brontë in Sarah Ladd's enthralling *The Letter from Briarton Park*. As Cassandra navigates the mystery of her own life, it is absolutely clear that family—either of blood or heart—are where she, and we, ultimately find our home."

—JOY CALLAWAY, INTERNATIONAL BESTSELLING AUTHOR OF *THE FIFTH AVENUE ARTISTS SOCIETY* AND *THE GREENBRIER RESORT*

"*The Light at Wyndcliff* is a richly atmospheric Regency novel, reminiscent of the works of Victoria Holt and Daphne du Maurier. The storm-swept Cornish coast is a character unto itself, forming the perfect backdrop for an expertly woven tale of secrets, danger, and heartfelt romance. A riveting and deeply emotional read."

—MIMI MATTHEWS, *USA TODAY* BESTSELLING AUTHOR OF THE PARISH ORPHANS OF DEVON SERIES

"[*The Light at Wyndcliff*] expertly deploys elements of gothic mystery . . . The descriptions of the dilapidated property add dark, delicious atmosphere . . . The atmosphere and intrigue keep the pages turning."

—*PUBLISHERS WEEKLY*

"[Ladd] faithfully depicts the rough Cornish coast of the 1820s, with its rocky coves and windswept moors, the slow-simmering romance between the attractive principals is skillfully done, the suspense is intriguing, and all is brought to a satisfying conclusion . . . This charmingly written, gentle tale of manners and romance hits the right notes."

—HISTORICAL NOVEL SOCIETY FOR *THE LIGHT AT WYNDCLIFF*

"Fans of Julie Klassen will love this."

—*PUBLISHERS WEEKLY* FOR *THE THIEF OF LANWYN MANOR*

"Cornwall's iconic sea cliffs are on display in *The Thief of Lanwyn Manor*, but it's the lyrical prose, rich historical detail, and layered characters that truly shine on the page. Fans of Regency romance will be instantly drawn in and happily lost within the pages."

—KRISTY CAMBRON, BESTSELLING AUTHOR OF *THE PARIS DRESSMAKER* AND THE LOST CASTLE NOVELS

"*Northanger Abbey* meets *Poldark* against the resplendent and beautifully realized landscape of Cornwall. Ladd shines a spotlight on the limitations of women in an era where they were deprived of agency and instead were commodities in transactions of business and land. The thinking-woman's romance, *The Thief of Lanwyn Manor* is an unputdownable escape."

—RACHEL MCMILLAN, AUTHOR OF *THE LONDON RESTORATION*

"Brimming with dangerous secrets, rich characters, and the hauntingly beautiful descriptions Sarah Ladd handles so well, 1800s Cornwall is brought vividly to life in this well-crafted tale that kept me glued to the pages."

—ABIGAIL WILSON, AUTHOR OF *MASQUERADE AT MIDDLECREST ABBEY*, FOR *THE GOVERNESS OF PENWYTHE HALL*

"Lovers of sweet and Christian romance alike will fall in love with Delia's strength amid the haunting backdrop of her tragic past and the Cornish coast."

—JOSI S. KILPACK, WHITNEY AWARD–WINNING AUTHOR OF THE MAYFIELD FAMILY SERIES, FOR *THE GOVERNESS OF PENWYTHE HALL*

"Absolutely captivating! Once I started reading, I couldn't put down *The Governess of Penwythe Hall*. This blend of *Jane Eyre*, Jane Austen, and *Jamaica Inn* has it all. Intrigue. Danger. Poignant moments. And best of all a sweet, sweet love story. This is by far my favorite Sarah Ladd book."

—MICHELLE GRIEP, CHRISTY AWARD–WINNING AUTHOR OF THE ONCE UPON A DICKENS CHRISTMAS SERIES

"A strong choice for fans of historical fiction, especially lovers of Elizabeth Gaskell's *North and South*. It will also appeal to admirers of Kristy Cambron and Tracie Peterson."

—LIBRARY JOURNAL FOR *THE WEAVER'S DAUGHTER*

"A gently unfolding love story set amid the turmoil of the early Industrial Revolution. [*The Weaver's Daughter* is] a story of betrayal, love, and redemption, all beautifully rendered in rural England."

—ELIZABETH CAMDEN, RITA AWARD–WINNING AUTHOR

"With betrayals, murders, and criminal activity disrupting the peace at Fellsworth, Ladd fills the pages with as much intrigue as romance. A well-crafted story for fans of Regency novels."

—PUBLISHERS WEEKLY FOR *A STRANGER AT FELLSWORTH*

"Ladd's story, with its menace and cast of seedy London characters, feels more like a work of Dickens than a Regency . . . A solid outing."

—PUBLISHERS WEEKLY ON *THE CURIOSITY KEEPER*

"A delightful read, rich with period details. Ladd crafts a couple the reader roots for from the very beginning and a plot that keeps the reader guessing until the end."

—SARAH M. EDEN, BESTSELLING AUTHOR OF
FOR ELISE ON *THE CURIOSITY KEEPER*

"My kind of book! The premise grabbed my attention from the first lines, and I eagerly returned to its pages. I think my readers will enjoy *The Heiress of Winterwood*."

—JULIE KLASSEN, BESTSELLING, AWARD-WINNING AUTHOR

"If you are a fan of Jane Austen and *Jane Eyre*, you will love Sarah E. Ladd's debut."

—USATODAY.COM ON *THE HEIRESS OF WINTERWOOD*

The
Letter
from
Briarton
Park

Also by Sarah E. Ladd

The
Letter
from
Briarton
Park

Sarah E. Ladd

THOMAS NELSON
Since 1798

The Letter from Briarton Park

Published in Nashville, Tennessee, by Thomas Nelson. Thomas Nelson is a registered trademark of HarperCollins Christian Publishing, Inc.

Published in association with the Books & Such Literary Management, 52 Mission Circle, Suite 122, PMB 170, Santa Rosa, California 95409-5370, www. booksandsuch.com.

Thomas Nelson titles may be purchased in bulk for educational, business, fundraising, or sales promotional use. For information, please email SpecialMarkets@ThomasNelson.com.

Publisher's Note: This novel is a work of fiction. Names, characters, places, and incidents are either products of the author's imagination or used fictitiously. All characters are fictional, and any similarity to people living or dead is purely coincidental.

Library of Congress Cataloging-in-Publication Data

Names: Ladd, Sarah E., author.
Title: The letter from Briarton Park / Sarah E. Ladd.
Description: Nashville, Tennessee : Thomas Nelson, [2022] | Summary:
   "In Regency England, one letter will alter a young woman's fate when it
   summons her to Briarton Park-an ancient place that holds the secrets of her
   past and the keys to her future"-- Provided by publisher.
Identifiers: LCCN 2021043227 (print) | LCCN 2021043228 (ebook) | ISBN
   9780785246725 (paperback) | ISBN 9780785246770 (epub) | ISBN
   9780785246787
Classification: LCC PS3612.A3565 L47 2022 (print) | LCC PS3612.A3565
   (ebook) | DDC 813/.6--dc23
LC record available at https://lccn.loc.gov/2021043227
LC ebook record available at https://lccn.loc.gov/2021043228

Printed in the United States of America

22 23 24 25 26 LSC 5 4 3 2 1

This novel is dedicated to KBR and KC—with gratitude

Prologue

DENTON SCHOOL FOR YOUNG LADIES
LAMBY, ENGLAND
AUTUMN 1811

Harboring anger against a woman on her deathbed was wrong. Cassandra Hale knew it to be true. How could any sensible, benevolent human feel anything but compassion for the dying?

Yet as she stared down at the woman who had been like a mother to her, indignation flared within Cassandra's chest. The words spoken just minutes ago had confirmed the unthinkable.

She'd been betrayed. Lied to. *For her entire life.*

One might surmise that Mrs. Denton had been speaking from her fever or was delirious with sickness. And yet, despite her illness, she was quite lucid.

A biting wind whipped its way through the open bedchamber window, as if eager to divulge its opinion of the current situation. It fluttered the curtains and stole into the room's corners. Eager for a diversion, Cassandra stood from her chair next to the bed and moved to the window. She nudged the heavy wool curtain aside and gripped the painted sash, preparing to close it, then stopped. The black murkiness of a stormy night met her. She squeezed her eyes shut as the cool air buffeted her face, her neck, her arms.

She shivered in spite of the fury raging within her.

This can't be true. None of it.

"Come here, Cassandra." The voice, even in its frailty, boasted an authority that would snap even the most iron-willed to attention. "I've more to tell you."

"More?" Cassandra scoffed and slammed the sash closed with more strength than she'd intended, then pivoted away from the window. "I'm not sure I want to hear it."

"Even so, it must be said. And you need to hear it before I'm gone."

Summoning fortitude, Cassandra returned to the bed and made herself gaze upon Mrs. Denton once more. The gaunt woman, a mere shadow of her former self, lay beneath thin white linens. She'd always been petite and wiry, but now those physical attributes worked against her, making her appear feeble and weak.

Life would not linger in her long.

Grief seized Cassandra in its numbing grip, forcing her anger at bay.

Oh, if only Mrs. Denton had shared this information sooner!

It had been nineteen years since Cassandra first arrived at Denton School for Young Ladies when she was but five years of age. In all the years she'd been acquainted with the headmistress, first as a student and then as a teacher, she'd known—nay, believed— Mrs. Jane Denton to be honest, loyal, worthy of every esteem. Never had Cassandra known her to misrepresent the truth or bend facts to suit her needs.

Until this moment.

A struggle raged within Cassandra—a devastating struggle between the need to respect the woman who'd raised her and the compulsion to demand the truth.

"You're furious with me. 'Tis understandable. But what have I told you time and time again? Such emotion will only cloud your judgment and diminish your ability to react rationally. You must listen to me now."

"I—I don't understand," Cassandra faltered, willing her tone to remain steady when it so earnestly insisted on brashness. "You told me you didn't know who my parents were or if they were even living. You declared so numerous times."

Mrs. Denton's sparse eyebrows rose, even as her chin remained tilted proudly, defiantly. "I told you only what was necessary. To protect you. To protect . . . others. I made a vow."

"A vow? To whom?"

Mrs. Denton's icy eyes sharpened with conviction. "That, I cannot say."

Cassandra's heart pounded. "Then why say anything if you are unwilling to divulge the entire truth? All these years I trusted you when you said—"

Airy coughs racked the older woman's body, silencing Cassandra with their severity. In a single instant Mrs. Denton's vulnerability and fragility reappeared, reminding Cassandra of just how afflicted the woman was. She retrieved a fresh handkerchief, drew close to her former headmistress, and pressed the embroidered fabric into her wrinkled hand.

After the coughing fit subsided, Mrs. Denton's head lolled back against the pillow. "There, on the bureau. That letter is for you."

With her attention redirected, Cassandra approached the mahogany chest of drawers. The missive's red wax seal was broken, and when she lifted the letter, money shifted from within, nearly dropping to the ground.

"That is yours," whispered Mrs. Denton. "Take it."

Cassandra stared at the banknotes balanced on her palm. "But I—"

"Take the money, read the letter, and I'll say no more on the matter." Violent coughs seized her body, and she pressed the cloth to her mouth. "Now I've nothing to regret."

Cassandra cringed at the sight of the crimson stain on the handkerchief.

Blood.

"Mr. Duncan!"

The surgeon, who'd been waiting in the corridor, rushed in at Cassandra's call, pushed past her, and hastened to the bed. "You must leave now, Miss Hale."

She heard the order but could not move. Panic, even more powerful than betrayal's sting, paralyzed her.

"Leave, now! And send the housekeeper for the vicar."

Cassandra staggered backward, as if the earth shifted beneath her feet. She promptly located the housekeeper, sent the woman on her task, and retreated to the darkened corridor outside of the sickroom. For where else could she possibly go?

As she paced the narrow space, the uneven wooden floor groaned beneath her weight, as if commiserating in her agony. She strained to hear anything from within the chamber, but all was quiet.

Now, with nothing left to do but wait, a rare, solitary tear slid down her cheek. In the last quarter of an hour, everything Cassandra thought she knew about her life had changed, and in the coming hours, there would be no returning.

She swiped away the moisture with her long cambric sleeve, unfolded the letter, and held it up to the candlelight flickering from the sconce.

My Dear Cassandra,

You must forgive the silence these many years, but surely you understand that some situations are delicate. I have a great deal of information to share with you about your family. Circumstances have evolved, and now the time has come when we may speak of such things. I sincerely hope that doors that have been closed may open.

I would not presume to intrude, but I invite you to come to my home, Briarton Park, in North Yorkshire, at your earliest convenience. My health prevents me from traveling, but if the trip is agreeable to you, send word and a carriage will be sent to convey you here.

The enclosed funds are rightfully yours and for your personal needs—some of which I hope you will use for the journey. I know you must have many questions, and if you are willing, all will be shared in due time.

With optimism,
Robert Clark

Who was Robert Clark? And why would this money be rightfully hers?

She hungrily scanned the letter again in case she'd missed any information.

The date struck her: 24 June 1809. Two and a half years ago. Two and a half years! Had Mrs. Denton kept silent about the letter all this time? It clearly had been read, judging by the broken seal and wrinkled paper.

Hysterical voices and haphazard footsteps echoed from behind the closed door, snapping her back to the present.

Mrs. Denton, the woman who had raised her, taught her, cared for her, and now employed her, was going to die.

And the life that Cassandra thought she knew was going to die with her.

Chapter 1

North Yorkshire, England
Autumn 1811

James Warrington met his half sister's determined gaze. A pink flush on Rachel's high cheekbones emphasized her tightly drawn lips. Shimmery tears brightened her silver eyes but did little to dim the rage brewing within them.

He braced himself for a battle.

A battle he was not entirely sure he would win.

"You are to have no more contact with Richard Standish," James articulated. "No more secret letters or clandestine meetings. Am I clear?"

Rachel met his stare with unmasked defiance, yet she remained silent.

He steadied his resolve. "Tell me you understand and that you'll obey me."

For the briefest flicker of a moment, he thought she might soften and perhaps even comply, but then in a sudden whirl of patterned saffron chintz, she spun away and stormed to the broad window. "You are cruel, James! How dare you behave so meanly!"

It would be simple to be drawn further into an argument, but where would such a response take them?

The gray morning light slid in through the front parlor's tall windows, highlighting the tremble of her thin shoulders. He was not sure when this metamorphosis from content child to morose sixteen-year-old had occurred. Regardless, he hated to see her cry.

He tempered his voice. "'Tis for your own good, Rachel."

"How do you know that?" she challenged.

"Because I know his sort."

"His sort? How would you even know what *sort* he is?" Her voice shrilled. "You've refused to even speak with him! You're the most prejudiced, condescending, ridiculous—"

"Enough, Rachel."

"But you know nothing about him!" She hurled her words like shots from a cannon. "Richard is kind. Considerate. You'd do well to emulate him, and I—"

"I said, enough!" His words reverberated from the plaster moldings on the ceiling, silencing her. He cleared his throat and straightened his neckcloth, buying himself time to soothe his mounting frustration and select his words with care. "I'm your guardian. You will abide by my instructions, and nothing else need be said on the matter."

Rachel's nostrils flared as she pivoted to face him. "Very well then, Brother. What do you suggest I do? You and you alone forced us to sever ties with everything and everyone that is familiar in Plymouth. Then you bring us out to some godforsaken place where there is no polite society whatsoever. So, what now? You decide whom I speak with? Whom I love?"

Love? He jerked at the word. He didn't know whether to laugh or cringe. What could this green girl possibly know about romantic love?

He sniffed. "When you are old enough to make decisions *responsibly*, then you may decide such things. Until then, I must intervene. As for Standish, the boy is penniless, with no respectable connections. He's undoubtedly learned of your inheritance. How he even managed to speak with you in the first place is beyond me."

"So my only attractive quality is my inheritance?" Her left eyebrow arched. "You are quite right. He could not possibly love me for any other reason."

"That's not what I said."

"Need I remind you that you were penniless once too?"

"Yes, I was. Very poor indeed. But I did not acquire my wealth through marriage."

She tipped her chin upward, color flooding her cheeks and certainty curving the corners of her mouth. "You could not be more wrong. My inheritance is not why Richard loves me."

James hesitated. How could he make her understand? Men like Richard Standish were after one thing—money. It did not matter if he was eighteen or eighty. His intentions would not change. When Rachel came of age, she'd have plenty of money at her disposal, thanks to their father's shrewd business practices late in his life. How would Standish be then, once he owned every farthing she brought to the union? James would wager not the charming, considerate man she believed him to be.

He heaved a sigh and crossed the room before he dropped onto the wingback chair flanking the fire grate. He allowed several seconds of silence to settle, hoping it would calm them both, and then leaned forward and propped his elbows on his knees. "Rachel, you've much more to offer a suitor than an inheritance. Much more. But as a woman of fortune, you must be certain that the man you choose truly loves *you* and not your pocketbook."

"And what about what I want?" she snapped back in offense before his last words left his lips. "What about whose company I choose?"

"You should choose someone who is stable and steady, proven and established. Standish is reckless. Consider, he risks your reputation by sneaking onto our property at night. By sending you letters under an assumed name. You can't think for a single moment that his behavior is in any way appropriate. And his surreptitious actions—the underhandedness and the furtive nature of it all—are precisely why I forbid it."

"You won't permit him to call any other way. Of course he must resort to ploys! You have created an impossible situation for us."

"For us?" James stood once more. "Rachel, for all intents and purposes, you are still a child. There is no *us*. Not with him. Not with anyone."

Tears now flowed unrestrained down her round, ruddy cheeks. "Are you so miserable that you must destroy not only your own life but also the lives of everyone around you? This is your fault. All of it. If Elizabeth were alive, she would understand. She always did."

James winced at the sound of his deceased wife's name. Two years since her death and he still tensed when he heard it, especially when it was hurled at him as Rachel just did. But she was right in one aspect: Elizabeth would have known what to say to soothe his sister's anger.

"I hate you. I hate this house!" Rachel choked out the words between fresh sobs. "I hate this sad, despicable village. I hate everything about it!" She bolted past him out of the parlor, the soft soles of her slippers echoing on the stone floor.

He stared at the empty spot until the footsteps subsided, trying to make sense of the words they had just flung at one another.

No, he had not won that battle. He'd not even come close. He might have even made it worse. But how was one to handle such a situation?

After being alone with his thoughts for several minutes, he heard light footsteps approaching. He turned to see his mother-in-law, Mrs. Margaret Towler. An air of condescension accompanied her every movement, and she smoothed a rare wayward silver curl from her brow with a long, bony finger.

"That young woman has a dangerous attitude about her." Her voice was calm. Dignified. Measured. "And thanks to her unconscionable clamoring, every last maid in the house knows of it. Best to tame that audaciousness while there is still time to do so."

This woman's similarity to her late daughter was evident. They both had tall frames, narrow faces, and straight noses. But their similarities ended with their physical attributes.

Mrs. Towler clicked her tongue with assumed authority. "If not controlled, she'll bring about her own ruin, not to mention that of the rest of the family."

James knew she spoke the truth, but he'd not speak critically of Rachel to another—especially to a woman who was already disposed to dislike her.

The layered ebony bombazine of her mourning gown rustled as she stepped closer to the fire in the broad hearth, her thin hands clasped firmly before her. "You must be strong and firm, James. It's the only way to handle such a child."

He stifled a huff. What could Margaret Towler possibly know about handling a girl like Rachel? Elizabeth, Mrs. Towler's only child, had been reserved to a fault and eager to please those around her. Nothing like his spirited sister.

Mrs. Towler reached to straighten a porcelain figurine on the stone mantel, and only once it was angled properly did she resume speaking. "You're right to forbid contact with that rogue. These past years have been difficult on Rachel—first Elizabeth's passing, then the relocation, and now this. He's playing to her vulnerabilities. I would speak with her, but you know her nature. She would only heed Elizabeth's word."

James did not look away from the fire. He and his mother-in-law disagreed on so much, but where Elizabeth was concerned, they'd both sing her praises. Elizabeth had been the one to navigate their family through every situation.

But her unexpected death upended everything.

In one single night a fever swooped in, as diabolic as any incubus, and claimed her. He'd found himself the widowed father of two small daughters, sole guardian to a feisty adolescent, and honor bound to provide for his mother-in-law without a clue as to how to proceed on any front.

He crossed to look out over the pristine grounds through the parlor window. A glittery morning frost settled over the gardens that formed the front lawn of Briarton Park, capping the ash trees and the manicured hedges. A small bit of blue sky fought its way through the rolling pewter clouds, and bare branches in the nearby copse of trees swayed in the menacing wind.

But something caught his eye—a willowy figure in a pelisse of dusky plum traversed the neatly paved path approaching the house. He retrieved his watch fob and popped it open, then frowned. It was too early for callers. "Who's that woman?"

Mrs. Towler joined him at the window, bringing with her a heavy scent of rosewater and hyacinth. "No doubt one of the parish women collecting for the poor again. According to Mrs. Helock, they've been here twice already this week." She shook her graying head and scowled. "I do wish that vicar would monitor such actions more closely. I'll tell Mrs. Helock to send her on her way."

His mother-in-law's footsteps padded in retreat, but James did not move.

He'd never seen the woman before. Surely he would have remembered. She wore no bonnet, leaving her chestnut locks free to flutter about her face. Her movements suggested a measure of demureness and grace—the sort that resulted from a gentle upbringing. No, she could not be a village woman.

When he snapped from his momentary trance, he could almost laugh at noticing such details. Had he not spent the bulk of the morning discouraging his sister from entangling herself in infatuation and fancy? He'd be wise to take the same advice and avoid such thoughts altogether. His responsibilities were with his family and his business, and he had no reason to contemplate implausible associations.

But even as he considered this, the inexplicable sense stole over him that this woman, with her wild hair and delicate movements, was not here by accident.

And whether he was avoiding the task at hand or merely seeking a diversion, he was determined to unearth what would bring such a creature to Briarton Park.

Chapter 2

Be brave, Cassandra.

She pinned her attention on the iron gate just before her—the last physical barrier separating her from Briarton Park. It had been nearly five days of arduous travel since she departed the tiny village of Lamby, and now that she'd almost arrived at her destination, her resolve wavered.

"What have I told you?" The late Mrs. Denton's words haunted her as Cassandra placed a gloved hand on the gate. *"Emotions will cloud your judgment and weaken your ability to react rationally."*

She paused long enough to rub her thumb over the small bit of rust bleeding through the intricately formed, beautiful black ironwork. If the gate alone boasted such elegance, she could only imagine the magnificence of the country house waiting beyond the road's bend. Cassandra leaned into the gate and it swung open, creaking in the morning stillness, giving a bleak voice to the noisy qualms and foreboding misgivings that had been her constant traveling companions.

Once inside the grounds, she ran her other hand down the front of the worn violet wool traveling pelisse one of the teachers had gifted her prior to the journey. The deeply set wrinkles and the mud spattered on the hem bore testament to the long days of travel.

She'd departed Lamby with all her earthly possessions—her money, both her earnings from teaching and the remaining amount from the letter; the letter of recommendation Mrs. Denton had written on her behalf before she died; a small dagger the school's manservant had given her for protection; and her few items of clothing.

And, of course, the letter from Mr. Clark.

With the exception of the money and letters, which had been safely stowed in her reticule, and the dagger, which was carefully tucked in her boot, she'd left the other items at the Green Ox Inn in the village of Anston, where she'd spent an uncomfortable, sleepless night.

A chilly gust swept down from the fading ancient ash trees lining the walk, bringing with it a shower of russet-colored leaves and the whisper that this place might hold the key to her past.

And, more importantly, her future.

Forcing her hesitance to remain at bay, she placed one foot in front of the other. For what choice did she have? Mrs. Denton was dead. The school had been sold to the master of a boys' school, and female teachers were no longer required. She had nothing, no connections, save for the hope that Mr. Clark's letter might uncover information about her family and ultimately a situation where she might belong.

She'd responded to the letter the day after she received it, when the sting of Mrs. Denton's betrayal still pricked her heart and grief dominated her emotions. Nearly a fortnight had passed since then, and she'd received no response. Had she been more prudent, she'd have waited for a reply before embarking on such a grueling journey, but with circumstances as they were, she had no time to waste, and every passing day was a day lost.

Armed with more questions than answers, she tightened her grip on her reticule and continued down the path, noting the deep ruts and hoofprints that suggested the road had recently been traveled.

She rounded yet another bend, and the sight that met her stopped her completely.

Briarton Park.

She'd expected it to be large, stately, but this . . . this might be a castle.

The stately home rose three stories above the polished grounds, with symmetrical gables at each end and pale gray sandstone chimneys randomly dispersed over the slate roof. Even the fading ivy clinging to the facade added to the home's imposing grandeur. Not even the vicar's house at the end of the lane in Lamby could compare in scope.

Summoning courage, she followed the graveled path to another iron gate in a sturdy stone wall that separated the formal grounds from the more wooded area. She stepped through, noting how the road continued parallel to the house before it split into two on the other side at an orchard's edge.

It was there she noticed a flash of indigo amid the orchard's subdued grays and beiges. A girl of seven, or perhaps eight, perched in the branches of one of the apple trees. Ebony hair lashed about her small, pale face, and she appeared to be watching her.

They were too far apart to speak, so Cassandra lifted her hand in greeting.

Instead of responding, the girl dropped from the tree and disappeared behind the wall. Almost simultaneously, the tortured cry of a poorly played pianoforte wailed from somewhere within the house.

With her curiosity growing, Cassandra made her way to the paneled door, richly ornate with delicately carved vines and leaves. She lifted the round metal knocker and tapped it against the wood. It echoed, deep and hollow, in the morning's quiet.

The music from inside did not stop, nor did she hear any other movement. She knocked again, eased away from the door, and waited.

At length a stout-looking footman opened the door, dressed neatly in emerald-green and tan livery.

She tightened her grip on her reticule and forced confidence to her voice. "I'd like to speak with Mr. Robert Clark, please."

The footman, with a shock of black hair and a deeply clefted chin, only stared. Had he not heard her?

Before she could repeat herself, a portly woman, clad in crisp black with a severe, disapproving expression, stepped in front of the servant. "I'll see to this, John."

Cassandra squared her shoulders. "I wish to speak with Mr. Clark, please."

The older lady raked her sharp gaze over Cassandra's traveling clothes, landing on the mud streaking the gown at her ankles. "Mr. Clark is dead."

Cassandra winced at the words. She did not have time to contemplate them further, for the woman began to close the door.

"Wait." Cassandra reached her hand forward to prevent the latch from catching. "Please, a moment."

With a huff of annoyance the woman gripped the edge of the door and nodded to the footman, dismissing him.

Determined to keep the woman's attention, Cassandra blurted, "My name is Cassandra Hale. I've come a very long way. May I speak with the master? It's very important."

The woman shook her head. "Mr. Warrington is very busy and will not be able to take callers today."

Mr. Warrington. She had the name of the current owner at least.

Sensing her time was limited, Cassandra spouted the first question that came to mind. "And are you the mistress of the house?"

"I should say not!" The woman's scoff denoted superiority. "I'm the housekeeper, Mrs. Helock. And if you are here to seek employment, I suggest you come around to the servants' entrance."

"No, no, you misunderstand," Cassandra hastened to correct her. "I'm not here about employment."

"Even so, you should not be using this entrance at all. You should—"

"May I be of help?"

The masculine voice startled them both. A tall man with sandy hair and broad shoulders approached from the corridor. He did not appear annoyed. Indeed, his presence and affable tone immediately put her at ease in light of Mrs. Helock's brashness.

The woman cast Cassandra a warning glance. "I can see to this, Mr. Warrington. You needn't bother yourself."

"Nonsense, Mrs. Helock. The young lady asked to speak with me." He rubbed his hands together before him. "I've a few moments before I leave. Tell me, miss. How can I assist you?"

Chapter 3

Cassandra's stomach fluttered as she followed Mr. Warrington from the entrance hall to the much larger great hall. After all that had transpired over the past few weeks, she'd finally arrived at the place where her questions could possibly be answered.

Even as fresh optimism soared, a stinging prick of inadequacy enveloped her as she lifted her gaze to the stately oak beams running the length of the high plaster ceiling. Her gaze fell to the chamber's two paned windows that framed the scenic grounds. Ample gray morning light flooded through, illuminating the long, narrow table centered in the hall with the serving pieces atop it, the presence of which suggested this space was one used for receiving and entertaining guests on formal occasions. The absence of the pianoforte music upon her arrival had only intensified the stillness—and magnificence—of the room. All around her paintings and portraits in gilded frames adorned the paneled walls, bringing the chamber alive with rich history.

She did not belong in a place as grand as this. Not with her sullied attire and wrinkled gown. She was a simple teacher with no real connections to speak of. Yet the man who had invited her here had lived within these walls.

And she was determined to unearth every detail he'd wanted to share with her.

She steadied her thoughts and tempered her expectations. Like Mrs. Denton instructed—emotions could not be permitted to interfere.

As they walked to the chamber's center, Cassandra ignored the thudding within her chest and focused instead on her host, who was likely her best source of information.

Mr. Warrington epitomized everything she imagined a country gentleman to be, not that she had ever really met one. From his tall, straight stature to his buff buckskin breeches and polished top boots, his very presence boasted confidence and authority. The cut of his dark blue coat and its defined lapels emphasized the broad expanse of his shoulders, and an easy smile added to his charm. He was handsome, with a strong jawline and thick, light hair that curled just wildly enough to make him appear approachable. But it was his own easiness in his surroundings that made her feel even more out of place in this elegant room. She'd invaded his territory uninvited. Unannounced.

A shimmer of color through the arch at the room's west end caught her eye. It was a young woman, younger than Cassandra, in a winter gown of rich, dark yellow. A mass of unruly sable curls rippled down her back, and a loosely woven shawl draped over her shoulders. She appeared pale. Sad. She paused in the doorway, staring at Cassandra, but said nothing and continued slowly on her way.

"Did I hear you say you're seeking Robert Clark?" Mr. Warrington, who apparently had not noticed the young woman, said, bringing her back to the conversation at hand.

"Yes, sir. I am."

"He is dead, I'm sorry to say." Mr. Warrington moved to the fire and stoked the waning embers.

"Yes, Mrs. Helock told me." Cassandra joined him by the fire as it roared back to life, grateful for the warmth after the chilly walk.

He returned the poker to the stand, wiped his hands together, then nodded toward the portrait to the left of the mantel. "That's Clark's likeness, or so I'm told. The paintings were all here when I acquired Briarton."

A thrill of connectedness surged through her at the bit of information, and she leaned forward to assess the man in the portrait. Sorrel hair. Obsidian eyes. The man in the painting was young, but even so, she was drawn to his soulful, somber expression. Robert Clark might be dead, but having this image to carry with her made him seem more real and heightened her enthusiasm about this search.

What secret did that man hold?

What secrets did he hold about *her*?

"Odd that you came to visit and did not know he was deceased." Mr. Warrington turned from the painting back to her.

His voice held no cynicism, and yet Cassandra suspected if she was to be successful in her quest, she needed to develop a new tactic. And quickly.

Perceiving that it would be best to appeal to his sense of rationality, she pulled the letter from her reticule. "I've never met him, but you see, I received this letter from Mr. Clark. Clearly it was written years ago, but it only recently came into my possession. I did write a response a couple of weeks ago, but I am not sure it ever arrived."

"You sent a missive here?" A frown shadowed his otherwise congenial expression. "That is likely my error then. Occasionally I receive letters addressed to the former owner, and I never open them."

Encouraged by his interest, she extended the missive toward him. "He indicated that he has—well, *had*—news to share with me about my family."

He accepted the letter and unfolded it.

Cassandra studied his face as he read it, hoping for some spark, some hint of familiarity, that would help her draw conclusions. But after several seconds he refolded it, tapped it against his hand as if pondering what he'd just read, and then extended it to her. "It's definitely intriguing, but I'm afraid I can't offer much information. I purchased this house after his death. I never met him either." His voice held a tone of finality to it, as if he was done with the conversation.

She shifted, resisting the urge to panic. So many questions lingered. She could not give up. Not yet. "Is there nothing that you know of him? Please, I've traveled a very long way. Any bit you can think of would be so helpful."

He drew a deep breath and looked upward, as if searching his memory. "In addition to this house, Mr. Clark owned two mills near here. I now own Briarton House and the Weyton Mill, but his son, Peter Clark, inherited and operates the other wool mill, Clark Mill. I suggest you speak with him."

His son! Surely, of all people, his son would be able to shed light. "Peter Clark, you said?"

"Yes. He lives in Ambleton. Next village over to the east."

The distant, dissonant pianoforte music she had heard earlier resumed.

Mr. Warrington cringed. Then his expression softened to an easy grin. "That would be my sister, Rachel. She's the musician of the family."

Cassandra let out a little laugh. "Yes, I—I heard it as I came up the drive."

"I think everyone's heard it from here to Bristol," he teased, as if amused at his own little joke, before he redirected their conversation back to the topic at hand. "You said you've traveled far. Where is it you are from?"

"Lamby. A small village outside of London."

"London? That's a far piece."

"Five days of travel." She nodded as some of the more treacherous legs of her journey flashed in her mind. "But if I can find some of the answers I seek, it will be worth every mile."

"I admire your optimism." He sobered, and concern momentarily darkened his features. "Do you have lodgings? Or other family nearby?"

"No, sir, no family, but I do have lodgings. At the Green Ox Inn."

He raised his brows. "The Green Ox Inn? I wish you luck. Perhaps you should try to meet with the vicar—a man by the name of Vincent North. He was the one to identify Mr. Clark as the man in the portrait when he called a few months back. I've heard only positive things about him, and I assume he's well connected with the people who have lived in the village. I don't know him well at all, but he'd be a better resource than anyone at Briarton Park."

As she opened her mouth to respond, the door behind them flung open. Two men, the taller one more finely dressed than the other, sauntered in comfortably, as if they'd done so a thousand times, and then both stopped short when they noticed her.

"Apologies," the larger man blurted, his narrow face still ruddy from the cool outside. "I wasn't aware you had company."

"Milton. Shepard." Mr. Warrington waved the men in, seemingly not surprised at the intrusion. "May I present Miss— Oh, wait." He turned his attention back to her. "I don't believe I caught your name."

"Cassandra Hale."

"Ah, very good. May I present Miss Cassandra Hale from Lamby. Miss Hale, this is Mr. Isaiah Milton, my associate, and Mr. William Shepard, the local magistrate."

"Miss Hale." Mr. Milton bowed politely, and she curtsied. As soon as the formalities were complete, an awkward silence hovered.

Mr. Warrington had been as accommodating as he could. Kind, she might even go so far as to say. But these men were here to speak with him, and Mr. Warrington made no other comments regarding her plight.

With a jolt the sense of intrusion intensified. "Please, Mr. Warrington, do not let me keep you from your business. I can show myself out."

"Did you walk here?" he inquired, as if an afterthought. "I can call the carriage if you're returning to the village."

"No, no, thank you." How silly she must seem, chasing after a letter in her crumpled pelisse and mud-caked nankeen half boots. She bobbed a quick curtsy, let her gaze fall one last time on the portrait to fix the image in her memory, and hurried back through the vestibule and out into the fresh air before another word could be uttered.

With her face flaming and the letter still gripped in her hand, she did not slow her pace or look back until she again reached the iron gate. Once she was under the privacy of the ancient ash's low-hanging boughs, she leaned against the sturdy tree and allowed herself the luxury of a few deep, cooling breaths. She turned her face upward to the intermittent bits of sunshine filtering through the leaves that were fighting to remain in their place as autumn strengthened its hold.

She struggled to make sense of what had just transpired.

She should be happy, she supposed. It would have been foolish to think that all her questions would be answered on her first visit to Briarton Park. At least now she knew the name of Mr. Clark's son and where he lived. And yet, despite these advances, she felt even more forlorn and isolated than before.

Mr. Clark's portrait, which had so entranced her in the moment, now haunted her, and she feared it would for a long time to come. Yet she forced the thought at bay. Lingering on sentiments was perilous, and like Mrs. Denton had said, emotions were of little use.

Cassandra tucked the letter in her reticule once more and trudged back over the arched stone bridge to the village.

She had to manage her expectations. She had to remember how important it was to protect her heart and her mind as she sailed through this voyage of discovery. For if she did not, no one would.

Chapter 4

It was not uncommon for Milton to stop by Briarton Park. He was, after all, Weyton Mill's supervisor. It was also not unheard of for Shepard, the local magistrate, to visit. It was, however, unusual for both of them to call at the same time, let alone before noon.

Sensing something was amiss, James focused his attention on the two men after Miss Hale had quit the chamber. "What is it?"

Milton's expression sobered, and he narrowed his gaze. "Riddy was found beaten outside the mill's south entrance this mornin'."

"What?" Shock lowered James's voice. "Is he all right?"

"Prob'ly will be, but right now he's in a pretty bad way."

Thomas Riddy, a man of near fifty, was a mainstay at Weyton Mill and had been instrumental in the ownership transfer when James purchased the business.

Rachel's piano music in the adjoining chamber fell silent. Fearing their conversation might be overheard, James ushered the men to his study in the house's east end. Once they were inside and the door closed, James turned to face his guests. "Tell me what's happened."

Milton shrugged his thin, stooped shoulders. "Some of the workers found Riddy on t' side of the road outside the gates. When he came to, he said he'd been pummeled by three men—the boys from o'er in Desdale."

Heat rose beneath James's cravat, and he folded his arms over his chest in contemplation. Both Riddy and Milton had warned James that the laborers from the nearby towns feared the new milling machinery he'd installed would take their jobs, and they had threatened violence as a means of intimidation.

Perhaps he should have paid the warnings greater heed.

Shepard pulled his enameled snuffbox from his waistcoat. "I can't say I'm surprised. That lot's been causing trouble for the mills up and down the river for weeks. *If* it's them, of course. They're not happy about the new looms coming up from the south."

James huffed. "They can't stop progress, no matter how many men they accost."

"Agreed." Shepard opened the box and offered it to James. When he refused, Shepard pinched a bit of the black powder between his thick fingers and inhaled it. "You know the Greycombe Mill north of here? Someone attempted to set fire to it after they had dismissed twenty workers. It set Mrs. Greycombe to such a state that she up and moved to London. And just the other day someone tried to set fire over at Tutter Mill some five miles west of here. Chased off by the dogs though."

In a sharp turn Shepard wiped his bulbous nose with the back of his pudgy hand. "Who was that woman? Hale, was it?"

James nodded, distracted by the change of topic. "Yes, Cassandra Hale. She stopped by inquiring after Robert Clark. She had a letter from him and said she had business with him. Family business, sounded like."

Shepard snapped his head up at the mention of Clark's name. "The man's been dead for years now. Didn't she know?"

"Apparently not. She seemed surprised to learn of his demise."

"Odd." Shepard's bushy brows drew together as he returned his snuffbox to his striped waistcoat. "Family business, was it? Bah, no telling what it could be. Clark always was a secretive fellow. She seemed harmless, but mind there's suspicious activity afoot. I'd be mighty careful who I allowed in my home, that's what I'd say, even someone as unintimidating as her. In fact, I'd consider hiring extra men to patrol at night if I were you. Dangerous times."

James stepped back as the corpulent man moved toward the door and placed his bell-shaped hat atop his auburn hair. "I'll be taking my leave now. I'm off to Desdale. Surely someone there knows something. Good day, gentlemen."

When all was quiet and he was alone with Milton, James dropped to the chair behind his desk.

Milton followed suit and sat in the chair opposite the desk. "'Twas a matter o' time, and we've both known it. Truth be told, we've been lucky 'til now."

James raked his fingers though his hair and recalled the events of the last several weeks. "Shepard's right. Hire men to watch the mill and the house, will you?"

"Figured you'd say that. Already sent out word." Milton smirked as he slouched, resting his bony elbow on the armrest. "You never met ol' Clark, did ye?"

"No. But it's strange that a woman is here asking after him after all this time. Isn't it?"

"'Course it is. But you didn't know Clark. Was a character, he was."

"How so?"

Milton cocked his head to the side and scratched his chin. "Ask twelve people what they thought of 'im, and you'd get twelve diff'rent answers. As for me, well, I respected him. I did. He was mighty shrewd but impulsive to a fault. 'Twas his downfall. Once he gave his word, it was solid as stone. That stubbornness, rightly or wrongly, is exactly why the mill was in such a sorry state when you bought it."

Shrewd. Impulsive. Stubborn.

Milton's words stayed with him even after the supervisor quit Briarton Park and James was alone in his study. The clock on the mantelpiece had not even struck the noon hour and already he'd argued with his sister, encountered a beautiful if not slightly mysterious woman, and learned of an attack on one of his workers.

As he absently tapped his fingers on the desk, he took fresh notice of a stack of unopened letters tucked under a newspaper. Miss Hale indicated she'd written a response, and sure enough, a letter addressed to Robert Clark was in the pile. He slid his finger under the seal and opened it.

Mr. Clark,

Please forgive this late response. I only just came into possession of the letter you wrote me dated 24 June 1809. I would very much like to meet you and discuss the family matters you referenced. My present circumstances have changed abruptly, so it is my intention to depart for Briarton Park and arrive in a few days. I sincerely hope this is still agreeable to you.

Until then, I thank you for your kind invitation.

Cassandra Hale

James doubted her arrival was part of a larger conspiracy against the mill owners, as Shepard had implied, but even so, questions lingered. Why was she here unaccompanied and without a carriage? What had she expected the outcome of this visit to be? Would she have need to return to Briarton Park?

He had more pressing matters to think on. His half sister. His mill. The locals determined to destroy it.

He studied the delicate penmanship on the missive's exterior. In all likelihood, he would never see Miss Hale again, even though he suspected the memory of her bewitching hazel eyes and the soft dimple at her mouth's corner would linger in his mind's eye for quite some time. Instead of returning the letter to the stack, he opened the drawer, tucked the letter inside, and closed it. He would just have to leave it at that.

The noon hour was approaching by the time Cassandra returned to Anston's high street. Sulky clouds now blotted out morning's earlier brightness, the effect of which conjured a dimness that matched her spirit.

The Green Ox Inn would be her temporary home for as long as she remained in this village. It stood just across the high street from the stone bridge. Presently, a muddy carriage with four bay horses stood in the broad, sodden courtyard, unloading a group of passengers. Two adolescent girls pealed with laughter and were quickly reprimanded by their mothers. At the sight, a pang of homesickness stabbed.

At this time of the day, her students would have been preparing for their midday meal. They would have just finished their arithmetic and reading studies. It had all been so predictable—a patterned comfort to which she'd grown accustomed.

But there was no school anymore.

No Mrs. Denton.

No *home*.

She missed her cozy chamber at the school—the one space that had truly ever been her own. She missed having others around her who cared for her, and for whom she cared in return. Mostly, she missed Mrs. Denton.

She sniffed and tossed her hair from her face. She would waste no time reminiscing. She'd remain steadfast. What other choice did she have? She had to focus on her remaining options, not the disappointments and the emotions threatening to dissuade her. Briarton

Park was only the first inquiry in her search. There had to be other people in this village who knew Mr. Robert Clark. And there was still his son.

She turned her attention to the cobbled high street with renewed interest. Modest shops with slate roofs and quaint thatched cottages lined the road, and at the far end loomed the church, ascending in stone blackened with age.

Perhaps Mr. Warrington was right. Perhaps the vicar could assist her. And there was no time like the present to find out.

The leaves swirled around her ankles and clung to the rough fabric of her pelisse as she made her way to the church, pausing to allow a group of plainly clad women to pass. At the iron gate to the churchyard, she slowed to assess the ancient structure. The grave-yard was tucked into the building's far side, sleeping eerily amid the ashes and oaks.

She hesitated. Cassandra had always avoided graveyards. Even as a child she'd shied away from them and squeezed her eyes shut as they crossed through the one at Lamby to reach the church's entrance. The idea of death, and the finality of it, unsettled her. Mrs. Denton had always said she did know Cassandra's parents' identity, but she'd also said she did not know if they were living. In Cassandra's young mind, that meant they could be in any graveyard—and that had unnerved her.

She pushed open the gate and stepped through. The graveyard was larger than she had initially imagined. As she traversed the path, she realized it curved around the back of the church and stretched beyond. Gravestones of every shape and size, darkened by age and now rain, dotted the grounds and family plots. An ancient stone wall, tinted with moss and covered with ivy, encircled all, as though not to allow anything to disturb what was sleeping within.

She swiped a drop of rain away from her face as she plodded forward, pausing to read each carved inscription. Then, after nearly a quarter of an hour of searching, she found what she sought in a small plot beneath a copse of ash trees.

Robert Clark 1745–1809

Cassandra froze in a desperate attempt to decipher the feelings brewing within her. Loneliness? Sadness? Grief?

She shifted her gaze to the name of the stone next to his, and she sobered. *Katherine Clark*. His wife.

But it was the three little stones next to them that jolted her. Small graves, all marked *Infant*.

She stood transfixed. The memory of the man in the portrait plagued her as she stared at his final resting place. She could not shake the sensation that they were connected. But how? Was she related to him? Was she related to these infants?

She gathered her skirts and knelt to brush fallen leaves and twigs from one of the infant's headstones.

"Were you acquainted with the Clark family?"

Startled, Cassandra jumped to her feet and whirled to face a man clad in a black coat standing a few feet from her, his hands clasped casually behind his back, the brisk wind lifting his molasses-colored hair from his forehead.

"O-oh," she stammered. "I—I didn't realize anyone else was here."

Ignoring her discomfort, the man continued closer until he was directly next to her. "I never had the pleasure of meeting Mrs. Clark. She died before my time here. I did speak with Mr. Clark a handful of times before he passed. A good man."

Cassandra took a step back, reestablishing an appropriate distance between them.

He was a stranger.

Speaking to her in a graveyard.

As if taking notice of her caution, he gave a little laugh and adjusted the black broad-brimmed hat he was holding. "Forgive my lack of manners. We've not met. I'm Vincent North, Anston's vicar."

The tension in her shoulders eased. "Pleasure to meet you, sir. I'm Cassandra Hale."

"You're not from Anston, are you, Miss Hale?"

"No, sir, I'm not. I arrived only yesterday."

"Then allow me to formally welcome you to our lovely village. And is your trip here for pleasure? Are you visiting family, perhaps? Or friends?"

"Actually, I'm in search of some information, and I was hoping to speak with you. I—"

Before she could continue, the heavy wooden door to the church opened, and a wiry woman toting a large basket and wearing a white apron over her old-fashioned round gown exited. She stopped suddenly and stared at Cassandra. "Merciful heavens, Mr. North. Who've we 'ere?"

"Ah, Mrs. Pearson." He pivoted to include the older woman in the conversation. "This is Miss Hale. A visitor to our parish."

"A visitor!" Her weathered complexion brightened. "Well now, we don't see many new faces here, do we, Mr. North?"

He shifted back to her. "Miss Hale, may I present Mrs. Pearson. She's the housekeeper at the vicarage, but she is instrumental in overseeing the charitable work for the church. She keeps things working as they ought here."

"Now, now, 'nough about that. It's startin' to rain, can't you see?" Mrs. Pearson blinked up at the gray sky and wiped away a bit of rain from her blotchy cheeks. "None of us need catch our death talkin' amid the stones. I've a mind to get Mr. North's tea brewin' early, and you'll come into the vicarage and take some. That way we can get acquainted, and you can tell us how ye came to be in Anston."

For a moment Cassandra felt robbed of speech. She could not

think of a time when a person had been so forthcoming—and expectant—with an invitation.

As if sensing Cassandra's hesitation, Mrs. Pearson continued. "Now, not a soul goes wanderin' among these stones without a reason, and there's a story behind yours, I'll wager. So come with me, child, lest the rain soak you clean through."

Mr. North chuckled. "Mrs. Pearson knows everything about Anston. If it is information you seek, she is, no doubt, an excellent resource."

At this Cassandra could not refuse.

The walk to the vicarage was a short one—just across a narrow road next to the church. It was a fine house, with dark gray stone and white trim, paned windows, and a tidy walkway. By the time her foot crossed the threshold, the rain fell mercilessly, and she was grateful for the shelter. Mrs. Pearson quickly took her pelisse and gloves and ushered her into a modest low-ceilinged parlor. Despite the gray skies, ample colorless light filtered in through the three broad windows overlooking the road, making the space appear quite bright. A warm, cheery fire was quickly brought to life, and when it was offered to her, she settled into a highback chair next to the hearth.

She'd met Mrs. Pearson and Mr. North but minutes ago, and already she found herself easing into their good-natured company. Mr. North was nothing like the old vicar in Lamby. He boasted amiability. His large brown eyes contributed to his youthful appearance, but the soft lines around them suggested that one should not judge his age by appearances alone. As he sat across from her in the faded green wingback chair, with his tea in hand and easy manners, Cassandra could feel her anxieties subside, even if just for a moment.

"Please pay no mind to the mess." He waved a dismissive hand at a pile of newspapers and books on a table beneath one of the windows. "Mrs. Pearson is always after me to find a place for these things. My office in the church is often quite cold this time of year, so I do a great deal of my work right here in this room."

"Ah, the young miss doesn't care 'bout your mess, Mr. North. No need to draw attention to it." Mrs. Pearson pulled a padded side chair close, sat down, then patted Cassandra's arm with her wrinkled hand. "Now then, why don't you tell us what brings you to Anston."

Cassandra gave them a brief overview of her situation—careful to impart enough information while still guarding her privacy. She did show them the letter, and she observed them for any reaction as they read it.

After they'd both read the letter, Mr. North handed it back to Cassandra, and for several seconds no one spoke. Then Mr. North sat back in his chair and crossed one long leg over the other. "So I must ask. Did you not find what you sought at Briarton Park?"

"No, sir. Unfortunately, I did not."

He stood, crossed the room to the fire, and reached for the poker. "In fairness, the Warrington family has been at Briarton for about a year. I'm not surprised Mr. Warrington did not know much of the history."

She scrutinized his every movement, as if the motions alone might hold some secret. "Perchance do you have information you could share with me?"

After several seconds the young vicar straightened, returned the poker to its stand, and turned. "Unfortunately, I did not know Mr. Clark at all. I only arrived a few months before his death. Not nearly enough time to forge any sort of true acquaintance. Mrs. Pearson? Did you know him?"

"Aye, yes. I remember Robert Clark well." Mrs. Pearson settled back in her chair. "They were a quiet family, the Clarks. Kept mostly to themselves far as I knew. Mr. Clark traveled often for the wool mills. He owned two, you know, Weyton Mill and Clark Mill. He conducted a great deal o' business in London, I believe it was, and Mrs. Clark remained behind at Briarton Park. She was frequently ill as I recall, but they had a son, and he resides over in Ambleton, not an hour from here."

"Yes, Mr. Warrington mentioned a son—a Mr. Peter Clark." Cassandra tried to mask her enthusiasm with a steady tone. "Do you know him?"

"I've met him, of course, once or twice at social gatherings," responded Mr. North. "He now runs Clark Mill. Passed down. I could manage an introduction if it would be helpful."

"Oh, it would." Cassandra nodded. "Immensely."

Mrs. Pearson leaned forward, her cobalt eyes bright with interest. "And do you recall, Mr. North? Mrs. Susannah Hutton was the housekeeper at Briarton Park for many years. She lives at the end of South Lane now with her sister. People in service to great families know everything about them, so perhaps she'd entertain a question or two. But I caution ye. She's not the friendliest sort. Guarded and severe. But never mind that. I'll see to it that all will go well. Tomorrow we'll call."

"T-tomorrow?" Cassandra stammered.

"Of course. I've not called on her in quite some time. I'll take you there myself."

It all seemed too fortuitous. "Are you sure? I wouldn't dare think of intruding on your time, and I am sure you have—"

"Nonsense! I'm forever telling Mr. North that he should call on all of his parishioners. Not just the agreeable ones."

Mr. North slapped his knee. "That settles it. A visit to Mrs. Hutton tomorrow is in order. And setting a time for an introduction to the younger Mr. Clark will take some doing, but these things have a way of coming together."

Cassandra was stunned at all that had been discussed. "You are both being so gracious."

"Everyone deserves to know who their people are. Where are you staying, child?" Mrs. Pearson asked.

"I have a room at the Green Ox Inn."

"What? No." Mrs. Pearson shook her head emphatically. "No, no, no. That place is one step above a hovel."

"I'm rather content, really," Cassandra urged. "In truth, I don't know how long I'll be in town, so for the time being it suits."

"Nonsense." Mr. North stood. "Mrs. Pearson is quite right. When we've finished our tea, I'll escort you over to Mrs. Martin's house myself. She takes on boarders, and she is a particular friend of mine. I'm sure she can offer assistance."

The afternoon passed pleasantly and quickly. As the rain subsided and it was deemed dry enough to venture out of doors once more, Mrs. Pearson retrieved Cassandra's now-dry pelisse and gloves.

After opening the front door, Mr. North turned to face her, his usually pleasant expression growing almost grim. "In light of all that lies before you, I'll offer this word of caution. As a rare visitor to our village, you will pique everyone's interest. You have kindly shared your story with us, but I think it prudent if you keep the details to yourself until more can be discovered. Mr. Clark was a mill owner, and regardless of his pleasant demeanor, that alone will cast a shadow on your search. I hate to admit it, but people love their gossip and will reinvent truths in a minute. Discretion, my new friend, is advised."

Cassandra nodded, but the warning cast a long shadow over her blossoming optimism, staunchly reminding her to guard her heart.

Chapter 5

Mr. North fell into step next to her as they traversed the cobbled street from the vicarage to the boardinghouse. With fortified tenacity and revived hope, Cassandra glanced toward him. He was a handsome man. His face was long and narrow and his complexion quite fair, but high cheekbones added to his air of authority. The directness of his personality, the candor and verisimilitude, relaxed her in his presence.

"The boardinghouse is not far from here. Just down the high street there. See?" He pointed down the street as they walked.

Her gaze followed his direction to a building that, in truth, looked very much like a smaller version of the Green Ox Inn. It, too, was built of stone and rose two stories high. Its facade featured tall, narrow paned windows and green trim, and the shingle outside of the brightly painted yellow door read *Martin's Boardinghouse*.

"Mrs. Martin will take care of you. I'm confident of it," Mr. North explained. "It isn't a palace, by any means, but Mrs. Martin keeps a tight rein over her boarders and only takes on ladies. It will be much safer and, I daresay, quieter for you there."

Cassandra adjusted her grip on her reticule. As humbling and difficult as it had been to ask for help, it was almost as challenging to receive it. Mrs. Denton had taught her that self-sufficiency was to be prized. She'd never known anyone, male or female, to truly help another without expectation for more, as Mr. North seemed to be doing. But he was, after all, a vicar. Perhaps he was sincere.

A sharp breeze swept down from the shop roofs, and with her free hand she clutched the collar of her pelisse tighter about her. "I am grateful to you for all you are doing for me, Mr. North."

"'Tis my job, and my joy, to help others." His manner was light as he opened the gate. "Come, through here."

Once at the door Mr. North knocked, and a young servant girl with plump cheeks answered. She took Cassandra's pelisse and gloves before ushering them into a modest parlor with a low ceiling. Two sofas and several mismatched chairs crowded the narrow room, and the silence of the space struck her. She had expected it to be more like the girls' school, which was forever echoing with the sounds of footsteps and instruction. Here, the absence of sound was disconcerting.

Before long a woman who could be Mrs. Martin appeared in the doorway. The slender, striking woman was every bit as tall as Mr. North. Her coppery hair, although faded, was coiffed in an intricate display of tight curls around her long face, and her gown of gold piping and blue embroidery was anything but retiring.

She paid no heed to Cassandra but focused her attention familiarly on the vicar. "Mr. North. What business brings you to my parlor today?"

He bowed in greeting. "I must beg a favor from you yet again, Mrs. Martin."

"What, again?" She swept into the room and sat in one of the highback chairs. It was only then that she looked to Cassandra and motioned for them both to be seated. "More charitable work?"

"Not exactly." Mr. North adjusted his coat as he sat down. "I've had the pleasure this day of meeting Miss Hale. She has come to our village on a personal matter and has need of lodging. It had been her intention to reside at the inn, but I'm certain you'll agree that your boardinghouse would be more suitable to a young lady of her standing. I'm having my maid bring her things here, pending your consent, of course."

"You were right to bring her to me." Mrs. Martin addressed Cassandra, "And where are you from, my dear?"

"I'm from Lamby. Near London."

"Near London, is it?" Mrs. Martin examined Cassandra from the top of her hair to the toes of her boots. "My, my. Not many visitors from London come all the way to my boardinghouse. And what sort of business brings you here?"

Mr. North interjected, "Miss Hale has had a trying day, Mrs. Martin. I think it best to show her to a bedchamber forthwith. We don't want anyone succumbing to fatigue."

"You are right, Mr. North, as usual." Mrs. Martin's voice rang hollow. She stood and clasped her hands primly before her.

Cassandra and Mr. North followed her lead and stood. He turned toward Cassandra, his expression encouraging, and he softened his voice. "Now, Miss Hale. I'll be by in the morning for the errand we discussed, if that is still agreeable to you."

Cassandra nodded. "It is indeed."

"Good. Then I leave you in Mrs. Martin's capable hands." He bowed to both of them. "Mrs. Martin, you, of course, are a treasure."

Cassandra watched Mr. North almost sadly, as if just realizing they were about to part. She turned to see Mrs. Martin watching him as well. The older woman's jaw twitched. In that instant it became clear: Cassandra was not the only one who did not want him to leave.

Cassandra shifted awkwardly after Mr. North had disappeared from view. She gripped her reticule tighter, as if by doing so she could regain control of the situation.

"There, now." Mrs. Martin's warmhearted tone tightened to one much more direct. "He's seen fit to bring you to my boardinghouse, has he?"

Cassandra pressed her lips together at the woman's perceived displeasure. "Mr. North has been very considerate."

Mrs. Martin's head tilted to the side. "And why would he do that, I wonder?"

The question hung heavy in the silence, interrupted only by muffled, distant voices and creaking footsteps crossing the floor above.

After several seconds Mrs. Martin let out a drawn-out sigh, and her gaze dropped to Cassandra's hand. She reached out, grabbed it in her own, and turned it over. "These hands have not seen much by a day's work, have they?"

"On the contrary, Mrs. Martin." Cassandra pulled her hand back. "I've worked very hard. I'm a teacher in a girls' boarding school. Or rather, I have been until recently."

"And what would bring a teacher to a village like this? And to have sought lodging at the inn, no less?"

Cassandra could only stare at the impertinent woman. It was one matter for her to share her quest with the vicar, a trusted man of the cloth. It was another thing entirely to share her story with someone whom she'd only just met, whose capricious gaze and curious eye seemed more bent on gossip than a sincere desire to be of help. Mr. North's words of caution took on an entirely new level of truth.

"You must forgive me, Mrs. Martin. As Mr. North indicated, I'm quite tired. I'd very much appreciate a chance to rest."

Mrs. Martin's thin brows rose, and she crossed her arms over her chest. "All my proper rooms are full, even the double ones, but I've an empty servant's room in the back by the kitchen. That will have to do, unless you're too proud, of course. And assuming you can pay the rent. I require a week's amount in advance."

Disappointment—or perhaps frustration—surged. Cassandra resisted the urge to let her posture slacken. She was in no situation to make any demands. "I'm certain it will suit very well, Mrs. Martin. And yes, I have funds."

"Well then, I've far too much to do to stand here in the corridor. Come now. And be quick about it."

With impatient steps Mrs. Martin led Cassandra down a corridor, through a cramped, low-ceilinged kitchen, and to a small door at the far edge. Cassandra looked around as she followed, quickly absorbing her surroundings. Heavy, dark beams extended the length of the room, and from them dried herbs and flowers hung. Pleasing scents of meat and boiled vegetables intermingled with wayward smoke that escaped the chimney, and a large orange fire raged in the hearth. Two girls with white aprons glanced up from cutting vegetables as they walked past.

Mrs. Martin's linen skirts swished as she reached for a key on a hook next to the door. She extended it to Cassandra. "This will be your room. As I said, there's not much to it, but it is dry, which is more than I can say for the condition in which the innkeeper keeps the Green Ox Inn. If another chamber becomes available, you will be the first in line."

Cassandra accepted the key and stared at the small wooden door.

"The morning meal is early on account of the other boarders going to the next village for work. If you want to eat, make sure you're not late. You'll hear 'em, no doubt. There is a blanket in the trunk. If you need water in the basin, ask one of the kitchen girls."

Cassandra could sense the two maids staring at her during the exchange. She turned and offered a smile, which was not returned. Bewildered, Cassandra pushed on the unlatched door.

The space was cramped, and the ceiling was even lower than the kitchen's, making it almost uncomfortable to stretch to her full height. A small bed was pushed up against the far stone wall. One of the windowpanes was broken, and a determined stream of wind fluttered the threadbare window covering, bringing with it an unforgiving chill.

Mrs. Martin produced a single candle from the kitchen and set it on the rickety table positioned between the two deep-set windows. "There's a hook on the wall for your pelisse, and a trunk for your things."

Cassandra's gaze fell to the tiny trunk. Sadness and the desire to be alone overwhelmed her. She resisted the urge to shiver. "Thank you, Mrs. Martin."

As quickly as she had ushered Cassandra to the room, Mrs. Martin departed. Cassandra hurried to close the door to ensure her privacy, desperate to be away from the maids' listening ears. She set her reticule and gloves atop the bed and rubbed her hands together to generate warmth.

A fresh gust rushed in, flickering the candle's single yellow flame and whipping at her hair. She wrinkled her nose at a stench she could not quite identify. She supposed now would be a good time to cry. And yet, it was not an act she was prone to. Yes, she had cried when Mrs. Denton died. Other than that, Cassandra could not remember the last time.

But now she was in a situation she'd never quite experienced. Very little had gone according to plan. She had hoped for a gratifying outcome, but now there were more questions than answers. More disappointments than successes. And more loneliness than ever.

Cassandra sniffed and wiped her nose with her handkerchief. She could not give in to emotion. She had no choice but to keep her wits about her. After all, there was still a chance. Mr. Clark's son was living. His former housekeeper would surely have information. But now she was cold and hungry, her feet hurt, and her head throbbed. She dropped to the bed.

No, crying would not help. When had it ever?

Chapter 6

James pulled the high collar of his caped greatcoat closer to his neck as he returned home from the mill. Night had fallen, bringing the bone-chilling autumn mists that could only come from a day beleaguered with drizzle and fog.

He'd lived at Briarton Park long enough to uncover the property's mysteries—the hidden dips in the road that might cause his horse to stumble, the secret shadows that concealed tree roots and disguised low-hanging branches. He'd become well acquainted with what lay ahead of him—he'd round a bend near a cluster of trees, cross the arched stone bridge spanning the River Sinet, and then come upon the house.

There should be comfort in returning home—in being among things that were familiar. But as he approached the river, tonight of all nights, melancholy plagued him.

The day had been onerous. He hated to quarrel with Rachel. The attack on Riddy had agitated the workers, and the menacing threats against the other mill owners made him apprehensive for his own family's safety.

James paused as his horse crested the hill that marked the edge of his property. The clouds that had hounded them with rain earlier that afternoon had thinned for the time being, and the moon's fragmented light flooded the ancient home with a silver glow. Briarton

Park—and the peace and solitude it could potentially afford—had been the dream he and Elizabeth had shared. A quiet life, away from the hustle of Plymouth's business responsibilities, where his days had been spent overseeing the sales and shipping of the broadcloth that came from several Yorkshire mills.

It had been a profitable and necessary time to fund their purchase of a mill of their own. They'd been patient and made their sacrifices—travel had kept him away from their home, and his long hours had caused tension and disagreements. He had told himself that soon it would all be worth it.

But then the unthinkable happened.

Elizabeth's death shattered that dream and propelled him into uncharted territory, personally and professionally. He'd done his best to keep their family strong and secure, but he could not lie to himself—their current existence was but a shell of their former plans. Despite his good intentions, disarray reigned. His relationship with his sister was tense, the relationship with his mother-in-law was strained, and his business, the very livelihood they had worked so hard to establish, now faced adversities he could not avoid.

After returning to Briarton's courtyard, James took his horse to the stables and entered the house through the workers' entrance. He discarded his greatcoat and hat, shook the remaining moisture from his boots and hair, and took the servants' stairs, two at a time, to the family wing. The hour was late, and no doubt both girls were asleep, but he needed to see them.

He nudged the nursery door open. A fire blazed in the grate at the room's far end, casting long, flickering shadows on the two canopied beds positioned beneath the draped windows. A rush of heat met him, warming his face and hands, and immediately the tension he'd been carrying in his shoulders relaxed.

As he eased the door open farther, it squeaked, and his older daughter, Maria, sat up. "Papa!"

He held his finger to his lips, nodded toward sleeping Rose, then moved to Maria's bed. He planted a kiss on the top of her head and sat next to her.

"You're so late!" she exclaimed as she fussed with the cotton sleeve of her white nightdress. "We tried to wait up for you, but Grandmother insisted we go to bed."

"I know, I'm sorry." He picked up a book on the table next to her bed. "Ah. Have you been reading?"

"Grandmother was supposed to read with us, but she didn't feel well this evening. So we read with Matilda."

He jerked, surprised. "The kitchen maid?"

Maria nodded. "But she doesn't know how to read, so I read it to her."

James stiffened and thumbed through the book's pages of pictures of bunnies and trees. He did not care for the idea that his daughters were reading with the kitchen maid. He and his mother-in-law had made an agreement that she would oversee their education and activities until the new governess they had engaged was available, which was still a few months away. Their agreement did not—under any circumstances—allow for the kitchen maid to be responsible for their care.

"Who was the lady who came by this morning?"

James frowned, pulling his attention away from his thoughts. "Who?"

"The lady who knocked on the door? I saw her from the garden."

The memory of Shepard's warning battled with the strange emotion the sight of the woman had incited in him. "She was here to inquire after the man who used to own this house."

"Why?"

"She was looking for some information." He patted her hand. "Nothing to concern yourself with."

Her small shoulders slumped slightly, and she fidgeted with the end of her long plait. "I miss it when people come. People always visited when Mama was alive. Do you remember?"

Yes, he remembered. How could he forget?

"I do."

Maria sighed. "Grandmother says there isn't anyone around Briarton Park appropriate for us to visit with."

He leaned closer. "Now, that just isn't true."

She scrunched her brows together. "Then why do we never have visitors or visit anyone else?"

As much as he hated to admit it, he knew exactly to what she was referring. Margaret Towler had been decidedly opposed to the family relocating to Yorkshire, and now she refused to engage with society, claiming it was beneath the station they had enjoyed in Plymouth. James had grown up in the area and was familiar enough with the other mill owners to establish professional relationships, but that left little engagement for his daughters.

He brightened his tone. "Tomorrow I'll take you for a pony ride, just you and me. How does that sound?"

A hint of a smile tugged at her lips. "Do you promise?"

"I do. And do not fret. Briarton Park will feel more like home eventually. All transitions take time, some longer than others. And this has been a big transition, has it not?" He stood from the bed, kissed the top of her head once again, and tucked the blankets around her. "Now off you go, straight to sleep. You'll need rest for our ride tomorrow."

She nodded eagerly. Satisfied that he'd provided at least a little comfort, he withdrew from the warmth of the nursery back out into the drafty corridor. As he rounded the corner on the way to his own chamber, he was surprised to see Mrs. Helock pacing the broad landing area at the end of the hall.

When she took notice of him, she rushed toward him, her normally cool, unaffected exterior visibly shaken. "You must come straightaway. Miss Rachel is missing."

"Missing?" James flinched as if struck as the words hit him. "What do you mean, *missing*?"

Rare tears appeared in the woman's rheumy eyes as she pressed a handkerchief to her nose. Her voice quavered. "Earlier this evening I thought I heard something odd coming from Miss Rachel's chamber as I did my rounds, but when I looked in, all was empty. She was gone."

Needing no more explanation, James rushed past the woman. The door to Rachel's room stood ajar. Flickering light spilled out. He jogged in, only to stop short when he saw his mother-in-law pacing, a black shawl wrapped around her. She whirled as he entered and threw her hands in the air. "She's gone, James. Gone!"

He scanned the candlelit room, searching for an explanation. "Surely she's in another part of the house, the library or the—"

"At this hour?" Mrs. Towler strode toward the tall mahogany wardrobe and flung open the door. "Her things are gone. See for yourself."

James stepped over to the wardrobe and pulled the door open wider.

It was not empty, but it was in disarray.

He removed one of the remaining gowns, studying it as if it held the secret to her location. "Have you asked the servants? Surely someone saw something."

"Are you mad?" Mrs. Towler hissed back. "Of course I did not ask the servants. The last thing we need is for them to wag their tongues. Mrs. Helock, fortunately, is the only one who knows. Imagine! What could the girl have been thinking?"

James searched his memory for any indication she might have given him. Rachel had been enraged earlier that day. He'd thought she had calmed down.

But clearly he'd been mistaken.

Mrs. Towler tightened her shawl with an exaggerated pull. "Mrs.

Helock did ask the groundskeeper and stable hands if they'd seen anything unusual. They said nothing was amiss."

An aggravating sense of helplessness crept in as he dropped the gown atop the bed. "Why was I not sent for earlier? How long ago was this?"

"Not more than half an hour. There's not been time. I cannot believe the selfishness of this child!" Mrs. Towler's tone shrilled. "How could she do this to her family? To her nieces! Everyone's reputation will be affected by this."

"I couldn't care less about reputations," James blurted. "We must find her."

Margaret's gaze narrowed as her voice lowered. "You know, of course, where she's gone. It is that Richard Standish fellow. And there is only one destination where a couple their age and in their circumstance would go."

The suggestion reverberated with aching poignancy within him.

Of course that was where she went.

Gretna Green. Scotland. The one place they could go and marry without permission. Without having the banns read.

He was left with little choice. He had to find her.

If he could reach her in time.

Chapter 7

The pistol was heavy in James's hand as he paced his study.

He paused his steps, stared at the weapon, and tried to remember the last time he had held it with the intent of possibly using it.

But now his sister was missing. And even though he was not sure exactly where Rachel was, he was almost certain whom she was with.

Ignoring the hard knot in his stomach, he tucked the pistol away and reached for his wide-brimmed hat. With every second that passed, his anger intensified.

What a fool he'd been. He'd taken her quiet retreat as submission to his instructions.

Mrs. Towler appeared in the doorway. "What are you going to do?"

He wished he had an answer. He'd searched Rachel's chamber for a clue as to where she might be. But there was nothing—no letter. And despite the mess in her wardrobe, it appeared that nothing of significance was missing. "I'm going to the inn. If they departed by coach, someone there will know something or at least will have seen something."

"Assuming she didn't go to another village." Mrs. Towler swept farther into his study, the rustling of her black skirt disrupting the silence. "Oh, this is a mess! I warned you about this. Did I not? Something should have been done sooner."

He ignored the hard edge of her tone. He had to. Otherwise his exasperation toward her might flare, and he had to remain controlled. "I'll return as soon as I am able. Hopefully with Rachel."

Mrs. Towler squinted. "I hope she realizes what she's done. Not just to herself but to her family. To Maria and Rose."

He refused to think about Rose and Maria being affected by this. "Have Mrs. Helock tell the groundsmen to patrol the surrounding area for anything suspicious. I'll enlist more help once I reach the inn."

He didn't dare glance toward his mother-in-law as he quit the chamber. He couldn't. Yes, he was angry with Rachel too. The girl was headstrong. Determined. Inconsiderate to a fault. But she was still his sister and a member of the family. He would not join in his mother-in-law's denigration of her. It would do no good. Instead, he would put his every effort into retrieving her.

He made his way to the stables and quickly saddled his horse. Within minutes he was mounted and through the courtyard with his sights set on the Green Ox Inn.

He'd known she'd been infatuated with the lad, but to run off? To actually forsake them? Overwhelming guilt surged through him. He was the guardian. He should have been more forceful. More watchful.

Once he reached the main road, he allowed his horse freedom to gallop along the dirt road. There was no need for silence among the trees.

But above all, concern for her safety ruled his actions. Everything else could be sorted through once he knew she was safe.

Cassandra paced her narrow bedchamber, clutching a tarnished pocket watch in her hand. The watch, which had once belonged to Mrs. Denton, confirmed the lateness of the hour. She should be tired. She should try to get some rest. But everything within her resisted.

The day's events had been fraught with uncertainty, and now her thoughts refused to settle.

She did her best to silence the noisy doubts winging in her heart and continued to pace. If only there was someone to talk with—someone to distract her.

At the school, solitude had been a rarity. Students always surrounded her, and even in the evenings, when her duties for the day had been completed, two other teachers shared her bedchamber. It had been so easy to find a diversion, but here she had no choice but to contend with her own thoughts.

Cassandra moved to the window once again. As she did a shiver traversed her spine, and she reached for the blanket Mrs. Martin had left for her and wrapped it around her shoulders. She was already fully dressed in her heaviest wool gown and flannel chemise and petticoats, but without a fire in a grate and proper panes of glass in her window, the night's bitter chill made sleep nearly impossible.

She drew the window's thin covering aside. Her window overlooked an alley, and from her position she could see most of the Green Ox Inn's front courtyard. Fiery torches lit the space, illuminating the activity in an eerie glow. Shadowy figures darted to and fro. Even in the dark of night, a carriage arrived. She watched the movement for several seconds, allowing it to disrupt her anxious thoughts.

She should be grateful for this room, for Mr. North had been right in his assessments. She'd seen and encountered several unruly guests at the Green Ox Inn in her short time there, and even now shouts and raucous laughter echoed from its direction. Fortunately, the boardinghouse was only slightly more expensive than the inn. Between her savings and the money from Mr. Clark's letter, she had funds enough for now, but she needed to consider what would come next. Regardless of the outcome of her inquiries, she would need to find another teaching position somewhere soon.

A sudden, salient feminine cry froze her in her spot.

She jumped back and dropped the curtain.

Pointed whispers echoed, and hurried footsteps slapped the cobbles just outside.

Both alarmed and intrigued, Cassandra inched back to the window and strained to hear.

The voices seemed to have come to a stop. When the man's voice resumed, it was low. And closer. "It's too late to change your mind. You said you were certain."

The responding voice was soft. Fragile. Panicked. "I know what I said, but don't you think this is wrong? Surely it must be, to be—"

"I've given up everything for this. Everything, Rachel!"

Clearly this was a private conversation, one not intended to be overheard, but the harshness of the man's tone chilled Cassandra. She peeked around the curtain's edge. Light from the inn's distant torches mingled with the white moonlight to illuminate two silhouettes—a male and a female—just outside the window. The wind whipped through the tight space, tugging the woman's cape and tossing her long strands of hair violently about her head.

There was something strikingly familiar about the tight curls of the woman's dark hair.

And then it struck her—she was the young woman from Briarton Park, the one dressed in saffron who'd stared at her as she passed through the chamber.

The girl reached for his hand. "But don't you think that if we wait, just a little, we—"

"No. No!" The tall, lanky man shook her free with a yank of his arm. "I can't go back, do you see? I've broken all ties for you. Because you said you loved me."

"And I do! I know James is strict, but I can't betray him. I just can't."

Cassandra had been around enough females of that age to detect uncertainty, if not fear, in the girl's voice.

The man reached out and grabbed the girl's shoulder. "You will honor your commitment to me."

"I can't. I—"

And then the man started to pull her back toward the carriage at the edge of the inn's courtyard.

The young woman cried out in resistance, but the man wrenched harder, refusing to release her.

Incensed, Cassandra dropped the blanket around her shoulders, reached for the dagger she'd set on the bedside table, and wrapped her fingers around the cold leather grip. Mrs. Denton had taught her to take action when necessary, especially if the person was unable to act for themself, and it was needed now. Before fully considering the consequences of her actions, she was at the kitchen door and pushed out into the alley.

At the door's opening the pair immediately stopped shuffling and turned to look at her.

"Let go of her," Cassandra demanded.

But the man did not drop her arm. "This is a private matter."

"I wonder then, if it's such a private matter, why you're shouting and behaving as such in a public space?" Cassandra smoothed her thumb over her knife, refusing to break eye contact.

The man turned the full brunt of his annoyance on her. "And I am telling you now to leave us be, madam."

Heart pounding, Cassandra looked to the young woman, whose glassy eyes and unkempt hair made her appear more of a child than a woman.

No, this was not her business. Over the years she'd seen it happen far too many times to other teachers and even her older students—

girls at the mercy of a man. She hadn't assisted then. What was different now?

She locked eyes with the man and lifted her dagger. "You *will* step away from her."

He scoffed and shifted, moving with arrogance, as if he intended to reach out for the knife.

She jerked back and then straightened. "I wouldn't step closer. I doubt you'd know how to react when confronted with a woman who can properly defend herself."

They stared at each other before he turned back to the girl. "This is absurd. We're leaving. Now."

The young woman, taking advantage of the man's break in concentration, ripped her arm free and stumbled toward Cassandra.

Cassandra lunged forward, putting herself between them. "She's made her decision. Now you leave, or I'll scream and waken every single person in this boardinghouse. Then how will you answer for it?"

The inn's light and moonlight flooded onto every hard edge of the man's enraged expression. He sucked in a sharp breath and then pointed his forefinger at the girl and emphasized each syllable. "I've had enough! You've made your decision and it will not be undone. Oh, the wasted time and effort! Go then, return to your prison. I'll not extend another opportunity."

Cassandra stiffened and relaxed the grip on her knife ever so slightly. This was not an abduction or some sort of attack, as she had initially assumed.

This was a lovers' quarrel.

Cassandra waited for the girl's response, but she made none.

The man turned, and within moments his pounding footsteps and grumbling faded and were absorbed by the sounds from the inn.

Once they were alone, Cassandra glanced around to ensure privacy. She did not know the particulars, but she did know what was at stake if a young woman was discovered in such a situation. She placed her arm around the girl's shivering shoulders to guide her away. "Let's go, Rachel."

"H-how do you know my name?"

"I heard him say it."

"Where are we going?" A sob shook the girl's shoulders.

"Your home. Briarton Park, isn't it? We must hurry."

"We?" Rachel's steps stopped short. "I can't ask you to do that."

Cassandra huffed. "I'm not about to let you walk alone in the dark of night, especially after what's transpired. Let's be quick."

They reentered the boardinghouse long enough for Cassandra to grab her own cloak and extinguish her candle before they were back outside. Fortunately, the path to Briarton Park was fresh in Cassandra's mind, and the shadowy darkness lent privacy. They crossed the high street undetected, crossed the arched stone bridge, and were on the road leading to Briarton Park within minutes.

Intermittent clouds floated in front of a large moon, shedding just enough light on the surroundings to make them vaguely familiar. Night sounds of wind whistling through the last dry leaves clinging to branches mingled with an owl's distant mournful cry. They kept to the side of the road, taking full advantage of the tree line to hide themselves, lest anyone should happen by.

"You're the woman who was at Briarton Park this morning," Rachel said once they were under the protection of the forest.

Cassandra nodded. "Yes. I'm Cassandra Hale."

"Are you acquainted with my brother then?"

The memory of the handsome, amenable man with dark blond hair flashed in her mind. "I only met him today."

They walked in silence, and then Rachel asked, "Why did you help me just now?"

"I heard you from my chamber and thought you needed assistance. Did you?"

"I—I did." She heaved a sigh and tightened her cloak around her. "I wonder if James knows I am gone. He'll never understand this."

When it was clear Rachel was going to say no more, Cassandra spoke. "It's none of my business, of course, but I can only assume that you had some sort of agreement with the young man."

Rachel sniffed. "There is no sense in trying to hide it from you, especially after what you witnessed. We were to be married. In Gretna Green. He'd made all the arrangements. None of my family knew. We'd planned to meet this night and depart. But—but just hours ago I changed my mind."

Cassandra had suspected something of the sort, but the similarities of this story to her own at this age were poignant—and heartachingly familiar. "And I take it your brother did not approve of this young man."

"No. Not in the least." Her voice was barely above a whisper.

Cassandra had to choose her words with care. She did not know this girl or her family situation, but she did know how strong the attachment of the heart could be and how damaging others' opinions could be. At such a moment this girl might just need a friend. "How old are you, Rachel?"

"Sixteen."

"We are not acquainted, and I doubt my opinion will hold much weight, but I think you made a very brave decision."

Rachel scoffed and impatiently swiped a tear from her cheek. "Brave? Nothing about this feels brave."

"I'm sure you faced him knowing it would be a painful, maybe frightening, conversation, and yet you did it anyway."

Rachel swatted at a low-hanging branch as they walked, her face hidden in shadows. "I'm not sure my brother would agree with you. He, no doubt, will think me foolish and irresponsible."

"Perhaps, but in the end, I'm sure he would prefer this decision than the one to leave."

"I did love him." Rachel choked on a sob, her shoulders shaking. "I think I still do."

Cassandra allowed several moments of silence to pass. How well she knew the power of such sentiments. Over the years she had learned, at Mrs. Denton's urging, to suppress emotions, but she remembered how intense some emotions could be. It would do no good to tell her to ignore them or focus on something else, not when the sting of her pain was so fresh. "Those feelings are strong. And I say that not only to make you feel better but from my own experience. I was in a similar situation, years ago. But I was seventeen, a little older than you."

Rachel stopped short. "You were?"

Cassandra's recollection of her own indiscretion rushed back to her. How she recalled the empty loneliness in the days following the incident. It had been raw. Painful.

Normally, Cassandra never would have dreamt of sharing such a personal detail, but she did not know this girl, and once her business in this village was concluded, she would likely never see her again. What harm would come in sharing a bit of solidarity and support?

"The details aren't important, but I could have left with him. But someone, my teacher, intervened on my behalf and refused to let me leave. I was so angry at her at the time, but now I see the wisdom in her response. I needed someone to make the decision for me. Thankfully you came to your senses on your own. It speaks to your maturity."

Rachel drew a shuddering breath and tightened her cape about her as they walked. "How long did it take for the pain to subside?"

But before Cassandra could respond, a distant pounding echoed from the road ahead.

Rachel stopped. "Is that . . . ?"

The sound sharpened into rhythmic hoofbeats.

Someone was coming. And fast.

Chapter 8

Raw, frigid air blasted James as he and his horse thundered away from Briarton Park and toward the bridge that marked the edge of his property and the start of the village of Anston. A sharp kick of his heel urged his horse faster down the lane and under trees he knew so well. He had to get to the Green Ox Inn as soon as possible.

Despite the evening's persistent chill, perspiration moistened his brow. He refused to think about what would happen if his assumptions about where she was going were incorrect. He didn't even have time to do so, for before his horse even reached the bridge, two shadowed figures appeared.

Two cloaked figures.

Two women.

On instinct he yanked the reins, and his horse neighed and reared in shock, sending a plume of wintery breath into the night air.

As he regained control of his horse, one of the figures let down her hood. He'd recognize those wayward curls anywhere.

Rachel.

Relief flooding, he slid from the saddle and rushed toward his sister. "What are you doing here? I could have trampled you!"

Rachel crossed her arms and met his gaze defiantly.

Her indifference and lack of response sent fresh fire surging through his veins. Words seeped through his clenched teeth. "Where have you been? What on earth are you doing out at night?"

The moonlight highlighted the glint of rebellion in Rachel's expression. "Well, you got what you wanted. Richard's gone."

"What are you talking about?" Her words made no sense. "What do you mean, he's gone?"

"Richard. He's gone now. And he'll not be returning."

James recoiled. "So you came upon this knowledge now? At this hour?"

A voice from behind Rachel reminded him another woman was present. "It's been a trying evening, Mr. Warrington. Perhaps if you take her home and get her warm, this conversation might be easier."

He stared at the cloaked woman. How dare a stranger comment on a personal conversation with his sister? "Who are you?"

"She is Cassandra Hale," spouted Rachel, stepping closer to him. "She offered me assistance. She was the only one to help me, I might add."

He looked closer at the woman. The hood of her cloak masked many of her features, but it did not hide the elegant slope of her nose or the attractive fullness of her lower lip. He could not fully make out her profile, but the honeyed tone of her voice confirmed that this was indeed the same woman who had graced his great hall earlier in the day.

The surprise of seeing Miss Hale again, here of all places, overtook his frustration with his sister's cheekiness. But his consternation quickly turned to suspicion. "I have to ask, Miss Hale, how is it that you have come to be with my sister at this late hour?"

Miss Hale lowered her hood. "Like she said, your sister required assistance. I happened to overhear."

His jaw twitched in irritation. Why would no one give a direct explanation? "Nothing will be solved standing here. Let's go."

"This is where I leave you then." Miss Hale turned toward Rachel. "Perhaps tomorrow we—"

"No, no!" Rachel clutched Miss Hale's arm with both of her hands. "You must come. You must help me explain."

Not giving Miss Hale an opportunity to respond, James straightened. Whatever had transpired, this woman had something to do with it, and she could not be dismissed so easily. "No, I agree with Rachel. I think you had better come with us."

Cassandra stood by the fire, fixing her eyes on the flames to avoid eye contact with Mr. Warrington or Mrs. Towler. Discreetly, she tugged at the sleeve of her heavy wool gown. She donned this gown in her chamber when she was desperate for warmth. Now, as she stood in this family's house, its stifling heaviness only added to her discomfort.

She shouldn't be here observing this intimate family conversation. She'd only intended to help Rachel Warrington return home safely. But now she found herself at Briarton Park—again.

This time, she was not standing in the great hall, as she had earlier that morning. Instead, she was in a more private sitting room one floor above. The ceilings were not as high on this level, and the walls were papered with images of bluebirds and emerald-green leaves. The surroundings were much more comfortable than the sterile stone floors, white plaster walls, and austere, carved wooden furniture. A cheery fire blazed in the grate, bathing the space in a golden glow.

But despite the chamber's coziness, the conversation within its walls was anything but pleasant. Cassandra remained still and silent as she inched closer to the bank of windows lining the east wall, feeling more like an intruder than a guest.

Rachel was seated in a highback chair next to the fire. Mr. Warrington stood in front of her, arms folded across his broad chest, and Mrs. Towler, to whom she'd just been introduced upon her arrival, stood just behind him. With her gown of ebony crepe with black velvet trim and a chemisette of inky lace that covered her throat, the older woman appeared to be in mourning, which only compounded Cassandra's mounting questions.

Cassandra returned her focus to Briarton Park's master. Gone was the general easiness Mr. Warrington displayed when she had met him earlier that morning. Instead he appeared poised, ready for a battle. His disheveled sandy hair and askew cravat bore evidence to the turmoil churning within him. He fixed his stormy charcoal eyes on his sister, his attention unwavering. "Let me make certain I completely understand. You had agreed to meet Standish to run away and elope. He was to meet you at the inn, and then you were going to flee to Gretna Green. But you changed your mind, and the two of you argued. Miss Hale happened to overhear the argument and intervened."

Tears trailed down Rachel's cheeks, yet despite the display of sadness, a hint of youthful brazenness glinted. "Yes, that is exactly what happened. I told him I would not see him again. Isn't that what you wanted?"

"It's not just what I wanted, Rachel." His response was impressively calm amid the emotional state of the chamber. "It is what needed to happen to protect your future. I wish you could see that."

"Well, it's done!" she flung back, a flush of crimson rushing to her round face. "It's done, and every chance of happiness I had is gone with it."

At the outburst, Mrs. Towler left her perch to the left of the fire. "Let's hope he decides to keep the details of this incident to himself. One slip of his irresponsible tongue and your reputation, not to mention the entire family's, will be ruined."

"Oh, I am so sick of hearing about reputations!" Rachel jumped from her chair, her hair in disarray and her muslin gown rumpled. "We are so far removed from Plymouth or any society whatsoever. What does it even matter? And who in Yorkshire could possibly care what I have to say or think or do?"

"Watch what you say, child." Mrs. Towler's gaze tightened. "You will want to marry well one day. Actions like this can follow you."

"Enough," Mr. Warrington interjected, holding his hand palm out toward his mother-in-law. "Rachel, you should go to bed. The hour's late. Everyone's tired. We can discuss this further in the morning."

Rachel pursed her lips and clenched her fists at her sides. She squared her shoulders and jutted her pointed, trembling chin upward. In a vibrant display of excluding her family members, she whirled to face Cassandra and articulated, "Good night, *Miss Hale*." Without waiting for Cassandra's response, she fled from the room.

Initially no one moved or spoke, as if Rachel had taken the room's energy with her. And then Mrs. Towler threw her hands in the air. "This is messy business."

"Give her time to calm down." Mr. Warrington shoved his fingers through his hair before pinning his gaze on his mother-in-law. "Give us all time to calm down."

Then he turned to her. "Miss Hale, I apologize that you were brought into this."

Cassandra's discomfort grew by the second. What could she possibly say that would be useful in this family disagreement? "I—I only wish I could help in some way. I hate to see anyone that upset."

"She brought it on herself," snipped Mrs. Towler. "We've been warning her as such for months."

In an attempt to lighten the room's heavy atmosphere, Cassandra shrugged. "Who among us has not made ill-advised decisions in our youth?"

Both turned toward her at the statement.

Mrs. Towler folded her hands in front of her. "Rachel is hardly a youth, Miss Hale. She is a young woman of sixteen. Far too old to allow romanticism to cloud her judgment. You cannot be so ignorant. You know as well as I that if anyone learns of this her reputation will be in tatters."

The harshness in the woman's tone irked Cassandra. It was clear that Rachel had made a poor decision, but regardless, Rachel needed understanding, not censure.

Cassandra was not exactly sure what came over her. She was extremely hot, after just being extremely cold, and she was tired. Annoyed. And the words rushed out of her mouth before she checked them. "I would think that at a time like this, Miss Warrington's well-being would be more of a concern than what others say about her."

Mrs. Towler jerked her head up. "My goodness. You've an awfully strong opinion on something—and someone—about whom you know very little. It borders on the offensive."

The frigid response echoed in the silence and made it clear that she had, indeed, overstepped her bounds. Cassandra looked down at the Persian rug beneath her feet before she raised her chin. "My apologies, then, if I have offended."

At this Mr. Warrington intervened. "We are in debt to you, Miss Hale. By Rachel's own admission you were instrumental in helping her successfully navigate the situation."

Mrs. Towler followed his words. "I hope we can trust you for discretion."

Cassandra raised her eyebrows in incredulity. For whom would she even tell? "Discretion? My only concern was her safety, Mrs. Towler. I certainly would never intrude if I didn't think it necessary, and I'd never reveal anything that would cast a young woman's integrity into question."

Cassandra's irritation mounted as Mrs. Towler's smug expression intensified. She might not know much about family dynamics, but she hoped they were kinder than this to Rachel. Her inability to mask her true opinions had always been a downfall, and she now teetered on the cusp of saying more than she ought. "I must be going. I can see myself out."

Fortunately, no one had taken her cloak when she arrived. She snatched it from the chair next to her, fixed her eyes on the door, and headed toward it.

But Mr. Warrington stepped in front of her, blocking the way. "You can't leave alone. It's far too dark and late."

"Yes, I can." She met his gaze, stopping a few feet before him. "I am quite capable of walking home."

He shook his head. "I do not doubt that, but it is now the middle of the night. No need for you to leave. We can certainly offer you lodgings here."

"Thank you, no." She almost laughed at the ridiculousness of the suggestion. "I will take my leave."

Chapter 9

James stared at Miss Hale, noting her tightly pressed lips and the flush on her high cheekbones. She was angry, and rightfully so. She'd offered them a service, a kindness, and now his mother-in-law's behavior toward her was inexcusable.

He could not blame Miss Hale for wanting to leave, but he needed to speak with her privately. He now had more questions than answers, and he must ensure that Standish was truly out of his sister's life. After all, she was the only one who could answer his questions without bias. Complicating the matter further, Mr. Shepard's warnings of violence and turmoil were fresh in his mind. What if this woman walked home and was attacked?

No, this could not be permitted.

Miss Hale wrapped her cape over her arm and moved around him toward the door.

He stepped forward just enough to prevent her from exiting completely. "Then allow me to call the carriage. There's no need to walk."

Miss Hale's jaw twitched, and fire smoldered as she glared once again toward Mrs. Towler. "If we are to speak of reputations, then returning in the carriage from Briarton Park would not only wake everyone on the high street but severely damage mine. I thank you for the offer, but a carriage is not necessary."

How could he make her comprehend? "Then I'll escort you myself. I cannot allow a young woman to be walking alone on Briarton property. There are certain dangers of which you might not be aware."

Miss Hale tossed her hair away from her face in annoyance. "As Mrs. Towler has so adeptly indicated, the last thing I—or any other young woman, for that matter—would want is to be seen walking alone with a man in the middle of the night."

Mrs. Towler smirked. "So you do care, then, what others think?"

James ignored his mother-in-law's ill-timed comment. "I must, in good faith, see you back to the village safely, especially after the kindness you have shown Rachel. Moreover, I would like to ask you a little more about what exactly happened—in private."

Miss Hale stared at him, and then her shoulders, which had been held in tight defensiveness, slumped slightly. She sighed and adjusted the cloak on her arm. "Very well, for the sake of Rachel."

Without another word or glance in his direction, Miss Hale exited from the room.

James did not look at his mother-in-law. He knew she would not approve of his escorting Miss Hale home.

And he did not care.

For Miss Hale alone had answers to their questions that were presently the most important thing in the world.

He grabbed his discarded greatcoat and followed her from the sitting room.

Miss Hale traversed Briarton's corridors as if she'd done so a dozen times. She swept down the angled staircase and through the darkened great hall toward the main entrance, with swift motions indicating that she could not exit the house soon enough.

And could he blame her?

Without a word he followed her out into the cold, still night. Above them the clouds had cleared and stars twinkled. He'd not even had time to grab a lantern. At least the moonlight was bright enough to light the way. He trotted to catch up and then fell into step next to her. "That was inexcusable. I'm sorry."

Her pace slowed slightly, but she did not divert her gaze from the path before her. Even in her haste her movements exuded grace. "She certainly has her opinions."

"My mother-in-law has good intentions, but if she's angry or disagrees, there is no changing her mind." He tried to lighten his tone. "We've not even been able to retain a butler for longer than a month because of her *opinions*."

Clearly not interested in his attempt at lighter conversation, she lifted her cape, shook it out as she walked, and wrapped it around her shoulders.

He didn't dare offer assistance.

They walked in silence until her cloak was fastened. "A teacher once told me that opinions, thoughts, and actions are the only things a woman can truly own. Everything else is subject to the influence of others. 'Tis one thing for Mrs. Towler to express her anger to me. I'll likely never see her again. But it's another matter entirely to take it out on Rachel. I don't know specifics, but I do know that young women of Rachel's age require patience and understanding. If you do not offer these, you risk pushing her away forever."

He could not fault Miss Hale's brashness. She'd been roped into a difficult situation in the middle of the night, and to intensify the situation, she'd been insulted. Even so, the walk to Anston was not a long one. He needed to keep the facts at hand and find out what really transpired. "Can you tell me what happened? Please. I—I need your help."

She slowed at his request and expelled a breath, pluming frosty air into the night. "I'm residing at Mrs. Martin's boardinghouse, and

I heard them arguing outside of my window. As far as I witnessed, everything transpired as Rachel said. The young man wanted her to leave with him, and she did not want to go. He began to get violent, so I let him know his actions were being observed."

"And that's it?" Miss Hale was quickly becoming one of the most unusual women he had ever encountered. "You just interrupted?"

"Of course."

"You had no idea who they were! Were you not frightened for your safety?"

"No. I only saw a woman who needed help. Besides, I always carry a weapon with me."

He stopped walking. "A weapon? Surely you jest."

Miss Hale shook her head. "I've a dagger in my boot this very moment. Do you really think I'd have agreed to walk alone with a man in the middle of the night without one?"

He was not exactly sure how to respond.

"It surprises me that not every lady takes such precautions when out alone," she continued matter-of-factly. "At the school where I taught, the manservant was a retired soldier who had lost his leg in battle. He was determined to teach every student the art of defense. It was not ladylike, of course, but women must be able to protect themselves. I think we can agree that men do not always have a woman's best interests at heart."

Never had he heard a woman speak so openly on this topic. James tried to imagine Rachel, Elizabeth, or even Mrs. Towler with a dagger. It was almost comical, and yet he could see the benefit of such a skill. How would Rachel have reacted differently this night if she had known how to protect herself?

They were nearing the edge of Briarton's property, and he still had so many questions. "Did you see Standish leave?"

"I saw him head toward the inn, but I did not see him depart. He said there was a carriage waiting."

Disappointment stung. James wanted to know for certain that this man was miles away from his sister and that he could never do her harm.

This entire evening—this entire day, actually—had been strange, but this was perhaps the strangest way to end it. They walked over the bridge in silence and drew to a stop at the foot of the bridge as it opened up to the high street.

She turned to him, and it struck him as the first time she had fully met his gaze, and even in the dark he could make out the charming slope of her nose. "You should be proud of your sister, Mr. Warrington. She made an error in judgment, and I know you must be frustrated, but she rectified it before permanent damage could be done. We all learn as we grow, and she, in the end, acted with bravery instead of cowering to a man's will."

He had not thought of the night's events in that manner. He considered her actions selfish. Foolish even. But brave?

As they prepared to part, he found himself surprisingly reluctant to bid her farewell. He was curious—genuinely curious—as to what else she would have to say on the matter. She'd witnessed his family at their worst. In spite of it all, he could appreciate her unique view on her surroundings. "How long do you intend to stay in Anston?"

"I'll stay here as long as necessary to find out what I can about my family, as I told you this morning. At your suggestion I did meet with the vicar and his housekeeper earlier today, and he seems to think he will be able to help me."

"And what then?"

"I'm not sure." She gave a little shrug. "I'll go wherever I secure a teaching position, most likely."

"Well, my family is in your debt. If there is ever anything I can do for you while you are in Anston, all you must do is ask."

She finally offered the subtlest of smiles. "There is no need for gratitude, Mr. Warrington. I'm happy to have been a help to your sister. And if I ever do need assistance, I will ask."

She curtsied, and then, after a cautious glance to her right and to her left, her cloak-covered figure retreated across the mist-laden road, passed the now-quiet inn, and disappeared into the shadows of the alley.

All was silent, yet he thought he could discern the scraping of wood against wood as the door opened and closed.

As he stood there, alone, a familiar feeling of emptiness plagued him—the loneliness that had been his companion since Elizabeth's death. And as he walked back through the silence, he was painfully aware of what had just occurred. He was intrigued by her.

He'd experienced a similar feeling about a woman only once before. The day he'd met Elizabeth.

And the realization of that fact alarmed him.

Chapter 10

Cassandra reentered her chamber at Mrs. Martin's boardinghouse the same way she had left—through the alley door of the darkened kitchen. She found her room just as she had left it—dark and frigid, with only the faintest bit of moonlight filtering through the window. The rag plugging the hole in the windowpane had fallen, and a frosty chill cloaked everything. Even the blankets atop her bed were cold to the touch.

She lifted the corner of the curtain, just as she had a few hours ago, to see if she could glimpse Mr. Warrington. But she didn't have the proper angle to see the bridge's end.

Without removing her cloak or the dagger from her boot, she dropped down atop her bed. As she did, the ropes supporting it creaked. One press of her hand against the cotton mattress ticking confirmed the flatness of the chaff inside. She groaned at the discomfort of it and reached for her pocket watch, which she had left on the rickety bedside table, and squinted to see in the faint light. The hour was almost two.

She sighed, gripped the metal timepiece between her fingers, and relaxed her head on the pillow, which was every bit as rough as the mattress. She might get a couple of precious hours of sleep before she had to awaken. But even though her body cried for rest, she was haunted by the pain in Rachel's expression.

No, she did not know the details of what had transpired between Rachel and the young man, but she was confident that despite the mother-in-law's overly strict criticism, Rachel was in a good home and the situation would right itself with time. But it was the reminder of Cassandra's own turbulent past, conjured by the similarities to her own dalliance, that resounded.

It had been a long time since she'd really thought about Frederick and pondered how different her life could have been if they had indeed eloped.

It had been cold that night, too, when Mrs. Denton disrupted their clandestine departure. She'd been absolute in her demand for Cassandra to return, and Cassandra had acquiesced out of both respect and fear. After that moment they'd never spoken of it again.

Mrs. Denton might not have been her mother, but she'd taught her more than anyone else and had undoubtedly been the most influential person in Cassandra's life. But the recent betrayal of the letter—the blatant deceit—was unforgivable. Unconscionable. Agonizing beyond belief.

One action, one opinion, one lie did not define a life. But sometimes it could alter the course of an entire existence.

A solitary tear, hot as fire, slid down her cold cheek. Now more than ever she was homesick for what was familiar. Just how much of her reality had been part of Mrs. Denton's lie she did not know, but she yearned for the predictability her life had once boasted. She wished she could go to her trusted advisor like she had so many times over the course of her life for wisdom and guidance. But that counselor would never return, and even worse, she'd taken with her the peace Cassandra had previously relied upon.

Shivering still, she tightened the blanket around her and rested her head against the coarse pillow. There could be no changing the past—no changing the shock and pain, which would shape her, undoubtedly, for years to come. She could question past actions, but to what end? The only thing she could do now was be wiser, more discerning, and act not out of comfort and predictability but out of self-preservation. She had to be smarter. Shrewder. And braver.

It was not the bright white light of dawn that woke Cassandra the next morning. Nor was it the nipping, stubborn stream of air that curled relentlessly through the window's cracked pane. The shuffle of feet over a stone floor and animated feminine chatter pulled her from slumber.

Cassandra sat up, blinked away the sleep, and took stock of her surroundings. She was still fully clothed. She even wore her boots and cloak. Her pocket watch had slid from her grip during sleep and was on the bed next to her pillow.

Then the events of the past night rushed her.

Rachel.

Mr. Warrington.

A midnight intervention and the rude Mrs. Towler.

Cassandra stood, stretched her arms above her head, being careful not to hit the low ceiling, stepped to the window, and pulled the thin covering away. Outside, the inn was visible. Carriages, horses, and men all moved about in the morning's low-hanging fog.

A bout of laughter from the kitchen captured her attention as the scents of ham and bread met her senses. Her stomach grumbled. She'd forgone the previous night's evening meal. If she was to be effective today in the meeting Mr. North had promised, she'd need her wits about her.

She removed her cloak and quickly changed yesterday's gown to a lighter gown of soft peacock-blue twill with long sleeves and a Vandyke hem. After letting down her hair, brushing the long tresses, and pinning them tidily against the back of her head, she checked her reflection in the cracked looking glass on the wall. The shadows under her eyes bore the only visible evidence to the previous night's events.

She pinched her cheeks for color.

This would have to do.

Mr. North had indicated that several seamstresses lived here. From what she could hear, they sounded chatty. Happy.

When she entered the kitchen, all attention turned to her. Six women, all of whom were plainly dressed and appeared to be about her age, stared in her direction.

Silence engulfed the chamber.

Cassandra forced a smile and gave a nod in the direction of the others.

A woman whom she recognized as one of the maids stood next to the fire and pointed toward the table with the spoon in her hand. "Sit there. We'll bring 'bout your plate."

Cassandra took the closest open seat and sat down.

The whispers started once again in the room, and Cassandra was reminded of her first day at the new school nearly nineteen years prior. She generally considered herself confident and self-assured. Had not Mrs. Denton taught her to be such? But as she sat here, the object of conspicuous scrutiny, her confidence wavered.

A tawny-haired girl from the end of the table stood, picked up her plate, moved toward Cassandra, and dropped into the chair next to her. "So, you are the vicar's friend, eh?"

"Mr. N-North?" Cassandra stammered at the odd line.

"Of course! He's the only vicar around here." The girl laughed at her own little jest before she took a bite of the salted pork on her plate. "I heard he recommended you to Mrs. Martin."

Cassandra tried to read the inflection in the woman's cheery tone and carefully chose her words. "I met Mr. North yesterday. I needed some assistance, and he was very kind to help me."

"Ah yes. Kind indeed. But then again, he has to be, hasn't he? He's the vicar. Besides him, most other people are suspicious about newcomers." A twinkle sparkled in her pale green eyes. "My name is Betsy Tilken."

"I'm Cassandra Hale."

A giggle emerged from the other end of the table, and Cassandra looked up to see that the women were staring at her slyly, as if a jest had just been made at her expense.

Fresh self-consciousness wound its way through her. She shifted uncomfortably.

"Don't mind them." With a toss of her frizzy locks, Betsy glanced over her shoulder at the other women and lowed her otherwise high-pitched voice. "Like I said, many people are suspicious about newcomers. But not me. Where are you from then?"

"Lamby. A village outside of London."

"London, eh? I've never been to London. Heard it is a wonder to behold. Anston must be a sight different."

"I rarely had cause to venture into the main parts of London. Lamby was quite small. This reminds me of it, actually."

"So, what brings you here? Not many people come to Anston for no purpose."

Mr. North's warning about sharing too many details flamed in her mind. "Family affairs."

"Ah." Betsy raised a playful brow. "Family affairs, is it?"

A distant bell rang, and all the women at the table shuffled up. Betsy grabbed a piece of bread from the table and stood. "Well then, Cassandra Hale, that's my call. I must be going. Tomorrow is Sunday, and Mrs. Martin requires us all to attend church. Even you, I reckon. The girls and I walk over together. You should join us. I will wait for you in the morning, if you like."

Perhaps it was the friendliness in her tone, or simply that she offered a sincere smile that eased Cassandra's tension. "Of course, Miss Tilken. I should like that."

"No, no. Not *Miss Tilken*. Nobody calls me that. Betsy's fine."

"And please, call me Cassandra."

As the room cleared and once again fell silent, Cassandra looked to her plate. She scarfed down the bread and salted pork she found there. She wanted to spend a little time before meeting the vicar and his housekeeper to plan her questions.

This was the time for her to find answers.

This was the time for her to finally seek what had never been divulged to her.

As dramatic as it seemed, this conversation could affect the future course of her life, and she was ready for it.

Chapter 11

The quietude was unnerving.

James sat at the breakfast table. Rachel sat across from him. They were alone in the chamber, and all was still save for the morning fire popping in the grate and the tap of the rain on the windowpanes. Neither of them had as of yet acknowledged the previous night's happenings, but even so, a melancholy cloak shrouded them. Her capricious actions needed to be addressed.

In that moment, perhaps more than in any other, Rachel's appearance garnered his attention. Even though they were half brother and sister, they bore little likeness to each other, apart from sharing their father's steely gray eyes. Whereas he had his mother's sand-colored hair and square jaw, she boasted her mother's tightly curled tresses and round face.

But this morning, that usually wild mass of disorderly curls was tamed neatly at the base of her neck. Despite the pallor of her skin, a delicate flush had replaced the childish ruddiness of her cheeks. Even her posture was different. No longer was she hunched over with her arms folded across her chest and her lips fixed firmly in an ever-present pout. She sat straight. She was still. Restrained. And unusually reserved.

When had this change from rowdy child to willful young woman occurred? When had she become the young lady before him?

She pushed her food around on her plate with her spoon without gazing in his direction. "You're staring at me. I know you're angry. You might as well say it."

James had to remain imperturbable. "No, Rachel. I'm not angry."

"Not angry?" she scoffed, still refusing to look at him. "I don't believe you."

He didn't want to argue. They'd already exhausted the subject of Mr. Standish. What mattered now was reestablishing peace in their home. Clearly she regarded him as the enemy—as if he alone was the very hurdle to happiness and freedom.

He had to make her see otherwise.

"Do you know why I insisted that you come and live with me when Father died?" James leaned back in his chair.

She raised a thin brow at the question, then shrugged one shoulder nonchalantly. "I suppose you had to."

"No, I did not have to. You were seven. Your mother's sister wanted you to come and live with her. But I fought her. I actually petitioned the courts, although I don't expect you remember any of that now."

She sat motionless, eyes diverted.

He forged ahead. "Maria and Rose were not even born, but Elizabeth and I felt it was important that family stay together."

"Well, things were different then, weren't they?"

James sensed the hurt in his sister's words. Elizabeth and Rachel had been very close, and given the fact that Elizabeth had been the only real maternal influence in Rachel's life, the resulting chasm was evident. "No, it's not the same, but you're missing the point. We must look out for one another, you and I. We're family."

She flicked a defiant gaze up at him. "Does family mean Mrs. Towler too?"

He swallowed, unprepared for the challenge hidden in her arrow-like question.

As he considered his response, her words lashed out. "If it is family you prize so much, why do you allow Mrs. Towler to be so cruel to me? In fact, why do you allow her to remain here at all?"

"That's not fair, Rachel."

"How can you say that?" Her spoon clattered to the table. "Of course it's fair. She scowls at me all the time, and you do not intervene. Nothing I do is ever good enough for her. Poor Elizabeth! Could you imagine growing up with such a mother?"

He shouldn't have been taken aback by Rachel's outburst.

Yet he was.

Yes, Elizabeth was graceful. Elegant. She was indeed a result of her mother's meticulous efforts. But he doubted it was vanity alone that urged her to raise her daughter in such a manner.

James softened his tone. "Elizabeth loved her mother. She'd want us to make the best of things. Mrs. Towler is alone. Think of how awful that would be. If it weren't for Briarton Park, where would she go?"

Rachel scoffed. "She is very high and mighty for someone who has nowhere to go."

"She's family."

"She's not *my* family."

"She's our family," he said, louder. "We don't turn our back on family. Ever. If anything, I believe she is harsh because she's scared."

"Scared?" Rachel huffed a sarcastic laugh. "People are scared of her. Not the other way around."

"She is scared, Rachel. Scared of being alone and without. She knows and understands the genteel world. For her, money is security. And where you're concerned, she believes that pristine manners and behavior will position you to catch a wealthy husband, and then you'll be set for life."

"You don't agree with that, do you?"

When he didn't respond, she slumped her shoulders.

He gave her several moments to think on things before he said, "Regarding last night—"

Rachel's groan and eye roll interrupted him.

"As I was saying about last night, we'll say no more on the subject."

She wrinkled her face. "What, no punishment?"

"Oh yes. You'll be staying on the grounds and will not leave for any reason without permission. I'll personally collect any letters you receive and deliver them to you, and any letters you send out will go through me as well. Additionally, you owe a few people, including Mrs. Towler and even Mrs. Helock, an apology. And you must find a time to thank Miss Hale. As I recall, you scurried off from her with a huff and a pout."

Rachel lowered her face and nodded.

"And about Mr. Standish . . ."

At the name Rachel stiffened. Her silver eyes flashed upward.

James continued. "I think it goes without saying, I am not to hear another word—or see any evidence of him—at all. If I do, then—"

"You need not concern yourself on that account," she added in haste. "I saw last night what a brute he is. I never want to see him again."

Something in his heart ached for all the heartbreak his sister had endured. He wanted to protect her. He could never forgive himself if something untoward should happen. And this near calamity had been too close.

He also thought of Miss Hale's words that his sister had been brave, in her own way.

After several seconds she looked down at her sleeve and fussed with the hem of it. "And for what it is worth, I am sorry. I should have listened to you."

Her contrition took him a bit by surprise. She was not one to apologize—not willingly, anyway.

"Let's put it behind us then."

"If any good has come of this, I do believe that Miss Hale will be a friend for me." Her lip quirked into almost a smile. "If I am allowed to see her, of course."

He thought of Miss Hale, with her sharp wit, her definite opinions, and the dagger in her boot. He did not know her well, but at first blush she was exactly the sort of woman he wanted to influence his sister. "One thing at a time, young lady. All in good time."

Chapter 12

Cassandra was not sure what she expected the former housekeeper of Briarton Park to look like, but this woman was certainly not it.

The severe image of Briarton Park's current housekeeper, Mrs. Helock, glowed fresh in her mind—a neat, tidy woman with graying dark hair.

Mrs. Susannah Hutton could not be more different. Her hair was faded, frizzed with wiry curls, capped with a frilly mobcap, and closer to white than blonde. Lines etched her plump, florid face, and her pale eyes were narrowed in suspicion—and annoyance—at having to receive unexpected guests.

Confidence and charm flowed from Mr. North's words in spite of the chilly reception. "Mrs. Hutton. It's always a pleasure to see you. Thank you for agreeing to meet with us."

"I didn't really agree to anything, did I?" Mrs. Hutton snapped as she wiped her hands on her linen apron, the statement more a declaration than a question. "I received your message that you were to call, and, well, here we all are."

Mrs. Pearson thrust a basket of bread and apples into Mrs. Hutton's arms. "Come now, since when is there a reason for formality when meetin' among friends? Your name was spoken in conversation yesterday, and I thought a visit and a chat was long overdue. Is your sister at home?" Mrs. Pearson turned after moving next to the fire and adjusted her reticule in her gloved hands.

Mrs. Hutton handed the basket to a young maid in the corridor. "No, she is not. She's gone to visit our cousin over in Northumberland."

"Oh, I had no idea," Mr. North exclaimed, his ever-present smile unaffected. "I'm sorry we've missed her."

"Did you not notice she's been absent from church these past four weeks?" Mrs. Hutton raised one gray eyebrow dubiously before turning her attention to Cassandra. "And who have we here?"

Before Cassandra could respond, Mrs. Pearson came and took her arm, then drew her farther into the sitting room. "I have the privilege of introducing Miss Cassandra Hale. She's come to Anston seeking information 'bout her family."

Cassandra curtsied to mask the butterflies within her.

But instead of returning the greeting, Mrs. Hutton grimaced. "You look awfully young to be traveling alone."

Mrs. Pearson forged ahead. "Miss Hale had reason to call on Briarton Park askin' after Mr. Robert Clark. 'Course he's dead now, and she had questions I could not answer. But then I recalled your long-standing tie to the family. I thought there could be no harm in bringin' her for a visit. I'm sure you two would have a great deal to talk about."

An odd quirk tweaked Mrs. Hutton's lower lip. "I don't know what I could tell you. I have not stepped foot in that place in nigh onto seven years."

"Be that as it may, it might be a pleasant way to pass some time. Come now. Surely a few questions won't hurt anythin'."

Mrs. Hutton, almost as a sign of defeat, motioned to the sofa and chair next to the fire grate. "Well then, since you're here, you might as well be seated."

When they were all situated, Mrs. Hutton lifted a fat orange cat to her lap. "So now. Tell me what this visit is really all about."

After sharing brief details about her past and the letter, Cassandra retrieved the missive from her reticule, extended it to Mrs. Hutton, and waited for her to read it.

When Mrs. Hutton was done with the letter she lowered it, removed her spectacles from the bridge of her wide nose, and returned it to Cassandra. "I can confirm that that is, indeed, Mr. Clark's penmanship. I'd recognize it anywhere."

Optimism flared, and Cassandra leaned forward. "Do you have any idea what he could mean or to what he could be referring? This was the first I'd ever heard from him. It's really quite cryptic."

Mrs. Hutton's gaze alighted on each of her visitors. The displeasure she'd displayed at their arrival seemed to have intensified. "I was indeed the housekeeper to the Clark family for nearly three decades, but one of the first priorities of such an occupation is discretion. I tended to the running of the house. Their private lives were their own concern."

"Goodness, Mrs. Hutton. We aren't askin' after any deep, dark secrets." Mrs. Pearson laughed, her hand flying to her chest. "The child merely seeks family information."

But Mrs. Hutton's mood did not lighten. "Just so I'm clear on what you are asking, you are in search of information about your *parents*? That is what all this is about?"

Cassandra nodded. "Yes, ma'am, it is."

"And you think Mr. Clark knows who your parents are?"

Cassandra glanced toward Mrs. Pearson, as if searching for reassurance. "Does not the letter suggest as much?"

Mrs. Hutton fixed her stare pointedly on Cassandra. Her tone sharpened. "Do you think Mr. Clark is your father?"

Cassandra's throat went dry, and she shifted uncomfortably.

It was a condemning, weighted question—one she could not answer without more certainty.

Mrs. Hutton stood abruptly and set the cat on the floor. "If you've come to me for information about Mr. Robert Clark, then you've come to the wrong place. I suggest you call on their son. But a word of caution, Miss Hale. I can only assume someone went through a great deal to keep your parentage a secret. Perhaps the secrecy is a gift."

As Cassandra, Mr. North, and Mrs. Pearson walked away from the thatched cottage at the conclusion of the awkward visit, Mrs. Pearson looped her arm through Cassandra's. "La, I told you she wasn't the friendliest sort. I'm sorry she didn't shed light on the subject for ye."

"It's all right, Mrs. Pearson." Cassandra gave a little shrug as she traversed the cobbled road. "I had hoped for easy answers, but that was unrealistic."

Mrs. Pearson's thin face lit up. "I've an idea, Mr. North. Perhaps you should check the birth records an' see if any Hales were born in the area. Or death records, for th' matter. I can't recall any parishioners by the name of Hale, but perhaps history will. How old are you, child? When were you born?"

"Four and twenty. I was born in November of 1787."

"Excellent thought, Mrs. Pearson," added Mr. North. "I'll review them later today."

They walked in silence on the high street, passing tidy shops and small clusters of people. It was late in the day now, and even though it was a couple of hours from nightfall, the dark canopy of clouds and the bitter blasts of wind made the hour seem much later than it was.

As they prepared to bid their farewells outside of the church's graveyard, Mrs. Pearson reached out to grab Cassandra's gloved hands in her own. "Don't give up hope, dear. There are still avenues to explore with this search of yours."

Before Cassandra could respond, Mr. North leaned closer, his chocolate-brown eyes twinkling with a hint of mischief. "And I, for one, refuse to give up hope. It's a mystery to solve, isn't it? I think Mrs. Hutton was right about Peter Clark. I will write to him yet today and see if we can have an interview with him."

"We?" Cassandra asked with a little laugh. "I've already taken up enough of your time already."

"I meant *you*, of course, but I'm invested now. Besides, you'll require a proper introduction, and given the topic it could be an uncomfortable conversation. He does have a certain reputation for brashness. But fear not. People are usually on their best behavior around me."

Something across the high street caught Cassandra's eye. Near the baker's shop, a large man with white hair and a black cloak stood partially behind the building's corner.

Though the day's light had grown dim, there was no mistaking what she saw. He was staring. At her.

Once the man realized she noticed him, he quickly withdrew around the corner.

Cassandra's blood ran cold.

Mr. North's question drew her back to the conversation. "Is something amiss, Miss Hale?"

"N-no," she stammered, shaking her head. "I thought I saw something, but I was mistaken."

"What did you see?" He leaned against the gate and angled his head to see what she had been looking at.

"It was nothing, really." She toyed with the strings of her reticule. "I thought I saw a man in the shadows there. But clearly no one is there."

"It's the graveyard." Mr. North nodded toward the stones behind them. "It plays tricks on one's mind. Ghosts and mists and thunder and such."

Bemused, she grinned at her own foolishness. "How odd to hear a vicar speak of ghosts."

"A vicar, yes, but a man first, and a superstitious one at that."

They bid their farewells and made plans to speak the next day, and she departed. Mr. North and Mrs. Pearson both held such optimism about the day's visit, but Cassandra wanted to get back to her room to ponder what she had experienced.

The truth was, she was no further along in her search than when she first arrived. If anything, discouragement was setting in, and the weight of it overwhelmed her.

A cold wind fluttered the folds of her pelisse as she walked back across the high street to the boardinghouse. She cast a glance in the direction where the man had been standing.

No one was there except for a few women crossing the high street to the haberdashery.

She had allowed herself to imagine something that was simply not true. Perhaps Mr. North was right—her mind was playing tricks on her.

Chapter 13

Cassandra adjusted the collar of her Prussian-blue spencer and settled on the hard wooden pew. She leaned over to Betsy, seated to her left. "Is it always this cold in here?"

Betsy nodded. "It'll get colder. Just wait until winter really arrives."

Cassandra rubbed her gloved hands together quickly to generate heat as they waited for the sermon to start and glanced around with piqued curiosity. The only church she had ever attended was the one in Lamby, where Frederick's father had been the vicar. Every Sunday the girls from school would line the four pews at the very back on the right, and the occupants of the nearby boys' school would fill the pews on the left.

"He is handsome, isn't he?" Betsy whispered.

Cassandra followed her friend's gaze to see Mr. North enter near the altar. His thick, straight hair was combed neatly to the side, his tidy side-whiskers emphasized his high cheekbones, and his warm eyes appeared bright against his fair, clean-shaven complexion. She'd only seen him in his somber black coat and trousers, but the flowing fabric and white band at his throat transformed him from friendly helper to a more official capacity.

"You're fortunate." Betsy's voice was barely above a whisper.

"Here not even a week and already you're catching the eye of one of the most eligible men in the village."

Cassandra shifted uncomfortably. She knew all too well how gossip could grow, especially on such a topic, and she had no desire to be fodder for such chatter. Not again. She gave a little laugh to lighten the matter. "Don't be silly. I only just met Mr. North a couple of days ago."

"And that is all it takes sometimes, is it not?" Betsy raised her fair brow playfully. "There is much about you that I don't know, but I do know there is hardly a young woman who would not benefit by a match to such an influential man."

Cassandra looked toward Mr. North again. Yes, it was important to be self-sufficient, but it was every woman's goal—not to mention hers—to one day marry well. And Mr. North had been very eager and attentive and did seem fond of her. With the school gone she needed to seriously consider that her future might soon include marriage. "Yes, I'm sure he would make a fine match for someone."

"I'd say so, but he's never given anyone else a second glance. At least not someone like the girls or myself." Betsy motioned to the other boarders at the end of the pew and in the pew behind them.

Cassandra did not miss the hint of sarcasm—or disapproval—in her new friend's voice. "I'm not sure I understand," she lied.

Betsy smirked. "Putting it plainly, the girls and I are a little too lowly for our vicar's society preferences. Every man has a reputation, vicar or not. Mr. North prefers to keep company with those who are more socially affluent than the likes of us."

"How can that be? For just yesterday I witnessed him stopping with Mrs. Pearson to deliver some bread baskets to the cottages along the river."

"Oh yes, Mrs. Pearson is inarguably cordial. I've never met a more thoughtful soul. But I suspect Mr. North had other motives for his display of generosity, like perhaps impressing a pretty visitor to our village. You're entitled to your own opinions on the matter, of course, but I've lived here for well over a year now and have not missed a single Sunday since my arrival—Mrs. Martin has made sure of that—and I'm certain that our vicar does not even know my name."

The reproachful words were sobering. Cassandra would have expected the vicar to be accepting of everyone. The mere suggestion of the contrary clouded the high regard she'd held him in until this point.

Their conversation fell silent, and Cassandra returned her attention to the activity around her. The gathering in the church was much larger than the congregation at Lamby. For the most part the congregation was plainly dressed in drab shades of grays and browns. Mrs. Pearson had told her that many of their parishioners were millers, weavers, or other occupations that worked wool, and judging by appearances only, the congregation seemed to match her description.

Cassandra noticed Mrs. Hutton sitting near the front on the far end of a pew. She was dressed in a dark green pelisse with elegant braiding and a high collar, and her silvery hair was much tidier than it had been at their visit. She spoke with no one but sat rigidly, her focus straight ahead.

A strange sense of defeat settled over Cassandra. She was convinced that Mrs. Hutton knew much more than she was letting on. But what could be done for it? She could not force the woman to divulge what she wanted to keep secret.

Cassandra was so lost in thought that she almost didn't notice when the Warrington family appeared in the nave. It strangely warmed her to see familiar faces, even though the circumstances surrounding their interactions had been tense. Mr. Warrington led them, clad in a smart coat of olive-green broadcloth. He held a little girl with an abundance of blonde hair in his arms, and another young girl held his hand. He looked different today, lighter. Rachel followed him in an elegant campanula pelisse, and Mrs. Towler followed her.

Of the family, Rachel was the only one to look out over the congregation, and she quickly caught Cassandra's eye and nodded.

Cassandra smiled in response.

"Are you acquainted with them?" Betsy asked, clearly noting the subtle nod.

"The Warringtons?" Cassandra considered how much to divulge. "Yes, but I have only been introduced. I don't know them well."

"Introduced? Ah, that makes sense then."

The judgment in Betsy's voice was difficult to ignore. There was more to the story than Betsy was letting on, but now was hardly the time or the place to investigate such things.

Mr. North climbed the pulpit, and the service began.

Cassandra tried to focus on his sermon, but it was not for lack of an impressive delivery, for Mr. North's effectiveness as a speaker could not be disputed. His clear voice commanded attention, his dedication to his topic was decided, and his appearance was captivating—even more so now as the light streamed through the tall windows and the situation allowed her to study his features without being accused of staring.

But it was the Warrington family that now captured her thoughts. Mr. Warrington had not looked in her direction. In fact, from her angle, she could see only his profile. But the two little girls next to him wiggled and chattered during the sermon. Given Mrs. Towler's demand for propriety with Rachel, Cassandra was astonished that she would allow it. Furthermore, Cassandra was surprised there was no governess. At least not one of whom she was aware.

Rachel glanced back at her a couple of times. Cassandra was genuinely happy to see the girl in a better state than the one she had left her in during their previous interaction.

As her gaze drifted back to him, she noticed it. Ever so slightly.

Mr. Warrington, with his cool gray eyes and calm demeanor, had glanced in her direction.

But only for a moment.

An unexpected jolt shot through her.

And then, as quickly as he had glanced her way, the moment was over, and he leaned to his side to quiet a chatty child.

He was a handsome man. Very handsome. And the gentleness in his nature was attractive. Despite the frustration she had felt after the churlish treatment by Mrs. Towler, her experience with Mr. Warrington had been quite different. She supposed that at one point in her life, it would have been easy to consider such a time romantic. All the elements were present on their walk back to the boardinghouse—they'd just endured an intense event and were alone under the cover of darkness. But time and experience had a way of dulling the allure of such a situation. And once tarnished, she doubted the luster would ever return.

At one time, securing a husband would have been first and foremost on her mind. But now she needed to remain focused on answering the questions that would complete her.

After the morning's service, Cassandra trailed Betsy from the nave, past the stone font, and through the ancient wooden doors. Just outside, on the path leading to the high street, Mr. North greeted each of his parishioners as they departed.

He smiled, familiarly and almost affectionately, as she approached, and he bowed. "Miss Hale! I wondered if you would be joining us today."

She curtsied. "I would not miss it."

He cast a glance toward Betsy and gave a nod before returning his attention to her. "I hope while you are in our village you'll join us each week."

As he spoke to her, enthusiasm animated his expression, but the manner in which he ignored Betsy added vibrance to the haughty picture of him Betsy had painted earlier.

Other parishioners were queuing behind her, so she bid farewell and moved farther down the path, through the very graveyard where she had first encountered him. Betsy muttered something about needing to speak with someone, and she stepped away, leaving Cassandra alone.

She was but a few steps away from the Clark gravestones. Her gaze drifted over to them.

Dread, sadness, and the desire for answers pushed forward.

What secrets, if any, did everyone besides her know?

At the call of her name, she turned to see Rachel Warrington approaching her. Genuine happiness to see the young woman filled her. "Miss Warrington!"

"I am so glad to see you." Rachel descended in a quick curtsy, her eyes bright and her cheeks pink from the chill in the air. "I was afraid I would not get a chance to see you again. James told me you were not sure how long you would be in the village."

A strange thread pulled within her at the thought of Mr. Warrington speaking of her. "I would not leave without saying goodbye. Besides, I'll be in Anston awhile yet, I think."

Rachel looked down to the gravestones at Cassandra's feet. "James also said that you're searching for information about your family. Are you having any success?"

Cassandra shifted. Somehow it felt safer to speak with the Warringtons on this topic as opposed to Betsy. After all, Cassandra and Rachel already shared a secret—a solidarity—which held with it an understood discretion. "Not quite yet, but I've not given up hope."

Rachel fiddled with the strings of her reticule and glanced over her thin shoulder before speaking. "I never did thank you for your assistance to me."

Cassandra shook her head. "In truth I did nothing. I just happened to be there."

"Nothing? How can you say that?" Incredulity clouded Rachel's expression. "Who knows what would have happened or where I'd be if you'd not intervened. I'm not sure I would have been strong enough to resist Richard on my own."

"You are much, much stronger than you think you are." Cassandra squeezed Rachel's gloved hand. "Have you heard from the young man?"

Rachel's face fell. "No. And I doubt I ever shall again. It is for the best. I see that now."

"And your brother and Mrs. Towler? Are you on better terms with them than you were the other night?"

Rachel bit her lower lip. "Things are set to right with James. We often don't see things the same way, but we always come 'round. I fear I'll never be on good terms with Mrs. Towler."

A giggle rose from the direction from which Rachel had come. The two Warrington girls were playing on the walkway, clad in matching dove-gray pelisses and chip-straw bonnets adorned with white ribbons. Cassandra recognized the older brunette child from the orchard on her first visit to Briarton Park. "Are those young ladies your nieces?"

Rachel looked over her shoulder, lifting her hand to still the curls wild about her face in the wind. "Yes. Maria and Rose. James's daughters. They are quite spirited."

Cassandra watched as the little one dropped to the ground and pulled some of the grass. "Do they not have a governess?"

"No. They would benefit from one, I'm sure. As it is they run Mrs. Towler ragged. She is supposed to be in charge of them, but she often does not pay them much heed, or rather, she doesn't know what to do with them."

Cassandra frowned. She was definitely in favor of allowing young girls plenty of fresh air, play, and sunshine, but there was a time and a place for such behavior. "And does your brother not intervene?"

"He tries, but he knows nothing of such things. He is like a big child sometimes. He encourages their wildness, I think."

Mr. Warrington swept in and gathered the child in his arms, attempting to redirect the determined girl from the grass and dirt.

Rachel tilted her head to the side, and a glint glimmered in her eye. "Did you not say that you were a teacher? It would be so nice for them to have a teacher—a governess—like you."

"I'm not a governess. Anyway, I'm sure Mr. Warrington will make arrangements for them on that front when the time comes."

"Mrs. Towler has already selected one, a fancy one, or so I'm told. But she will not arrive for several months. Apparently she is traveling with the family she's currently engaged with." Rachel raised her brow. "But I know my brother would like a governess for the children sooner rather than later. And besides, isn't a governess really a teacher who lives with a family?"

It was impossible not to interpret Rachel's meaning.

How had Cassandra not at least thought of it? She was in need of a position. Mr. Warrington had said that he owed her a favor. Could it even be a possibility?

It would not do to raise false hope. "I very much doubt that I am the sort of person your brother and Mrs. Towler have in mind."

Rachel shrugged. "I meant nothing untoward by it. Anyway, I must be off, but will you come to call at Briarton Park presently? My brother has expressly forbade me from leaving the grounds without his permission, but he's said nothing about not having visitors."

The girl exuded eagerness. How could she tell her no? She'd been through a great ordeal. If Cassandra could help her, it would make her feel like she was doing something worthy. Plus, she really would cherish the company. "I should like that very much."

"Good. Tomorrow, perhaps late afternoon?"

Cassandra nodded and watched as Rachel rejoined her family. She said something to Mr. Warrington, and they both looked in her direction. Mr. Warrington bowed from a distance.

She watched him with the youngest girl. She could help him. She was capable of being a governess. She needed a position. And it was right in the village where she needed to be.

The crowd that had gathered began to thin, and she spotted Betsy, who motioned for her to join her. "My, my. Speaking with the Warringtons. The next thing you know, you will be speaking with the Prince Regent himself."

"Don't be silly. Miss Warrington is my friend, just like you are."

Betsy clicked her tongue. "She's kin to the owner of a mill. Most people here work in a mill or are related to someone who does. Lines are drawn very quickly. Just be cautious as to which side you are on."

Chapter 14

Cassandra lifted her face to the sunshine, allowing its bright light to flood over her face and cloaked shoulders. She closed her eyes and let its subtle warmth caress her cheeks.

At this very moment she felt free. Here, outside in the fresh air, she could pretend it was an early spring day back in Lamby and nothing at all had changed. That she was surrounded by the children in her care and confident in her role.

And then she opened her eyes.

The rosy memory faded into her current reality.

She was not surrounded by the girls at her school, but by the other female boarders who were scattered over the hill on patchwork blankets and clad in dark cloaks. There was no green grass or cheery spring buds, only the muted colors of an autumnal terrain, a colorless sky, white sun, and bare, gray trees.

Their picnic was situated on a hill at the end of the high street near the road that turned off to the mills and other buildings. From where they sat, not too far from the church, they overlooked the village of Anston. A stone wall separated them from the high street and the activity that bustled along the cobbles.

Cassandra shifted her gaze to her companions. She was grateful to be included in the outing, but despite the kindness from Betsy, she felt like an outsider. She'd belonged to one place for so long, would she ever really feel comfortable anywhere else?

"Did you ever go on picnics in Lamby?" Betsy removed a piece of bread from their basket sitting between them.

"All the time." Cassandra leaned forward to select a slice.

"With your family?"

Cassandra stiffened. It was a simple question—one that any friend might ask another. Given her current confusion over Mr. North's character, she decided to disregard his warning about sharing too much of her personal life. "No. I don't have any family in Lamby. I was a teacher at a girls' school. During the warm months I would often take my pupils on picnics after church."

Betsy took a bite of the bread. "Ah, a girls' school, was it? Very fancy."

Cassandra could not help but chuckle. "I'm not sure *fancy* is how I'd describe it, but it was my home."

"Where is your family then?"

"I've never known them." Cassandra looked down to the bread in her hand, her appetite gone. "The school was the only family I ever knew, first as a student and then as a teacher."

Betsy leaned back on her fist and tilted her head to the side. "So I ask again. What brings a teacher from a small village to Anston?"

Cassandra returned the bread to the basket and wiped her hands. "My position at the school ended when the owner died recently, and at that time I was given information that hinted that I might be able to learn about my family here. It may all lead to nothing, but with the break in my employment, I thought it would be as good a time as any to search."

"Will you seek a teaching position then?"

"Eventually. I need to start sending out inquiries. It is just that so much has changed in a brief period of time. I wasn't really prepared."

Not prepared was an understatement. In truth, the suddenness of Mrs. Denton's illness was one of the few shocks in her life. And then to find out that she knew the identity of Cassandra's family, but had concealed it from her, compounded the blow.

Betsy noisily wiped her hands together, showering bread crumbs to the ground. "There aren't many schools around here, not the sort you would be used to anyway. Mostly mill people here. The children work alongside the families. Do you think you'll stay in Anston?"

Cassandra shook her head. "I've no idea. I have no employment and, right now, no prospects."

"There's always matrimony."

Cassandra belted out a laugh.

"I do not jest." Betsy took a piece of cheese from the basket. "If a man were to offer for my hand in marriage, I'd accept him straight-away. And I wouldn't be that particular."

"In order to get married, one would have to know a young man," reasoned Cassandra, "and I have spent my life in a girls' school, barely having any contact whatsoever with men."

"Well, it seems that you have no shortage of admirers since you've arrived, Mr. North standing at the front of the line."

Cassandra, eager to shift the focus from herself, asked, "And where are you from?"

"Heyton. A tiny village about a day's travel from here."

"And did you leave family to be here?"

She nodded, tucking her tawny hair under her straw poke bonnet. "My mother is there. With my sister and her family."

"You must miss them."

"Of course. I haven't seen my mother in almost six months, but I am able to send home some money, which makes me feel like I am with her in some small way. Plus, my matrimonial prospects are much better here. One day, perhaps I'll be wed. I hope I am. But for now, this suits as well as anything." Suddenly Betsy straightened. "Oh dear."

Concerned, Cassandra stiffened her posture. "What is it?"

Betsy nodded toward the road, squinting her chartreuse eyes against the strong breeze. "Look who's coming this way."

Cassandra followed her friend's gaze to see Mr. North on the high street, on the far side of the stone wall, walking alongside a man.

"We've picnicked at this very spot nearly every Sunday since spring, and he's never once made an appearance."

Cassandra frowned, unsure what was so unusual about a vicar walking in his own village. "Surely he walks on the high street all the time."

"At this end? By the meadow? On a Sunday? *Tsk*. No."

Mr. North laughed at something his companion said and then looked in their direction. He tipped his hat, said something to the man accompanying him, and then stepped through the gate toward them.

When it became clear they were the object of his interest, Betsy and Cassandra stood from their blanket, and Cassandra brushed a bit of dried grass from her cloak and smoothed her hair.

"Ladies." Mr. North let the gate close behind him and approached. "What a surprise to see you here."

Betsy tilted her head to the side. "Really? That's odd. For we gather here every Sunday, weather permitting."

The cheek in her friend's voice shocked Cassandra.

Betsy continued, almost as if she enjoyed implicating the man for his disregard. "Actually, 'tis odd that you have never noticed us here before."

Mr. North, in true form, beamed a practiced, genial smile, projecting an unruffled disposition, and bowed. "Then you must forgive my oversight."

Betsy glared toward Cassandra. "Please forgive me, Mr. North. I am expected elsewhere."

Before he could respond, she bobbed a curtsy and departed, leaving Cassandra and Mr. North alone.

He glanced down to the quilt and baskets scattered on the ground. "Are you enjoying your picnic?"

Cassandra laced her fingers before her, trying to ignore the stares she sensed from the others in the party. "Very much."

"Today will probably be one of the final mild days of the year, so I am glad you can take advantage of the fine weather." He took a step closer, and his demeanor sobered. "But I confess, I am surprised to see you here, in this company."

Cassandra winced at his bluntness. "Oh? Why?"

Mr. North chuckled good-naturedly and rubbed his hand over his chin before speaking. "Mrs. Martin is a fine Christian woman. One of the most dedicated women I know. But she cannot control the actions of her boarders. When I suggested you stay at the boarding-house, I did not necessarily mean that you needed to associate with the residents on a social level."

No, she did not know these people well, but Betsy had been kind and welcoming. She was not about to judge an entire group so abruptly. "I appreciate the concern, but we're having a lovely time. It's a fine day, and it is much better to be out here in the fresh air than to sit alone in my chamber. Besides, I've been enjoying their company."

He straightened. "I understand such interactions might be a diversion for now, but some of these people—not all—might not be the sort of people you are accustomed to associating with. 'Tis only a friendly observation, of course, with your best interests in mind."

Cassandra looked down to hide her dismay. If spoken by any other person, she might not be surprised, but to hear such words from a vicar about members of his own parish was disconcerting.

When she did not respond, Mr. North continued. "I saw that you were speaking with Miss Warrington after the service. I could not help but wonder if they had any more information regarding your search."

"No, sir. They did not."

"Well, it is fortuitous that I found you here, for I have news." His lighthearted congeniality returned as he produced a letter from inside his coat. "I wrote to Mr. Clark last night, as promised, and had one of the boys run it over to him after we returned from our visits yesterday. After the service a boy brought around this note from Mr. Peter Clark to the vicarage."

His seemingly arrogant offense momentarily forgotten, she forced herself to stay calm.

"It may not be exactly what you want to hear, but Clark departs for London tomorrow and will be gone for at least a week. But he did say he will meet with you upon his return, so that is something to anticipate."

A week? Cassandra's nerves intensified. How long could she afford to pay for such lodgings without a position?

Mr. North tucked the letter away. "And, of course, if it is agreeable to you, I thought I'd join you. Perhaps then you can put voice to some of your inquiries."

She battled the disappointment and tried to focus on the positive. "That is wonderful, truly. I cannot thank you enough."

Expecting their conversation had come to an end, Cassandra prepared to bid him farewell, but he stopped suddenly. "There is one other thing I had hoped to talk with you about."

Cassandra brushed her hair from her face. "Oh?"

"Last night I took the liberty of checking the birth and death records for the year you were born, 1787, as we discussed."

Cassandra's chest tightened as she studied his face for any clues. "And?"

"Unfortunately, I did not find anything in our parish records that would support your search. With your permission I will contact my colleagues in the neighboring parishes and see what I can uncover."

She shook her head to mask her further disappointment. It seemed every door was being closed before her. But she had to remain cheerful—she did not want Mr. North to feel as if he had failed her. "This is all very helpful. Really."

He hesitated and looked toward the young women gathered before he fixed his gaze on her. "I did not mean to take you away from your picnic, but I thought I would be forgiven by sharing that bit of information with you. You must have guessed by now that I feel a personal interest in your situation. I'm so very sorry for what you are going through, but if I am being quite selfish, I am happy that it has brought you to Anston."

After a bow, he retreated back in the direction of the vicarage, and a strange sense wound through her. Initially, perhaps naively, she had thought he was helping her out of the goodness of his heart. But after hearing Betsy's remarks and after encountering the hidden meanings behind his actions, she sobered.

If she did not want to be hurt again, she had to be smart and guard herself . . . and her heart.

Chapter 15

After the picnic concluded, Cassandra did not return to the boardinghouse with the rest of the young women. Instead, with her discussions with both Rachel and Betsy fresh in her mind, she felt her task was clear before her, and she set out over the bridge leading from Anston to Briarton Park.

A week ago she never would have had the courage to ask someone for a position of employment. It just was not done.

It was presumptuous, really. She had a decent education, but it did not extend to the exalted level of ladies of the Warringtons' station. There were etiquette rules and languages that she did not likely know that Maria and Rose would no doubt require.

But she had witnessed their lack of ladylike decorum. They needed guidance. Guidance she could offer. And if anything positive had come out of this debacle, this past week taught her that she was capable of initiating difficult discussions and accomplishing difficult tasks.

The worst Mr. Warrington could say would be no.

After traversing the wooded path from the bridge to the Briarton property, Cassandra pushed open the gate to the side of the front lawn. A fire burned somewhere on the grounds, and the earthy scent of burning leaves and timber lent a bit of familiarity.

She recalled the housekeeper's ire at Cassandra's knocking at the main entrance on her first visit, so she continued on to the other end of the house, where the road curved to the stone stables and slate-roofed outbuildings behind them.

She rounded the path and was met with an unexpected sight. Mr. Warrington and another man, presumably the groom, were in the courtyard supervising the young girls on small ponies.

They all had their backs to her, but then the younger girl spotted her and pointed her riding crop in her direction, and both men turned to face her.

They were having a riding lesson.

At the sight her confidence fled, and she felt like a fool. How it must appear for her to come wandering up, uninvited. Unexpected.

She wanted to disappear. To turn and run to escape her embarrassment. But she'd been observed. She had no choice but to muster courage and proceed.

Mr. Warrington handed the lead rope to the groom, patted the girl's arm, spoke to them both, and then walked toward her.

"Miss Hale," he said as he approached, "we did not expect you today."

She made a quick study of his expression, hoping to gauge his reaction to her surprise appearance, but his demeanor struck her as affable and genuine, which put her mind slightly at ease.

"I—I was hoping I might speak to you." She gripped her reticule tightly. "But I see you are busy, and I do not wish to disturb."

As he glanced back at the girls, the wind swept down from the trees, disrupting the pale hair over his forehead. "No, not busy. The groom is giving riding lessons to my daughters. We're just about done. I'll see them inside. Please, go on into my study. It is through that door, the first room on the left. You can't miss it."

She followed his instructions and went to his study cautiously, as if stepping into his private space was a glimpse into who he was.

It was a sizable room, with two large windows overlooking the very courtyard from which she had just entered. She did not intend to spy, but she watched as Mr. Warrington helped the two girls down from the dappled ponies. The little one twirled dramatically about him, and the older one tugged at his arm. He said something to the groom, and then they entered the house from a door on the courtyard's far side.

She turned back to the center of the room, shrugged her pelisse from her shoulders, and held it in her arms. She smoothed her hand down the front of her best celadon muslin gown and patted her hair.

Cassandra drew a fortifying breath. She could not allow doubt to take hold. Instead, she made a quick study of the space. The paneled walls were painted dark green, and a large desk stood in the center of the room. Two worn chairs flanked the fire, and tidy stacks of paper dotted the furniture. She was about to turn her attention to the landscape paintings on the wall when heavy footsteps sounded in the hall.

Mr. Warrington lingered in the doorway, his broad shoulders filling the space. Even though she anticipated his arrival, his sudden appearance caught her off guard.

She did not know when she had been so nervous—not even when she had first knocked on Briarton Park's door.

His very presence unsettled her, with his windblown sandy-colored hair and distractingly sharp gray eyes. He stooped to pass through the door's opening and brought with him the scent of the outdoors and horses and the faintest hint of wood smoke. "I'm sorry to have kept you waiting. I wanted to get the girls settled back in the nursery."

"No apology needed." She forced her voice to be as calm as possible. "I interrupted your day."

"Think nothing of it. As I said, it was just a riding lesson. Please, be seated." He motioned to a chair across from his desk. "When

Rachel was young, we lived in the city, in Plymouth, so riding lessons weren't a priority. Now that we're in the country, it seems like something they should know how to do. Do you ride, Miss Hale?"

"N-no," she stammered. She settled into the chair. "I do not."

He sat in the chair behind his desk, pausing to adjust his cravat, pulled his striped waistcoat straight, and smoothed his fingers through his tousled, curling hair. "There now. What is it I can do for you?"

Cassandra opened her mouth to speak, and the words she had so carefully planned felt thick and clumsy on her tongue. She lifted her chin. She had to at least appear confident. She met his gaze directly. "The other night you mentioned that if I needed any assistance to come to you, and you would help if you were able."

He nodded. "Yes. Of course. And I meant it."

Her words came out in a rush. "I understand you are in need of a governess for Miss Maria and Miss Rose."

At this he raised his brows and shifted in his chair. "Well, we do have a governess engaged, but she will not be here until the spring."

"But spring is many months away, and it is my understanding from Rachel that you are in need of one now."

"She did, did she?" Mr. Warrington leaned his elbows on the top of his desk. "I see. And who exactly is it you would suggest to fill that role?"

Cassandra straightened her shoulders. "I would like to recommend myself for the position."

Mr. Warrington stared at her. If he was shocked at her suggestion, he gave no indication.

After several seconds he stood from his chair, stepped out from behind the desk, and leaned against the desk's edge. "It was my impression, Miss Hale, that you're in Anston with your sights set on finding family. I was not aware you were seeking employment as well."

"That is true—I am looking for my family, but one must be

practical. Even if I'm successful, I doubt my professional situation will change."

He pushed himself off the desk and moved to the window, where he stared out at the courtyard.

Unsure of how to interpret his actions, she could only fill the awkward silence. "I've taught young girls for the past four years, am proficient in French, and I—"

"Did you observe my daughters at church today?" he interrupted, not turning away from the window.

She hesitated at the odd diversion of topic. "Yes, sir. I did."

He then turned around to face her. "And what was your opinion of their behavior?"

Cassandra recalled how the little one was playing in the grass and running with the other children. "I think they are spirited little girls. And isn't that what you want to see? Children who are vivacious and enthusiastic for life? But for young ladies, this enthusiasm must be channeled appropriately."

She bit her lip and mentally prepared herself to be thrown from the room.

But he did not expel her.

Instead, he rubbed his hand over his chin and narrowed his gaze on her. "And how does one do that?"

She shifted in her chair. "Discipline has its place, but I think a better approach is to praise children when they are doing something well. All children, by nature, want to please. I am sure your girls are no different. Over time they will seek to do right and will find less pleasure in doing something wrong. Today, for example, I would have looked for ways to praise them during the times when their behavior was appropriate, and then, if they did misbehave, redirect them to those very activities and behaviors that were more proper. Of course, it requires consistency, but I've found that it's infinitely more effective than pointing out their faults."

He again fell into silence for several moments, making his stoic expression even more difficult to interpret. "They lost their mother two years ago and moved here but a year ago, away from everything they had ever known. They've experienced much loss and change in their young lives. I fear another change would be trying. A governess is not a decision I undertake lightly."

"Or perhaps a new change could be a saving grace." She was determined to keep the conversation positive. "I know what it is like to interact with children who have suffered loss. All of the girls at the school where I taught had endured it, in one form or another. They were all separated from their families, and many were uncertain when, or even if, a reunion would come."

"And what of your search for your family? How would a commitment to my family affect it? Would you abandon it, I wonder?"

"No. Not abandon it. But as I said, I don't expect my situation to change. I seek answers. Information. Beyond that, I have no expectation. I need to work, Mr. Warrington. If I do not find employment in Anston, where I believe my search lies, then I will have to move elsewhere, which would make my search much more difficult."

Eager to continue her momentum, she retrieved a missive from her reticule, stood, and joined him at the window. "This is my letter of recommendation. It was written by Mrs. Denton, the headmistress of the school where I taught and where I was educated."

He looked at her, took the letter, and unfolded it.

Cassandra gazed out the window to the courtyard—the dirt grounds and the line of stone stables on the far side. She could not bring herself to watch his face as he read the words. As for the letter itself, she knew it by heart.

How much time had passed? Seconds? Minutes?

"Miss Hale? Maria told me you were here!"

Cassandra whirled at the sudden shout to see Rachel, wide-eyed and smiling, in the doorway. She hurried in, hands outstretched, and took Cassandra's gloved hands in her own. "You did come!"

The high pitch of Rachel's voice tweaked Cassandra's already tense nerves, and she was unsure if she should be grateful for the interruption or perturbed.

Rachel swung their joined hands side to side, and her words rushed forth seemingly unchecked. "I'm so glad you are here. But why are you in this study? It is so gloomy in here. Shall we go out for a walk? It will be dark soon. The gardens are so lovely this time of day, even if the sun is hiding. I just need to get my pelisse."

Cassandra cast a glance back to Mr. Warrington, who seemed unfazed by his sister's interruption. He lowered the letter and folded it before extending it back to her. "Yes, you ladies go on your walk. If you want to take advantage of the daylight, you'd best be about it. Miss Hale, we can finish our conversation another time."

She bit her lip to hide the bitter disappointment welling within her. His dismissal and distracted expression seemed like a rejection. Then again, perhaps he needed to think.

Or perhaps this was his way of declining her politely.

Either way, perhaps a bit of fresh air and a walk with Rachel would do her good.

Chapter 16

Rachel had been right. The ornate gardens that stretched out before Briarton House were beautiful in the late-afternoon light.

Despite the fallen leaves and faded hues of autumn, the boxwoods and intricate stone paths were a sight to behold. Cassandra and Rachel strolled beneath the canopy of ash trees, as if old friends instead of new acquaintances.

"I'm so glad you came by today." Rachel glided her bare fingertips over the tops of the boxwoods as they traversed the stone path. "It's so quiet here. Don't you agree? Never a soul around besides those who reside at Briarton."

Even though it had been partly due to Rachel's suggestion, Cassandra thought it best to keep the topic of the conversation she'd had with Mr. Warrington to herself. "But you have visitors, don't you?"

Rachel shrugged her narrow shoulders. "Not really."

As a mill owner, surely Mr. Warrington was connected socially. But as the meaning of Rachel's words struck her, the young woman's behavior began to make sense. Perhaps she was searching for friendship and camaraderie and not necessarily a romantic attachment. Could that sentiment have contributed to her actions with Mr. Standish?

Loneliness could drive one to make decisions they would not ordinarily make. Did she herself not know that to be true?

Rachel brushed her hair away from her face, her brows drawn together. "Do you really not know who your parents are?"

Cassandra shook her head. She shouldn't have been surprised at the personal nature of the question given their interactions, but the topic seemed sudden. "No. I don't."

"Both my parents are dead," Rachel offered matter-of-factly. "My mother died of fever when I was two years of age. My father died of pneumonia when I was seven. That's when I came to live with James and Elizabeth."

"Elizabeth was your sister-in-law?"

"Yes, and she was wonderful. She was beautiful and genteel and everything a lady should be." Rachel's face brightened. "It's hard to believe she was raised by Mrs. Towler, the old bird."

Cassandra had to mask her amusement at the sudden disgust in Rachel's tone. "That's hardly kind."

"Well, she's hardly kind to me. And she never has been. One time, several years ago, I heard her telling Elizabeth that I was standing in the way of the family being resplendent because of my parentage, which is ridiculous because James and I have the same father. Can you imagine? I was just a child."

Sadly, Cassandra could hear Mrs. Towler saying those words. "What an awful thing to say."

"I lack 'natural grace,' or so she says."

"Well, if it makes you feel any better, I think your grace is brilliant. But why does she still live with Mr. Warrington if her daughter is dead?"

Rachel scrunched her face and fussed with the fabric-covered buttons of her pelisse. "It's James's own fault. He claims it's what Elizabeth would have wanted him to do. Mrs. Towler came to live with them when her husband died, before I arrived. She has no money of her own or any close family. James says it's important that she remain with us because she is the only family Maria and Rose have left, and family must be respected and protected."

The words struck her. How would it feel to be treated like that—respected and protected? To know Mr. Warrington felt that way eased her. He might not know the answers she sought, but he seemed sensitive to her plight.

"But surely your brother intends to wed again one day. One would think that having a mother-in-law living under the same roof would discourage that."

Rachel shrugged. "James cares only for his work, plus he still mourns Elizabeth. He doesn't say as much, but I know."

Their conversation was treading on very personal information. Cassandra needed to shift it. "After what happened, I am glad to see you happy and smiling, Rachel. You seem to be recovering well."

Rachel nodded and drew a deep breath. "I suppose. It's frightening how close I came to changing my life so completely. What could I possibly have been thinking?"

"Do not be too harsh on yourself, my dear. You are not the first woman to find herself in this situation. And that includes me, as I told you. Maybe one day I will tell you the details, but right now, they aren't important. What is important is that you find that your strength is in your character, not in the person to whom you are married. Find happiness and contentment from within, not in your circumstances."

The words she uttered struck her.

Circumstances.

Was she not battling the same thing? She had spent the last few days waiting for information. Waiting for truth. Endless waiting. But what if this was as far as her journey took her? What if she never found her family? Would she be able to find happiness then?

Indeed, she'd be wise to take her own advice.

The hour was growing late, and the crowd was growing rowdy at the Green Ox Inn.

As James sat alone at a table waiting for Milton to rejoin him, he took a swig of cider and returned the pewter mug to the table with a thud before once again assessing his surroundings. He should be satisfied. He and Milton had just concluded business with two local sheep farmers regarding wool prices. But the news the farmer shared sobered him. A wagon transporting new power cotton looms had been attacked in broad daylight. Two men had been injured, and the loom had been destroyed with axes. The incident had taken place two villages over, but the violence was increasing in its frequency.

James toyed with the mug and glanced at the faces around him. He'd grown up in a village very much like this, where his father resembled the men around him: hardworking, suspicious of authority, and eager to make names for themselves yet deeply rooted in tradition.

After James's mother had died when he was seven, he and his father lived in the countinghouse at their struggling textile mill, spending every waking hour surrounded by wool and workers and learning the value of hard work. His father remarried to Rachel's mother when he was sixteen, and it was then he was sent to Micah Towler in Plymouth to learn the shipping details of the trade.

James became acquainted with the business quickly, but even more importantly, he earned Mr. Towler's respect. He'd been treated as a member of the family, which gave him the opportunity for his attraction to Mr. Towler's daughter, Elizabeth, to grow.

He married at twenty-two years of age—ten years ago now—much younger than his mentors advised and much to the chagrin of Mrs. Towler, but neither he nor Elizabeth would be deterred. She had possessed every quality he ever could have dreamed of. She'd been divinely beautiful. Poised. Elegant. But what was more, they'd shared a passion for their future—one that they hoped would take them out of the bustle of the city back to his roots in Yorkshire.

Their plans changed when apoplexy claimed Mr. Towler's life not even a year after their marriage. Mr. Towler's holdings transferred to one of his nephews, leaving Mrs. Towler in reduced circumstances with very little to live on. James took all the knowledge he had learned from both his father and Mr. Towler and established his own shipping company, and for the next several years he continued to single-handedly grow their finances and dealings until he was a respected businessman in his own right: Shrewd. Calculated. Clever. They had surpassed either of their fathers before them, but when Elizabeth died, his world shattered. There seemed little point in remaining in Plymouth. He sold the business and purchased Briarton Park and Weyton Mill to return to the work his father had taught him.

The entire experience had been one difficult decision after another, and now he had a new decision to make. Miss Hale had presented him with a very interesting proposition. His girls did need a governess, and the governess his mother-in-law had chosen was not available for several months. Maria and Rose needed guidance, and Mrs. Towler was not providing it.

And he genuinely liked Miss Hale. She was direct and to the point, sure of herself and determined, and dignity and integrity seemed to rule her actions. She was unlike any woman he'd ever encountered.

But something about her gave him reason to pause. She possessed the sort of beauty he thought about at the oddest times. It was unnerving. She was the first woman he'd taken notice of since Elizabeth.

Initially it didn't really matter, he'd told himself. For she would eventually leave the area.

But she was gradually weaving herself into the fabric of their lives. First as a friend to Rachel, but a governess? Living in his home?

He could be professional, of course, for he did think her a good influence for his girls. But to be faced with that temptation, day in, day out, was another matter entirely.

He missed Elizabeth.

He always would.

But he also missed feeling connected to someone. And attraction was just the start of how those feelings could develop and deepen. He was strong enough to face a great many things, but was he willing to risk the idea of losing someone again?

"Warrington, if I am not mistaken?"

The deep voice pulled James from his thoughts, and he looked up to see a finely dressed stranger approach his table.

The white-haired man nodded to the empty seat across from James. "May I?"

Oddly grateful for the reprieve from his own thoughts, James leaned back in the chair. "Be my guest."

The man sat down. "Name's William Longham. You don't know me, I reckon, but I know you. You own Weyton Mill. You live up at Briarton Park."

It was not surprising that the man should know his identity, but with the recent unrest at local mills, it was a little disconcerting. "I do."

"Believe it or not, I've passed many a day at Briarton Park. That was years ago, of course. I was—am—the late owner's man of business."

James raised a brow. "Robert Clark's man of business?"

"Yes, yes indeed. Never thought I'd be back here though." Mr. Longham lifted his gaze to the ceiling's roughly hewn beams. "But duty calls."

"And what duty is that?"

The older man pulled a pipe from his coat. "I understand you had a caller at Briarton. A Miss Cassandra Hale."

When James did not immediately respond, the man pointed his

pipe at James and continued. "You're suspicious. I don't blame you. Never you mind. It is impossible to keep secrets in a village like this. And no one's business is ever really private, is it?"

Now James's interest was piqued. A few days ago he'd never even heard the name Cassandra Hale. Now it seemed that her name, not to mention Clark's, was on everyone's lips. It was odd—he almost felt defensive for the young woman. Yes, they'd only just met, but she'd helped his family and he felt honor bound to watch out for her. Besides, if he was in any way considering her for a governess, he'd need to know why such a man would be inquiring after her. "What business have you with Miss Hale?"

"Normally I'd say it's personal and not share a word. But it is urgent I speak with her. I'd hoped you could help."

Mr. Longham hadn't answered his question. Not really. James took another swig of his cider as the battled raged within him. He should not get involved.

He should *not*.

He returned his mug to the table, but before he could speak, Milton returned to the table and stood next to it. "Longham! That you? Ye a ghost?"

Longham guffawed and extended a thick hand toward the man. "Ah, Milton. Good to see you, man. No, not a ghost, but might as well be some days."

Milton slapped a heavy hand on the much taller man's slightly stooped shoulder and dropped to the chair next to him. "What brings ye back to these parts then? Ol' Clark back from the grave bringin' us trouble?"

Longham chuckled. "You'd think so, wouldn't you? But no, no. But it is the Clark estate that brings me here."

"You should be callin' on Peter Clark then, eh?" Milton leaned on the table with his pointed elbows. "I shouldn't think there's much to do with th' estate here at ol' Green Ox."

"I will need to speak with Peter eventually, but not yet. It is quite another person I am here to see." Longham pivoted toward James. "I'm told that Miss Cassandra Hale was at your place asking after Mr. Clark."

James did not like how the man asked after her so boldly. "And how would you know that?"

"The innkeeper here and I go way back. I asked him to keep an ear out for her name since so many come through his doors. He notified me when he saw her name come across the travel ledgers. Glad he did too. Devilishly hard woman to track down."

A strange sense of satisfaction spread through James. He was right to be cautious about this man. After all, perhaps Miss Hale didn't want to be found. But then again, wouldn't she want to know anything associated with the Clark estate given her quest?

Oh, his interest in her was intensifying.

Longham folded his aged, gnarled hands on the table before him. "I have business with her. Rather, Mr. Clark's estate does. Do you know how to reach her?"

He knew what he needed to do, even though he suspected it would pull him down into the depths of whatever was going on.

"I can get a message to her," James offered, "but I must know the nature of it before I agree to assist you."

"There are matters related to his estate that pertain to her, namely his will."

James exchanged glances with Milton, who shrugged. Milton seemed to have a good rapport with Longham. And had James not told Miss Hale specifically that he would offer any assistance?

"Very well. Come by Briarton Park tomorrow evening at dusk. I will reach out to her, and if she is amenable, you may speak with her there."

Chapter 17

Cassandra simply could not make sense of it.

Earlier that morning she'd received a letter from Mr. Warrington. She'd assumed it would be regarding the governess position, but it didn't even mention it. The message had been simple: Mr. Warrington had encountered a solicitor who wanted to speak with her regarding Mr. Clark. He was facilitating an introduction at Briarton Park, and he'd send a carriage to convey her there. Now, as Briarton Park's carriage rumbled through the main gates, her nerves fluttered within her as she mulled over possible scenarios.

When the carriage finally drew to a halt, Mr. Warrington was standing in the main drive, hands clasped before him. As she exited the vehicle, he offered his hand to assist her down. A sober expression replaced the much more congenial one he usually boasted, and once her feet were on the ground, he spoke low. "I hope it was all right to write to you."

"Of course. I was grateful to receive your message."

"His name is William Longham. He approached me at the Green Ox last night. He was Robert Clark's solicitor," Mr. Warrington explained in a hushed tone as they walked toward the house. "He found out you were here looking for information. He asked questions about you, and I was not comfortable having the discussion without you present. I hope I did not overstep my bounds by inviting him here. Forgive my assumption, but I thought it best that you meet him somewhere familiar."

Once they reached the wooden door, Mr. Warrington leaned forward to rest his ungloved hand on the door's brass knob, but he did not open it. Instead, he inched closer to her and lowered his voice. "He's here, just inside in the great hall."

Cassandra jerked, and her face flushed hot. "He's here? Already?"

"He arrived quite early. He's been here nigh half an hour. He's quite keen to meet with you, but rest assured, I've told him nothing about you or what you've shared with me. Are you ready?"

She nodded, and he ushered her directly into the great hall. There stood a large man, finely dressed, with broad shoulders. No one else was about—no servants, none of the family. The guest towered over Mr. Warrington. His white hair was thinning and was combed over the top of his head, and his bushy eyebrows and side-whiskers were decidedly gray.

A grin cracked his leathered face when he saw her, and he bowed. "Miss Hale, I'd know you anywhere."

Her eyes narrowed as recognition blazed. Emboldened by the fact that she was perfectly safe within Briarton's walls, she could not be silent. "I saw you! Earlier this week. You were watching me when I was walking with the vicar and his housekeeper. Why?"

Mr. Longham chuckled. "I was just making sure it was really you and I'd not been misinformed. It wasn't the right time to approach you. I did try to find you to speak with you afterward but was unsuccessful."

"Hmm." She removed her straw poke bonnet and placed it on the table. "Well, you have my full attention now, sir. I have to admit I am curious to hear what business you have with me."

Mr. Longham rested against his walking stick. "You would not remember, of course, but you and I have met before."

"No, I don't think so." She eyed him suspiciously, noting the deep creases around sagging jowls. "I'm sure I would have remembered."

"Oh no." He shook his head emphatically. "You were far too young. You were just a babe then. My name is William Longham, as Mr. Warrington might have told you. For nearly forty years I was Robert Clark's personal solicitor. I have been searching for you for these last two years. Ever since your father died."

Cassandra seized at the word.

Father?

Surely the air had left her lungs.

She'd suspected it, of course. But to hear it so plainly, so bluntly, caught her off guard. Her confidence in this situation crumbled, and she felt as if she might be ill. She grappled for words. "My . . . my father?"

"Yes, yes, of course. Robert Clark." A shadow fell over his face. "You did know, did you not?"

She cleared her throat and straightened her shoulders. She could barely force her voice above a whisper. "No."

The older man's good-natured expression faded. "She really never told you?"

Stunned, Cassandra could only shake her head. She needed answers quickly, or else she might dissolve into a puddle. "Who told me what? Mr. Longham, I'm afraid I'm not following your meaning at all."

Mr. Warrington stepped in, his tone calm. Soothing. "You've startled Miss Hale, Mr. Longham. I think you'd better explain yourself, sir."

Mr. Longham tilted his head. "This is where the matter is confidential. The young lady and I should speak privately, for everyone's sake. I assure you, Mr. Warrington, no harm will come to her. Believe it or not, I've actually spent these many years protecting her."

The sleeve of Mr. Warrington's coat brushed her arm as he drew near, his voice barely audible as he whispered close to her ear. "Do you want to speak with him alone? I can stay with you if you'd like."

Cassandra liked the thought of Mr. Warrington being near her and the confidence he afforded. But she had never needed anyone for a difficult conversation before. She had her dagger in her boot, not that she would need it. "No, that is not necessary. I'll speak with him."

"Very well." He motioned to the corridor. "You may use my study if you wish. But know I'll be right outside the door."

Cassandra drew a deep, steadying breath as she waited to be ushered into Mr. Warrington's study. Her stomach quaked.

Mr. Longham had just confirmed her father's identity. Suddenly. Without ceremony.

After twenty-four years of wondering, she now knew the truth.

She glimpsed Mr. Warrington's supportive nod as he held the door for her and Mr. Longham, then closed it behind them.

She had to focus and keep her wits about her, in spite of what she'd just learned. She needed to absorb everything this solicitor could tell her. Feeling warm and slightly dizzy, she removed her pelisse and gloves, placing the pelisse on the back of a chair. Not trusting her legs or her balance, she quickly sat in one of the chairs by the desk and folded her trembling hands in her lap.

The older man ambled in behind her. A satchel was slung over his hunched shoulder, and he relied heavily on his cane with each step.

"Perhaps we should begin anew." With frustratingly lackadaisical movements he placed his greatcoat and hat atop the desk. He sat in the chair opposite her, seemingly oblivious to the anxiety this situation was producing in her. "As Mr. Clark's man of business, I am responsible for seeing that his estate is settled. A task that has been very difficult."

She could not help but blurt out her question. "You're certain, then, that Mr. Clark was my father?"

"Oh, very certain." Mr. Longham leaned back in the chair, and a frown crossed his wrinkled brow. "But I can see that I've shocked you. I am sorry for it. I had assumed you knew."

Fresh tears burned as she employed every ounce of discipline to remain calm. "Why would you think that? How would I have known?"

"I assumed Mrs. Denton would have told you at some point." He studied her for several seconds before he retrieved a handkerchief from his pocket and extended it to her.

Cassandra eyed the handkerchief and then accepted it warily. How did he know of Mrs. Denton? She wiped her nose. "Well, she did not."

Several moments passed in awkward silence before Mr. Longham spoke again. "I know he wanted to tell you himself. He told me he had written to you. That was a few months before he died."

At the mention of the letter, she hastily retrieved it from her reticule. "This letter?"

He took the missive, retrieved his spectacles, balanced them on the end of his arched nose, and read it. "I don't know if it is the exact letter. But the date is accurate. June 1809. He died in October of that year."

She accepted the letter back, frustrated with how slowly the conversation was proceeding. "I only came into possession of this letter two weeks ago."

"Two weeks?" He winced. "How's that possible?"

"Mrs. Denton gave it to me on her deathbed. She said she was sorry she had kept a secret from me, but she had made a promise."

"Yes. I'd heard she had died, but it makes no sense that she should have kept this from you." Mr. Longham frowned. "Her promise has long since been fulfilled."

"What promise?" Cassandra cried out. "Mr. Longham, clearly you know a great deal about my life, but it is all a complete mystery to me. I'm confused about who I am, who my parents are, how I came to even be at the school, and it seems you are the only person to have any answers to my questions. So please, I beg of you, do me a kindness and start at the beginning. Tell me everything you can."

He nodded and crossed one leg over the other, as if settling in. "Twenty-five years ago, it was brought to Mr. Clark's attention that one of the maids in his home was with child. *His* child. Mr. Clark was, of course, married to Mrs. Clark at the time, and it was his chief concern that his wife never find out about the child. About you."

Illegitimate.

She found her voice. "Go on."

"In an effort to conceal his actions, Mr. Clark secretly, but legally, assumed full custody of you and placed you with a family in the country until you were old enough to be placed in a school—Mrs. Denton's school."

"And my mother did not oppose this?"

"She was young and in no position to raise a child on her own. Mr. Clark could provide for you much better than she ever could. He gave her funds for a new life, and in return she agreed never to have any contact with you."

Cassandra swallowed dryly. It felt as if her hands had grown numb. Her arms. "What is my mother's name?"

"Mary Hale."

"And is she still living?"

Mr. Longham nodded his white head. "After the agreements were signed, I never had contact with her again. But news does travel, and I did hear somewhere along the way that she eventually married and is living somewhere near here. Her married name is Smith, if memory serves."

"So if I understand you correctly, all these years that I have been at the Denton School for Young Ladies, Mrs. Denton knew of this arrangement?"

"Of course. No expense was spared for your education and care."

Unable to be still any longer, Cassandra jumped to her feet. "So why tell me all this now? Why even look for me?"

Mr. Longham released a deep sigh. He removed his spectacles and casually returned them to his pocket. "After Mr. Clark's wife died, he tried to contact you. He was gravely ill at the time, close to death himself. When he received no response, he sent me to the school to speak with you, but when I arrived, Mrs. Denton said you had taken a position elsewhere and she had no idea where you were."

"What? But that's a lie! I lived under her roof since I was a child!"

"Well, be that as it may, I was told that the two of you had quarreled, and you departed without providing a forwarding address."

The false words swam in her mind, refusing to come into focus. Determined to make sense of what she was hearing and take full advantage to learn every detail she could, she sat back down. "But that does not answer my question. Why were you looking for me? Why did you track me down here?"

He blinked, as if shocked at her naivete. "You father's will, of course."

"His will?" She flinched. "What will?"

His expression softened. "Take heart, Miss Hale. I fear I've given you a great deal to think on, but I also come bearing news that should be beneficial to you."

Mr. Longham reached for the portfolio by his feet. "Your father was a very wealthy man, and he was haunted by guilt, especially considering how luxuriously his son, your half brother, lived."

She eyed the portfolio. "Yes, I was told he had a son."

"He never forgot you, and after his wife's death, he altered his will to include you. When you did not respond to his inquiry, he was not sure if you would be found, so he gave a very specific time frame for you to obtain your inheritance. The will clearly states that if you were not located and did not claim your inheritance within three years, it would pass to another party—the Stricklin estate. That time expires in about a year from now, and that is why I've been so keen to locate you. But now we have time. We should be able to set everything to right."

"But it cannot be." She shook her head in disbelief. "He never knew me."

"I am not disputing the fact that he was a poor father to you. But he was still your father. He was there the day you were born. I was as well. He received regular updates on you as you grew into adulthood, and I know it was the greatest regret of his life not knowing you."

She sat frozen, transfixed, stunned at the news she'd just been given.

How different her life could have been if only she'd known.

She wiped her hand impatiently across her eyelash. She would not cry. Not here.

She straightened her posture. "What's to be done now?"

Mr. Longham stood. "It was Mr. Clark's intention that you should inherit the plot of land to the east of here—the land where Clark Mill now stands. The locals call the land Linderdale. You'll not inherit the mill or the business, mind you, just the land. They are two separate entities, and it was set up this way so if the business ever encountered trouble, the land would be protected as an asset. It is all quite complicated, but it comes down to this. You own the land. Peter Clark, your half brother, owns the business. The business will pay you a lease for as long as it is there. Furthermore, the will is written in such a way that you cannot sell the land, nor can your children, should you have any, for a period of up to fifty years. The income from the land should give you funds or provide a nice dowry. But I caution you, there are still hurdles to cross."

"Hurdles? Such as?"

"Peter knows the name Cassandra Hale. It is clearly stated in the will, but he does not know you are Robert Clark's daughter. He will certainly contest your claim to the will, which could drag this out for years. But I have all your paperwork in line, including this." He produced a piece of paper from his satchel. "This is a copy of the signed agreement between your mother and your father stating that your father is to have full custody and that your mother is not to contact you."

She skimmed over the words until her eyes landed on her mother's signature. Tears blurred her vision. Her mother had written this.

Her mother.

"This document, along with my official statement as Robert Clark's man of business, should be enough in court to prove your identity. I also have a few other documents, letters, and payment receipts to the school that further support this claim."

"This is all amazing." Cassandra managed a little laugh through her tears, and then, as the reality of what she was hearing started to sink in, her excitement began to grow.

"It is my pleasure to see you realize what is rightfully yours. Of course, I doubt anyone would question it based on your looks alone."

She jerked. "What do you mean?"

"That slight cleft of your chin. You appear more a Clark than Peter."

She felt stunned.

He chuckled. "If you don't believe me, look at the portrait in the great hall and tell me if you don't see a resemblance. Now," he said, slapping his hand against his knee, "our next step is that I must speak with Peter Clark. No doubt news of your arrival has spread, and in my experience, gossip travels faster than the truth."

"Yes, I believe the vicar has contacted him on my behalf. I was trying to reach him because of the letter."

Mr. Longham nodded. "He deserves an explanation as well. I am bound by both duty and honor to see that your father's wishes are carried out to the very jot."

She stared as she recalled Mr. North's observations. "Would my birth be part of the church records?"

"I'm sure it would be, but I doubt Mr. Clark's name would have been associated with it. Why do you ask?"

"Mr. North, the local vicar, said it could not be found."

"Ah, someone could have listed a false name. You were baptized, I do know that. In this parish as well. I will call on your half brother as soon as I am able to set a meeting for the two of you. You are residing at Mrs. Martin's boardinghouse, if I'm not mistaken."

"Yes, sir."

"Good. Then I can reach you there. This is not a secret, per se, but I would advise that you not publicize or act on any of this until all is made known to Peter Clark and the appropriate parties. As I said, the probate could take quite a long while. I wish I could stay in town and handle it immediately, but Peter Clark is out of town and I'm expected in London. Come now," he said with a smile. "I fear your friend Mr. Warrington is none too happy about my chatting with you."

Chapter 18

James paced the darkened corridor outside of his study. Inside the chamber Miss Hale was speaking with Mr. Longham, and James was not sure what to make of it.

The expression on her face at learning her father's identity would plague him. He could only imagine what the lady was thinking and feeling after learning such critical news.

Her plight was drawing him in. The struggle. The hope. The determination. For many reasons she was a mystery to him, and every interaction left him wanting to know more about her. How curious it would be to have no knowledge of your parents' identity and embark on a journey with only a vague letter as a guide.

Family had always been the cornerstone of James's life. He and his father had not always seen eye to eye, but it had been his father's legacy and foresight that influenced James's work. It was the sort of legacy he hoped would continue with his own children one day.

What must it have been like for Miss Hale never to have had a parent or a sibling? To live every day wondering who your people were and where exactly you were from? It was the very reason he had fought so hard to be Rachel's guardian. To prevent her from that very scenario.

James ceased his pacing and sank onto one of the wooden chairs lining the wall outside of his study. He remained very still in order to listen for voices, but the only sound that met his ears was indecipherable muttering.

At length the study door opened and Mr. Longham appeared.

James jumped to his feet.

"Our business is concluded, Mr. Warrington. Thank you for the use of your study."

James entered the study and sought out Miss Hale. She stood in silence next to the window. "I trust everything is all right?"

"Of course." Mr. Longham's voice rang with confidence as he gathered his satchel and held it in his arms. Seemingly unaware of Miss Hale's affected state, he lifted his gaze to the painting behind the desk. "You know, I spent many hours in this study when Mr. Clark was living. In his later years he spent the majority of his time in London, but when he was here, I'd come by monthly to go over papers and the like. I even had my own chamber upstairs. The Blue Room."

James lifted his brows.

Oblivious to his host's annoyance, Mr. Longham continued. "Many secrets and stories I could tell you about this house. For instance, let me show you one." Mr. Longham returned his bundle to the chair and crossed the room with languid, intentional movements. He knocked on one of the wall's painted panels, knocked on the one next to it, pushed it in, and surprisingly, it gave way, revealing a small alcove. He beamed back at James, as proud as a child with a new toy. "Concealed spaces."

James stepped forward to get a closer view of the exposed depository. "I had no idea."

Longham chuckled. "Ah yes. These recesses are scattered throughout this house, especially in the cellars. Mr. Clark used to keep French brandy in this one when it was his study, but as you can see, it's been cleared out."

As intrigued as James was about the hidden spaces in this

venerable house, the hour was growing late, and he was more concerned about Miss Hale than any secret the house might possess. "Perhaps the next time you are in town you can share with us the house's other mysteries. But it will be dark soon. I'm sure Miss Hale would like to return home."

"Again, it was never my intention to upset Miss Hale." Mr. Longham turned to her. "May I escort you back to the boardinghouse, my dear?"

James grew increasingly frustrated with the man's assumed acquaintance with her. "I'll make arrangements for a carriage to return Miss Hale."

"My goodness, you take the job of host very seriously." The solicitor turned to him, unhurried, and extended his hand. "Very well, very well. I wish you many happy and successful years here at Briarton Park, Warrington."

James shook the extended hand.

Mr. Longham bowed toward Miss Hale. "I leave for London in the morning. But I will send word to you as soon as I am able after I arrange the meeting we discussed."

She nodded.

He handed her a card. "Should you need to write me, this is where to reach me."

Miss Hale accepted the card and tucked it in her reticule.

The three of them walked through the corridors to the great hall, where James and Miss Hale saw Mr. Longham out.

And then they were alone in the great hall.

James was uncomfortably aware of her presence, her nearness. Of the change in her disposition. Of how much he wanted to help her or offer some sort of comfort, but he didn't know how.

"That Mr. Longham seems a long-winded fellow," he said in an attempt to lighten the mood. "I hope whatever news he had for you was pleasant."

At length she looked up at him absently, the expression that curved her full lips forced. Her cheery tone could not mask the melancholy underneath. "He answered a great many of my questions. I thought any information would bring consolation, but now it seems there are even more questions."

He wanted to bring her encouragement, but how? "I'm certain that once you have time to contemplate what you learned, you will feel more at ease with it."

"You are right, of course. I should be grateful. And I am. I just—" Her voice broke off, and she struggled for words. "I think it best that I return home."

He studied the expression in her golden eyes, in the downcast set of her lips. For the first time since he'd met her, her customary poise and tenacity waned. Whatever had transpired in the study had affected her. "Of course. I'll call the carriage. And do not bother to argue, Miss Hale. This time I will not take no for an answer."

He half expected her to refuse—to insist on walking as she had so emphatically done in the past. But there was a sense of exhaustion, almost defeat, in her disposition. "Thank you, Mr. Warrington. I'd be grateful."

He left her alone in the great hall to make arrangements for the carriage, and when he returned, he found her standing in front of the portrait of Mr. Clark.

He did not want to interrupt her. Her attention seemed quite focused on a rather somber piece of artwork.

"Do you think we share a likeness?"

The personal nature of the question took him aback.

When he did not respond, she adjusted the plum pelisse in her arms and looked back to the somber expression, captured in time. "I know you heard Mr. Longham say that this man was my father. He said I resemble him."

James moved closer to her and gazed up at the portrait. No fire burned in the fireplace, but even in evening's dull gray light, he could see it.

Yes, there was a resemblance. But whereas his umber eyes appeared stern, her hazel eyes were soft, full of emotion, and feathered with dark lashes. The cleft in the man's chin was severe, but the cleft in Miss Hale's chin was so slight he'd not even noticed it at first. "Perhaps. But I'm hardly an expert on such things."

She crossed in front of him to the other side of the mantel to the portrait of Mrs. Clark.

Once again, he stepped next to her to assess the painting of the titian-haired woman with a decidedly full face and pale, almost sallow complexion. "I don't think your resemblance to her is as strong."

At first Miss Hale did not respond. Then her voice was barely above a whisper. "She's not my mother."

He sobered.

Suddenly it all made sense.

Miss Hale was Mr. Clark's illegitimate child.

The sound of the carriage crunching over the drive in front of the house as it came around from the carriage house drew their attention. She donned her pelisse and fastened the buttons with shaky movements, then they moved through the foyer and door. Her eyes did not meet his as she spoke. "I fear I have trespassed upon your kindness once again, Mr. Warrington."

He followed her out, wishing he could offer a compelling reason for her to stay.

She climbed into the carriage, and before long, the conveyance had departed down the drive.

He stood still, out in the brisk night air. As the carriage disappeared around the bend at the copse of trees, he felt her absence keenly.

And that surprised him.

It was ridiculous, really. He hardly knew this woman. A week ago he didn't even know she existed. But she'd swept in from Lamby, and her very presence was awakening a part of him that had been locked in grief. What surprised him the most was the blossoming realization that he wanted to care about someone again. To help heal the broken places and be loved in return. And their fleeting yet usually poignant interactions were starting to fill those cracks or, at the very least, make him aware of how desperately he wanted to feel whole. It was not reasonable for him to think that this woman might be that person, but the very fact that she was awakening such a sense in him was alarming indeed.

Cassandra swayed with each movement of the Briarton carriage as it jostled over the stone bridge leading back to Anston.

Darkness had fallen over the Briarton Park grounds. Faint wisps of faded light slid through the carriage windows, falling across her gloved hands and lap.

So much had been confirmed to her in a single, tidy conversation with Mr. Longham.

Yes, Mr. Clark was her father.

Yes, she was illegitimate.

Yes, he knew her mother's name, but he did not know her whereabouts.

Yes, she had a brother—one living relative.

This was what she wanted, wasn't it? Answers. Names. Details.

Then why did her heart still ache?

She expelled a shuddery breath and leaned her head back on the seat. After all the time she'd spent thinking about this very moment, she'd not been prepared for the discomforting feelings that accompanied it.

The carriage wheel hit a rut, lurching Cassandra forward. She cried out and caught herself with her hands on the opposite bench.

There had been no one to catch her or prevent her from falling. No one to witness her awkward attempt to right herself.

She was alone.

Completely alone.

She scrambled back to her seat and bit her lip, fighting back tears.

Yes, they were answers, but oh, how they pushed so many other questions to the forefront.

And more waiting for even more answers that may or may not come.

She tried to encourage herself. After all, Mr. Longham had mentioned an inheritance—land. An income was associated with it, but he'd also said her half brother would likely contest it. She was certainly not versed in matters of the law and wills, but she'd heard stories. It could be years.

That was why it was just as important as ever that she find a way to support herself. If she'd had even a glimmer of hope that Mr. Warrington would consider her as a governess for his daughters, it now dimmed. He knew she was illegitimate, which would almost certainly disqualify her from such a close role to his children.

The carriage slowed to a stop as it arrived at the boardinghouse. Firelight gleamed from inside the front windows, but it was hardly a warm, welcoming home.

For what was home now?

Chapter 19

Determined to keep her hands busy and her heart calm in light of Mr. Longham's revelations, Cassandra rose early the next morning and planned a day of tasks. Once the other boarders departed for their occupations, Cassandra had the large copper tub brought to her chamber and a hot bath poured, and then she washed her hair. She cleaned her gowns, cloak, and pelisse as best she could. She organized her belongings. She did whatever she could think of to prevent her mind from wandering back to Briarton Park.

How she wished she would receive word from Mr. Longham. He'd said it would be days before she received any letter from him or his office, yet she yearned for any new bit of information. But even as life-changing news dominated her thoughts, another topic battled for her attention: Mr. Warrington.

She was not an overly romantic woman. Frederick had crushed any such inclinations. But the expression in Mr. Warrington's eyes had caught her unaware. Perhaps it was that he did not jump to a conclusion or project a judgment. Nor did he dismiss her as insignificant. He'd been concerned. Kind. She had wanted to lean into it. Find solace in the warmth and gentleness.

She sniffed and straightened her brush and comb atop the small bedside table. She knew the danger to which that feeling could lead.

After all, Frederick had been gentle and kind too.

Later in the morning, as she sat next to the fire in the kitchen brushing her still-damp hair, Mrs. Martin swept in. As usual, the older woman's hair was tidy and neat and her gown of crimson muslin was freshly pressed, but her expression revealed her annoyance. "You've a gentleman caller in the parlor. I've told you before that I don't approve of gentlemen callers."

Cassandra whirled. "For me?"

"Yes, for you," Mrs. Martin snipped as she fussed with her lacy fichu. "Who else?"

Cassandra stood quickly. Her first fanciful thought was that Mr. Warrington would check on her. Or perhaps it was Mr. Longham with some sort of news.

As if reading her thoughts, Mrs. Martin interjected, "You're fortunate it's Mr. North. I would have sent any other gentleman on his way. You'd best tend to your hair. You can't meet someone like him in such a disheveled state."

Cassandra tightened her grip on her hairbrush. Of course it was Mr. North. He was the most logical person.

Yet why did her heart fall a little at the mention?

She ignored the woman's insult of her hair and nodded. "Thank you, Mrs. Martin. I will be out presently."

Cassandra remained still as Mrs. Martin bustled back in the direction from whence she came, and then Cassandra quickly returned to her chamber and pinned her long locks against the base of her neck. She smoothed her hand down her milky-white cotton gown, printed with dainty primrose flowers, and pinched her cheeks for color.

Betsy's words about Mr. North's interest in her echoed in the back of her mind. She was not ignorant. Mr. North's attentiveness went beyond a vicar's concern for a parishioner. At the end of the day, marriage would be the ideal solution to her problem.

Eager not to keep him waiting, Cassandra made her way through the kitchen and to the sitting room, where she found Mr. North.

He stood as she entered the room. How attractive he appeared in his smartly cut double-breasted tailcoat of smoke-gray broadcloth, crisp white cravat, and sapphire waistcoat. His nearly black hair was smoothed tidily across his brow, and despite their darkness, his eyes were bright as the early afternoon light that reflected off them. What was more, he appeared genuinely pleased to see her.

He bowed. She curtsied.

"I hope I've not interrupted you, Miss Hale." He adjusted his black felt round hat in his hands, his affable expression eager. "I know I shouldn't call without notice, but I had to speak with you."

"You are interrupting nothing, Mr. North. I'm not used to being at my leisure like this. I'm not entirely sure what to do with it."

"Then what say you to a walk? Mrs. Pearson and I have business in the village and would like your company, not to mention your assistance." Then he lowered his voice and leaned toward her. "And I have news for you that is probably best discussed away from any listening ears."

Despite the shock afforded by the information she received the previous evening, news interested her, and the idea of fresh air appealed to her. She quickly retrieved her pelisse, bonnet, and gloves, and together they stepped outside.

"It is good to be out," Cassandra said once they left the boarding-house. The cold breeze and pewter clouds had returned, and she lifted her face to the sky. "I'm not used to being idle."

"Do you not sew or engage in needlework? I was under the assumption that that is how many young ladies pass the time."

"I'm afraid I've never been fond of it, nor do I possess the talent." She let out a laugh. "I find it tedious."

"Well, there is never a shortage of volunteer work to do, should you have any interest. Mostly delivering donations and supplies and the like."

"I should very much like to help."

"Good. I shall let Mrs. Pearson know. She coordinates all of those who are kind enough to extend charity."

They continued to walk down the middle of the high street toward the hill where she'd participated in the picnic the previous day. The cobbles were still wet from a brief morning rain shower, and several tradesmen had set up carts along the side of the road. They paused as a group of geese passed the road, and she laughed as a young boy chased after a dog. She was growing much more comfortable in Anston and more familiar with her surroundings.

With the events of the previous day still heavy on her, she decided to take advantage of her time with Mr. North. "I do have a question for you, if you don't mind my asking you for yet another favor."

"I'll help however I can, Miss Hale. I hope you know that."

"With the closing of my recent school, I'm in need of a position."

"A position?" He stopped and looked at her, his brow creasing into a slight frown. "You can't mean that."

His shock at the suggestion took her aback. "Of course. Sooner or later I will have to work again."

When he did not respond, her defenses rose. She stopped abruptly. "Teaching is an excellent profession. It is—"

"I do apologize, Miss Hale. I meant no offense. You're correct, of course. Teaching is the most commendable of endeavors. It's only that I assumed you would set your sights on something more permanent."

"Permanent?"

He chuckled and averted his gaze. "Work isn't the only future available to a young woman."

She understood his meaning. Matrimony. Nervousness surged through her. She wasn't ready to talk of marriage. Not with him. Not yet. "Work is the only option for me. At least until . . ."

She started walking again, more quickly this time. She'd almost forgotten he'd not been apprised of what Mr. Longham had told her.

"Until what?" he prompted, his eyebrows still drawn in confusion as he fell into step once more.

She swept her gaze over the street, ensuring none of the other villagers about were in earshot. "I learned some information last night, and I'm not sure what to make of it. But it's rather a sensitive topic. I was advised to be discreet."

"Miss Hale, I'm a vicar. Discretion is at the cornerstone of my profession. I can assure you anything you tell me will remain private, between us."

She drew a sharp breath. She had no reason not to trust him, and she really did need advice. "Very well. I had a visit yesterday from a man by the name of Mr. Longham. Do you know him?"

Mr. North shrugged. "I do not."

"He was—*is*—Robert Clark's solicitor, and he confirmed that Mr. Clark was my father."

"How extraordinary." His face brightened. "Surely that must make you happy?"

She stilled the ribbons of her bonnet as a breeze brushed past them. "I'm not entirely sure how it makes me feel."

"But this is an answer, is it not? If you are certain this Mr. Longham can be trusted, of course."

She recalled Mr. Longham's kind expression. "He was very knowledgeable about my situation. Besides, he had all the appropriate paperwork. He said he's actually been searching for me. Apparently my father included me in his will."

"A will. My dear Miss Hale, that is tremendous! Perhaps you will not have need of a position after all."

"You're more optimistic than I. My father may have included me, but Mr. Longham says that when he brings my claim forward, it will most certainly be challenged by Mr. Clark's son—the very one you contacted. He cautioned that it could take a long time, if it ever comes to fruition. So you see, regardless, I must give a care to my personal finances. But now, let's talk no more about that. You said you had something to tell me."

"Ah yes!" he exclaimed as he pulled a letter from inside his coat. "I have a surprise for you, and this surprise comes in the form of an invitation. I called on Mrs. Kent, a most generous patron of this church. She and her husband have their hand in a great many of the dealings and host a monthly gathering at their ancestral home for the leaders of the area. I'm always invited to attend, although I don't know why. She is fond of me for some odd reason. But anyway, I mentioned you to her, in the vaguest of terms, and she has sent you this."

He extended the missive to her.

Cassandra slid her finger beneath the wax seal, opened the letter, and read it. "It's an invitation for this week."

"Of course, this all took place before I learned of your news just now, but I think your prospects are brightening. I have it on good authority that Mr. Peter Clark will be in attendance."

At this she sobered. "But there is still so much I do not know. Maybe it is too soon. Perhaps I should wait for Mr. Longham to make the arrangements."

He waved a dismissive hand. "Oh, I don't think that's necessary. You said yourself this could take time, and it never hurts to have the local gentry on your side. Mrs. Martin always attends, along with a few of the other business owners on the high street. It's a very eclectic gathering. We often share a carriage, and I assume this time will be no different."

"I've never been invited to anything like this," she confessed, slowing to study the fine penmanship on the invitation. "I'm not sure what I would do."

"It's quite simple. You'll be yourself, and you'll be completely captivating. Don't look so perplexed! If you're to spend much time in Anston, you need to be in with the right sort of society. One never knows how these things will develop."

She sobered, attempting to comprehend. "It just doesn't make sense. Why would she invite me? She doesn't even know me."

"But she knows me, and I daresay she quite fancies me. Come, do say you will join us. It would brighten the event for me, that is sure."

A million thoughts darted through her mind. Perhaps it would do her good to meet some other people, as Mr. North suggested. She did, after all, need to look after her future and could take nothing for granted.

She folded the letter with her gloved fingers. "Again I must thank you for your thoughtfulness. You've really been most kind. I'm not sure what I have done to deserve it, but I am grateful nonetheless."

He gave a little chuckle and stared down at the ground, then glanced up almost sheepishly. "Do not credit me too much. I assure you my motives are quite selfish. Now that you are here in Anston, I find I can't imagine what it would be like without you."

Chapter 20

"Why, this is wonderful!" Betsy cried as she read Cassandra's invitation to the Kents' soiree as they stood in the boardinghouse parlor. "You must be beyond thrilled."

Cassandra accepted the invitation back and tucked it in her reticule. "I'm not even sure I should go."

"Why not? I don't know anyone who has been invited to one of Mrs. Kent's gatherings. Certainly not someone who boards here."

Cassandra stretched her hands out toward the dying fire to warm them from her recent walk outdoors. "I've never been to anything like that. I'm sure if it's as fine as Mr. North indicated, I'd not fit in at all."

Betsy sat on the sofa in the parlor and motioned for Cassandra to join her. "You worry for nothing. All you need do is smile and be polite. Besides, if Mr. North went to such trouble to secure you an invitation, he must have other thoughts on his mind."

Betsy's thoughts mirrored her own on that count. She could not plead ignorance. Mr. North's attentions had crossed the line from concerned vicar to a man whose interest teetered on something more.

Perhaps her continued conversation with him encouraged it. Perhaps not. But she could not think on that now. She had to keep her focus firmly in front of her. Cassandra joined Betsy on the sofa. "But I have nothing suitable to wear, and it's just under a week away. My best gown is the celadon muslin one I wore to church on Sunday. Mr. North said that Mrs. Martin would be in attendance. If I am using her as a guide, I'm far too shabby."

"I might be able to help on that count. A grin spread across Betsy's face and she motioned toward a candle. "Take up that light and come with me."

Cassandra did as bid, grabbed the candle, and followed Betsy up the stairs. It was the first time she'd been upstairs in the boardinghouse, or anywhere near the main bedchambers, for that matter. She paused as Betsy opened the door and went in.

This room was much nicer than her little space off the kitchen. The ceilings were not tall, but there were two spacious windows that overlooked the high street. Two beds stood centered in the room, along with a compact dressing table and chair. A single wardrobe stood in the corner, and a chest was at the foot of each bed. A fire grate was at the far end, and embers glowed softly.

Betsy knelt on the wooden floor next to the trunk, pushed a long tawny lock away from her face, and set the candle next to her. She lifted the lid, rummaged inside, and then pulled out two gowns. She stood and laid a gown of ivory brocade with gilt threads embellishing the bodice on the bed, and then she shook out the folds of a deep rose silk adorned with Mechlin lace and with white flowers embroidered on the sleeves and in the folds of the shimmering fabric.

"Why, those are beautiful!" Cassandra exclaimed. "Where on earth did you get them?"

"They're mine, of course." Betsy beamed with pride. "I haven't always lived in a boardinghouse, you know. One of these should do for the dinner, I should think."

"Oh no, no." Cassandra shook her head. "I couldn't ask that."

"You aren't asking. I'm offering. Besides, these gowns haven't seen the light of day in well over two years." Betsy extended one to her. "Someone might as well get to use them."

Cassandra took the soft fabric in her hands. "But why don't you wear them?"

Betsy shrugged and rubbed her finger along the ivory gown's delicate lace adornment. "They are far too fine for me to wear. Moreover, the other girls would think I was putting on airs."

As if interpreting the questions on Cassandra's face, Betsy motioned for her to sit next to her on the bed. "When I was young, my father was a merchant. Had a proper shop on the high street in the town we lived in, and there was no shortage of fabrics and bows and fripperies and bobs. In those days I only sewed for fun and to pass the time. But when my father died, everything changed."

"Oh." Cassandra realized how little she knew about this woman who was quickly becoming a friend. "I didn't realize."

"He had debts. I suppose most men do. When he died, everything was sold to cover them. My sister and I had to make a living the only way we knew how—sewing. She was lucky enough to marry soon after his death, but I, well, let's just say I didn't quite catch anyone's eye."

"That isn't to say you won't," Cassandra offered, sensing her friend's disappointment. "He could be the very next person you meet!"

Betsy laughed dismissively before she took the gown from Cassandra and waited for her to stand up. "Here, let's see. If I am to take it in before the dinner, it must be fitted. We're about the same height, but I am a bit plumper. It shouldn't need much alteration."

Energized by her friend's enthusiasm, Cassandra stood. "I wish you had an invitation. I hate the thought of attending alone."

"Alone? No, no. Mr. North will be there with you. And Mrs. Martin, of course," Betsy goaded, retrieving a measuring tape from the chest. "You know, Mrs. Martin has had her eye set on Mr. North since the day he arrived. She flirts shamelessly. Imagine, a woman of her age. He's so much younger than she is. It never would be. Besides, like I said, his sights are clearly set on you."

Cassandra pivoted to allow Betsy to take her measurements.

Betsy paused in her task. "While we are speaking about Mr. North, I hope I can say something to you as a friend and you will not be offended."

Cassandra's mood shifted as Betsy's countenance sobered. "Of course. Say whatever you wish."

"I know I tease you about him, but I do realize that Mr. North is very charming and handsome, and as much as I would love to see you happy and settled and wed with a dozen babies around you, I feel I must say something by way of caution."

Cassandra swallowed nervously. "Go on."

"Mr. North might be a vicar. And he is probably a very good man. But people do talk."

Cassandra remained very still, preparing her mind for whatever would pass her friend's lips.

"He has a certain reputation. While he is a friendly man, he's a guarded man. I have friends, male friends, who have been in his presence at certain events. It's said he has a darker side to him."

Cassandra struggled to understand exactly what Betsy attempted to convey. "Do you mean with women?"

Betsy leaned closer, her fair brows furrowed. "Not so much about women, but he's rumored to be greedy. He gambles a great deal, not around here, of course. I don't know details, but I think you should be fully aware of what is being said about him. Just take heed."

"If greed is his fault, what interest would he have in me?" She could almost laugh at the very suggestion. "I have nothing to speak of."

But then it struck her. She might be inheriting land.

Surely that had nothing to do with it. She had only just learned of it, and his interest in her had been evident since her arrival.

The conversation fell off as Betsy pinned the gown and marked the length, and in no time, Cassandra's measurements were complete.

When Betsy was done, she stood back, propped her hands on her ample hips, and tilted her head to the side. "Well, Cassandra Hale, when you meet your future husband at the ball, and after you marry someone fabulously rich, you will remember your friend who lent you a gown and will, in turn, find said friend an equally wonderful beau. Goodness knows I need all the help I can get."

Miss Cassandra Hale.

James thought about her as he leaned with his elbows on his rough desk in the mill countinghouse that had been here for decades.

He should be focused on wool. On buying and selling. On worker relations. On securing the safety of the new looms that were to be delivered in less than a fortnight. But all he could think of was the winsome brunette and her haunting expression.

A light rain tapped against the room's four windows late that afternoon. A dying fire popped in the grate. He should get up and stoke it.

It had been three days since the meeting at Briarton Park when Longham shared his news. Miss Hale had tears in her eyes when she'd hurriedly climbed into the carriage.

That was the last sight he had of her.

There had been no more talk of governesses or Mr. Clark. In truth, he'd thought about their last interaction far too much.

When he'd bought the mill and Briarton Park, he was all too aware of the effect Mr. Clark had on the wool industry in the area. To his credit, Robert Clark had single-handedly built three mills in different areas of Yorkshire and restored Briarton Park from a crumbling old house to an elegant home. Over the years, however, his actions led to one mill closing entirely and Weyton Mill and Briarton Park being sold so inexpensively.

James had not really considered Clark's legacy at the time. He'd been so intent upon making changes and implementing procedures that he'd considered little else. He'd not even accounted for the effects of the deceased man's decisions—including angry former employees and odd solicitors coming to his home.

James stood from his chair to look out the window. The rain still fell, and now the slick, shiny dampness covered the mill's looming, storied brick buildings and muddy grounds. His workers, both men and women, darted to and fro about their tasks to prepare for the shipment due to leave the next morning. His focus fell on a group of about five men loading a cart. The fact that each one of these people was employed by him—depended on him—was sobering.

"Are you going to Kent's dinner?" Cool air swept through the door as Milton entered the countinghouse.

"Ah yes. Of course." James turned from the window. "Tomorrow, isn't it?"

"Comes 'round like regular." Milton shrugged off his dusty, damp coat, hung it on a hook, and tossed a letter onto James's desk. "Might be worth it this time. Peter Clark's returned from the city, so I've heard. Cut the London visit short. If we want to team up with 'im about some shared security, it might be the right time."

James turned from watching the activity in the courtyard. "Did you hire extra watchmen along the route to the village and back toward Briarton?"

"Yes."

"The river too?"

"Yes, but 'tis costin' us. Threat of violence is high. No one wants to get involved."

The extra security was expensive, but did he have another choice? The locals were growing angrier by the day at the perceived slights.

Costs were increasing, demand was going down, and every farthing he had was invested here. "Given the week's events, I'll talk with Clark and see what we can come up with. Since the mills are in such close proximity, maybe we can find a mutually beneficial solution."

"If he's willin' to work with us, that is. 'Tis no secret you're not exactly one of his favorite people."

Very true. Peter Clark had made no effort to hide his annoyance that the mill and estate had to be sold to cover his father's debts. Peter had no doubt expected to inherit it and was as shocked as anyone at the business's state at the time of his father's death.

But that was out of James's control. It had been a family matter and had nothing to do with him. He owned the house and the mill outright now, and that was the start and end of his business with the Clarks.

Movement outside the window near the gate caught his eye. A drably clad youth with a flat cap was running in toward the courtyard. The boy paused to talk to a group of men, one of whom pointed to the countinghouse.

"Who's that?" asked James.

Milton joined him at the window. But before he could respond, the boy ran to the countinghouse and flew inside. "Letter from Briarton Park for Mr. Warrington." The boy extended the missive toward James.

Panic sliced. He'd never received a letter from Briarton while at the mill.

He snatched the letter and ripped open the seal and read it.

Maria injured. Fell from tree. Fear arm is broken . . . Surgeon's been called.

James pushed the letter toward Milton by way of explanation, snatched his own coat, and ran out the door. Within minutes his horse was saddled and they were galloping down the road toward Briarton.

He soothed himself with the thought that the injury could be small. He clung to this as his horse raced over the grounds. He had to. He could not allow his imagination to run away with him.

No one met him once he arrived at Briarton—only an eerie silence bid him a grim welcome. He quickly located a stable boy to take his horse, and he took the main steps two at a time, up two floors until he reached the nursery.

"Papa!" Rose, who had been sitting outside the nursery door alone, rushed toward him and jumped into his arms.

He embraced her, kissed her cheek, and smoothed her loose flaxen hair from her face. "Why are you sitting out here?"

"Grandmother told me to. Maria hurt her arm."

"I've heard." He lowered her back to the ground. "Wait here just a little longer, all right?"

A fire had been built in the grate in the nursery. Its glow flickered on the walls and fell on the people within. Mrs. Towler and the surgeon, Mr. Gardinar, both turned as he entered. Rachel, who was sitting by the window, stood. But Maria captured his immediate attention. She slumbered on her bed. A white bandage swathed her arm, and another white cloth bound it to her chest.

He stepped closer to her. She seemed peaceful. Her dark hair splayed over the pillow. Her long eyelashes fanned over her pale, slightly freckled cheeks.

He wanted to snatch Maria up. Hold her tight. Never let her go. But his hands remained still at his sides.

What would have happened if she'd been injured more? The possible scenarios struck him hard and fast, and fear wound tightly in his mind. He reached down to lift the fingers on her uninjured hand. So delicate.

The surgeon wiped his hands on a cloth. "She'll recover, Mr. Warrington. She broke her arm, but it's a clean break. Painful, but it'll heal."

He struggled to believe the words. "Which tree did she fall from?"

"One of the trees in the apple orchard, or so I've been told. 'Tis fortunate it was not a leg or an injury more complicated than her forearm. I've set the bone and given her something to ease the pain and help her sleep. I'll be by tomorrow to check on her, but I have left my instructions for recovery with your housekeeper and Mrs. Towler."

The surgeon's voice sounded muffled, as though it was coming from the next room. James could not look away from his daughter. He managed to mutter, "I thank you for coming."

The surgeon departed, leaving them all in the quiet and slight confusion that accompanied such an accident. James looked to Rachel, wide-eyed and uncharacteristically taciturn, whose face paled to as white as the linen swathing Maria's arm. "Will you sit with her a moment, please? If she stirs or wakes, call me."

Rachel nodded, and James motioned for his mother-in-law to join him in the small chamber adjoining the nursery.

Admittedly, there was much James didn't know about feminine etiquette, but he did know that ladies should not be climbing trees. Frustration mounting, he drew a deep breath. Once they were alone, he whispered, "What was she doing climbing a tree? She could have broken her neck!"

"I don't know what she was doing." Mrs. Towler's voice shrilled defensively. "She was out in the garden. I had no idea she'd climb a tree. The idea!"

"But why was she out there alone?" There had to be answers.

"Oh, don't be ridiculous." Mrs. Towler fussed with the black fichu at her throat. "Maria is a child of eight years. She's absolutely capable of being out in the garden alone."

He refused to let her avoid responsibility. "I thought you said that if we waited for the specific governess, then you'd be personally responsible for the girls until the governess's arrival. Is that not what we agreed?"

Mrs. Towler tilted her head to the side. "Are you suggesting that this is somehow my fault?"

"I'm saying that you promised me that if we delayed engaging a governess, then you would see to both Maria's and Rose's education and safety. Furthermore, I've made it clear that the children are not to be left alone outdoors. Not while this weaver business and violence is a threat."

"I'm not one of your hired servants that you can order about," she hissed, disgust emphasizing every word. "In fact, I insist you adjust your tone. This is hardly acceptable."

"Hardly acceptable? What's not acceptable is my child breaking her arm because she climbed a tree unsupervised."

Mrs. Towler's lips quivered. "I am Maria's grandmother. I will not be talked down to."

With every word she uttered, fresh anger raced through him. Anger that his daughter was hurt. Anger that his mother-in-law was not doing as she had promised. Anger with himself for not knowing exactly how to deal with it. And anger that Elizabeth was dead.

How had all of this become so complicated?

"We will no longer wait for a governess," James declared.

"Oh, the idea! Of course we will," she shot back.

"No, we will not." Miss Hale's offer flashed in his mind. "I'll see to the arrangements myself." He stomped from the small room to the main corridor and turned to walk downstairs.

Mrs. Towler trailed him. "But that was not our agreement! That is not what we—"

"I'm their father." He did not break his stride as he descended the stairs. "I make the decisions—let me be abundantly clear about that."

"And I'm here as a voice for Elizabeth." Her voice cracked as she called from the upper-level landing. "She would have wanted us to wait. She would have wanted—"

"Elizabeth is dead!" His bellowed words echoed from the plaster walls. He stopped short on the stair's landing and turned to look up the stairwell to face her. "She's not here, and she never will be again."

He spoke more harshly than he intended. But it was a truth they all needed to accept. Himself included.

Mrs. Towler's face blanched to ashen. She suddenly looked very small. Very frail. The assumed authority, the poignant sharpness of her voice, taunted. "How dare you speak to me in such a tone. After all I have done for you. For this family."

When he did not respond, she shouted even louder. "Pick your governess then. We'll see what happens. If you are determined to ruin your daughters' chances at success in society, then there is naught I can do."

Chapter 21

James glanced at his pocket watch, then returned it to his pocket. He needed to be off to the Kents'.

He was hardly in the mood for a social gathering. It had only been one day since Maria's fall, and today mill business had kept him away from Briarton Park. As much as he wanted to stay home tonight, he knew how important these monthly meetings could be—for so many different reasons.

He climbed the staircase to the nursery. He'd expected to find Maria in bed, but he found her curled up on the window seat, her face turned to look at the grounds below. Her long, sleek hair was loose around her shoulders, and she had her knees pulled up to her chest. Her arm was protectively cradled in her sling.

The sight was a difficult one.

Determined to brighten her mood, he forced cheer to his voice. "There's my girl!"

His smile quickly faded, however, when she turned. The light highlighted the tear tracks on her freckled cheeks.

Sobering, he lifted a wooden chair, crossed the room, placed it next to her, and sat on it. Silence prevailed, then she inched down from the window and approached him.

"What are these tears for? Does your arm pain you?"

She leaned against him and sniffed. "A little."

Sensing there was something on her mind, he put his arm around her narrow shoulders. "Is something else bothering you?"

"I shouldn't have been in the tree." Her pensive words were barely above a whisper. "I'm sorry."

"What were you doing up there?"

She shrugged. "Just looking. I like being up there. It is peaceful, and you can see all the way to the other side of the courtyard."

"Yes, I'm sure it was very pretty, but it isn't safe to climb trees like that. It's not safe for anyone. Those trees in the orchard are old. The branches may not be steady."

She bit her lip thoughtfully. "Would Mama be upset with me?"

"Your mama?" The whispered words jolted him and evoked Elizabeth's image in his mind. "Why would she be upset with you?"

The girl was still. "She never would have climbed a tree."

"Your mother would be relieved you weren't hurt more seriously, that I know for certain."

Maria sighed and leaned her head against his shoulder. "One of the maids told Grandmother that I was climbing a tree, and Grandmother told me to stop. She'd told me that before, but I disobeyed. I just like being up high. And that's when I fell."

"You knowingly disobeyed your grandmother?"

Maria stared down at the rug and nodded.

Guilt pricked his conscience. He'd been hard on Mrs. Towler. Too hard. He had made judgments without knowing this bit of information.

He cleared his throat. "If you disobeyed your grandmother, then you know what you need to do. You need to make it right with her."

Maria nodded with a little sniff. "I miss Mama."

"I do too." How inadequate the words seemed.

He forced cheerfulness to his voice. "But she would not want us to be sad. She would want us to start each day trying to do our best and to be happy, wouldn't she?"

Maria nodded again.

"Have you spoken with your grandmother today?"

Maria studied her hand. "She has been up a couple times, but I think she is very upset with me."

"I suspect you won't start to feel better until everything is resolved. Will you?"

She shook her head. "I'm always doing the wrong thing and saying the wrong thing."

"You do plenty right. But we all could use a change to the way things are done around here. A new start, of sorts. Don't you agree?"

At the suspicion in her eyes, he gave a little laugh. "You do not need to look so severe. Everything will be all right. I promise. But first things first. You need to apologize to your grandmother."

And he would need to do the same.

Chapter 22

By the time the gathering at the Kents' arrived, Cassandra still had received no news from Mr. Longham. Or Mr. Warrington.

And her confidence was waning.

So many significant questions lurked on the horizon, fuzzy and dim, and it seemed Mr. Longham held the answers to them all. To make matters more disconcerting, her meager funds were diminishing, and she could only interpret Mr. Warrington's silence on the governess position as a refusal.

She'd sent out a handful of inquiries about teaching and governess positions. She'd written to some of the women who had taught with her at Mrs. Denton's school, hoping they might have leads on new employment, but as of yet she'd received no response.

Despite the anxious waiting, the week had been quiet, especially during the daytime hours when the other boarders were occupied and she was the only boarder in the house. With the exception of a few outings to assist Mrs. Pearson in delivering food to the local poor, the hours had passed slowly, allowing time for her nerves to intensify as the gathering at the Kent house drew nearer. The only real social events she'd ever attended were the picnics and dinners at the vicar's house, but after her incident with Frederick, even those stopped.

What a sharp contrast the vicar she knew in her youth cut against the vicar who now was in her company. Lamby's vicar was severe and often cross. He rarely smiled and scarcely laughed, and almost every word uttered was in condemnation.

But Mr. North was so dissimilar. Perhaps it was the variance in age, or even just the difference in their personalities. But when she was in his presence, she felt no guilt or need for pretense. He was . . . a friend.

One she had never expected.

Perhaps she should make more of an effort to encourage him romantically. With each day Mr. Longham's suggestion of a possible inheritance faded, and she'd not be able to support herself forever. What was more, she did like Mr. North. He was charming, funny, and kind. He was attentive and grew more so with every interaction.

And yet Betsy's warning rang in her mind. It was the very reason she'd avoided him this week. Betsy may be prone to exaggeration, but she would never cast a shadow over his integrity without a valid reason.

At the moment, Cassandra and Betsy were in Betsy's bedchamber, and Betsy was fastening the small buttons on the back of the altered rose-hued gown. Once she was done with the task, she stepped back and tilted her head to the side. "There. I daresay it looks lovelier on you than it ever did on me."

Cassandra smoothed her hand down the pale pink gown's shimmery fabric, allowing her fingertips to linger on the embroidered flowers, admiring the newly applied lace overlay on the bodice and lace trim at the sleeves. "It's beautiful, Betsy. Truly."

Betsy propped her hands on her hips. "If there is one benefit to being a poor, overworked seamstress, it is that sometimes the shop's owner lets us have the extras, lace and trims in particular. Besides, it is nice to think that you might have a chance at catching someone's eye. Perhaps you'll make your match tonight, and my lace will have helped you. Perhaps Mr. North?"

Cassandra raised a brow. "I thought you didn't approve of Mr. North."

"Why? Because I shared a doubt?" Betsy reached forward to adjust the hem on Cassandra's elbow-length sleeve. "It's not my opinion that matters here, is it? It should be yours and yours only."

Cassandra returned her attention to the small looking glass on the wall. It would not do to give herself false hope. "I think it best not to jump to conclusions."

"You think I am jumping to a conclusion about Mr. North's intentions?" Betsy huffed. "La, Cassandra, he secured you an invitation. Do you not know what that means? Come now, turn. Let's put this last bit in your hair."

Cassandra sat at the small dressing table and was still as Betsy's hands worked the ribbon through her curls. She watched as the woman's round face sobered in concentration at the task, and a genuine fondness for her new friend tugged at her. "I do wish you were coming."

Betsy smirked and reached for the comb. "Girls like me do not get invited to such parties. I didn't go to a fancy school."

"Our backgrounds don't matter much now, do they?" Cassandra tilted her face to give Betsy a better angle. "We live in the very same boardinghouse now."

"But your path will take you farther. Somewhere bigger and better than a seamstress shop."

Cassandra's stomach sank.

Bigger and better.

Until everyone found out that she was illegitimate.

The cool air held the scent of rain as Cassandra alighted from the carriage to the drive before Kent House. Torches lined the drive leading to the elegant sandstone structure, providing flickering light to the guests arriving.

The drive from the village had been brief, and the hired carriage crowded. It conveyed not only Mr. North, Mrs. Martin, and herself, but two others as well. Now that they were here, Cassandra's emotions vacillated between anticipation and hesitation.

She could feel Mr. North, strong and supportive, at her elbow. "You look wonderful, Miss Hale. No need for nervousness. Everything is going to be fine," he whispered, almost intimately, as the flurry of activity of everyone departing from the carriage swirled around them.

The softly spoken words, and the compliment, caught her off guard and incited a flutter in her heart she had not anticipated, but before she knew it, they were swept into the grandeur of the house. Never before had she seen so many candles illuminating a chamber or so many elegantly clad people gathered and milling about. Voices echoed from the plaster walls, woven tapestries, and ancient stone floors. Laughter resounded from nearby rooms. The atmosphere felt happy. Engaging. Her nerves melted away and excitement flowed in.

Mr. North led Mrs. Martin in, and Cassandra followed to where a couple was greeting guests. Before she was even fully through the door, an older woman in a shimmering gown of vermillion lustring pushed past Mr. North and Mrs. Martin and took Cassandra's hands in her own. "So, you must be the young Miss Hale Mr. North has told me about."

There could be no doubt. The authority and perceived familiarity confirmed that this must be their hostess. Cassandra curtsied. "Yes, I am. And I thank you for your kind invitation to—"

"Ah, ah, none of that. My motives are purely selfish, I assure you. I'm so eager to have another young woman in our acquaintance that it is *you* who are doing *me* the favor." She looped her large arm through Cassandra's with a twinkle in her droopy russet eyes. "I'm taking her from you, Mr. North, Mrs. Martin. You've had her to yourself all this time."

Cassandra cast a glance to the woman who had claimed possession of her. Her hair was faded to a pale walnut brown, streaked with white, and wrinkles splayed out from the corners of her eyes, but otherwise, her high, proud cheekbones and delicately arched eyebrows spoke to another time in which she must have had the command of every room she graced. And, judging by the way the woman paraded around the room, she still did.

When they were nearing the hearth, Mrs. Kent paused and turned to Cassandra. "So, Miss Hale. How do you find our little village?"

"It's very lovely."

"You probably haven't seen much of it. How long have you been here?"

"Just above two weeks now."

"My, my. And what an impression you've made."

Cassandra was not sure how to take the last statement, but she was keenly aware of how the woman assessed her. Her gown. Her hair. She gripped her reticule to keep from fidgeting and focused on the conversation. "Mr. North and Mrs. Pearson have been kind enough to introduce me to some of the villagers."

Mrs. Kent snapped her fan open. "Mr. North is such a pleasant man. I knew it the first time I saw him. Do you believe in that sentiment, Miss Hale? That you can tell what you need to know about a person the very first time you meet him or her?"

Cassandra chose her words with care. "I think we can make some judgment at first glance. But I find that some people take longer to divulge the truth about themselves."

The ruby-and-diamond necklace about the woman's neck glittered in the light with the movement of her laughter. "Oh, you sweet child. I suppose that at one point in life I felt the same way, but now I am not so sure. Perhaps it is my old age that makes me so suspicious.

There now, I see the disbelief in your expression. I would shudder to know what you think of me upon this our first meeting."

"I think you're very kind to invite me without even knowing me." She wanted to change the conversation from herself. "How long have you been acquainted with Mr. North?"

"Three years, if you can believe it."

"And how did you become acquainted?"

"Mr. North's uncle was the vicar in Anston before him. He had been for decades. I was particularly fond of his wife, Alice. She always attended these gatherings."

"I was not aware that his uncle preceded him as vicar. That's very interesting."

"Yes, Mr. North first came to our parish as the curate, serving under his uncle, of course. His mother's brother, if memory serves. I was so taken with him that I moved heaven and earth to make sure he became the next vicar. Impressive young man. And he would be a fine catch for any young woman."

Cassandra's cheeks flushed at the recommendation, and yet a sensation of uneasiness quaked within her. She glanced back at Mr. North. When he noticed her looking at him, he nodded. Smiled. Based on what Mrs. Kent had said, perhaps the sentiment was spreading. Perhaps others were seeing her as a contender for his hand.

She allowed herself to be led through the hall, pausing to be introduced at Mrs. Kent's whim. It was clear Cassandra was here as the woman's amusement—to be shown off. But with every new introduction, she was watchful. Mr. North had suggested that Peter Clark might attend. She would never dare inquire so obviously, but her eyes and her ears were open.

When they ventured from the great hall to the parlor, another man entirely captured her attention—one she had not expected to see.

She was looking at none other than Mr. Warrington.

Chapter 23

Maria's sad expression refused to leave him as James arrived at the Kents', and he was in no humor for socializing.

His earlier conversation with Maria about Elizabeth was still alive and vibrant in his mind, and at a time like this, he'd much rather be alone with his thoughts. Duty called, however, and there was business to conduct. Peter Clark was supposed to be here, and if they were going to defend their mills against the angry locals, then they needed to find some way to collaborate efforts.

He looked around the ornate, candlelit parlor. All of the regular attendees were present: the mill owners, some of the gentlemen farmers, even the innkeepers and local breeders. He needed to remain focused.

Elizabeth would have laughed at his apprehension. She would have smiled, fussed with his cravat, and told him that he'd worked too hard on the mill and invested too much time to allow an opportunity—any opportunity—to go to waste.

She was right, of course.

She'd always been right.

Milton elbowed his arm. "This day just keeps gettin' more interesting. Isn't that your little visitor? The one Longham asked about?"

James turned from his place next to the mantel and looked in the direction Milton indicated.

Miss Hale.

She was the last person he had expected to see, being led around by Mrs. Kent, no less.

What was she doing here?

A general hush fell over the chatty room as other guests took notice of her arrival. It was not often a new face joined them, especially a lovely young woman.

James tried not to stare, but how could he not? Her chestnut hair was curled and coiled at the base of her neck. She was in an exquisite gown of a striking shade of palest pink—a fetching, decidedly feminine hue in a sea of sedate blacks and browns. The gown's empire waist accentuated the delicate curves of her body, and the candlelight reflected from the smoothness of her skin. She possessed a freshness, an overwhelming sense of radiance that seemed to awaken the very room.

Mrs. Kent had a possessive hold on the young woman's arm, and judging by the animation in the older woman's expression and the volume of her laughter, she was enjoying the role very much.

"What's her name again?" Milton lowered his voice.

"Cassandra Hale."

"Ah, that's right. I wonder if Longham was able to speak with her, as he had wanted to."

James took a drink of his beverage to mask his discomfort at discussing the topic. Yes, he knew Longham had spoken with her. And he also knew that Robert Clark was her father, but it was not fodder for gossip. And it went deeper than that. He'd seen the tears. This experience was painful for her, and he wanted to protect her from the local meddlers as best he could. "I'm not sure."

Oblivious to the battle within James, Milton continued. "Well, at least one of the rumors about her 'tis true."

"What rumors?"

"Well, she's a beauty." Milton pivoted. "Heard she was. I only saw her but the one time at Briarton, but I'd been so befuddled over Riddy's attack I hadn't really noticed."

James's gaze landed on the faint flush to her cheeks. The soft curl of the escaping locks of hair framing her face.

Alluring. Entrancing.

It was not a betrayal to Elizabeth's memory to notice.

Was it?

Not wishing to discuss that topic with Milton, James forged ahead. "And what other rumors did you hear?"

Milton smirked, as if enjoying his role as gossipmonger, and took a drink. "That old man Clark might have left her a significant inheritance—one that will no doubt shake Peter Clark to the core."

James winced. Longham had mentioned that she might have been left something in his will, but he'd assumed it was relatively insignificant. "Where did you hear this?"

"Various sources. Reliable sources. Apparently when the will was read after Clark's death, it named two individuals as heirs to parts of Clark Mill. 'Course that was a couple of years ago, so the details are murky, but I'd be willin' to bet a week's wages that Peter Clark's acutely aware."

James cleared his throat. "I'd be careful to put too much faith in a rumor. Change always brings about gossip—you know that."

"It certainly does." Milton watched Miss Hale as Mrs. Kent introduced her to a small cluster of people just inside the door. "Why do you think Mrs. Kent is being so nice to her?"

Annoyance arced through him, and he glanced toward the woman. Mrs. Kent's snobbery was legendary. "Poor Miss Hale. Someone should tell her to run away from here and never look back."

"I wonder if Mrs. Kent knows somethin' 'bout the will," speculated Milton. "She's not the sort to be kind for kindness' sake."

All the bits of information James knew began to coalesce. Mr. Longham was Robert Clark's solicitor, and as such would be executor of the will. He'd known that Miss Hale was Clark's daughter, and Robert Clark had tried to contact her just before his death. What was more, Longham had mentioned the will when they were at the Green Ox Inn. Based on that, it did seem likely that the rumors were true.

Milton drew a deep breath. "Regardless, a bonny face is never a bad thing, is it? Might give it a go myself. But there looks to be competition."

James turned to see Mr. North approach Mrs. Kent and Miss Hale. Miss Hale seemed to regard the vicar with friendly familiarity.

"Hard to compete with a vicar, but still," Milton mused. "I daresay someone will give him a challenge. Not every day we get a pretty girl from outside the area."

James smirked. "Who, you?"

"Why, I think I've as good a shot as anyone here. Although my pockets might not be as thickly lined as some, I do have charms that are worth more than gold."

James tried to focus on this conversation with Milton, but he was much more interested in the conversations Miss Hale was having.

A fresh curiosity had taken hold about what she was saying and with whom she was speaking.

It had not been intentional, but he and Miss Hale shared secrets. It had been so long since he'd shared a secret with someone. They both knew details about the other's life that were intimate. And damning. And yet he trusted that she would keep what she knew about his family private. And he would return the favor.

Mrs. Kent escorted her around the room, parading her about and introducing her to the other guests. Miss Hale's affable expression gave the impression that she was enjoying herself. And why shouldn't she? She deserved a bit of brightness after how upset she had been the last time he saw her. But at one point, Miss Hale excused herself and exited through the door to the corridor connecting the parlor to the house's entrance hall. A less observant person might not have noticed, but her gown's skirt did not swish out of sight. Instead, she disappeared just enough to give the impression that she was standing against the wall, alone.

Why was she standing in the corridor?

This was preposterous. It wouldn't do to be spying on the young woman. They were already introduced. There was nothing improper in speaking with her, and if he desired to do so, this might be his only opportunity, especially if Mrs. Kent reclaimed her.

He excused himself from Milton and a handful of other men who had gathered and made his way toward her. He found her, as expected, standing alone, her back against the wall. "Miss Hale. Is everything all right?"

She turned and snapped to attention. She ran a nervous hand down the front of her gown to smooth it, and a pretty blush flushed her cheeks. "Forgive me. I just needed a moment."

He stepped farther into the hall's shadow. "Is there anything I can do for you?"

"No, no." The tension in her narrow shoulders eased. "I saw you earlier and was hoping we would have a chance to converse. It is so nice to see someone I am already acquainted with. I wasn't entirely sure I'd be welcome here."

He leaned forward to take her into confidence. "To be honest, Miss Hale, I feel exactly the same way."

"You? Not welcome? But surely you're acquainted with everyone present."

"Am I?" He lifted his brow. "You forget I'm a newcomer."

"Well, you *belong* here, at least. Mr. North was kind enough to help secure an invitation for me. He said it would be beneficial to help me learn more about my family."

James stiffened at the mention of Mr. North and the memory of the warm smile she'd given him. "I thought Mr. Longham had been assisting you."

"He has, of course, but I've not heard from him since our interaction at Briarton." She stepped closer, tightening the space between them. Her voice lowered. "And concerning that, again I feel the need to apologize. I never would have expected to impose on you in such a manner."

"Miss Hale, how quickly you forget that you've assisted my family in the most extraordinary way. I think the use of my study for a rather short conversation is a small price to pay."

She tilted her head to the side thoughtfully. "Since you are, in a way, familiar with my story, might I ask you a question?"

"You may ask me anything."

"I'm told there are several mill men here. Is Mr. Peter Clark, by chance, present?"

Now it made sense. Perhaps Milton had been right. This was why she was here.

"No, I've not seen him," he said. "Actually, I'd hoped to speak with him on a different matter as well, but it appears we both will need to wait for another opportunity."

Disappointment furrowed her alabaster brow. "I was hoping to meet him, given what Mr. Longham had said. Do you know anything of him?"

He drew a deep breath. Peter Clark was a boorish man, that much he knew. Determined to profit at any cost. It did not bother James, for their interactions began and ended with the mills. He could only imagine the man's brashness in a conversation as personal as the one he would have with Miss Hale. But what good would it do to divulge that at this point? "He's married and has no children, but that is the extent of what I know of his personal life. Beyond that our interaction has been limited to specific mill talk."

James glanced back through the threshold to see Mr. North at a distance, yet staring in their direction.

"And how is Rachel faring?" Miss Hale asked, seeming oblivious to Mr. North's attentions.

He chuckled, returning his full attention to her. "Angry not to be here. She insists that she is old enough for such gatherings."

Miss Hale's amiable lightheartedness returned. "You do not agree?"

"She's still young. Her behavior and the choices she makes need to reflect her age before I consent to such."

"I daresay she learned a valuable lesson over the last couple of weeks."

"I should hope."

"And your daughters? Are they well?"

He sobered at the question. "Maria fell from a tree and broke her arm."

Miss Hale's hand flew to her chest. "Is she all right?"

"It's a painful injury, but she'll recover." He looked down at her, and he knew exactly what needed to be done.

He liked Miss Hale. He respected her. He already considered her a good example for Rachel. What could she also do for his girls? Furthermore, he knew the truth about her: she was Robert Clark's illegitimate daughter. It should matter, but for some reason, it didn't. "Speaking of the girls, I'm glad to have encountered you. We were never able to resume our conversation the other night."

At this, eagerness widened her eyes, as if they were sharing a secret. She lifted her face to him expectantly.

"I realize that this probably isn't the best place for this chat, but Maria's experience has shed light on the fact that I cannot, in good faith, wait for the governess my mother-in-law has selected. Someone is needed now to oversee them. I'm not, of course, sure what you have learned from the solicitor and how it affects your plans, but I am keen to learn if you are still interested in the governess position."

Chapter 24

Had she heard him correctly? Cassandra could almost laugh with relief.

In that single second Mr. Warrington's offer hoisted a great weight from her shoulders. Finally, something positive glimmered, something secure and concrete—a development that would propel her in the right direction.

She could not respond quickly enough. "Y-yes! I should like that very much."

He nodded, but his expression remained customarily stoic. "Excellent. If it is agreeable to you, I will take tomorrow to get things situated, and then you may come by early the next day to get settled at Briarton Park. I see no cause to delay."

With every new word spoken, her nerves flailed wildly within her. "That is wonderful. Thank you, sir. I am certain that—"

Her words were interrupted. She lifted her gaze slightly over Mr. Warrington's shoulder to see Mr. North approaching them, his expression unusually severe. "Oh, Mr. North. Forgive me. I did not see you there."

"I've been looking for you! I thought I'd quite lost you." Mr. North moved closer, giving Mr. Warrington a brief nod in greeting. "The hour is growing quite late, and the rain has started, I'm afraid. Mrs. Martin desires to return home. So as much as I hate to put an end to the festivities, I do feel the time has come to see you ladies home."

A pang of disappointment shot through her. She cast a glance up at Mr. Warrington, wishing there was some way he could intervene. She wanted to stay with him. To continue discussing their plans.

But it was impossible, of course.

Besides, in a matter of two days all would begin. Her new role. Her new pupils. Something to focus on outside of herself.

"Very well then." She pivoted back to Mr. Warrington. "Thank you, sir. I look forward to all we've discussed."

"Until later then." Mr. Warrington bowed.

Cassandra took the vicar's proffered arm and followed him as he led her from the quiet and privacy of the corridor back to the main drawing room.

When they were out of earshot, Mr. North whispered quite close, "It is none of my business, I know, but I could not help but overhear. Mr. Warrington mentioned something about 'later.' Do you have upcoming business with him?"

She saw no reason to keep it secret. "I do. Rather exciting news, at least on my part. I've been engaged as governess to care for his daughters."

She expected him to offer a bit of congratulations, but none came. In fact, his expression turned almost adverse.

She lowered her gaze to the ground as they walked. She was learning his ways—learning his moods and his dispositions. "I take it from your silence that you do not approve."

He hesitated. "It is not my place to approve or disapprove, but do you think it wise to tie yourself to a family—a position—so early in your search?"

"What could be wrong with it? It is employment, and quite necessary. Nothing more."

"You will need help from others," he cautioned, his tone worrisome. "There are still many questions to be answered, and people, whether you like it or not, are starting to talk."

A tingle skittered down the back of her neck. The same tingle she had felt when he talked about socializing with Betsy and the other boarders. He was turning this conversation in a direction she did not necessarily want it to go.

He stopped to face her. His resolute jaw twitched. "I hate to tell you this, for it reeks of idle gossip, and you know I detest such happenings. But you must know what people are saying. They are figuring it out, Miss Hale. Why you are here. They are saying there's an inheritance involved. A sizable one. If you are to inherit, what would it look like to serve as a governess—"

She raised her hand in hasty interruption. "I'm in no position to care what people think, inheritance or not."

"It's not just that. Mr. Peter Clark and Mr. Warrington are not exactly friends. Or even allies. It . . . it sends a certain message."

She recoiled. A message?

His voice softened and his face relaxed. He glanced around, ensuring privacy. "I only urge you to keep your options open. I do not mean to upset you, and I fancy you a friend. You—your presence here—fits a hole that was in my life. I've probably said too much, but it's important you know someone cares very much what happens and sincerely desires the best for you."

"A friend," she repeated. He seemed earnest, but the sincerity displayed slammed against Betsy's warnings. "Then as a friend I must ask: Does a title, such as a governess, mean so very much to you? Would you consider me less worthy to be a friend if I obtained such a role?"

"Of course I would not consider you less worthy. You misunderstand me. I only caution you to consider every scenario. After all, what do you know of the Warringtons? I barely know them, and we have lived in close proximity for quite some time."

"What does any governess know of any family who employs her?" Her tone sounded more churlish than she'd intended. "I do thank you for wanting the very best for me, but I assure you, I've lived my entire life without expectation. I can manage this situation quite fastidiously."

They continued on to bid their farewells to their host and hostess, but while their discourse drew to an end, the words exchanged continued to trouble Cassandra. They could be perceived as encouragement—like a friend encouraging another—but quite the opposite seemed to be true. Everything she thought she knew had shifted, which reinforced one fact: she needed to be very careful whom she trusted.

Sunlight streamed through the tall panes, illuminating the steam rising from the coffee before him as James sat in his study.

After the previous night's events at Kent House, he'd not slept at all. He'd not expected to encounter Miss Hale there. It was supposed to be a humdrum gathering with mundane conversation and perhaps one or two worthwhile business discussions.

But that had not been the case. And he'd done it. He'd offered her the position of governess.

Now she'd be in his home. Caring for his children.

Rachel would be thrilled, of course. The girls would, too, no doubt. But his mother-in-law was another story.

He leaned back in his chair, contemplating his tactics—and how he would tell Mrs. Towler he'd engaged a governess.

She'd be angry, of course. No doubt Mrs. Towler would think that a governess would diminish her own importance in the household. But it was clear the task of caring for the girls was beyond her. They had been allowed far too much freedom, and Maria's injury stood as testament to that.

So where did that leave them? Was Mrs. Towler destined to live under his roof until the children were grown?

Out of respect for Elizabeth, he could not—would not—alter the situation. Elizabeth's mother was welcome in his home for as long as she had need. But time was passing, and grief had evolved from a stabbing pain to an aching loneliness. He yearned to see beyond the anguish of loss to a new, different future for himself with someone else. But Mrs. Towler's constant presence, the continual reminders, were painful. Confusing. Heavy.

Mrs. Towler always took her breakfast alone in a small room off the parlor. Practicing what he would say, he ascended the stairs to her small breakfast room and rapped against the door with his knuckles. "Might I have a word?"

She looked up from her breakfast, expressionless, a piece of toast in her hand. "Of course."

He stepped into the chamber and sat in the chair opposite her. "I owe you an apology."

She lifted her pointed chin, as if she suspected him of foul play. "Oh?"

"Yes, regarding Maria." He rested his elbows on the table. "I should not have blamed you for her fall. I now know she disobeyed you. I'm sorry I jumped to a conclusion."

His apology caught her off guard, he could tell. She pierced him with her glare. "All is forgiven, James. I'm only glad she wasn't more seriously injured."

He cleared his throat, girding himself for the second part of his delivery. "There is one other thing I wanted to discuss with you. The matter of the governess."

She returned her toast to the plate. "We've been through this, or so I thought."

"The girls need more structure. More routine. We cannot continue as we are, surely you must agree. They're floundering. Their behavior is declining, they are sad, they—"

She scoffed and shook her head. "How do you know what children need? La, men. You think because you understand the running of a mill that you are fit to rear a child. It is hardly the same, and it is work best left to women."

James stiffened. True, he knew very little about children in general. But he did have instinct. "My decision is made. I've engaged Miss Hale to oversee the girls' education."

Mrs. Towler started, then released a sharp, bitter laugh. "You can't be serious."

"I am."

"But she's . . . she's . . ." Mrs. Towler's words trailed off, and then she straightened her frail shoulders with a renewed sense of vigor. "This woman shows up from only God knows where, and you think she is capable of raising your daughters?"

"She is an experienced teacher. She has references."

Mrs. Towler threw her hands up. "References. Bah. A meaningless piece of paper with contrived words. Have you personal references? I daresay you don't. If you're insistent, I can engage a temporary one until—"

"No. I've made my decision."

She pinned him with a sharp gaze. "Then you are a fool."

"Miss Hale is sensible and clever, and she is available."

"Available? High praise. And a very rational reason to select her to raise your daughters." Her face darkened. "I forbid it."

"Forbid it all you want, but my child fell from a tree. She could have been killed. And I may be completely ignorant of the ways of children, as you put it, but I am almost certain climbing trees is not an approved activity for young ladies."

At this she leapt from her chair and strode toward him, her

ebony skirt swishing about her. "I know what this is about. Miss Hale. She's attractive, I will grant her that. But are you so blind, so selfish and fixed on your own desires, that you'd invite her into our home? It's sickening."

The accusation threatened to enrage him.

Mrs. Towler jabbed her forefinger at him. "Elizabeth would be ill at this."

He stiffened. How the very sound of his wife's name stopped him short. Would it always? But Mrs. Towler knew this. She was using Elizabeth's name as a weapon. It was his weakness—a knife to an open wound.

But as painful as her words were, this arrangement, this sense of being suspended in time, was killing him. "This has nothing to do with any romantic feelings toward Miss Hale. But I assure you when and if the time comes when I shall feel such feelings again, such inclinations are mine and mine alone. I need no one's consent."

"How dare you. *How dare you!*" Tears pooled in her eyes. "You know full well what Elizabeth would have wanted."

"She's not here! How I wish she were, but she's not."

"So you are determined, then, to undermine Elizabeth's wishes?"

"This is not about Elizabeth."

"It will always be about Elizabeth, as far as her daughters are concerned." Her tone approached a shout.

James refused to break eye contact with her. "Maria and Rose are my daughters too."

A silent battle for control raged. He'd always treated Mrs. Towler with the utmost respect. She was, after all, his late wife's mother and his children's only living grandparent.

But the lines were blurred—and those lines needed to be redrawn.

The ice in her glare froze him. "I will never cease acting in their best interest."

"Neither will I. So you have a choice, Mrs. Towler. You are welcome here. You always will be. You are family. But I will not be crossed. Not on this."

Commotion sounded at the door. Rachel appeared in the threshold. "My goodness!" she exclaimed, a little laugh on her lips and an apple held loosely in her hand. "Why does everyone look so serious? You are not still arguing about me, are you?"

Mrs. Towler whirled to face Rachel. "For heaven's sake, girl, despite your best efforts, not every conversation in this house is about you." She threw her napkin down and brushed past Rachel as she exited the room.

Rachel, confused, peered at James for clarification. "What's upsetting her?"

He straightened in his chair and drew a deep breath. "I've come to a decision about the governess for Maria and Rose."

"I thought that was settled?"

"A change of plans. I've spoken with Miss Hale and decided that she will oversee the girls."

"You're in earnest? She'll be living here?"

"Yes, as a governess. I thought she'd be company for you as well."

"Oh, I adore her!" Rachel clasped her hands together in front of her and then dropped them dramatically as if a great idea had formed. "May I be allowed to prepare her chamber? I think there is one near mine with a window that—"

"She's not here as a guest, Rachel. You must remember. The room off the nursery will suit her fine."

"When is she to arrive?"

"Tomorrow."

She threw her arms around him, kissed his cheek, and was out the door as quickly as she appeared.

He listened as the tapping of her feet faded away. At least Rachel was pleased with his decision. It was good to see her enthusiasm after months of melancholy brooding.

Even so, doubt chided him. The silence that Rachel's departure left only magnified it, leaving empty spaces for the questions to reverberate.

Mrs. Towler's words about Elizabeth had stung. It was his biggest fear—to make a decision that would dishonor his wife. She was never far from his thoughts. He doubted she ever would be, regardless of what developments occurred. But Elizabeth had also trusted him. Had she not told him so many times during their marriage?

He departed the small breakfast room. He'd made one member of the household irate and one ecstatic. It was impossible to please everyone. He just had to do what he believed to be right.

Chapter 25

"I can't believe you're leaving the boardinghouse." Betsy sat on the bed in Cassandra's tiny chamber with a pout. "It feels as if you've only just arrived."

"I've actually been here a few weeks now." Cassandra reached for her cloak and hung it on the hook. "Sometimes it seems like forever, and other times it seems like it has only been a day."

Betsy looked to the ceiling and frowned. "And I can't believe you stayed in this room all this time! Poor dear. Had I known it was this unpleasant, I would have shared mine."

Cassandra glanced around the sad little chamber and folded her nightdress, then put it in her trunk. "Truly, it hasn't been that bad."

"Not bad? It is freezing." Betsy rubbed her arms and shivered. "No wonder you're eager for a new situation."

"I've no choice but to find a new situation." Cassandra reached for her pocket watch. "Things can't go on as they are. If so, my money will be gone. I don't think Mrs. Martin would let me stay just out of the goodness of her heart."

Betsy tittered. "I'm not even certain she has a heart. So tell me all about Mr. North last night. Was he doting? Everything a dutiful suitor should be? I saw him from the window as he was leaving. He did look handsome."

Cassandra considered Mr. North's behavior the previous night. Yes, he'd been attentive . . . and perhaps a bit too opinionated. His disapproval about the governess position still did not bode well with her. "I don't think that Mr. North approves of my taking a position at Briarton Park."

"But why would he object?"

"He said I'm ruining my chances to be taken seriously by society here. I think he wants me to be something different than I am, which is really just a poor teacher. It would be lovely to be a fine lady and be able to follow all of society's rules, but I must work. And I do think this will be a good position for me."

"You needn't convince me." Betsy lounged back on the bed on her elbows. "I understand completely. If I had your experience and education, I would take that situation in a minute over this overcrowded boardinghouse and the drafty sewing rooms."

"And why shouldn't I?" Cassandra stuffed a petticoat and her extra stays next to the nightdress. "It's a good position, with a good family. I'm grateful. And honestly a little excited."

"Well, I'm happy for you, but selfishly I'm heartbroken. I thought I was to have a fast friend here, and now you are to leave."

Cassandra sighed and sat next to Betsy. "I will still see you. Sundays, of course. And my days off. And at charity outings. Mr. Warrington is aware of my desire to continue the search for my family, and he has said he would support it."

Betsy's green eyes twinkled. "I've always thought Mr. Warrington a handsome man. Maybe even more so than Mr. North."

"Betsy," laughed Cassandra, "do you think of nothing else?"

"Not really."

"Well, such thoughts about my new employer would hardly be a good way to start my time in a new home."

A knock at the door interrupted their discussion. A maid appeared and extended a missive.

Cassandra jumped up and accepted the letter. "Thank you."

She opened it and located the signature. *William Longham.*

"Who's it from?" The earnest expression on Betsy's face was sincere.

How Cassandra longed to tell her friend every detail of the journey she was on. But she mustn't. Not now. Not yet. It almost felt like she was lying. But what could be done? "It's a letter from a friend."

If Betsy was offended, she gave no indication. Instead, she stood from the bed. "I will leave you to read your letter. I'll be back to help you later."

Once Cassandra was alone, she dropped to the bed and read the message eagerly.

> Miss Hale,
>
> I have news regarding Mr. Peter Clark. It pains me to report that he is not pleased with these developments, but then again, I warned you that he might not be. He has, fortunately, agreed to an interview with us this Thursday. I will collect you at the boarding-house at the noon hour and accompany you there personally. I will bring all of the necessary documentation. Don't forget, Miss Hale, my priority is to see the will fulfilled to Robert's specifications. Then we may all put the matter to rest.
>
> Until then,
> William Longham

The very next morning, Cassandra arrived at Briarton Park as not just a visitor but the new governess. Instead of the agonizing trepidation that had threatened to cripple her upon prior visits, she now regarded the stone walls and leaded windows with fresh perspective.

How ironic that it was, at one time, her father's home.

And now it was going to be hers.

She might only be a hired governess, but she would sleep here. Eat here. Live out her daily life here. Anston was officially her new village. She could make friends and establish routines without concern for the immediate future. Now, despite what would happen with Peter Clark, she was carving out her own prospects.

She gripped her reticule and small valise tighter as a thread of excitement wove through her. The hem of her cape grazed the tips of the frost-laden grass as she walked along the edge of the path. The sweet sounds of birdsong energized her, and with each step her mind raced with ideas for how best to spend time with the girls.

She could do this, and do it well.

Cassandra made her way back to the courtyard entrance and knocked. A young maid answered and showed her to one of the back rooms of the servants' area before leaving her to retrieve the housekeeper.

Within moments Mrs. Helock appeared. What her pointed expression lacked in warmth, her eyes made up in censure. "You're here then. Mr. Warrington told me to expect you, but he isn't in. The maid has gone to inform Mrs. Towler you've arrived. In the meantime, come with me. I'll show you to where you'll be staying." Her gaze fell to the small valise in her hand. "Where are the rest of your things? Surely you have more than that."

"Not much more, but Mr. Warrington said he planned to send a boy to the boardinghouse who will bring my belongings by day's end."

Cassandra followed the housekeeper up the servants' stairs to the upper level and the family wing. She'd not been this far into the house before. The nursery was at the end of the corridor. She followed her into a series of small, connected rooms—a schoolroom, a bedchamber—until they reached the last door.

Mrs. Helock pushed it open. "This is where you'll stay."

Cassandra ducked to get through the low doorway and looked around the bright space. The ceiling was low, but the curtains were pushed open and a small fire crackled in the grate. She warmed. They'd been expecting her. She slid her finger over the side table against the wall as she made her way to the window.

The chamber she'd shared at the girls' school had a small square window, but if she wanted to see out of it she had to pull a chair up to it, and even then she was just able to glimpse the tops of distant trees.

But here the window was as broad as it was tall, and it framed a landscape of the autumnal garden. Beyond that, the distant brown moors stretched for as far as she could see until they met the gray expanse of the sky.

She turned. A bed with tidy, clean coverings, a wooden chair, and a wardrobe completed the room's furnishings.

This was home.

A month prior she never would have dreamed that events would take her so far from the girls' school. The bittersweet sense of change raced through her.

She dropped the thin curtain covering the window and turned to remove her gloves and bonnet. She untied the ribbons, lifted the straw hat from her head, and placed it atop the bed. Commotion at the door interrupted her. She turned, expecting to see Mrs. Helock.

But there stood Mrs. Towler.

Cassandra had not seen the older woman since their interaction the night of Rachel's incident and then at church. Now she stood still in the doorway, her hands clasped in front of her.

"Mrs. Towler. You frightened me." Cassandra expelled a little laugh. "I didn't hear you approach."

At first the woman said nothing.

When the awkward silence grew noticeable, Cassandra turned to fully face her. "Was there something you needed from me?"

The woman took one step into the room, her ink-black skirts swishing with the movement. "Maria and Rose will be up shortly. But I wanted to speak to you first. It's important you know that *I* do not agree with your presence here."

Cassandra blinked, determined to hide her shock. She'd suspected the woman would oppose the arrangement, but to hear her disapproval blatantly expressed was unnerving. "I suppose we must trust Mr. Warrington's instincts as a father to know what is best for his daughters."

Mrs. Towler inched farther into the chamber. "I've seen girls like you before. Young women eager to change their status and situation. If you have any designs set upon this place other than that of a position as a governess, I suggest you reconsider your presence here. I will not allow you or anyone else to take advantage of this family."

Stunned, Cassandra tempered her tone. "I assure you, ma'am, I am quite capable as a governess."

"I'll be watching, Miss Hale. Nothing is more important to me than my granddaughters."

Footsteps sounded in the hall and then approached through the nursery. Cassandra was grateful for the diversion and, after quickly shedding her pelisse, followed Mrs. Towler to the schoolroom.

There stood the girls, holding hands—Maria, with her long black hair, light freckles across her nose, and her arm in a sling, and Rose, with hair a few shades lighter than Mr. Warrington's and the same pale gray eyes. They eyed her cautiously, and then Rose smiled ever so subtly.

Cassandra's heart softened immediately at the sight, and she knelt in front of them. "I am Miss Hale. I'm going to be your governess, and I very much look forward to all of the things we are going to do together."

Rose leaned closer to her sister, eyes wide. "What are we going to do?"

"Well, we will read together and sew, and I can teach you the pianoforte. What do you think of that?"

Rose and Maria exchanged curious glances.

Cassandra reached for Rose's hand. "I know what we can do right this minute. The day is fine out. I thought maybe the three of us could go for a walk together to get to know each other. Besides, I know of a game, a very special game, but it will require all three of us."

Maria looked down to Rose and then nodded approvingly.

Encouraged by their agreement, she drew an energizing breath. "Then it is settled. Now you ladies will have to show me where you keep your capes and bonnets, for I'm also going to rely on you to show me where everything is."

Cassandra could feel Mrs. Towler's gaze boring into her as they walked away. She would have to tread lightly. She had no desire to make an enemy.

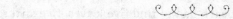

Laughter and happy chatter met James's ears before he entered the nursery. And the sound was sweet.

Moments like this, sounds like this, made him think that the family could truly be happy again. And that was what he wanted—to live life again, out from under the shadow of grief. Elizabeth would always be a part of them, and the last thing he wanted was for anyone to forget her. But he'd meant what he said to Maria. Elizabeth would not want them to live in sadness.

He stood silently, listening so as not to miss a minute of it. Then he turned the corner to the nursery to see Maria, Rose, Miss Hale, and even Rachel sitting at the small square table. Baskets were strewn across the top of it, and on it was a pile of leaves and sticks.

It was a beautiful sight, really.

When he entered the room, both girls jumped to their feet and ran to him. He swept Rose up in one arm and wrapped his other around Maria, careful not to jostle her arm. "Well now, how was your day?"

Rose wrapped her arms around his neck. "Look! Our new governess is here!" She wriggled down and bounced over to Miss Hale and grabbed her hand.

"I see." His gaze fell on Miss Hale as she stood from the table. "Welcome to Briarton Park, Miss Hale."

She curtsied in response, and before she could speak, Maria leaned with her good arm on the table. "Look at our collection!"

What initially had seemed like a haphazard pile when he had entered was really several piles separated into leaves, rocks, and sticks.

He sat in the chair to make a greater display of observing their work. "Ah, so I see! Tell me about it."

Rose climbed up on his lap and picked up one of the smooth stones. "Miss Hale said we each had to find five leaves, five sticks, and five stones. None of them could be like any of the others we found. And they all had to be from our garden and fit in our baskets. See? This one is my favorite."

"I hope you don't mind such outside activities," Miss Hale added quickly, twisting her fingers before her. "If you prefer that we remain indoors, we—"

"I think it's wonderful. As long as they stay in the walled garden with you." He bounced Rose on his knee. "What else did you do?"

He listened as the girls outlined their day, and warm satisfaction spread through him at their enthusiasm. After the girls finished, he left them to complete their sorting and approached Miss Hale, who'd been standing at the window, listening and watching. "Are you settling in all right?"

"Yes, I am. Your daughters are charming."

He looked back at them, encouraged by the joy radiating from their small faces. "Yes, they are. If you require books and so forth, just get a list to Mrs. Helock and she will see to it that they get ordered for you."

"Thank you. I will."

Miss Hale returned to the girls, and James watched for several minutes. Things were looking up for the Warringtons. And he did not want it to stop.

Chapter 26

Each day at Briarton Park divulged new revelations, leading Cassandra to believe she could indeed enjoy being a governess. She adored her young charges and discovered specific facts about them with each interaction. Maria enjoyed reading. Rose loved all things out-of-doors. Even Rachel, who no longer needed a governess, was becoming a friend.

It was Mr. Warrington who surprised her most, however. She'd always heard that governesses had little contact with the parents, but every evening he would spend at least an hour with his daughters, reading, playing, or talking. He spoke with her often about the girls' progress—what they were learning and how they behaved.

But now, as she sat next to Mr. Longham in Mr. Clark's stark countinghouse at Clark Mill, waiting for her half brother to join them, the peace and confidence that brought her such comfort at Briarton had fled, and a sickening anxiety flooded her. Other than the sounds of the persistent rain on the panes and the hissing fire in the grate, she and Mr. Longham sat in galling silence.

Cassandra glanced up at the clock above the mantel and shifted uncomfortably on the hard wooden chair. Mr. Clark should have joined them half an hour prior. "Do you think he'll not come?"

"He'll be here." Mr. Longham's tone exuded confidence. "I know

Peter Clark quite well, actually. He's stubborn. This is his attempt to seize control. We simply will not allow it. We'll wait as long as it takes."

She smoothed a wrinkle out of her sleeve for the dozenth time and fidgeted with the satin cords of her reticule. If only she possessed Mr. Longham's composure.

After what seemed like more than an hour, the door flew open, creaking on its hinges and thudding against the wall behind it.

Cassandra jumped, whipping around to see who caused such a commotion, and could only stare at the bulky man in the doorway. For weeks now she had wondered about meeting him. She'd envisioned him to resemble her father's portrait. He did, but only to an extent. His face was ruddy, either from frustration or drink, and his sorrel hair was wild, unkempt. His nose was strong and straight, and his forehead remarkably broad. But it was his eyes, the same obsidian eyes from the portrait, from which she could not look away.

Mr. Longham rose, his movements as casual as if this were a pleasure visit. "Clark. It's been a while."

Peter Clark did not respond immediately. He stomped in, his boots heavy on the planked floor, then went straight to the sideboard and poured himself a brandy. "So, you've not let this go, have you?"

Ignoring Mr. Clark's question, Mr. Longham extended his arm toward Cassandra. "I'd like to introduce Miss Cassandra Hale."

Mr. Clark returned the glass noisily to the sideboard and turned to fix a hard gaze on her. "So I hear you are claiming to be my father's illegitimate daughter."

Flustered—and slightly intimidated—by the accusations hidden in his tone, she lifted her chin. "I am only looking for answers."

He scoffed. "Answers, is it? Bah. Spreading vicious rumors, more like. What is it you want? Money?"

She shook her head, shocked at the animosity in his tone. "I'm not spreading rumors. And I don't want money."

"You know very well your father named Miss Hale in the will," Mr. Longham interjected, as if soothing an angry child. "Why act surprised now that she's here?"

Mr. Clark fixed a hard stare on Cassandra and squared his expansive shoulders. "I don't believe for a moment that you are Cassandra Hale. Furthermore, I don't believe you are my father's daughter, whatever this man claims."

"Do you know another Cassandra Hale then?" Longham reasoned, amused sarcasm dripping. "Be reasonable, Clark. She's a real person, clearly, otherwise your father never would have included her."

Her defenses growing, Cassandra forced confidence to her voice and retrieved her letter from her reticule. "I received this letter inviting me to Briarton Park and claiming to have information about my family. I think you will see for yourself that it is by your father's hand." She extended it to him.

His face hard, Peter Clark snatched it from her and glanced at it.

And then, in a sudden action, he turned and tossed it in the fire.

"No!" Cassandra lunged toward the fire and knelt next to it, but the note was positioned behind leaping flames. There was no way to reach it. Enraged, she stood and turned. Tears burned, but she would not cry. Not in front of this man. "Your father—*our* father—wrote me that letter. Nothing will change that fact. And I *am* Cassandra Hale, and I have spent my entire life wondering where exactly I come from. And now, thanks to Mr. Longham, I know. Whether you like it or not does not change it."

Mr. Clark widened his stance and leaned forward, towering over her, undoubtedly attempting to intimidate by size. "And what do you think will happen? That you will inherit land from my father? Nah, I'll never believe you are Cassandra Hale. For all I know, you are just an actress hired by Mr. Longham to get the money."

"It is not about money." Her voice shook with ire. "It is about truth."

"Ah, is it? So I suppose if I offer you money to leave and never come back, you'd refuse it? Doubtful." He jerked open a drawer full of banknotes. "I'm sure we can come to an agreement. You can walk out of this countinghouse a very wealthy woman. You would just need to sign an agreement never to return."

She looked at the banknotes. It was more money than she had ever seen.

But it wasn't right. None of this was right.

She was no longer intimidated. Fury and frustration replaced any such sentiment. "I am not about to sell the truth about myself."

"Foolish woman." He slammed the drawer closed and approached her, so close she could smell the brandy he'd just consumed and the dust from the courtyard, and forced words through clenched teeth. "You, madam, are not my sister."

At length Mr. Longham stood, his tone sobering. "She's named specifically in the will, Clark. Fight it if you will. It won't change matters."

"Oh, I've no doubt there is a Cassandra Hale somewhere. But this woman? No. Where is the proof?"

"I have my own personal statement and testimony as your father's man of business, not to mention the documentation." Mr. Longham lifted his satchel. "Every bit of it. It is all in order. Signed by your father. Signed by her mother."

"Papers? Hogwash. I'll fight this in court." He pointed his forefinger first at Mr. Longham and then at her. "Neither you—nor you—will ever see any of my father's property."

"It's not the money you are worried about, is it?" Mr. Longham's voice was impressively even. "You're not going to get the land, if that is what you are thinking. You've seen the will; you know it as well as I. Miss Hale had three years to inherit. If she did not, then the Stricklin estate would have three years to lay claim. And then it would go to you, but only as a last resort when all other options have been exhausted. It goes either to her or to the Stricklin estate. It's what your father wanted."

"And who is going to press the issue? You?" Peter Clark sneered. "What's in it for you to go and drum her up? Or the estate, for that matter? You must be getting something."

"I made a promise to your father."

"Bah. I don't trust you, Longham. Furthermore, I don't believe you. You have something to do with this. Something to gain. Oh, I've read the will. So has my solicitor. If the land is not claimed after a six-year period, it reverts to the estate, which I'm inheriting. It's all right there. Leave it alone. For all I know, you wrote that sham of a letter yourself and started this whole debacle."

Cassandra stiffened. She had trusted Mr. Longham from the beginning, but Mr. Clark's words struck a chord. She had no proof that Mr. Longham was truthful either. In her eagerness to have answers, she had accepted blindly.

Mr. Clark's sharp tone recaptured her attention when he pointed a thick finger at her. "I don't know who you are or where you come from, and honestly, I don't care. But if you are putting any trust in this man, your faith is misguided. I wash my hands of this matter entirely. You stop spreading rumors about my family, or you will pay. Pay dearly."

Stunned and dismayed, Cassandra eased back against the carriage seat as they departed the countinghouse and headed home toward Briarton Park.

The conversation with Peter Clark drummed in her mind. The animosity. The disbelief. The fact that he burned the letter from her father. She'd expected him to resist her and to protest Mr. Longham's words, but his reaction was more turbulent than she could have imagined. Furthermore, Mr. Clark had planted seeds of doubt toward everything Mr. Longham had told her. Uncertainty, even more potent and vicious than before, swirled within her.

As if sensing her distress, Mr. Longham expelled a long sigh and patted her gloved hand with his own. "Don't let this discourage you, Miss Hale. I'm not in the least surprised at Peter Clark's behavior, vulgar as it was. I've been a solicitor long enough to know that inheritances cause a great deal of turmoil in even the most basic of cases, let alone one with unusual circumstances like this."

"You said he'd be argumentative about it"—she tried to avoid saying too much until she worked out her thoughts—"but there was much I'd not considered."

Mr. Longham retrieved a pipe from his coat. "My business is in the letter of the law, Miss Hale, not in managing family dynamics, but here's what I know to be true. Your father had regrets and altered his will to include you to attempt to make amends. I have all the paperwork to satisfy a court, so please, do not fret. No doubt you were taken aback at Peter Clark's outburst, but I was not. I fully intend to see this through and fulfilled as soon as I get to London."

"I still have so many questions. Who's Mr. Stricklin?"

"Edward Stricklin was the man who gave your father his first loan that allowed him to build his first mill—Tutter Mill. It's the mill that was forced to close due to debts. Edward Stricklin's been dead for years, but Robert had always intended for the land to go to him, or at least to his family, by way of repayment. But in his later years he decided it should go to you instead. Since we could not locate you initially, he amended the will in the days leading up to his death to state that if you did not claim the land and then the Stricklin estate did not claim the land, then it would default back to the Clark estate and Peter Clark would manage it. It is all quite detailed and would easily be overlooked, and that's what Peter is counting on—that no one will pursue the details and that time will pass, allowing him to become the owner of both the business and the land."

She bit her lower lip in contemplation. "I just don't understand how that would work. How can I own the land and he owns the business on it?"

"It is quite a simple arrangement, on paper at least. Like any tenant leasing land from a landlord, the mill would pay you rent for occupying space on your property. You will receive a rather hefty sum regularly that will allow you to live very comfortably. And if the business should go under, the land will always belong to you. By the way the will is written, the land cannot be sold for fifty years after his death. You will always have income. Your father actually protected you."

Cassandra shook her head. "No wonder Peter Clark is upset."

"No doubt he sees it as a slight, but father and son had a difficult relationship. They did not see eye to eye. Never did."

Cassandra studied Mr. Longham, from his thinning white hair, to his bulbous nose, to the deep wrinkles etched around his muddy-brown eyes. Her heart trusted him, she realized, but her head urged caution. "And, if I may ask, what do you get out of this entire situation? It seems a great deal of work for you to track this all down and set it to rights. What benefit will you see if I, or even the Stricklin estate, for that matter, inherits?"

The corner of Mr. Longham's wide mouth quirked in a smile. "I'm a man of my word, Miss Hale, but I'm also practical. If you read the will in its entirety, you'll see that your father left me a rather small amount once the will has been served out. The more expeditiously this matter is resolved, the larger my payment. Naturally I'm eager to resolve this entire situation as soon as possible, but I also know this situation is not without its difficulties. Locating you was the most challenging part. Now, everything else should fall into place."

Cassandra could not share his optimism. "What if Peter Clark contests it in the courts? It seems almost certain he will. How will I fight that? I've no money."

"If you are worried about my fees, do not be. They will come out of your inheritance when all is said and done. That is, if he actually does contest it."

His words took her aback. "*If?* He seemed so angry. Surely he will."

"Bear in mind, my dear, any contesting will make this all public, you see. Such a scandal surrounding his name could very well bring about ruin or, at the very least, damaging gossip, especially in such a precarious business."

It all seemed so impossible and foreign to her. "So what do I do?"

"You must be patient. This will all work itself out in the end. These things always do, in time. I will assist you. You forget that I was there the day you were born. I was a witness as the paperwork was signed. It's my name you'll see signed beneath your father's. I personally watched as you were moved from the house. I was there when you were sent to Mrs. Denton's school. You may have felt abandoned all these years, but you were not without people watching over you."

A surprising lump tightened her throat. All this time she'd assumed she was alone, and now to find out that people were aware of her and even caring for her was overwhelming. "I don't know what to say."

"You need not say a word. I knew that, at the end of all, your father would regret a life separate from you. Now we must focus on moving this whole business forward."

My father.

She stiffened, trying to forget the resentment in Peter's expression. The thought that father and son did not get along unsettled her. "Was he a good father to Peter?"

Mr. Longham exhaled a long sigh. "I'm hardly the sort of person to give an account of another man's life."

Cassandra recognized hesitation in his voice, yet she persisted. "Was he funny? Serious? Harsh?"

Mr. Longham settled back against the seat, looking toward the carriage's ceiling as if the answers to her questions were written there. "Robert Clark was a very determined man. He was extraordinarily strong-willed when it came to his businesses. Not so much in his personal life. He built his fortune and then lost it, only to fight to rebuild what had been lost. He was a man of contradictions. Strict when it came to money, lax when it came to other matters in life.

"He loved his wife and put her on a pedestal, and in his son he would accept nothing but perfection. He was opinionated and boisterous and commanded attention wherever he went, but he was tormented by the mistakes of his past."

"And I was one of those mistakes."

"For many years he thought so, but toward the end, I believe the regret of knowing you were a carriage ride away and he never met you tore at him."

Seconds slipped into minutes, with naught but the sound of the crunching gravel and the pounding of horses' hooves to break the silence. Cassandra watched as autumn's grays and browns flashed by outside the window. Her life was changing, not only day by day, but hour by hour.

Before long, Briarton Park's chimneys emerged above the tree line, and the sense of arriving home warmed her. When she'd first arrived at the estate, there was no way she ever could have imagined how much her life would change, but now it was playing out right before her.

She squeezed her eyes shut. She had no way of knowing how all of this would end up, but she had to trust that it would be all right in the end.

Chapter 27

"Did you hear?"

James lowered the letter he was reading and looked up as Milton entered Weyton Mill's countinghouse, the scent of cold and rain accompanying him. "Hear what?"

"There was another attack on Greycombe Mill last night."

James straightened, his concern piqued. "No, I'd not heard."

Milton dropped a satchel onto one of the desks and removed his greatcoat. "Apparently they broke into the storage barns behin' the mill. Broke all sorts o' machinery, carding machines and his looms 'n' the like, set fire to the carriage house with the wagons already full with cloth for delivery. Caused all sorts of damage. Didn't injure anyone, but the mill will not operate. Likely for weeks."

James leaned his elbows on his desk. "When did you hear this?"

"Just now. We just received another shipment of wool, and the man delivering it told me."

He could not help but wonder if this was connected to the assault on Riddy. They'd still been unable to officially identify the men responsible. "Any idea who was behind it?"

"Not yet. He suggested we keep an extra eye out, but we're way ahead of that." Something outside the window caught Milton's attention, and he angled his head. "Speakin' of keepin' an eye out, looks like we have comp'ny."

James shifted his attention to Peter Clark's large form ambling up the road.

His first thought was that Clark, too, had learned about the violence and was here to discuss it. They'd all benefit by banding together to fight against such actions, and until now Clark had resisted any talks. But then he recalled that today Miss Hale and Mr. Longham were to visit Peter Clark, and he grimaced.

The man stomped toward the countinghouse, his fist clenched at his side. His lips were set into a hard line, and he was staring hard across the courtyard. The wind whipped at the hair beneath his black top hat.

James cleared his throat. "Perhaps you'd best leave this conversation to me."

James stood from his desk in anticipation of Clark's arrival in the chamber, and once Milton exited the room, he opened the door himself.

Clark did not wait for an invitation before he pushed his way in. He stepped to the desk and turned, his fists akimbo and his stare direct. "What are you playing at, Warrington?"

James closed the door and stifled an inner groan. The pointed question left no doubt that this had to do with Miss Hale and Mr. Longham and nothing to do with the mills. He just was unsure what about their visit had to do with *him*. "Good day to you, too, Clark. To what do I owe this pleasure?"

Clark huffed a sarcastic sneer. "You've bought the mill. And the house. But this—this is taking it too far. What is it you hope to gain?"

James needed to defuse this situation and keep calm. "Whatever is troubling you, I am sure we can come to some sort of—"

"You've retained a new governess," he stated. "One that claims to be my father's illegitimate child."

"I've employed a governess, yes. But I fail to see how who I take on to care for my children is any of your concern."

"Oh, it is very much my concern. That daft woman is spreading nefarious lies about my family."

James lowered his tone. "I required a governess, Clark. Nothing more. I've no interest in her personal life. Or yours."

"Oh, don't you? So the fact that she is set to inherit the land on which my very mill sits is of no concern to you?"

James winced. He knew nothing about Miss Hale inheriting *land*.

"Don't pretend you're unaware. If you are involved in something underhanded to get your hands on my property—"

"You're mistaken."

"You just happen to employ her? *Her*? Ha!" scoffed Clark. "What are you trying to do? Woo her and wed her so her land will become yours?"

James adjusted his stance. "Careful, Clark. You're crossing a line."

Clark's harsh stare narrowed. "These are precarious times. Dangerous. As mill owners and neighbors, we can either work together or we can work against each other. But I, for one, will not work with someone I cannot trust to have our mutual best interests at hand."

Clark stomped out of the door, then slammed it shut on his way out, rattling the windows in their panes.

James expelled his air in a puff and rubbed the side of his jaw. This issue surrounding Miss Hale was becoming a bigger and much more complex problem than he had anticipated. He did not wish to make an enemy of Clark, but Miss Hale had saved his sister. He owed her something. Furthermore, he believed her.

He returned to his desk, sank into the chair behind it, and stared into the fire. He had to get a handle on this, and quickly. There was just too much at stake.

❀ ❀ ❀ ❀

Cassandra stood outside Mr. Warrington's study, staring at the brass doorknob, garnering courage.

She shouldn't be surprised that the father of the children in her charge wanted to speak with her. But the hour was late. Murky darkness had fallen outside of Briarton Park's walls, and the girls were already asleep.

Fearing something was amiss, she smoothed her hair and shook out the folds of her gown, stalling for time as she mustered fortitude.

When she could delay no longer, she lifted her hand and rapped twice on the door.

"Enter." His response was deep. Calm.

She pressed the wooden door open with her fingertips and looked inside. Mr. Warrington was seated behind the desk. Papers and maps were strewn about him. Candles were scattered around the chamber, their yellow glow adding warmth to the deep-green walls and worn furniture.

He straightened as she drew inside. He wore no coat, and his wrinkled cravat hung loose about his neck. His sandy hair was disheveled, and his linen sleeves were rolled up to his elbows. She liked his appearance—comfortable and approachable. He gave a quick smile and then motioned toward a chair.

"You wanted to speak with me?" she asked as she traversed the faded blue rug.

"Yes." He waited for her to get settled in her chair. "How are you getting on with Maria and Rose?"

Her shoulders eased at the topic. "They are lovely girls. So spirited, so vibrant, so clever and bright. And I think your Maria might have talent with a paintbrush. Have you ever noticed?"

"I can't say that I have."

"You should see her painting of a goldcrest. There seems to be a nest in the boxwoods at the orchard's edge, and we took the easels down so she could paint it. I'll have her set it aside for you to see tomorrow. Quite impressive."

"Good. I'm glad it's going well. Do you have everything you need? Books? Paints?"

"I have given Mrs. Helock a list of a few more items I think we will need, but we're doing fine."

He did not respond to this last statement, and his expression shifted slightly.

At this a thread of alarm tightened within her. Was he upset? Disappointed?

He cleared his throat. "I asked you to come here not only to inquire after the girls but to let you know that I had a visit from Clark earlier today."

Heart thumping, she held his gaze, contemplating how best to respond.

Of course he knew about the visit. He'd given her permission to be absent from her duties. She wanted to be positive, but the visit with her half brother had been dismal and she prepared for the worst. "I see. What did he say?"

"He was livid." Mr. Warrington stood from behind the desk and came around to the front of it. "I do hate to pry, Miss Hale, but you are employed by me and live in my home. Peter Clark is both my ally and my competition. Given my tenuous business relationship with the man, I cannot afford ill will. If this situation is to continue, we must come to an understanding."

Cassandra's heart sank, and panic rose to take its place. The last thing she needed was for Mr. Warrington to be drawn into this predicament even further. "Yes, sir."

"Your personal life is your own, but I don't like to be caught off guard where business is concerned. I was aware there was a will, but he said that you are to inherit the land the mill is on. Is this indeed the case?"

She met his gaze as bravely as she could. "Yes. My understanding is that I am to inherit the land called Linderdale, I believe, and Peter has inherited the business."

He studied her, as if judging her veracity. "And you just now learned of it?"

"I learned some of the details upon my first meeting with Mr. Longham, but more details were shared today."

"Such as?"

"If I do not take ownership of the land within three years of my father's death, the land will pass to the estate of a man named Stricklin. And then, after a period of an additional three years, if the Stricklin estate does not claim it, the land will default back to the Clark estate, which means Peter would inherit it. That is why my presence is such a problem to him."

"I see. Clark also said he did not believe you were actually the Cassandra Hale referenced in the will."

She tensed. Her neck grew hot. This ever-present need to prove her identity was wearing on her. "I may not know much about my family history, but I do know one thing with certainty. My name is Cassandra Hale. You saw the letter that I received. Mr. Longham says we will likely need to prove my identity to the court, and he has the power to issue an official statement and the paperwork to do that."

They sat there in silence, awkward in the uncertainty.

"And where is Mr. Longham now?" Mr. Warrington inquired.

"He's staying at the Green Ox Inn tonight and will depart for London in the morning." Cassandra watched his face for any sign of a reaction. Annoyance. Displeasure. But Mr. Warrington's countenance was calm, his expression relaxed. He leaned back against the desk.

"Peter Clark has always been an intense fellow," he conceded at length. "In my experience people become quite aggressive when their livelihood or reputation is threatened."

"I suppose I threatened both." She looked up at him, finding that she really did care about his opinion on the matter. "You do believe me, don't you?"

He focused his full attention on her, as if he could see into the heart of who she was. "You assisted Rachel in the most selfless of manners, and people who are willing to take such risks to help another deserve respect. So yes, I do believe you, but you must understand that my children are now involved by default. I will be no stranger to this matter until it is resolved."

"Yes, sir." She nodded. "That's fair."

"Speaking of fairness, I think it only right to inform you what Clark accused me of, since it includes you."

She lifted her gaze, confused. "Accused *you* of?"

Mr. Warrington left his position at the desk and crossed to the mantelpiece. He paused to adjust a book on the mantel, as if fumbling for time, then turned to face her once again. "Clark suggested that my reason for engaging you as governess was an attempt, somehow, to gain ownership of the land. It's ridiculous, of course. I had no idea of your connection to the land until this very day. He suggested that I have you in my house to form an attachment to you, for if you owned the land, your, uh, husband would become the owner, and, well . . ." His voice faded away.

Cassandra winced. The heat of embarrassment rushed to her cheeks at the suggestion. It was one thing to speak of employment. It was another thing entirely to have someone suggest marriage, even in passing.

She looked down at her hands and muttered, "I—I never considered that."

When she regained her courage to look at him once again, his expression perplexed her. When had someone beheld her with such approval in his eyes? As if he wholly listened to her and her thoughts mattered? Surely she was not imagining it.

"Are you all right, Miss Hale?"

The simple words threatened to undo her. How she had yearned for someone to come alongside her. Support her. *See* her.

She could not allow herself to notice how deeply his direct attention affected her, or allow her mind to wonder how safe it would feel to stand closer to him. She had to keep her wits about her. She could not—would not—romanticize this conversation. "My only intention was to find my family, Mr. Warrington. In spite of all this, I promise you, I will be a good governess for your children."

"And I believe you will."

Chapter 28

Cassandra could not sleep.

Nestled in her small little chamber, she found her thoughts drifting from the anxious uncertainty to the confusing sentiments that had ruled her thoughts since quitting Mr. Warrington's study. It wasn't the topic of conversation that had unnerved her so. Instead, it was the vulnerability that the conversation conjured.

Perhaps this entire situation was all carefully orchestrated by someone with ulterior motives, as Peter Clark had suggested. Perhaps not. There would be no way to tell for sure until the truth finally emerged.

Her letter—her one truly personal tie to her father—had been destroyed, and yet she kept coming back to Mrs. Hutton's statement. *"I can confirm this is his writing."* Moreover, Cassandra had seen the same exact signature on the paperwork Mr. Longham possessed.

Yes, she believed Peter Clark was her half brother.

Yes, she believed Mr. Longham, in spite of the lingering questions.

But her sense of rationality longed for concrete evidence of truth.

Her mind raced, reliving every occurrence since her arrival in Anston and at Briarton Park. Her thoughts returned repeatedly to Mr. Warrington. His direct expression and the delivery of his tone had affected her. His strong physical presence and his gentle kindness attracted her. She recognized the undeniable draw that was developing between them. She had felt it with Frederick. But she had to check herself. Mr. Warrington was her employer.

Her employer.

It would be more appropriate for her to linger on thoughts of Mr. North. He'd given her plenty of advice, but unlike Mr. Warrington, he'd never inquired how she was doing or feeling.

It would be a slippery slope if she allowed her mind to think of Mr. Warrington as anything other than the man who paid her wages. But in the daunting loneliness of night, she craved that feeling of having someone care about her. How would it feel to have his arms around her? To trust him with the secrets of her heart and to know that he thought of her as more than just a governess? She desired honesty. Sincerity. Vulnerability. Their conversations had opened the door to those thoughts. And now that it had been opened, that door would be very difficult to close.

The next day, Cassandra awakened before dawn. Indeed, she'd never fallen asleep. She heard the maids creep in for their early morning stoke of the fire to make sure all was warm when everyone arose, so she rose from bed, dressed in a heavy wool gown, donned her cape, and would go out for a walk to watch the sun rise over the garden walls.

She encountered several maids on her way out, and as she passed Mr. Warrington's study, flickering firelight poured from it, suggesting he was already awake as well. She glanced at her pocket watch. Forty-five minutes remained before she would wake the girls for the day, ensuring enough time for some fresh air.

Outdoors, the air was cold and exhilarating, the freshness of which helped to clear her mind from the thoughts that had festered overnight. She traversed the courtyard to the manicured lawns, where even in winter the paths were trimmed neatly and the plants maintained their order. The hoarfrost was crisp and fresh beneath her boots. It crunched with each step, and her breath plumed before her in invigorating brightness.

She continued along the wall until she reached the edge of the garden, where a copse of ash and elm trees separated the gardens from the muted moors that stretched beyond. She looked back to Briarton Park, doing its best to appear gloomy in the morning shadows. But nothing could look sad in the pink morning light that reached from the east. So she decided to walk farther.

Then, as she turned the corner at the edge of the boxwoods, something caught her eye. Something black on the grass protruded from the corner, just where the fence met the trees. She walked down the road a bit farther to the edge of the fence and frowned.

A boot jutted out from behind the uneven stone wall.

Alarm pricked her skin at the sight. Every word of warning that Mr. Warrington had shared rushed her.

Cassandra held her breath and took another step. The black fabric of trousers became visible. As she took another step, her mind prepared her heart for what she was about to see.

A body lay there. Unmoving and awkwardly positioned.

But not just any body.

She recognized the white hair, the emerald coat from the previous day.

Mr. Longham.

The beauty she had enjoyed just moments ago dissolved around her into horror.

Disbelief slowed her limbs, making them feel thick. Heavy. Her throat felt too dry to speak, yet she managed to call out his name.

But she knew he would not answer.

She dropped to her knees by his side and touched his shoulder.

As she did, he rolled slightly, just enough for her to glimpse blood and his glassy stare.

The scream curdling within her bubbled, and she scrambled to her feet. She took one step backward, and then another, until she turned and ran as fast as she could back to Briarton Park.

James could hear it before he saw it—a desperate cry for help, a piercing scream.

He jumped from his desk and looked out into the courtyard. But from where he stood, all was still.

Had he imagined it?

But then he heard it again. This time there could be no mistake. He snatched his coat and punched his arms through the sleeves as he hurried down the corridor and out into the misty morning.

Running footsteps echoed from around the south entrance, and as he made his way in that direction, Miss Hale burst through the gate, her cloak billowing out behind her, her face ashen and her movements unconstrained.

Once she spotted him, she ran to him and grabbed his arms. "Hurry! You must hurry. It's Mr. Longham. I think he's dead!"

James started, sure he must have heard incorrectly. "What?"

Her hand slid down his arm and she gripped his hand tight. "In the garden. Please, he's not moving. We mustn't waste time!"

Before he knew it, she'd led him out into the courtyard. She dropped his hand, and he followed her hasty steps, unsure of where they were going until they were at the edge of the walled garden, where a break in it gave way to the main road.

Then he saw it, and his own frosty breath caught.

The foot. The leg. Then the man.

And he knew in an instant.

This man was dead.

He put his arm back to protect her from the sight and to make her keep her distance. "Tell the groom and send someone for Shepard. Go!"

The padded sound of her feet running the opposite direction faded into the morning stillness. Despite the cold, perspiration beaded on his forehead as he knelt next to the man and pushed his shoulders. He checked for a pulse, knowing full well he would not find one. Dried blood darkened Longham's face. James was no expert, but it appeared he had been dead for some time.

But why? Why here? How?

Unsure of what exactly to do, he rolled the man over, searching, hoping he was mistaken and that he would get some sign of life. But he'd evidently taken a blow to his head.

James glanced around for any sign of a struggle. Had he fallen? Been struck? If so, why here at the garden's edge?

Just to the side of him lay a satchel. It was the same one Longham had the first day he arrived at Briarton Park. His arrival that day had been suspicious too. The will. Peter Clark's anger. Milton's suggestion of the rumors. All the anger and speculation and possible scenarios regarding this entire situation struck James, and now a man was dead.

Suddenly things had taken a very dark turn, and whether he liked it or not, he was a part of it.

Chapter 29

Briarton Park had always been a quiet, sleepy place. That had been its allure—what had drawn him here. But now a death darkened the landscape. Not just an attack, but a seemingly violent demise that shook the entire household to the core.

James shuddered at the thought of what this man had endured. At what Miss Hale experienced upon finding him. At the possibility that one of his children or Rachel could have discovered the body.

The loss. The horrific, needless loss.

James stood at the edge of the fence watching the activity as it unfolded. Mr. Shepard and two constables had arrived shortly after being summoned, and the coroner shortly thereafter. A dozen or so men had joined to assist in the investigation—more people than had been on the property at one time since they'd arrived.

"What do you make of it?" James called out as Shepard approached him.

"'Twas no accident, I've a firm mind on that." Once Shepard reached James he turned, arms folded across his chest, to watch the scene. "Did you see that head wound?"

The horrific sight was burned into his memory, and he doubted he'd ever forget it. "Yes, I saw."

"Come on, let's let the coroner finish his investigation and we'll go back to the house."

James fell into step next to his guest as they headed toward Briarton. "Are you and the coroner in agreement that it was murder then?"

Shepard gave his head a hard shake. "No mere fall would cause that. It appeared he had two blows. One on top of his head, which likely came from someone higher than him, like on horseback or in a carriage. Then the other that seemed like he struck the stone wall. That was probably the one that killed him." He retrieved the snuffbox from his pocket. "You said your governess discovered the body? The same woman we met the morning of Riddy's attack?"

"Aye."

"Hmm. I just heard about Longham and her visit with Peter Clark yesterday. Shady business, all of this."

James grimaced. This situation was growing stickier and more complicated by the minute. "Do you suspect a connection?"

"Hard to tell. Normally I'd start by asking myself why anyone would want to kill a man like Longham. Aged. Generally well liked. He's an unlikely target."

The assaults on the millers ran through James's mind. "Do you think it was a random attack? Or maybe the men who've been targeting the mills?"

"Not sure. All that will be brought to light, though, surely. About that conversation your governess had with Clark, you don't happen to know what that was about, do you?"

"Something about Robert Clark's will." James was careful not to divulge information that was not his to tell.

"I figured as much. Rumors travel wide, but I needn't tell you that. I'd like to speak with her."

James had not seen Miss Hale since she'd run away from him back toward the house. But he could not stop the magistrate from doing his business. "Be my guest."

James led Shepard through the corridor, where they encountered a maid, and he requested that she fetch Miss Hale and bring her to the great hall, and then he led the magistrate there.

A cheery fire blazed in the grate, its light warming and brightening the space during the otherwise dismal day. They waited in silence until dainty footsteps could be heard on the landing, and then she slowly descended the great staircase.

James could tell straightaway that she'd been crying. The redness of her eyes made them appear more vibrant, and her dark gown emphasized the pallor of her cheeks. Her chestnut hair was loosely bound at the base of her neck, but long strands escaped, untethered and untamed.

"Miss Hale, this is Mr. Shepard, the magistrate," James said. "He wanted to talk with you about what you saw this morning."

Cassandra's head thudded with the day's painful realities, and now this man—this stranger—was going to ask her questions. Her throat felt raw and dry, as if lined with wool. How would she ever be able to speak?

She recognized Mr. Shepard from her very first visit to Briarton. He was a giant man, with a barrel chest and broad face. He stood several inches taller than Mr. Warrington, with a mass of dark auburn hair and thick side-whiskers of a slightly lighter shade. His eyes were small and intense, and Cassandra resisted the urge to shrink away from them.

She tightened her shawl around her shoulders to ward off the shiver that seemed to not want to leave her body before finding her voice. "Of course. Mr. Shepard, what would you like to know?"

"You discovered Mr. Longham's body." His question was more of a statement.

"I did. I was out for a morning walk."

"Did you see anyone else on this walk? Notice anything out of place?"

She shook her head. "No, sir. I did not."

"And I understand you were acquainted with Mr. Longham. And the nature of that relationship?"

Her insides tightened, and the nausea that had plagued her ever since the discovery swelled. She flicked her gaze toward Mr. Warrington. She would have to share the details, she knew. All of them. He was a magistrate, for heaven's sake. She could not lie. "I met Mr. Longham a short while ago, on this property. He said he was Mr. Clark's solicitor."

"And why did he want to talk to you?"

"He wanted to inform me that the late Mr. Clark was my father."

Mr. Shepard's bushy brows rose. "Robert Clark was your father?"

"Yes. According to Mr. Longham."

Mr. Shepard scoffed. "And you saw fit to believe him?"

"Mr. Longham said he'd been searching for me for a few years, and we only just connected. He had every manner of paperwork in his possession. A custody agreement signed by my mother, school payment records, and the like. And I had a letter written to me by my father."

Mr. Shepard turned toward Mr. Warrington. "Can you confirm any of this?"

Mr. Warrington nodded. "I can confirm that she did have a letter signed by Robert Clark. I saw it and I read it. I read a reference letter signed by the headmistress at the school where Miss Hale previously taught. Mr. Longham visited here, and he was clearly familiar with the property and the house. I have no reason not to believe anything that was said."

Mr. Shepard returned his attention to her. "And I heard an account that you both spoke with Peter Clark yesterday."

Cassandra's already tense muscles tightened. "Yes. Mr. Longham and I went to his office to discuss the matter of my father's will."

"And?"

She was not sure what to divulge. "Peter Clark was quite angry."

"What was he angry about? I presume he's seen the will prior to this."

"Yes, but he said he did not believe me to be Cassandra Hale, despite Mr. Longham's insistence and proof."

"I see. And this letter from Robert Clark? Do you have it?"

"It was destroyed."

"Destroyed?" Mr. Shepard jerked.

"Mr. Clark threw it in the fire."

Mr. Shepard adjusted a satchel slung over his shoulder.

At first Cassandra thought very little of it, and then, as she looked at it closer, she noticed the initials embossed on the front. Surprise jolted through her. "Is that Mr. Longham's satchel?"

Mr. Warrington nodded. "It was found by the body."

Casandra's heart gave a little leap in spite of herself. "All of my documentation should be in there. That is where he kept it."

Mr. Shepard shook his head. "I'm sorry, miss. It was empty when we found it."

The significance of his words showered over her, and she felt as if she'd been struck a blow. "B-but that's not possible. I saw all of my papers in it just yesterday."

Mr. Shepard extended it to her. "See for yourself."

Hungrily she grabbed for it and flipped the flap open.

Mr. Shepard was right. It was empty.

Her ears rung noisily with frustration, distracting her as she tried to complete the puzzle in her mind. "But I don't understand. Someone must have taken it."

It didn't make sense. Not any of it.

Their conversation was interrupted when Mrs. Towler entered

the room. "Mr. Shepard. Thank goodness you're here to make sense of this terrible tragedy. What have you learned?"

He bowed toward the older woman. "I have no specific answers yet, Mrs. Towler."

"This is exasperating," she cried. "How could this happen on our property?"

"That is what I intend to find out. Don't worry. Bad deeds never go unpunished. Not on my watch."

For once Cassandra was grateful for Mrs. Towler's presence, to put an end to the questioning.

With a rusty smile Mr. Shepard bowed toward her and took the satchel back from her. "Thank you, Miss Hale. I'm truly sorry for what you have endured today." He turned to Mr. Warrington. "Accompany me out, will you?"

The men bowed toward Cassandra, and she curtsied in response and watched as they departed.

As James and Shepard returned to the grounds, a fine, cold mist started to fall, shrouding the property in a filmy gray veil. But even so, the men who had gathered to help in the investigation continued with their search for any information on the circumstances of William Longham's demise.

"How well do you know this young lady?" Shepard asked as they walked the path back toward the garden.

"Well enough to let her be the governess of my children."

"How long have you known her?"

"Just over a month. It was the letter from Robert Clark she told you about that brought her to Briarton Park in the first place."

"And how did she make the jump from searching for information to being your governess?"

James considered his answer. He would not lie, but he would not divulge his sister's indiscretion either. "She needed employment and had appropriate references. My children took to her right away. It was a natural progression."

James had always had a cordial relationship with Shepard, but now a thread of tension stretched between them. He could almost tell what the man was thinking, and he wanted to be clear. "You certainly don't think she had anything to do with this, do you?"

Shepard clicked his tongue. "Unlikely. She's a small person, and Longham would have towered over her. He was struck from the top, you know. With the nature of the injury, I don't think she would have the physical strength for something like that. But you never know. More than likely it was a random attack, considering the activity with the weavers as of late, but my next call will be to Peter Clark, to be sure."

James adjusted his hat to deflect the drizzle, but as he did, one man in particular caught his eye.

Mr. North was approaching.

It was appropriate that he was here. He *should* be here. After all, a man was dead and he was the vicar. But instead of heading toward the scene of the death, he was walking toward the house.

Mr. North took notice of them as he came up the path and lifted his hand in greeting. "Shepard. Warrington. What a horrible event this is."

"It is," responded Shepard. "Did you know Mr. Longham?"

North shrugged. "Never met him before in my life, poor soul. This sort of discovery in our parish is a terrible shock. I believe I heard that Miss Hale was the one to find him. Is that true?"

"She was."

"I thought I might speak with her and offer some consolation. I can only imagine it was a harrowing event, especially for a woman of such a sensitive nature."

James eyed him. It was not fitting to question a vicar's motives, and yet he'd seen his behavior at the party. Nonetheless, James could not interfere. Not with this. "She's inside, I believe. You're welcome to go on in."

North bowed and continued down the path.

Shepard scoffed, and a flash of amusement brightened his otherwise somber face. "Consolation indeed. I'll wager he's something else in mind, vicar or not."

James did not respond, but he recognized the tightening in his stomach. As much as he hated to admit it, jealousy—or something fiercely akin to it—roiled inside him. He did not like the thought of North, with his sickly sweet smiles and elegant words, within any distance of Miss Hale. She was an intelligent woman—did she really not see past his facade? But to forbid a vicar from calling on a woman who had just been in such distress was cruel.

But what was the alternative to North's attention to her? That James would be the man to offer consolation? It was impossible. She was in his employ. She was caretaker for his children. And, if he were honest, there was a thin transition between consolation and romantic intentions.

Even so, a part of him wished he could be the man she would want during this time. But he had to be practical. She was the governess. There were questions about her parentage. Questions about her motives. They all had their role to play, and blurring any lines could be dangerous for everyone involved.

Chapter 30

Cassandra pressed her palms to her forehead as Mr. Warrington and Mr. Shepard departed the great hall. She squeezed her eyes closed as if by doing so she could shut out the horrible sight she'd seen earlier that day.

How her head ached with the day's events. She'd fully anticipated that someone would question her about discovering the body, but she'd not expected to feel like a suspect or to share family details with a stranger.

She opened her eyes and moved to the window that overlooked the front yard. There stood Mr. Warrington, speaking with the magistrate.

About her, no doubt.

Oh, what Mr. Warrington must think of her. How he must regret ever allowing her at Briarton Park. True, she had nothing to do with the death, but Mr. Longham never would have been on the property if not for her plight. She could not help but feel that she, in some way, had brought tragedy here.

To make matters worse, she could sense Mrs. Towler's presence, heavy and judgmental, from across the hall. Cassandra could barely bear the weight of it. She pivoted away from the window in preparation to return to the nursery, but Mrs. Towler's snipped words stopped her short.

"I'm sure now you see what you have brought on this family."

Stunned at the accusation, Cassandra shifted. "I did nothing."

Mrs. Towler moved in a rustle of charcoal bombazine, blocking the way to the staircase. "You presume to tell me that your presence at Briarton had absolutely nothing to do with that man's death? La. I took you to be shrewder than that."

Cassandra swallowed dryly, feeling her tenacity buckle under the scrutiny. She did not feel that she could bear an altercation, and she refused to engage in one. But then the door creaked open behind her and heavy, masculine footsteps echoed.

She turned. Mr. North stood in the threshold.

Relief flooded her at the sight of him. A friendly face—the expression on which suggested he already knew the details, and he was concerned. *For her.*

Mr. North held his wide-brimmed hat in his ungloved hand. He bore no smile. He entered and bowed toward them both. "Ladies. I understand it has been a most difficult morning."

Mrs. Towler folded her hands before her and raised her chin. "I'm surprised to find you here, Mr. North. It has been months since your last call to Briarton, has it not?"

If he was affected by the coolness of her tone, he gave no indication. "My sincerest apologies, if that is indeed the case. I was summoned, of course, with the discovery of the body. I would be remiss not to check and see how you are faring and to offer comfort, if possible."

"I thank you for the effort, but it is wholly unnecessary," Mrs. Towler said in a clipped tone. "Need I remind you that Miss Hale is a governess, an employee of this house, and is not in the habit of accepting visitors? Especially *gentlemen* visitors."

He gave a little laugh, as if stunned—or amused—by the woman's insinuation. "My dear Mrs. Towler, you misunderstand. These are extreme circumstances and Miss Hale's experience this morning was, no doubt, unprecedented."

Mrs. Towler turned her attention to Cassandra. "Very well, but the girls require their lessons. I trust you will not be long."

Once the sound of Mrs. Towler's footsteps had faded, Cassandra expelled the breath she'd been holding. Finally, she could interact with Mr. North as friends.

He stepped much closer to her, and his scent of sandalwood encircled her. He lowered his voice to an almost intimate level. "How are you, really?"

"This is unbelievable." She, too, pulled closer to him, grateful for someone she could relax around. "Have you been to the site?"

"Yes, I have. Ghastly. The coroner was there, along with some other men from the village."

"What are they saying?"

"They suspect he was attacked in some way. Have they given you any information?"

"No one has told me anything." Cassandra shrugged. "The only thing I know is what Mr. Shepard told me just now, which was not much. Oh, how will they ever know what really happened?"

"Things, as unpleasant as they are, have a way of coming to light." He adjusted his hat in his hands, left her side, and walked farther into the room before facing her once more. "I have been called to such scenes before, but I must confess, Miss Hale, that this one was most distressing. As soon as I heard you were the person to discover the body, all I could think of was your well-being."

She gripped her hands before her to calm her nerves. The earnestness in his gaze was unlike any she had seen from him before.

Mr. North sighed. "These are the most precarious of times, especially with the unrest of the weavers. You've heard of it, of course."

She nodded. How many times had Mr. Warrington warned her of such—of staying close to the main house and not letting the children outdoors without supervision?

He continued. "After the Kents' gathering I feared I had overstepped my bounds in cautioning you against this position. But now, as your friend, I feel even more compelled to ask you to reconsider remaining here."

She swallowed, surprised at the strong inflection in his voice.

He glanced over his shoulder at the door before he spoke again. "I have shared that they suspect it was an attack. Mr. Warrington is a mill owner. He's seen as the enemy by many. I can't help but fear this will happen again."

She nodded her agreement and tucked a wayward lock behind her ear. "I will keep watch. I am perfectly safe. But I do appreciate your concern. And your friendship."

"You will always have my friendship, Miss Hale. I knew the moment I encountered you in the graveyard that you would be an important person to me. Now, circumstances, and my feelings and reactions toward them, are making me realize how important."

Commotion sounded, and one of the maids entered to tend the fire.

Mr. North straightened at the interruption. "I should be going. They will need me at the site. You must promise that if you need anything at all, you will call on the vicarage. Mrs. Pearson is also eager for you to stop by if you have need."

"Thank you. I shall."

He took his leave. It had been kind of him to check on her, and the visit had brought her solace. But as she turned her attention to the front gardens and the men scurrying about, a heaviness once again fell over her heart. Would she ever be able to find true peace again?

By the time James returned home, darkness had descended, and a heavier rain now fell. His coat and hat were soaked, and his hair dripped with its effects.

Once in the corridor just inside the workman's entrance, he shed his wet coat and shook the water from his hair. He was not hungry. He could hardly think about food after what had transpired that day. But he did want dry clothes and a hot fire.

He started toward the great hall when he heard footsteps in his study. He stopped short. No one should be in there, especially at this hour. He slowed his steps and looked inside.

There, pacing before the simmering fire, was Mrs. Towler. She lifted her head as he entered, and they stared at each other for several seconds before he entered the study. His dry clothes would have to wait.

She tapped her long fingers against the edge of his wooden desk. "So, this is where we are."

He remained silent. He hadn't talked to his mother-in-law all day. In fact, he'd avoided her. But now he had no choice. "It's unfortunate."

"Unfortunate! Unfortunate? One of the girls could have discovered the body. I never thought I would live to see the day when my granddaughters would be in such close proximity to something so vile. You invited this entire mess into our house when you asked her to be governess," she accused.

Cold and tired, his sarcasm slipped. "Very well. What would you have me say? Yes, I asked Miss Hale to be the governess here. Yes, there has been a tragedy. Yes, I have no idea what to do about it or even what to think about it. So did I invite it in? Apparently so."

She stepped quite close. "I have tried to do everything I can for you, James, out of love for my daughter, love for my granddaughters. But I cannot stand by and watch this. For if I do, I am party to it, and that I cannot abide."

James was in no mood for games. "What are you saying?"

Her chin shook with each word. "You are permitting mayhem to prevail in this house. I've lived with your family for several years now. Through triumph. Through tragedy. But this is beyond the scope of what is reasonable for anyone to take." She paused dramatically and then jutted her chin upward. "The governess must go."

Resentment surged at her continued interference. But he would not lose his temper. Not again. She was threatening him—playing a frustratingly dangerous game of dominance. "Or?"

"Or I will go."

In his current state of bitter irritation, he could almost laugh. "And where would you go?"

"I do have a cousin, or have you forgotten? I've been loyal to my daughter, but this, this is too much. I know you think I'm completely dependent upon you, but nothing is further from the truth."

"So you have just issued me an ultimatum," he clarified.

"I suppose I have."

And with that, she swept from the room.

He tugged his damp cravat free, pulled it away from his neck, and dropped into the chair. He forced his fingers through his wet hair and then shook off the moisture from his fingers. The day's events ran through his head swiftly and angrily. The morning cries from Miss Hale. The vision of Longham's body. The endless discussions. Miss Hale's interrogation, and then Mr. North's annoying visit. And now this. What was worse, he was at a loss as to how to right this dangerously leaning ship. If only there was a clear answer—a clear path out of this mess. But there was nothing to be done but see it through, and he had no idea how long that would take.

The one thing he did know was he would never cower to the demands of an ultimatum—from anyone.

Chapter 31

By the time James had returned to his chamber to exchange his wet clothes for dry, he had begun to calm down. Surely Mrs. Towler was merely trying to prove a point with her demands. She often exhibited certain patterns, so surely by morning her stance would soften.

But for now, he wanted to find a bit of peace—and check on Maria and Rose. The activity had kept him away from the house, and he needed to reinforce with Miss Hale that in light of the day's events, the girls were to remain indoors in the coming days. He could not rest until he was certain they were clear on that matter.

With a candlestick in his hand, he made his way to the nursery suite and pushed open the main door. Save for the firelight, all was dark, and he could see both girls asleep in their canopied beds.

He leaned in farther. Miss Hale was seated by the fire, reading. A shawl was draped over her thin shoulders, her chestnut hair bound at the nape of her neck and trailing down her back. Her feet were tucked casually beneath her.

It was such a peaceful sight—one that conjured pleasant memories of happier times.

He shifted, and the floorboard squeaked beneath him. At the sound she looked up, lowered her book, and joined him in the corridor.

Once she had pulled the door to the nursery closed behind her, he said, "I'd hoped to see the girls before they went to bed."

The shadows from his candle played on the smooth surface of her fair cheek as she spoke. "I know they would like to see you. They missed seeing you for your regular evening visit. I can wake them if you wish."

"No, no. That's not necessary. But I do wish to speak with you. Can you join me in the drawing room?"

As soon as his request left his lips, he realized that he'd put them both in a precarious situation. It was one thing to speak briefly just outside the nursery door. But no good could come from a quiet chat with her in the hushed night hours after such a tumultuous day. Not when emotions ruled his thoughts and the future remained so uncertain.

She hesitated momentarily, and yet she complied and together they made their way to the drawing room. Once they were in the firelit chamber, it was clear that the day's events had taken their toll on her. Every other instance he'd been in her presence, her countenance had been alert and bright, her manner sanguine and confident. But tonight her face was pale, and shadows darkened the soft skin beneath her eyes.

The sight of Miss Hale's sorrow, her pain, affected him. He wanted to help her, to alleviate her distress, but he wasn't sure what to say.

How long had it been since he consoled a woman?

Snippets of time and fragments of conversations with Elizabeth flashed in his mind.

And the battle raged.

He had to remain focused. "Are the girls aware of what happened?"

"Rachel is, of course, but Maria and Rose are not. We managed to keep them in the nursery. They saw the men in the gardens from the window, but they quickly lost interest. They did ask after you though."

"I'll depart for the mill early in the morning, but the girls are indoors for the time being. They may venture to the courtyard, but no farther than the courtyard gates. We have no idea who was behind this, and I don't want to take any chances."

She nodded. "I couldn't agree more."

They stood in stiff silence, and he regarded the tear tracks on her face. It was not his place to make such a personal observation. The sight tugged at him, touching his heart more than reason. At this moment the rules that should dictate such an interaction were fading away, and they were no longer employer and governess, but a man and a woman. "You've been crying."

"Oh." She touched her cheek in absent distraction. "I'm sorry."

"What are you sorry for? It's been a sad day. I'd be surprised if you shed no tears at all."

"That's not what I meant." She raised her shoulder in a half-hearted shrug, her gaze still downcast. "I'm apologizing because of what I've brought into your home."

He sighed and shifted his weight. "There's no way anyone could have foreseen this. It was a tragedy, a—"

"But if it weren't for me and my presence here, Mr. Longham never would have been on Briarton Park's property in the first place."

He drew closer. "That might be so, but no one thing is completely dependent on another. There are threads that, if pulled, affect everyone and everything, whether those effects were intended or not. If Mr. Longham had never returned to Briarton Park, he very well might still be alive. Or he might not. He might have fallen and struck his head. He might have suffered an affliction or fallen prey to a highwayman. We've no way of knowing, and we needn't speculate."

Her tone hinted at disbelief. "That is very gracious to say."

"Graciousness has nothing to do with it." He watched as she toyed with the cuff of her sleeve. He was close to her, closer than he should be, yet she made no effort to increase the distance between them.

He wanted her to meet his gaze. What better way to judge the true feelings of a person than to see into her eyes? Her soul?

She tucked a wayward lock of hair behind her ear. "I don't know what to do now. Not only is Mr. Longham gone, but so are the contents of his satchel. I've no way to prove my identity. Now it really is as Mr. Peter Clark suggested. I could be anyone claiming to be Cassandra Hale."

"There has to be a way around it. You've known a lot of people in your life, I'm sure. Witnesses who can vouch for you. Surely there is a way to collect your inheritance."

"It's never been about the inheritance." Her voice hovered barely above a whisper. "I didn't even know about it until recently. I came here thinking that if I could just find out the truth about my family, I'd be happy. Now I have found the truth, but it is far more painful than I ever could have imagined. I believed Mr. Longham. I still do. But the sad reality is that I still have no family. No hope for what might be."

"No hope?" He ached for the pain he saw in her. "There is always hope."

Her expression dimpled her cheek. "Well, come to think of it, hope may be all I have left."

The response struck him.

They might as well be talking about him.

He'd thought all hopes for happiness had died with Elizabeth, but slowly, surely, another truth was emerging. He studied the manner in which Cassandra's hair was parted at the side, how her otherwise straight nose turned up ever so slightly, how she bit her lower lip in times of uncertainty. How, in this short period of time, this entrancing young woman had touched many parts of his life. A stranger just weeks ago, she was now a part of everything.

Oh, he needed to be careful. For she was sweet. Beautiful. Endearing. And now he could feel a tug he'd not felt in years—the desire to be in someone's company and not leave her side.

He was not prepared to deal with these feelings again—to come to terms with the idea that another woman might be working her way into his thoughts and his mind.

He stepped toward the door to increase the distance from her, for his muscles ached to reach out and take her in his arms, and his heart longed to connect to hers.

This interaction had already gone too far, and she had to know it too. In that moment he was certain—she could not possibly have feelings for North. Not with the way she was looking at James now. They were in a dangerous situation, and if he allowed it to continue, there could be no turning back.

He cleared his throat. "It's getting late. With your permission I'd be happy to write to some of my contacts in London and see if I can find out anything more about Longham. Perhaps he has a partner or business associates who might have information regarding his clients. It's worth a try."

She nodded, wide-eyed, the hesitation of which suggested that she, too, was struggling to make sense of the strange, invisible pull between them. She gave a hasty curtsy and was out of the chamber within seconds, leaving him alone with only his thoughts and the sounds of the fire popping in the grate.

Mrs. Towler's warning echoed in his mind.

He had no idea how this would all work out, but he would not send Miss Hale away. That, he could not do.

Rose pressed her small face against the window in the nursery and looked out to the front garden. "May we go outside today?"

Cassandra stacked the books on the table. "No, dearest. Your papa wishes us to stay inside. Besides, it is far too cold."

Rose slumped to the chair, a pout curving her lips. "But it's sunny out. We always go outside when it's sunny."

"Come now. Let's practice letters." She reached out her hand to the girl.

With a toss of her long, golden braid, the girl reluctantly sulked to the table and lifted her book, and Cassandra listened as the girl read the letters aloud.

She tried to focus on the task at hand, but like her young charges, her mind kept drifting. She was haunted by the previous day's events, and she supposed she always would be, but it was her conversation with Mr. Warrington that lurked in the corners of her mind.

She'd always considered Mr. Warrington a gentle, if not somewhat aloof, man. But any thought she had about his indifference toward her and her plight had been squelched by their last interaction.

Never had a man looked at her with such sincerity, concern, and even affection before—not even Frederick.

It frightened her.

It excited her.

In a different world, under different circumstances, Mr. Warrington would be everything she could ever desire. He was gentle, strong. And so very handsome.

And yet as these thoughts threaded through her, they were met with a darker thought.

Her mother had been in service in this very house. Perhaps this very chamber. She had been seduced, or taken advantage of, by the master.

Could this simply be a matter of history repeating itself? Mr. Warrington seemed kind. But all men could *seem* kind. His intentions could be another factor altogether. Could she be allowing herself to imagine a future that could never actually be?

Too many things were occurring all at once. Too many questions that needed to be answered. She needed to keep her focus firmly on her goal of learning the truth, at any cost. She had no idea where things would go from here. Mr. Warrington had said he would make inquiries on her behalf. But without Mr. Longham's guidance and without proper documentation, what hope did she have? She needed to either find out who took the paperwork or find someone else who knew the truth.

Chapter 32

Cassandra fell into step next to Rachel as they trailed behind Mrs. Pearson on the charitable rounds for the day.

It had been several days since Mr. Longham's body was discovered. The shock was subsiding, but the resulting melancholy draped every action, every thought. Mr. Warrington agreed that Rachel needed a diversion, so he granted permission for her to accompany Cassandra, Mrs. Pearson, and a few other ladies.

Cassandra was used to these outings now and even looked forward to them. Every few days she would accompany the parish women on some act of charity. Once they had visited the nearby poorhouse. Another week they had called on a young mother who had just lost both of her parents to fever. Today they were to visit a woman whose husband had suffered an apoplexy and was near death.

The visits were rarely easy, but Cassandra found solace in knowing she could offer a little consolation, in addition to feeling renewed gratitude for her own situation. Her circumstances might not be ideal, but she was healthy. Content. And as Mr. Warrington had suggested, she was not without hope.

With Rachel next to her, the outing took on a new purpose. The activity afforded them time alone, away from the little girls, where they could talk about life and growing to adulthood.

As they walked together side by side, Rachel cradled a basket of bread. When they were out of earshot of the other ladies, she said quietly, "You said you would tell me one day about what had happened to you, in regard to the young man. Is now a good time? I don't think Mrs. Pearson is paying attention to us."

Mrs. Pearson, who had organized the outing, was speaking with one of the other ladies from the village. Cassandra considered how best to respond to Rachel. While it was something they could relate to each other about, she did not necessarily care to revisit it. Not that she was ashamed of it—the experience was a turning point in her life, one where she made an important decision and learned a valuable lesson on discernment and trust. But reliving it was never pleasant.

And yet she'd promised.

Cassandra adjusted her own basket on her arm. "I met him when I was quite young. His name was Frederick, and he was the vicar's son. I'd see him at every church activity, and we became quite close one summer in particular. We'd find time to be alone at picnics or walk together. His father was preparing to send him away to school, so we decided we had no options but to run away together. It had been a foolish thought, really, and I think I always knew it would not actually come to pass, but I felt the emotions so intensely—I thought surely they had to be real.

"We planned and schemed until the day before we were to leave. I made an offhanded comment to the girl I shared a chamber with, and she informed the headmistress. Mrs. Denton interrupted our departure and that was the end of it. Afterward, he was immediately sent off to school. He returned a year later, rumored to be engaged. Now he is married."

Rachel shook her head sympathetically. "You must have been heartbroken."

"I was. But, looking back, it was for the best. I see that now. After it happened, I was so sure he would find a way back to me, and I held on to that thought much longer than I should have. But when he did finally return, it was as if he never knew me."

"I'm so sorry for you." Rachel swiped a dark curl from her face as they continued down the path. "It is just so painful."

"But I survived, you see?" Cassandra forced cheer to her tone. "And I am wiser for it. Or at least I think I am."

"In my mind I know I am better off here, but in my heart I still miss Richard."

"I think you miss the idea of him," Cassandra offered. "Don't forget, never forget, that he showed you his true self that night when he grabbed you. That is not the man you want in your life, as your partner and as the father of your children."

They fell into an easy, comfortable silence until Mrs. Pearson nodded toward a small cottage. "Here we are, my dears. This is the house of Silas Smith, the man who suffered an apoplexy and has not regained consciousness. He and his wife have three sons. It is my hope that we can bring her some comfort or, at the very least, distraction."

Together the women waited at the door, baskets in hand. It was a humble cottage, like so many of the other miller cottages lining the row, with a low thatched roof and deeply set square windows.

At length the door opened, and Cassandra started. The woman who answered the door was strangely familiar. She was older with straight, faded chestnut hair, but it was the slight upturn of her nose and the dimple at the corner of her mouth when she spoke that captured Cassandra's attention.

They were both like her own.

Had she not been aware of the woman's name, Cassandra might not have noticed. But Mrs. Pearson had said this was the Smith residence.

Hadn't Mr. Longham said her mother's name after marriage was Mary Smith?

But it was such a common name. Surely there was no connection.

After stepping inside the dark corridor, she leaned toward Mrs. Pearson and whispered, "What is her name again, please?"

"This is Mrs. Smith, dear."

"No, I meant to ask about her Christian name."

"Mary Smith, I believe. Why?"

Cassandra did not answer. She could not answer. Control seemed to flee her body. Her arms felt weak and tingly. Her breath fluttery and airy.

Could this woman be . . .

No, surely not.

Mrs. Pearson continued the introductions, oblivious to the panic bubbling within Cassandra. "This is Miss Rachel Warrington. She lives at Briarton Park."

Mrs. Smith's sternly set jaw twitched ever so slightly.

"And this is Miss Cassandra Hale," continued Mrs. Pearson, "governess at Briarton Park."

At this all color drained from Mary Smith's face.

Cassandra knew there could be no doubt—this woman, fearing for the life of her husband, was her mother.

And they both knew it.

The next minutes blurred. Mrs. Smith's words were brusque. Abrupt. Baskets were emptied. Food was left. Prayers were said. It was as if Cassandra was watching the events unfold instead of participating in them.

She wanted to say something, but what? It was hardly the time. Her mother's husband could very well be on his deathbed. And there was no privacy.

But as they prepared to leave, Mrs. Smith called after her, "Miss Hale. A word before you leave, if ye don't mind?"

Cassandra separated from Mrs. Pearson and Rachel and stayed behind at the cottage. For several moments the women stared at each other. No words were exchanged, and then Mrs. Smith's words rang cold. "So, ye found me."

Cassandra's mouth dried. She could only stare at the petite woman she'd thought about, wondered about, every single day of her life.

Mrs. Smith pushed on. "I heard you were in the village askin' questions. Mrs. Hutton told me 'erself. Why? What are ye hopin' to do?"

"I—I just want to know the truth about who my family is. I received a letter from Mr. Clark. He told me he wanted to share information—"

"Robert Clark is dead, as ye well know," she snipped. "Why are you here, at me house?"

Cassandra didn't know whether to be hurt, angry, or anxious. She didn't have time to formulate her response, for Mary Smith's churlish words barreled forth.

"What right have ye comin' here, pokin' 'round where ye don't belong? I've a life now. You have yours. My husband and boys know nothin' 'bout you, and Silas must never know what my life was like before. Leave the past in the past, where it belongs. Dead. Buried. You upended my life once. Don't do it again."

Mary Smith spun back into the house and disappeared before Cassandra fully understood what had just happened.

Tears threatened, and a sob caught unexpectedly. She was not prepared for this. She was not prepared to meet her mother.

And she was being rejected.

It was as if the breath had been siphoned from her lungs as Cassandra stared at the empty space where her mother had been standing.

The words—the dismissal—hurt more than any dagger ever could.

The one person she had dreamt about wanted nothing to do with her.

Chapter 33

Cassandra knocked on the door to Mrs. Hutton's cottage. And waited. When no response came, she lifted her gloved hand and knocked again. Harder.

The shock from earlier in the day had been almost more than she could bear.

Her mother was alive.

Now there seemed to be no one who could help her find the truth. Except for one person—Mrs. Hutton.

She continued knocking rapidly until Mrs. Hutton appeared at the door. Immediate recognition—and irritation—flashed. "Miss Hale."

"I'm intruding, I know." Cassandra held out her hand to keep the door open. "And I am sorry for it, truly. But I have questions to which I need answers, and I fear you are the only person alive who can answer them."

At first Mrs. Hutton only stared at Cassandra after the rush of words. But then she expelled a puff of air, rested against the door, and cocked her head to the side. "So you spoke with Mary Smith, did you?"

"How did you know?"

"I figured you'd find her eventually. I heard the church women were headed to her house, what with Silas's current state. Thought you might be there."

Cassandra nodded. "It did not go well at all."

With a sigh that teetered on defeat, Mrs. Hutton pushed the door wider to allow Cassandra to pass.

Once they were settled in the parlor, Cassandra recounted the events that had occurred at the Smith residence. "She was furious, but she did mention you. She said she'd spoken to you about me, so I am hopeful that means you know something about my birth and history. Please, I have so many questions, and now that William Longham is dead, I fear you may be my last hope."

Mrs. Hutton's expression remained aloof as she folded her wrinkled hands primly on her lap. "Mrs. Smith has a right to her privacy."

"I agree wholeheartedly," Cassandra hastened to say, "but have I no right to know the truth about where I am from?"

Mrs. Hutton hesitated.

"I promise I will not bother Mrs. Smith," continued Cassandra. "I'll leave her alone completely and never contact her again. Any information you share will be with me only."

Like she had on the first day they met, Mrs. Hutton picked up the big orange cat coiling around her legs and petted it before responding. "Mary Hale was not the first young woman in service forced to give up a child. She had no choice, really. She had to leave you and start a new life."

Cassandra held her breath, eager to capture every detail.

"I was the housekeeper when Mr. Clark, your father, bought Briarton Park. This was decades ago, mind you. I was immediately fond of his wife, Mrs. Katherine Clark. She was the kindest woman I ever had the pleasure of knowing. She deserved a much better life than the one Mr. Clark gave her."

Cassandra's question rushed out. "Was he unkind?"

Mrs. Hutton pressed her lips together thoughtfully. "There were occasions he was very kind, but he was a most selfish man. At times even harsh. Your mother was a chambermaid, and he pursued her, as if he had a divine right to. When she became with child, he denied it, of course, but when she threatened to inform Mrs. Clark, he became quite cruel. He all but coerced her into hiding until you were born, and then he bullied her to sign an agreement to sever all of her ties to you."

Cassandra's chest tightened with every new bit of information. "But how could he force her to do it if she did not want to?"

"Oh, I don't believe you are so naive that you don't know the answer to that," she scoffed. "What choice did she have? None. She could not afford to raise you. She could not even afford a roof over her own head."

"So she simply walked away?"

"What else could she do? She had no family. No other employment." Mrs. Hutton stroked the cat's fur. "Do not judge her too harshly. We all could have found ourselves in her position."

Cassandra stiffened as the statement wound its way through her mind. Had she not had romantic thoughts about the current master of Briarton House? Had she not thought she saw something in Mr. Warrington's expression that made her think his interest in her went beyond that of servant and master?

She pushed the unsettling thought aside and returned to the topic at hand. "You speak as if you and Mrs. Smith were friends."

"Not friends, no. Allies? Perhaps. She worked under me, and I saw things. I did everything I could to protect her, young as she was, but your father was a very powerful and persuasive man. She and I kept in contact after she left. I was able to help coordinate references and the like. But her life moved on, as did mine. As did everyone's."

Cassandra could not shake the image of the fuming Mrs. Smith from her mind. "Is she happy now?"

"Of course this illness with her husband is devastating to her, I'm sure, but otherwise I suppose she is as happy as any woman could be, given her status."

"That does not sound very convincing."

Mrs. Hutton lowered the cat to the floor and then pivoted to face Cassandra. "You know, I was there the night you were born."

Cassandra raised her head, eager for details. "You were?"

"Yes. I was the only staff member in the house then. When the time drew near, Mr. Clark was concerned that his wife would find out. He was a man driven by obsessions and suspicion. So he brought Mary back to Briarton and sent his wife and all the staff away. But Mr. Longham remained with us, of course."

The murky picture of how the specifics were connected was starting to materialize. Bits and pieces were beginning to connect, like a puzzle taking form. Mrs. Hutton's recollections matched the information Mr. Longham had shared with her. But there were still pieces missing—pieces essential to gaining full clarity. How did Mrs. Denton fit into it? To whom did she make a promise? Whom was she protecting?

Now was the time to ask.

"Did you know Mrs. Jane Denton?"

Mrs. Hutton nodded. "I did."

Cassandra's heart pulsed. She'd expected Mrs. Hutton to say no, and the familiarity with which she spoke about Mrs. Denton shocked her. "Mrs. Denton told me she'd purposely kept my father's identity from me—that she had made a promise to someone. Do you know anything of that promise?"

"I do. And I hesitate to tell you"—Mrs. Hutton shifted uncomfortably—"but I suppose everyone involved is dead now. Well, mostly everyone."

Cassandra held her breath.

"Mrs. Denton was Mrs. Katherine Clark's sister."

"S-sister?" The word tasted thick and strange on her tongue.

"Yes. Sister. A few months before you were born, Jane Denton was visiting Briarton Park and overhead Mr. Clark and Mary, your mother, arguing about her situation. To my understanding Mrs. Denton confronted him. She clearly loved her sister very much and wanted to protect her from the pain and humiliation that infidelity would inflict. At that time Mrs. Denton had already been a widow for some years, and her school was quite established. She had a pristine reputation, and she was persistent. She, along with Mr. Longham, advised Mr. Clark to permit you to live at her school. She said she would raise you and keep your identity hidden. I, being one of the few people to know about you, was forced to keep that secret as well, on pain of dismissal. Oh yes, Mrs. Denton despised Mr. Clark, but she was devoted to Katherine."

"But why, then, after Mrs. Clark died, do you suppose Mrs. Denton did not tell me the truth?"

Mrs. Hutton retrieved a handkerchief from her apron pocket. "Young Peter Clark would be my guess. She loved that boy as much as any aunt could love a nephew, never having had children of her own, and she never wanted to cast a shadow on her sister's memory. And, of course, to keep scandal at bay."

The words struck, numbly at first and then with increasing intensity.

Could that be true?

Did Mrs. Denton really sacrifice telling Cassandra the truth to protect a person as brutal as *Peter Clark*?

Mrs. Denton had loved her and cared for her.

But apparently she had loved her flesh and blood more.

"I can see this is affecting you," Mrs. Hutton said after a space of silence. "I confess, it's been a burdensome secret to bear. But I leave you with this. Do not judge your mother too harshly. Mr. Clark robbed her of so much. Her confidence. Her innocence. Like I told you in our first encounter, sometimes secrets are a gift. You seem to have done well for yourself. A young woman could do worse than a governess position in a house like Briarton Park. Maybe you'll find yourself a husband. 'Tis no secret you've caught the vicar's eye. Word's all over the village, not that I pay mind to gossip, but everyone seems to be expecting a wedding by summer. I've experienced a great deal in my day, and my advice is to forget this business and focus on what comes next."

Cassandra needed to return to Briarton Park before she was missed.

It would be dusk soon, and as much as she would prefer to walk in complete solitude to contend with her thoughts, the fastest way back to Briarton was through the village.

She passed through the small maze of cottages off the high street and trod the cobbled road. But as she reached the church, her steps slowed.

Mrs. Hutton had said bluntly that the vicar was taken with her. She even said the villagers expected a wedding by summer. The thought should have flooded her with optimism and given her hope for a future and a family.

So why didn't it?

Since her arrival in Anston, Mr. North had been gracious and obliging. His visits to Briarton had been regular since Mr. Longham's death. And he really was undoubtedly attractive. But she could not deny that the more time she spent in his company, the more acquainted she was becoming with his other qualities—insistent, possessive qualities that, to her, sullied his otherwise congenial nature.

She tried to force her mind to look past the misconduct. They were minor failings, and after all, who was without faults? But another thought—another person—pushed the idea of Mr. North to the back of her mind. Mr. Warrington. But it was impossible. Implausible. For look what had happened to her mother when she set her sights on someone in an unattainable position.

Yes, she should want to marry. She should want to marry *Mr. North*.

As she passed the vicarage, Mr. North emerged, donning his black coat as he did so. She'd half expected to see him, for his study overlooked the high street and he observed all comings and goings. He waved a hand and jogged toward her.

"I wasn't expecting to see you in the village today." His pace slowed, and he fell into step beside her. "But I'm glad, for I have news for you."

"Oh?"

"Yes. But first, how are you?" His brow creased. "Mrs. Pearson said you were not yourself after the visits. She worried you were ill. In fact, I called out to Briarton not an hour ago and was told you were not able to be found. I was concerned."

The words should warm her, or at least make her feel supported, but something in her resisted it. "Do not worry on my account. I'm quite well, as you see. After our outing, I called on Mrs. Hutton."

"Mrs. Hutton?" He jerked. "Why?"

She immediately wished she had not divulged the last bit. He was getting too close. His intentions might be innocent enough, but she was suffocating under the weight of them. "I'd rather not talk about it, if you don't mind."

His dipped his head and raised his hands submissively. "Fair enough. We'll say no more on that subject, but there is a matter, a serious matter, I wanted to discuss with you. But perhaps you are not up for it."

Her patience was growing thin. "If you've something to disclose, then please do."

"They arrested a suspect for the Longham murder."

She lurched to a stop and faced him, squinting as the late-afternoon sunlight slid over the church's roof. "What?"

He nodded. "As we all know there have been several attacks on mills and mill owners, and they suspect that Mr. Longham simply got caught in the crosshairs of one of these attacks. It seems Mr. Warrington's new carding machines have caused quite a commotion among the workers, and that is why they were on Briarton Park property. It's not common knowledge, not yet at least, but I thought you'd want to know."

She started walking again, and he followed suit.

"There's more. The man who was arrested was employed by Peter Clark."

Peter Clark. The very name seemed to be haunting her, following her in every situation. "What evidence do they have against this man?"

"I don't know exactly, but apparently something was found in his house that tied him to Mr. Longham. Something about documents. I can only surmise it was the documents from Mr. Longham's satchel that you had told me were missing, but that's merely an assumption."

The documents. *Her* documents.

A little flame of hope flared.

With the documents missing and her mother refusing to acknowledge her, there would be no way to help her prove her identity. Cassandra could hardly push forward without any evidence whatsoever. But now, just maybe, there was a chance the documents would come to light and offer the support she needed.

Chapter 34

The afternoon was growing late when James returned to Briarton Park from Weyton Mill. He needed to speak with Miss Hale. Rumors that Shepard had arrested a man on the suspicion of murder were rampant, and he wanted to make sure she knew.

But as he entered the parlor, music echoed, and he found Rachel at the pianoforte. He stopped short. "I thought you were spending the afternoon with Miss Hale."

The music halted and she turned to him. "I did."

"Back so soon?" He popped open his watch. "I thought she said you wouldn't be back until evening."

"I thought so, too, but after our first call, Miss Hale said she had a headache and wasn't feeling well, so we returned."

He snapped the pocket watch closed and tucked it away. "Is she all right?"

"Well, I thought so, but then she left in a hustle on an errand. She said she'd return for the girls' supper. I—I'm afraid I upset her."

"Oh, I doubt that." Sensing she needed to talk, he dropped to the sofa next to the pianoforte, stretched one arm over the back of it, and crossed one leg over the other. "It is her free afternoon. Perhaps she really had errands."

"You didn't see her. She was not herself at all." Rachel lowered her hands from the keys and shifted to face him. "Then Mr. North called, and when I went to tell her, she wasn't in her room. I'm worried she is upset with me."

Mr. North.

His visits were growing in frequency and duration. And how could James possibly tell a vicar to limit his calls, especially after what had transpired on the property?

He cleared his throat and returned his focus to his sister. "That seems unlikely. What could you possibly have asked that would upset her so?"

"I asked her a question about her past. It was too personal. I should've known better. She told me the very first day we met that she'd experienced a similar situation to what I had with Richard. She almost eloped with a young man but was stopped. She said she'd share the details of it with me one day, but she seemed upset after I brought it up."

A disrupted elopement?

So Miss Hale did have a bit of a past.

No wonder she'd acted defensively on Rachel's behalf.

He refocused on his sister. "That doesn't sound right to me. Perhaps there is something else. Or she really did not feel well. I wouldn't worry over it."

But with everything that had transpired and all of the suspicion, he remained uncertain. There was so much he didn't know about her—but it was not her past that concerned him. It was the present, and how it would affect the days, months, and years to come.

Dusk was already starting to fall, and shades of purple and blue covered the autumn's browns and golds as Cassandra ambled back toward Briarton Park. The bare-branched trees swayed and creaked in sharp gusts, the urgency of which reminded her that she needed to get home.

She was late—much later than she should be. It was her free afternoon, but Mr. Warrington had repeatedly made it clear that no one was to be out alone on the grounds, given the recent violence, after dark.

In the courtyard a riding lesson was in progress. The girls were clad in their new riding togs that Betsy had been engaged to fashion for them, and both Mr. Warrington and the groom were instructing them.

She lowered her cape and approached, and memories of the day she arrived to ask for a position rushed her. But now, instead of anxiety and uncertainty, a sense of calm cloaked her. This place—Briarton Park—was home, and the people in it were becoming a source of comfort. Rachel was a friend. Maria and Rose, her purpose. And Mr. Warrington . . .

Cassandra paused to take a deep breath.

Mr. North might be winsome, but Mr. Warrington enchanted her.

And now he was approaching her.

She waited, still and silent, as he strode from the courtyard, hatless, casually and confidently. His silhouette cut an impressive figure against the backdrop of the leafless trees and winter shrubbery as he drew nearer, through the gate by the orchard and to the path along the front drive, where she stood.

"Miss Hale," he greeted. "Rachel said you weren't feeling well. She was worried."

"I didn't mean to worry her. I should have told her where I was going."

He did not ask for details, yet the ensuing silence and his raised brows asked the questions his voice did not.

She owed no further explanation, but until this point she had not realized how badly she wanted to tell someone.

To tell *him*.

Her mother had made it clear that she wanted it kept a secret, and Cassandra had planned to keep it a secret. But Mr. Warrington already knew so much about the situation. And she trusted his advice. "As it turned out, the woman we visited on one of the calls today was named Mary Smith. And she is my mother."

"Your mother?" he repeated. "And this is good news, isn't it?"

The words fought her as she spoke them. "I'm not certain. She wants nothing to do with me. I'm never to call on her again."

"I am sorry," he said softly.

"At least I know the truth." She infused her voice with as much optimism as possible. "I know who my father was. I know who my mother is, and I know where she's living. And thanks to Mrs. Hutton, who used to be the housekeeper here, I know the circumstances surrounding my birth. It is everything I wanted to know."

The breeze lifted his hair from his brow, and he studied the distance as if pondering what she'd said. "But it's not enough, is it?"

Alarmed by his insight, she looked away from him. "It should be. But no. It's not. I suppose I will have to be satisfied and leave it as it is."

"If we, myself included, wait for complete satisfaction, we'll always be disappointed. There will always be unanswered questions and things we wish were different. If we dwell on those, though, we risk missing the good that is before us. I know that to be true every time I look at my daughters."

He could relate, she knew.

He'd lost his wife. He surely wanted resolution to unanswerable questions, just like she did.

She distractedly pulled her kid glove tight. "Well, I know I have a brother, a mother, and my father's dead. So now what?"

"You have an inheritance."

"True, but I have no way to prove my identity. Mr. Longham possessed every pertinent piece of documentation, and now—"

"I don't know if you've heard, but Mr. Shepard made an arrest regarding Longham's death."

"Yes, Mr. North told me."

At the reference to Mr. North, Mr. Warrington's jaw twitched. Or had she imagined it?

He adjusted his stance. "I'm not familiar with the details, of course, But Shepard did stop by Weyton to say the man in question was also a suspect in some of the mill attacks. He also said he had evidence that tied him to Longham's assault as well, but I'm not sure what that evidence was. Perhaps this development will lead to the papers you need."

She indulged in an exasperated sigh. "Everything, every aspect of this search, feels so convoluted. Mrs. Hutton informed me that the woman who raised me—Mrs. Denton, the very one who wrote my recommendation letter—was actually Mr. Clark's sister-in-law. Can you believe it? Apparently she was Peter Clark's maternal aunt, and they were quite close. It seems as if everything I know is a lie or a shifted version of truth. I don't know what to do or where to go. Perhaps no one can be trusted."

He took one step closer to her. "You can trust me."

She looked up at him, suddenly very aware of his scent of sandalwood and the outdoors, of horses and fresh air. The pewter of his eyes was vibrant in the early evening light. How she wanted to believe his words were true. Yet she could not shake her mother's experience from her mind. Had her mother believed that she could trust Robert Clark?

All she knew for certain, in spite of her conflicting thoughts, was that she did not want to leave Mr. Warrington's side. There was strength, a comfort in his presence, which until now had been quite foreign to her. Perhaps it was the space he gave her when they spoke, or the manner in which he seemed to focus on her wholly, without agenda or motive, that affected her so.

A gust of evening wind swept in, dislodging her hair and whipping it around her face.

He reached forward, slowly, and lifted the wayward curl away from her face. His finger brushed her cheek and lingered there. Intimately. Tenderly.

At the touch, a thrill shot through her—the thrill of being connected to someone, of being understood or, at the very least, cared about. This was the feeling she'd been searching for. The feeling she'd been chasing. And yet it was in its infancy. If allowed to grow, where could this feeling go? What could this become?

His eyes fixed on her, poignantly, as if she were the only person, the only thing that mattered.

"But how could this . . ." Her questions felt inadequate. "If this goes on, how do I . . . ?"

His thumb caressed her cheek. "I don't know the answers. All I know is that I care very much about what happens to you. And you've come into my life for a reason. I know that as surely as I've ever known anything. And I think we should explore why."

Could this feeling be trusted? Could *he* be trusted?

Cassandra had trusted before—Mrs. Denton, Frederick—and she'd been hurt. And now everyone seemed to be aware of her possible inheritance. Was that what he was attracted to? Had not Peter Clark insinuated that very thing?

Movement over his shoulder snagged her attention. There, in the study window overlooking the main drive, stood Mrs. Towler. Watching them.

He followed her gaze and looked over his shoulder to the house. His touch on her cheek grew rigid, and he dropped his hand to her shoulder. "You should go on inside now." His hand fell from her shoulder completely.

Suddenly she felt very pathetic and inched backward. She looked back up at Mrs. Towler, feeling very much like the seventeen-year-old version of herself having just been discovered in compromising circumstances with Frederick.

In that moment Mrs. Denton's words screamed loudly. *"What have I told you? Emotions will cloud your judgment and weaken your ability to react rationally."*

She was doing exactly what she'd been warned against. Her emotions regarding Mr. Warrington were gaining dangerous power.

Her cheeks flamed. What a fool she'd been.

Chapter 35

James braced himself. He was outraged. He curled his fists at his sides as he stalked back to his study.

He respected his past with Elizabeth. He loved her; he always would. Her presence would always be felt with Rose. Maria. But he could not remain frozen in grief and in the past, not when new feelings were flourishing. His interest in Cassandra Hale was not wrong. It was a natural progression—one afforded by time. Attraction. Mutual trust. A desire for something more.

It didn't matter that she was the governess. Not to him. Those onlookers would judge him for it, but what did he care? What did he have to lose?

The disparity in their stations was not as uncommon in his upbringing. He was from a humble place. This new world in which they existed—Elizabeth's world—cared much more for those social strictures.

Now, as he approached the study, he was going to be called upon to defend his thoughts. His actions. To the woman who was closer to his late wife than anyone.

Mrs. Towler stood in his study, as expected, in her customary black gown and severely arranged silver hair. Her expression was pinched, but she was pale. She spoke before his foot even crossed the threshold. "I'm leaving Briarton Park at week's end."

He had been prepared to hear a lecture from her, but not this.

A strange guilt crept in, and he searched for words. "There's a misunderstanding, I think, that—"

"No," she snipped. "No misunderstanding. Things are abundantly clear."

He cleared his throat. "Where will you go?"

"To my cousin in Devon. She will be happy to see me."

"The girls will miss you," he offered. "Have you told them yet?"

"No. But I think this is for the best. 'Tis past time."

James suddenly felt shame, as if his actions had contributed to this departure. "Is this because of what you witnessed just now?"

"I already told you the day of that murder that I was leaving if Miss Hale was not removed as governess. But as for what I saw just now, did I not tell you this would happen? That she was looking to advance herself? At one time I did respect you. I thought you above such things, but I'm surprised at nothing anymore."

She said nothing else but stormed past him, out to the corridor.

And he was alone.

Control was slipping. He felt it. The past as he knew it was falling further away, and something entirely new was taking its place, whether he was prepared for the transition or not.

He looked to the portrait of Elizabeth sitting atop his desk— where it had sat every day since they arrived here. How familiar the shape of her face was.

He ran his finger over the image lovingly, as if trying to recapture the feel of it.

But it was impossible—she was gone forever.

The pain, although still present, had dulled to an ever-present ache. He lifted the miniature closer. "I miss you. Everyone misses you," he whispered. "Tell me what to do."

Yes, he was torn, but deep down he knew she would not want sadness—not for him and certainly not for the girls.

He returned the portrait to its spot on his desk and stared out the window. The last bits of light were fighting their way through the gathered clouds, and he looked to where he had stood with Cassandra.

He and Elizabeth had talked about death. They'd always said if something happened to one of them that the other should marry again. And now, years after becoming a widower, he found his heart pulling in that very direction.

What was more, he believed that Miss Hale might return his regard.

So where did that leave everyone?

His heart was in dangerous territory, but it was not just his heart that he had to consider. He knew the truth. And he had to let her know where he stood.

It was late by the time James and Milton prepared to leave the Green Ox Inn. The day had been an unsettling one, with the interaction with Miss Hale and the talk with Mrs. Towler.

But it was not over yet.

Night had already fallen, and they'd just concluded their business with a handful of sheep farmers from the southern villages. The atmosphere at the Green Ox Inn was the same as it was every time James had been there—smoke from the broad fire hovered in the air, locals and travelers alike filled the tables, and rowdy, raucous laughter rang out. And yet, chatter of the supposed arrest was on everyone's lips. But no one had concrete details—merely hearsay and rumors that became more elaborate with each telling.

He and Milton bid their farewells and were about to vacate their table and depart, just as Vincent North was entering.

James knew the man had designs on Miss Hale. Everyone knew

it. Even so, he did not believe that she returned the regard—especially not after the moment they'd shared earlier in the evening.

But he was not ignorant.

She may not feel romantic affection toward North, but young women were often eager to marry. And no doubt Mr. North was considered a catch. His eagerness suggested he'd be ready with a proposal any minute. James was not at that point yet.

The very thought of actually offering a proposal startled him. Had his feelings really developed to that point?

Yet here he was—his thoughts never far from her as of late. She'd wrapped her way around every part of his life.

James had no right to stand in the way of her happiness, her security, especially when he was not prepared to act. But it did not mean he had to like it.

"Ah, Mr. Warrington. Mr. Milton." North stepped next to them, just inside the door. "May I join you?"

James nodded toward the empty chair in response.

North placed his wide-brimmed hat on the table and reclined against the chair's high back. "I was just out there earlier today to call on Miss Hale after I heard the news about the arrest. I'm sure you've heard, of course."

"Yes, Shepard was out to the mill to tell us and to suggest vigilance. I'm surprised you've heard of it, though, considering it's a milling matter. News must travel fast."

"Ah, 'tis a part of the profession. People tell me things, ask my thoughts on matters. Doesn't change the fact that it was a nasty business. I feel for Miss Hale. What an awful experience. I don't suppose you know if they've found anything out regarding the documents that were lost. She was so counting on it."

He should not be surprised that the vicar knew so many details, but the familiarity with which North spoke irked him. Even so, he was not so distracted that he failed to notice the subtle challenge in North's tone.

Perhaps he saw James as a rival too.

"Miss Hale seemed quite upset this afternoon," North continued matter-of-factly. "She has confided in me a great deal on the matter, and I feel quite conflicted as to how to proceed."

James exchanged glances with Milton before biting on the leading statement. "Oh? And why's that?"

"She's my parishioner now that she resides at Briarton Park, of course, but more importantly she's my friend. My good friend. I'm sure you don't see her in that light, given that she is the governess of your children. But still, I worry for her."

Irritated, James adjusted his hat. "Miss Hale is the governess in my household, yes. I'm not in the habit of discussing those under my roof, but I will say this. She's under scrutiny, details are emerging about the inheritance, and rumors are flying about Mr. Longham's death. I'm sure you know all about it. She obviously trusts you, and I'd hate to think that someone in your position would abuse that trust to advance a personal agenda."

"A personal agenda?" Mr. North scoffed as if thoroughly amused. "Are you saying that my interest in Miss Hale has more to do with her inheritance than the lady herself?"

James shrugged. "She's endured much, and it's understandable that she'd confide in a man in your position."

"You seem to be paying very close attention to matters." North raised a dark brow. "One might question it."

"Question all you would like. I'll not permit anyone to be taken advantage of."

"Careful how you speak." North's gaze narrowed. "Such a statement borders on the offensive."

"Interpret it how you will."

North chuckled, but his wry expression held anything but humor. "Are you this particular about all the servants in your employ, or is it just the pretty governess? Very well, Warrington. I consider Miss Hale capable of making up her own mind. I wonder what she would think of you making decisions for her regarding with whom she can and cannot speak. Perhaps I will discuss it with her tomorrow when she comes to assist with the baskets."

The familiarity. The possessiveness in his voice. It all swirled together, antagonizing and provoking his sense of duty. James lowered his voice, leaned as close to North as his position at the table would allow. "Let me be absolutely clear. Yes, I do question your intentions with Miss Hale. She is quite capable of handling whatever comes her way, I'll give you that, but I'll be watching and will not hesitate to intervene if necessary."

James thought the vicar might challenge him further, but instead, the tension in North's face eased, and he forced the simpering grin once more. "Well then. I think our conversation here is done, Warrington. I do believe my party is waiting for me."

North stood, straightened his ridiculously ornate scarlet toilinet waistcoat, and pushed past them. Not able to wait another second to be free of the inn, James jumped to his feet and exited into the cold, damp night. The rush of chilly air felt calming against his face, and he did not stop walking until he arrived where his horse was secured on the far edge of the courtyard.

"That's one way t' talk wit' the vicar." Milton caught up with him. "What was that 'bout?"

When James did not respond, Milton chuckled. "I see."

"You see what?" James shot back.

Milton shrugged, amusement creasing his face. "I know you don't care for North, but he might have a point."

James huffed as he adjusted the horse's saddle. "Doubtful."

"Are you sure?" Milton prodded. "'Tis no shame, no shame at all, in admittin' ye are attracted to someone. Happens to most people, sooner or later. You included."

"I'm not discussing this with you." James turned his back to Milton and mounted his horse. "We'll stick to the topic of wool and mills."

Milton quipped, "Whatever you say."

As they rode toward the bridge leading to Briarton, the conversation weighed heavily on James's mind, mostly because he was annoyed at himself for allowing his emotions to control him. But beyond that, he'd been honest when he said he didn't trust the man. His manner was too familiar. His nature too complimentary in general. Something seemed amiss, and James was determined to find out what it was.

Chapter 36

As Cassandra and Rachel gathered with other village women just inside the church after distributing baskets, Cassandra's tensions eased, and her heart felt light. She was content with her role at Briarton Park, but she had missed the companionship of the other people she'd met, especially Mrs. Pearson and Betsy.

Mrs. Pearson was helping Rachel organize donated cloth, and Cassandra stood with Betsy returning undistributed apples to a barrel. They'd not spoken all week, and yet news had traveled far and wide. With the exception of Cassandra's mother's identity, Betsy seemed to know almost as many details about the entire murder and inheritance as Cassandra knew herself.

As they stood folding linens and preparing to finish up their tasks, Betsy wiped her hands together. "I just can't believe how quickly all of this happened. You must have been so frightened to find a body like that. I'd have been terrified."

"I was more sad than frightened." Cassandra placed more apples into the barrel. "Mr. Longham was very kind to me. So helpful."

"But to see his body in such a state," continued Betsy. "It must have been horrific."

"It was."

"Did he have family? Do you know?"

"I don't think so. From what I understood he was a bachelor."

Betsy's tawny brows drew together in question. "And no one knows for sure who might be responsible?"

"Mr. Shepard and a couple of constables have visited Briarton Park this week, and he spoke to me once, but most of his interactions have been with Mr. Warrington. Honestly, I hear so little where I am. Almost my entire time is spent with the girls. I did hear, however, that one man was arrested, but I can't seem to get a clear answer of what the evidence was."

Betsy pivoted and propped her hand on her hip. "Oh, that is suspicious."

"It is, and it isn't." Cassandra removed the linen from a basket and began to fold it. "Mr. Warrington had said numerous times that there are men who are retaliating against the mill owners and their property, so that is a possible motive as well."

Betsy leaned closer and lowered her voice, her gaze very direct. "Is the rest of it true? About the inheritance? Everyone says that you will inherit land. Land, Cassandra!"

She nodded in response. "It's in the will, but I must prove my identity. That, I cannot do. Not without Mr. Longham's statement and the documents he possessed. Besides, I have no funds to pay a solicitor to assist me in the courts now. I fear the cause might be lost."

As the day's activity began to fade, Mrs. Pearson took Rachel and the other young volunteers to the vicarage for tea. Betsy and Cassandra and the rest of the women were left at the church to finish organizing the donations. Over time the others dispersed, and before long Betsy and Cassandra were alone in the church's nave.

A glance through the window confirmed the hour was growing late. It would be dark soon, and Briarton's carriage was waiting for them. She looked over at Betsy, who was fiddling with her cloak. "Hurry, Betsy! I promised Mr. Warrington that Rachel would be home by nightfall."

And yet Betsy tilted her head to the side and made no steps to the door. An impish grin curved her lips. "I've never been in here by myself before."

"That's because everyone else has gone and it's time to go."

Even in the dimly lit space, her mischievous expression twinkled. "Didn't you say you were searching for birth records or something of the like?"

"Mr. North already said they weren't here. He looked."

"And you're not the least bit curious to see for yourself? I never trust what anyone says. Not unless I see it myself."

Uneasiness wound its way through Cassandra. "I think it's best we leave."

Betsy stood firm. "I've heard the parish chest is in there, in the vestry."

The wooden door to the small office stood ajar.

She had to trust Mr. North, didn't she? He was her friend. He would not knowingly lie to her.

But the last several weeks had taught her the danger of being naive, and her interest was piqued. If she'd been born at Briarton, as Mr. Longham and Mrs. Hutton had claimed, her name would be there, for she'd been told she was baptized, and that would be one step closer to proof of her identity.

In an intentional flick of her wrist, Betsy tipped a basket on the stone floor, and the apples rolled through the open door. "Oh bother. We should pick those up."

Her friend's intentions were clear. "Betsy, I—"

"I'm only picking up the apples. Help me."

With a sigh Cassandra put her basket down as well and began to retrieve the apples that had rolled onto the floor. She paused at the door to the office and watched helplessly as Betsy stepped inside. Betsy motioned for Cassandra to join her.

Against her better judgment, Cassandra cast a glance over her shoulder and joined Betsy to look around the narrow space. A desk stood in the middle along with two chairs. A tall wardrobe was against the far wall, and on the far end stood the parish chest.

She'd never been in this part of the church before, but she knew right away that this was the office Mr. North had referenced upon their first meeting. This little room was frigid and dark, with naught but light from one narrow window to brighten the space.

No wonder he had not wanted to meet with people in here.

But someone had been in here recently. A half-burned candle sat atop the table. Papers were strewn over the desk haphazardly.

Betsy hurried to the parish chest and tried to lift it. But it didn't budge. "Locked."

"It is a sign we shouldn't be here." Cassandra gaped as Betsy started to rifle through the papers on the desk. "What are you doing? Put those down!"

"I'm only looking." She moved to the drawer and opened it. Then another. "After all, if these were truly private, this door would have been locked."

Cassandra pressed her lips together. She was about to reprimand her friend when shuffling could be heard. "Someone's coming!"

"Ladies!" Mr. North's voice echoed in the tall room. "What is happening here?"

"I dropped a basket of apples." Betsy emerged from the room with a congenial laugh. "How clumsy of me. We're to put them with the donations that came in, but they fell and rolled in here. Miss Hale was helping me retrieve them."

"Ah. I am sure the poor will be most grateful to receive them. I was about to lock up, but—"

"We were just about to leave," Cassandra said hastily. "Then I was going to head to the vicarage to collect Miss Warrington."

"Ah, then I will join you. I was hoping to speak with you privately anyway. If you don't mind?"

Cassandra nodded nervously.

"Very good," added Betsy. "I'll finish up here and see you by the vicarage then."

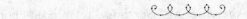

Cassandra's nerves tightened as she fell into step with Mr. North when they exited the church.

One sideways glance at him confirmed he seemed quite calm and unsuspecting of their snooping.

Even so, his customary good-natured smile was absent. His jaw clenched with unusual solemnity before he spoke. "I've battled my thoughts on this matter, but I cannot remain silent. So I'll just say it. I had a most distressing encounter with Mr. Warrington last night at the Green Ox Inn."

She stiffened as they drew to a stop on the path. She had not been aware that Mr. Warrington had gone to the inn last night. But why would she? "A distressing encounter with Mr. Warrington?"

"Yes. He seemed quite out of sorts. And bluntly, I'm concerned." He turned to face her directly. "Men like him, with position and power, are used to having their way."

Surprised at his grim opinion of Mr. Warrington, Cassandra studied Mr. North a little more closely.

He, too, seemed a bit out of sorts.

His thick hair, which was normally so tidy, was ruffled and windblown, and his cravat was uneven and hung slightly askew. A strange tension coiled around his mouth.

But as quickly as she made these observations, he continued, his words rushed. "Has he said anything or made any suggestions to you regarding your father's will?"

Her shoulders tensed at the question. "Why?"

At this, he reached out, touched her arm, and then dropped his hand. "I hope by now you know I'm not a suspicious man, but you must keep one thing in mind. There is no one in the area who would benefit from owning Linderdale more than James Warrington. Personally, I know you to be good. Kind. Trusting. Be wary, my dear, dear Miss Hale. Be wary of who you trust. Men like him are clever and not what they seem."

Her blood iced in her veins as the meaning behind his words sank in. She had no idea how to respond. She would never speak ill of Mr. Warrington. Why would Mr. North have reason to do so?

She needed clarity. "Are you accusing Mr. Warrington of being involved with Mr. Longham's death?"

"No, nothing like that. I don't think him involved at all. But I think he might take advantage of the situation."

She could not let this go. "Then who do you think is involved in Mr. Longham's death?"

"Unfortunately, I think the answer to that is very clear. I'd confess my thoughts on this to no one else besides you, but by now you know that Peter Clark is a volatile man. Normally I pay no heed to gossip, but then again, never have I felt that someone I cared for was in danger. His groom reportedly gave a very different account of that night than he or his wife did. Very different."

She felt as if she would be ill. If Mr. Clark was involved with the murder, then the logical conclusion was that Mr. Longham was killed to ensure silence.

And she was the reason why.

"I've said too much already," he continued, "but I will say one more thing and then be silent. It is just that I . . . I do care for you, Miss Hale. Very much. I want you to be careful."

A shuffle sounded at the church door behind them, and they turned to see Betsy.

From their safe distance, Mr. North said, "Your friend's not very fond of me."

"Betsy?"

Sarah E. Ladd

Mr. North spoke low but did not look away as Betsy approached them. "As the vicar here, of course I would like for her to be comfortable around me, at least. But these days I find myself caring less about what others think about me. My concern lies more with what one person in particular thinks."

There could be no doubt now of his meaning. These were not the words of a vicar to his parishioner. These were the words of a man to a woman.

A strange sense of panic surged through her. "Mr. North, I—"

His words silenced her. "How long do I have to—"

But he quickly stopped talking as Betsy drew nearer.

"I got all of the apples! One rolled under the desk. It took me a while to retrieve it." She glanced from Cassandra to Mr. North. "If I am interrupting, I—"

"No, you're not interrupting at all." Surprisingly relieved to be released from what could have been a much more serious conversation, Cassandra reached for Betsy's empty basket. "It's getting late. I must retrieve Rachel." She turned and curtsied. "As always, thank you, Mr. North, for your concern and help."

A flash of disappointment, or perhaps annoyance, splayed across his handsome face, but a smile quickly replaced it. "Of course. If you are done in the church, I will just go lock the office."

Betsy looped her arm through Cassandra's as they walked toward the vicarage and lowered her voice. "What did Mr. North want?"

Cassandra hesitated. His intentions were clear. Had his help been a mask for his romantic intentions all along? But he had repeatedly stated the importance he placed on social rank. What exactly was his interest with her? It didn't make sense. "I'm not entirely sure."

"Hmph." Betsy's voice dripped with sarcasm. "You are now the most interesting person in the area, what with the inheritance looming, and every man will want to speak with you."

"I don't know what to believe, Betsy. It seems that everyone has different stories. Different expectations. If only I had some definite new proof."

"Yes. Too bad you don't have any documentation." A sly smirk crept over her face as they walked along, and she pulled back the linen over the basket in her arms. Inside was a sheet of paper.

"Betsy!" cried Cassandra as she looked down at the page. "What have you done?"

"While you were talking, I just took a look and found something very interesting in the bottom of a drawer, tucked away in a portfolio."

"But you can't just take things." Cassandra glanced over her shoulder to see if anyone was watching them.

"Are you sure? Because . . ." Betsy stepped off the road and tugged Cassandra with her. "Look." She removed the paper from the basket and held it out.

It was a vellum paper with a list of names and dates on it. The page had clearly been torn from some sort of bound book. Shock nearly stole Cassandra's speech as the significance of what she was holding dawned on her. "These are baptism records."

"I know. Look here." Betsy pointed at the page.

Cassandra's name was listed next to a date about a month after her birthday. "Why, this is me! But Mr. North said he did not find my records."

"Well, I guess he did not find you because he, or someone else, did not want you to be found."

"But he started searching for these before I even spoke with Peter Clark. It makes no sense."

Betsy smirked. "Do you still want to return this paper to the vestry?"

With a roll of her eyes, Cassandra took the paper and tucked it in her pocket.

Betsy covered the basket again. "I thought you might feel that way."

Chapter 37

When Cassandra and Rachel returned to Briarton, the sun was just starting its descent over the trees. The temperature was dropping, and the wind pressed hard against the side of the carriage. It would rain soon, and Cassandra would be grateful to be back in the warmth and privacy of her chamber to peruse the paper Betsy had provided.

But for now, she tried to relax and enjoy this time with Rachel. They rarely had time to themselves without the younger girls. Rachel's company was effervescent, and it was good to see her blossoming.

"I had no idea that Mrs. Pearson could be so kind!" Rachel's face glowed bright as she recounted the day's activity. "And amusing. Did you know there were so many young ladies my age in the area? I thought I must surely be the only one. I am confident Mrs. Towler will not approve of them, but I truly don't care."

Cassandra could only smile as the young woman chatted on gleefully about the afternoon. She'd suspected that it would only take a few introductions and time out from under Mrs. Towler's watchful eye for Rachel to feel more settled.

After the carriage crossed the bridge and turned onto the road leading to the main house, Cassandra frowned. An unfamiliar carriage stood in the drive. It was not unusual for Mr. Warrington to have visitors, but most of them, especially those with mill business, would pull into the courtyard in the back.

Rachel leaned forward. "Who is that, I wonder?"

They drove past the carriage toward the courtyard, where they alighted the carriage.

Initially all seemed quiet, but then two maids scurried across the dirt ground, and one of the stable boys ran past. As they approached the house, Cassandra stopped one of the kitchen girls as she crossed the yard. "Whose carriage is that? What is going on?"

The young girl tightened her grip on a bundle of linens. "That carriage belongs to the surgeon. Mrs. Towler collapsed."

Cassandra winced and exchanged glances with Rachel. "Collapsed? How? When?"

But the girl did not respond. She scurried back inside.

Cassandra gripped Rachel's hand and together they ran in, not even pausing to shed their cloaks. They darted through the empty kitchen and the narrow, paneled corridors until they finally encountered Mrs. Helock pacing at the foot of the great staircase.

"Is Mrs. Towler all right?" Cassandra gasped, reaching out to take Mrs. Helock's hand in her own. "What has happened?"

The housekeeper stopped and fixed her gaze on Cassandra. The sadness in her red-rimmed eyes shifted to haughtiness, and she tipped her chin and jerked her hand free. "Clearly the recent happenings in this house have been too much for Mrs. Towler to bear. The surgeon suspects her heart."

Cassandra ignored the thinly veiled insinuation that her presence contributed to the episode. She could not focus on that now. Mrs. Helock turned to leave, and Cassandra called, "And the children? Where are they?"

Mrs. Helock paused dramatically and turned to face her once again. "As the governess, should you not know that?"

Annoyed, Cassandra dropped her shoulders. "Will you just tell me where they are so I may go to them?"

"Miss Maria and Miss Rose are in the nursery."

Cassandra hurried up to the nursery to assess the situation. She'd left the girls in Mrs. Towler's care, but now they were with one of the maids. After instructing Rachel to sit with her nieces, Cassandra discarded her cloak and made her way to the family's sleeping chambers.

The door to Mrs. Towler's bedchamber was ajar. Cassandra peered inside.

Mr. Warrington was sitting in a chair near the fire. His side was to her. His elbows were on his knees, and his head was in his hands. He wore a striped waistcoat over his linen shirt but no coat. His sleeves were rolled up to his elbows. His boots still had mud on them, suggesting he had been caught by surprise by Mrs. Towler's condition when he returned home as well.

She angled her head to look in farther.

Sure enough, Mrs. Towler was in the bed. She appeared to be sleeping, but Cassandra knew it was more than that. The man she assumed to be the surgeon was seated at the side of the bed.

She hesitated. Perhaps she was overstepping her bounds by being present. Mrs. Towler did not care for her, that was certain, and despite their interactions, Mr. Warrington was still her employer. But as she watched him sitting there, her heart tore.

Surely now, after all they had experienced together, her presence would be welcome.

She entered the chamber. Mr. Warrington lifted his head at the sound.

For the first time since she had known him, he appeared tired. Worn. "Have you heard?"

She nodded, and without waiting for an invitation, she inched forward and sat in the chair opposite him. She leaned toward him and kept her voice low so as not to disturb the surgeon. "What is it?"

"She had an episode. Her heart." Mr. Warrington sat upright and settled against the back of the chair. "He's certain."

Cassandra's chest tightened. "Will she recover?"

"He doesn't know." He forced his fingers through his sandy hair. "I don't know how the girls would handle another loss."

"Let's pray it does not come to that." Cassandra swallowed the dry lump forming in her throat and then looked back toward the sickbed. Memories of the pain of sitting at Mrs. Denton's side enveloped her—the anger, the sadness, the sense of betrayal. It all seemed so distant now, as if it had happened in a nightmare. She felt as helpless now as she had felt then. "I wish there was something I could do."

"There is," he said. "Sit here. With me."

Sit with him?

Simple as his entreaty was, it was not the sort of request an employer should make of his governess.

Yet what about their interactions had fallen into any semblance of normalcy?

She looked down at his hands as they sat across from each other. His fingers were laced before him. How she wanted to reach out and cover those hands with her own. She could no longer deny the truth. Her feelings for him were growing in both depth and intensity. She didn't care what Mr. North—or anyone—thought of him.

Even now, she could still feel the softness of his finger lingering on her cheek from their previous moments together. She wanted to be there again in that feeling of intimacy and closeness, of attentiveness and solidarity.

Did he think of it too?

The chances of a woman like her and a man like him having a personal relationship was so improbable. Even to find a match with a man like Mr. North was far-fetched for her.

She was an illegitimate, poor governess.

Dare she even let her thoughts drift there?

Or if she did follow her heart in such a manner, would she end up dispossessed like her mother?

She remained seated with him until after the surgeon left and all was still once again.

"I should like to help, if I can," offered Cassandra as they sat in the quiet chamber. "I'm happy to sit here and do whatever is necessary. Does she have any family that should be notified? Any other children?"

"No. The girls and I are the only family she has, other than a distant cousin." He folded his arms and looked toward his mother-in-law. A storm brewed in his gray eyes. His jaw clenched, then released. "My last conversation with her was an argument."

She had no doubt what the argument with Mrs. Towler must have been about. Her.

"I understand how that feels. I do." Cassandra tempered her voice. "I've shared with you that Mrs. Denton was like a mother to me, but what I didn't tell you was that she waited until she was on her deathbed before she told me the truth about my past. All along she knew who my parents were. She said her silence on the matter had been to protect me, but in my final hours with her, I felt so betrayed. My last words to her were spoken in anger. How I regret it."

He nodded. "It's no secret that Mrs. Towler and I have not always seen eye to eye. We never have. Even before Elizabeth and I were married. She thought my background unbecoming for her daughter. She probably was right. But if something should happen I would hate to think our last conversation was one in which we were both so livid. And to think her state of mind might have contributed toward . . ."

"You can't think that way. You mustn't. Nothing you did, or didn't do, contributed to her current state."

He stood and stepped closer to the bed, increasing the distance between them. "Elizabeth would have been devastated by this. She adored her mother."

Cassandra stiffened. She did not know much of love between a child and her mother. But she did know what her relationship with Mrs. Denton had been like. "Mrs. Denton knew I was furious that final night. But she also knew I loved her and respected her, and ultimately, nothing she could say to me would change that. I'm sure Mrs. Towler knows that even though you might not have the most cordial relationship, you respect her. It's evident to those around you."

"I hope so. How did life get so complicated?"

She managed a small laugh. "I ask myself that question nearly every day."

He sobered again, his expression distant, as if the day's events had opened a door to the past, allowing memories to stream in afresh. "I was not there the night my wife died. But Mrs. Towler was."

He stared straight ahead as he spoke the words. "Mrs. Towler was the one who comforted Elizabeth in the end. Knowing that Elizabeth was not alone in her final hours—for that I will always be grateful."

Cassandra remained quiet, sensing his need to share.

"I was only supposed to be gone for a few days, you know. I had traveled to Yorkshire, of all places. But the weather had changed and the roads to return home were impassable. I didn't even know she'd been sick until I'd arrived back in Plymouth. By then it was too late. She was already gone. And now we're here. And it seems like a version of it is happening all over again."

His shell was falling away. With every word, with every memory he shared with her, their bond was deepening. She couldn't care less about convention. He'd experienced loss. It was a different kind of loss than hers, but she could understand the pain.

She resisted the magnetic urge to draw nearer to him—to rest her hand on his arm in comfort. Instead, she tilted her head to the side and was about to speak when the door opened and Mrs. Helock appeared.

Sarah E. Ladd

Cassandra straightened. She could only imagine what this must look like, Mr. Warrington and her engaged in hushed conversation.

But then again, perhaps it was exactly what it looked like.

Mrs. Helock swept in with a fresh candle and set it atop a table. "Thank you for staying with her, Mr. Warrington. I've arranged things in the kitchen for the time being. I'm happy to sit with her now."

He nodded and looked down to Mrs. Towler's still form. "Very well. I'll be back to check on her soon."

Mrs. Helock turned to Cassandra. "No need for you to remain either. I've got things quite in hand."

"I don't doubt it, Mrs. Helock. But you can't stay here indefinitely by yourself. I will come by in a few hours and take your place so you can get some rest."

At first Mrs. Helock's eyes flashed with indignation. But then her expression softened to one Cassandra had never seen before. Was it sadness? Exhaustion? Defeat?

Cassandra did not wait for a response before she followed Mr. Warrington from the room to the small landing just outside.

They paused in the shadowed corridor, next to a bay window that framed the courtyard below as dusk was falling. As he turned to face her, he ran his hand down his face, scratched his fingers through his hair, then shook his head. "I'm sorry. I've said more than I ought. I'm afraid I put you in an awkward situation."

"No, no. I—I'm glad you did. I'm glad to know more about you. About your family."

He appeared almost nervous. "With everything happening I forgot to ask you how your day with Rachel was."

"I think she enjoyed herself. It was good for her to be around other women closer to her age. She's social by nature."

"And you? How did you enjoy the day?"

She hesitated. "I hate to bring it up to you in light of what is happening."

"A diversion, Miss Hale, would be very much appreciated."

She retrieved the folded vellum from the pocket in her gown. "Something happened. That is, something was found, and I am not sure what to make of it."

His brows drew together. "What is it?"

"Here." She unfolded the paper and extended it, pointing to her name. "See? That's me. It has to be. 1787. That is the year I was born."

He turned the paper over. "This has been ripped out of the record book, hasn't it?"

"It appears to have been."

"Where did you find this?"

"Betsy came across it in the church vestry. At the bottom of a closed drawer of all places. She shouldn't have been searching there, but her intentions were to help. Who would do this?"

He folded it and returned it to her. "Clearly someone who doesn't want your identity confirmed."

"But Mr. North checked days after I arrived in Anston. So it was before anyone, even Peter Clark, would have known I was here."

Mr. Warrington raised a blond brow.

There was only one way to interpret his expression. "What—you think Mr. North tore it out?"

Mr. Warrington drew a deep breath. "He does have access to these sorts of things."

Silence hovered awkwardly between them in the darkened corridor.

"May I be blunt?" he blurted suddenly, almost forcefully, as if the words he was about to speak could no longer be withheld. "It's obvious that Mr. North is taken with you. His intentions are glaringly evident, and not a soul could question him on that count. After all, you are, well . . ." His words faded and he cleared his throat, as if changing his tactic. "Of course he'd find you charming. But think for a moment. What if he was already aware of your inheritance when he arrived? He said himself that people tell him things. Maybe he has reasons to keep you from knowing the truth. I, of course, don't have the answers or any evidence as such, merely an observation."

Cassandra bit her lower lip. Firmly. In the space of two hours, each man had warned her of the other. She'd considered Mr. North a bit conceited and arrogant perhaps, but deviant?

And yet, the confident set of Mr. Warrington's jaw challenged that thought.

His tone lowered. "I would hate to see you taken advantage of, by anyone."

"I've made my way so far alone," she said proudly. "You needn't worry about me."

"I know. You have your dagger." His tease lightened the mood only slightly until the directness of his words refocused them. "What I mean is that I've grown very fond of you. I think you and I share similar thoughts. Perhaps similar views of the world."

At this, she could only stare.

Did he know how his words were affecting her?

"But then again"—his tone darkened—"perhaps now is not the time to talk of such things."

Not ready for their conversation to end, she nodded, battling disappointment.

After they bid a rather solemn farewell, Cassandra returned to the nursery. As she did, Mr. Warrington's steps echoed in retreat in the opposite direction. She was not exactly sure what had transpired between them, but one thing was certain: not only did she have to worry about her future, but now she had to guard her heart.

Chapter 38

The next morning, Cassandra awoke with a start.

She immediately winced and rubbed the crick in her neck, stretched, and glanced around the sick chamber. Around midnight she had relieved Mrs. Helock of sitting with Mrs. Towler, and apparently sometime during the midnight hours she'd fallen asleep.

Cassandra stood, tightened her shawl around her shoulders, and crossed over to Mrs. Towler's bed. A gentle, bright glow from the early sun filtered through the filmy curtains, and the fire simmered in the grate. Mrs. Towler appeared as she had the night before. Her chest rose and fell evenly with her breathing, but her skin was even paler than normal. Cassandra sat next to her on the bed and, unsure of what else she should do, took one of Mrs. Towler's limp hands in her own, just as she had many weeks prior with Mrs. Denton.

As much as she tried to fight it, at the sight of Mrs. Towler she was transported back to Mrs. Denton's final days. Their illnesses were quite different, and yet there were so many similarities in the way the events transpired. Cassandra understood this woman did not like her and did not approve of her. In fact, Cassandra was probably the last person Mrs. Towler would want sitting with her. But perhaps this would be a turning point for them both. Cassandra wished she had handled her final hours with Mrs. Denton differently. Perhaps now was the chance to change the tide with Mrs. Towler.

Approaching footsteps sounded in the corridor, and Cassandra turned to see Mrs. Helock in the doorway holding a tray.

"She hasn't woken yet." Cassandra shook off her own sleepiness and nodded toward the tray. "I don't think she will take anything."

"This isn't for Mrs. Towler," the housekeeper said. "This is for you."

Surprised, Cassandra looked at the tray of tea, bread, and jam. "For me?"

"You've been kind to sit with her." Mrs. Helock set the tray at the end of the bed and moved to the other side to adjust the blankets.

Shocked by the change in the woman's attitude toward her, Cassandra studied her from the corner of her eye. Mrs. Helock had been crying. A handkerchief was tucked haphazardly in her sleeve, and she was still dressed in her wrinkled muslin gown from the previous day.

Despite the coldness Mrs. Helock had shown her, Cassandra's heart went out to her. After all, she knew what it was like to be at the bedside of a loved one, not knowing what the outcome would be. She wanted to be a comfort. "You two seem as if you are very close."

Mrs. Helock nodded. "I've been with her since I was a girl myself. I was a chambermaid when she was not much older than you, and I eventually became her housekeeper when she married Mr. Towler."

"This has to be quite difficult for you then." She motioned for the woman to draw closer. "Why don't you sit down? Surely you could use a rest."

Mrs. Helock hesitated and then sat tentatively on the other side of the bed. She took Mrs. Towler's other hand in hers and sniffed. "She's scared. She might not admit it, but I know it to be true. That's why she's been so opposed to you being here."

"Why is she scared?"

Mrs. Helock smoothed the ruffle on Mrs. Towler's sleeve and sighed. "She was scared that you'd come in and change everything. Take her place. Take her Elizabeth's place. She didn't say so exactly, but I know her so well. Fear takes on many faces, you know."

Cassandra looked down again to the ill woman. It made sense, in a way. Did she not know what it was to fear the unknown? "I have no desire to take anyone's place. I only want to find a bit of security, if that's even possible. I'm quite fond of this family. I would not hurt it or try to push anyone away for the world."

They sat in silence before Mrs. Helock cleared her throat. "I think I owe you an apology."

Cassandra recoiled. "Me?"

"In my defense of Mrs. Towler, I'm afraid I've acted unkindly. You've been good to the girls, and very good to sit up with Mrs. Towler. I was wrong."

There was more motion at the door, and Cassandra looked up to see Rachel standing in the threshold. She was still clad in her linen nightdress and wrapped with a heavy wool shawl. Her unruly curls were bound in a single thick plait, and she was pale. Very pale.

Cassandra stood from her spot on the bed and moved toward the young woman.

"Is she doing any better?" Rachel whispered so as not to be overheard by Mrs. Helock.

"I'm afraid there's no difference."

Tears filled Rachel's eyes. "Do you think she's going to die?"

"I don't know, Rachel." Cassandra put her arm around the girl's shoulders.

Rachel impatiently wiped a tear. "I've been so awful to her. All we do is argue. What if it is too late to apologize? It's all I've been able to think about."

Cassandra forced optimism to her voice. "I am sure she'll improve. We must pray that she does."

"If she gets better, I will be nicer to her." Rachel gave a decided nod.

Cassandra squeezed the girl's shoulders affectionately. "Sometimes it takes a tragedy to appreciate the things you have."

"But we've already had a tragedy. Isn't one enough?"

It was true. The entire Warrington family had experienced a tragedy in Elizabeth's loss. "I wish I had better answers for you, other than to say that everything you experience will make you stronger. More resilient."

As Cassandra left Mrs. Towler in the capable hands of Mrs. Helock, she returned to start her day with the girls. All through the morning the events of the past two days stayed with her. She had thought Mrs. Towler was harsh, but now Cassandra realized the woman might just be frightened of the future. She'd believed that Mrs. Helock did not like her, but it turned out her coolness came out of loyalty to another.

That night, James found Miss Hale in the parlor, alone.

He'd been looking for her ever since he returned from the mill. He needed to speak with her. He had tried to suppress his feelings until he was certain, but if the previous day's events had reminded him of anything, it was that time was not promised.

Was he ready to open himself up like this again? To imagine a life with another woman? And yet, everything he had seen from her embodied the sort of ally he wanted in life. The role model he wanted for his daughters. The partner he wanted for himself.

Yes, he was ready. Renewed enthusiasm rushed through him as he entered the room. She looked up and started to stand from her position on the sofa, but he motioned for her to remain seated.

"Are the girls asleep?" he asked as he walked in farther.

"Yes, they are."

And then he saw the paper in her hand—the record of her baptism.

Without another word he sat next to her on the sofa and took the document from her hand.

She did not move away from him. If anything, she seemed drawn to him.

He could feel her warmth, her nearness. He could also sense the frustration and sadness emanating from her. "I've been thinking about this. About you. With your permission I am going to ride out to Shepard and share this with him tomorrow. Someone wanted your identity concealed, even before Longham arrived. Shepard needs to know. I don't believe Longham's death was connected in any way with the mill violence. A random laborer would not have the forethought or access to make this page disappear from the registry or to steal Longham's documents. This assault cannot be lumped into the attacks on mill owners, and that's what Shepard was doing with the recent arrest he made. Someone knew exactly what they were doing when Longham was killed and had a specific motive."

For some reason he'd expected her to share his enthusiasm, to share in the urgency that this was the correct step. But she did not respond right away. She pushed herself off the sofa, stood, and paced the narrow space.

"If this is indeed connected to Mr. Longham's murder, then yes, Mr. Shepard needs to know. But as far as my identity is concerned, I'm not sure it even matters at this point. Everyone knows now. My father's dead. I'm to be a stranger to my mother. I'm illegitimate. And you know how people talk."

He set the paper on the sofa and stood. He wanted to erase her uncertainty on this matter. But how? It would be easy, simple, to take her in his arms and hold her until her doubts subsided, but he had no idea if she would be receptive of his touch. Instead, he asked, "Do you think it matters to me?"

He stepped even closer, until she was just inches from him.

He could feel her uncertainty. Her questions.

Her gaze did not leave his as she whispered, "Does it?"

In a moment of impassioned determination, he reached out to grip her soft, trembling hand in his. At the touch, fire ignited. He felt it with every fiber of his being. She had to feel it too. "It would probably make a lot of things easier if it did, but the truth is, I care very much about you, regardless of where you are from or who your parents are."

She looked down at their joined hands and remained silent.

He'd already said too much to turn back. Eagerness surged, and he drew nearer. "I tell you this with no expectation, but I can't deny my feelings grow stronger each time I see you. I know you have other things pressing on your mind, but I—"

"Yes, there are other things on my mind," she interrupted, flicking her gaze up to him.

He steeled himself, waiting.

Then her expression softened. Her shoulders eased. "But you are in my thoughts too. Of course you are. How could you not be?"

She closed the space between them even more. Her fingers entwined with his. "I can't explain it, and I don't know how it happened. But somehow between all of the things that have transpired, you have steadied me. But what if we find out something even worse? I don't want you to feel—"

"Cassandra."

The use of her Christian name silenced her.

"Please let me be very clear," he continued, his voice barely above a whisper, his eyes locked with hers. "None of that matters to me. Not a bit of it. I never thought I'd feel this way again, and now that I do, nothing will stand in the way of it."

She quickly diverted her gaze again to their hands.

He reached out to cup her chin and gently lifted her face to meet his gaze. "I promise you, Cassandra Hale, I will be by your side through all of this, if you will allow me. And then for every day after that."

And then he kissed her, sweetly, gently, until she wrapped her arms around his neck and returned the kiss.

Chapter 39

The next morning passed quickly for Cassandra as if nothing was amiss or different.

She ate breakfast with the girls. They dressed for the day, read their stories, practiced embroidery, and worked on their sums.

But the day was far from ordinary.

For the girls, their grandmother was sick in the other room and unresponsive. Cassandra tried her best to distract and encourage her young charges, but their sadness and the situation's uncertainty shadowed every hour.

As heavy as the situation with Mrs. Towler seemed, Cassandra's heart soared with the secret she and James shared.

He cared for her.

He'd held her. Kissed her.

And for the time being, the knowledge of it was theirs alone.

But with every flutter of her heart, another thought rushed her: Was that how it had started with her mother and father? Stolen kisses in the parlor?

During the late-afternoon hours, as the girls worked on their painting, a knock sounded at the nursery door.

One of the kitchen maids stood at the threshold. "There's a woman to see you downstairs."

"To see me?" Surprised, Cassandra stood from where she was sitting and shook out the folds of her skirt. "Who is it?"

The maid shrugged. "She wouldn't give me her name."

Cassandra instructed the maid to wait with the girls and made her way down the staircase, through the hall. She rounded the corner to see Mary Smith standing just inside the corridor.

Cassandra stopped short, shocked into silence.

A gypsy straw bonnet was atop Mrs. Smith's head, and a dark blue shawl caped her shoulders. Her expression was much softer than when they had first met. Even so, Mrs. Smith fixed her cognac eyes on Cassandra and gripped her shawl fiercely. "I know I have no right to come here after how I spoke to you, but I was hoping to speak with you again. Alone."

With her doubts—and curiosity—quaking within her, Cassandra nodded and led the way to a small parlor off the great hall. Once they were inside, Cassandra closed the door for privacy. "We can speak in here."

Her mother lifted her gaze to the plaster ceiling and then stroked her fingertips along the flowered wallpaper. "So many memories in this house."

Still not sure what to say or how to account for the woman's change in disposition, Cassandra motioned to one of the sofas, and together they were seated.

"How is Mr. Smith?" Cassandra asked, trying to make sense of the visit.

"He's better, praise be. Doctor says he'll be good as new in time. And I thank ye for the inquiry, but he's not why I'm here." Her mother drew a deep breath, folded her worn hands on her lap, and jutted her chin upward. "I must apologize."

Cassandra shook her head, resisting the urge to shrink under the directness of the statement. Their last interaction had inflicted so much uneasiness that she was not sure how to interpret the words.

She eyed her cautiously. "There is nothing for which to apologize. I shouldn't have—"

"Please." Her mother placed her hand over Cassandra's, silencing her. "Let me speak, else I might not say it at all."

Cassandra bit her lip and looked at her mother. Really looked at her.

How different she looked by the light of day. The ample afternoon white light spilled through the room's tall windows and highlighted the mahogany strands in her hair, which closely resembled the color of her own.

Her mother took Cassandra's hand in both of hers. "I haven't been able to stop thinkin' 'bout what I said to ye. How I said it."

Eager to make her mother feel more comfortable, Cassandra said, "My presence was a shock, and you were under duress."

"Doesn't matter. I gave the impression that I never thought of ye. That was not true. I've always wondered about ye. Where ye were. What ye were doin'. What ye looked like. If ye were happy." Her voice grew raspy, and she cleared her throat. "I've three boys now. But you—you're my only daughter. It has haunted me. All these years."

Cassandra remained silent as the meaning behind the words soaked into her heart. Her mind.

"Robert Clark was a mighty influential man. Intimidatin' man. Ye must know I had no choice but to leave ye wit' 'im. I didn't want it, but it was how it had to be." A sob broke her words. "I hope ye can understand that, an' forgive me."

Cassandra knew how quickly such events could change a life. How it could have happened with her and Frederick, or Rachel and Mr. Standish. "Honestly, I do understand."

"And I also want to tell ye that not a day goes by that I don't regret not having fought harder. But I was so young. And he was so . . ."

Her words faded, and Cassandra placed her other hand over

her mother's. A powerful desire to soothe the pain this woman had evidently experienced seized control. "I can only imagine what an impossible situation that was for you."

A tear escaped down her mother's aging cheek, and she impatiently wiped it away. "Look at me, fussin' on. I was wrong when I said I wanted nothin' to do with ye. It was grief talkin'. I hope we can be friends at least. I'd like to know ye, if you'd allow me."

Excitement began to surge through her. "There is so much I want to ask you."

"I told me husband about you," she blurted. "The guilt of lyin' ev'ry day caught up with me."

Startled, Cassandra winced. "What did he say?"

"I should have waited until he was stronger, and I ain't ever seen him angrier, but he's a proud man. A good man. But he deserved the truth, didn't he? I've lied a long time, and 'tis a stranglin' weight to bear. I got to thinkin' how hard this must be on you—to come to a new place. But I see ye doing well for yourself. A governess in such a house." She gazed around the room. "I wish you more happiness here than I had."

Cassandra's heart leapt again at the memory of the moment she had shared with James the previous evening. "Were you not happy here? I wasn't sure, because . . ."

"If ye are askin' if I loved your father, then the answer is no." She withdrew her hands and folded them in her lap. "He took advantage, and that's that."

Mary Smith sniffed, signaling the end of the topic.

So it had not been a relationship of passion or love.

Eager to learn more, Cassandra straightened. "Have you ever met Peter Clark?"

"No, ain't ever met him, but I saw him once. Looks somewhat akin to his father, he does. Does he know about you? About how you're related?"

Cassandra nodded. "Mr. Longham and I met with him, but he doesn't believe either of us. He thinks I am only trying to get the inheritance."

"I've heard about the inheritance. Word travels fast, and of course, Mrs. Hutton knew of it an' she also told me what had happened to Mr. Longham and his papers and such."

"The challenge now is proving my identity. But if you and Mrs. Hutton could be persuaded to speak for me, that would be a start. Plus, this was found in the church." Cassandra retrieved the slip of paper from her pocket and handed it to her mother.

"'Tis the baptism registry," her mother exclaimed.

"You know it?"

"Yes. My name is there, see? Along with yours. Notice no father was listed, or any other details. Mr. Clark insisted you be baptized but refused to have his name registered. I wasn't even allowed to witness it. He paid the vicar off to keep it all very quiet. They were chummy, of course."

Cassandra tilted her head to the side as a thought struck her. "The vicar was his friend?"

"Yes, their families went way back. The vicar was always here for some reason or t'other."

Cassandra searched her memory. Did Mrs. Kent not say the vicar back then was Mr. North's uncle? And he had a wife?

Cassandra furrowed her brow in thought. "There's no signature from the officiant who performed my baptism, but there are various signatures with the other names. Do you remember the officiant who conducted it?"

"I do."

Cassandra recalled the name of the vicar Mrs. Kent had given her. "Did this vicar have a wife?"

"Yes, he did. A pretty wife. Name of Alice Stricklin, if I'm not mistaken."

"Stricklin?" The name flew from Cassandra's mouth as recognition flared. "Edward Stricklin?"

"Yes. I think so."

Suddenly, Cassandra's mind raced to map all of the pieces together.

Mr. North's uncle.

Mr. North's tie to the will.

Mr. North's proximity to baptism records.

Mr. North's ability to manipulate situations.

Perhaps James's suspicion about his character was right all along.

"Stricklin, or his estate, was named in my father's will," Cassandra shared.

"Wouldn't doubt it. 'Twas said that the vicar had loaned money to Robert Clark."

"Mrs. Kent said that the living of the vicar had been passed down through the family," expressed Cassandra, trying to piece the information together. "I wonder if Mr. North would have any tie to the Stricklin estate."

"Don't know 'bout all that. But I do have something for ye. My pride shouldn't stand in the way of you claiming what's rightfully yours, an' when I heard the solicitor lost his papers, well, I thought this might help ye. Robert Clark owed you that much at least." She opened her bag, pulled out a piece of paper, and unfolded it.

Cassandra's hand flew to her mouth. Her breath caught in her throat. It was a copy of the custody agreement. The very same one Mr. Longham had possessed.

"I never told me husband, ye ken, and I'd made up me mind to forget ye. Even so, I could not bring myself to feed this t' the fire. I kept it hidden under the floorboards. Perhaps it will help you."

"And I have your permission to share this? With the magistrate? And the court?"

Mary Smith nodded.

"Why, this is wonderful!"

"I hope it will help ease things for ye."

Cassandra embraced her mother. "This makes all the difference in the world, truly. Thank you for sharing this with me."

As James returned home and crossed the great hall, Cassandra was on his mind.

Their kiss and the moments they shared the previous evening had complicated matters but also offered a fresh sense of hope. The very thought of her was a bright spot in the sea of darkness he'd found himself in, but he would be lying if he thought there was not a multitude of issues that would stand in their way.

He was on his way up to check on Mrs. Towler when the sound of muted feminine chatter echoed from the small parlor off the hall. Curious as to who it was, he made his way to the parlor door at the hall's edge and pushed it open.

Inside sat Cassandra and a woman.

Cassandra jumped to her feet as he entered. Happiness lit her face, and she strode toward him. "Mr. Warrington, this is my mother, Mrs. Smith."

The happiness on her face warmed him, and the other woman stood quickly at the introduction. He could see their similarities instantly. They were both petite women with narrow shoulders. The shape of their faces was nearly identical, and they both had large hazel eyes fringed with dark lashes. "Ah, Mrs. Smith. Welcome to Briarton Park."

The woman glanced toward Cassandra nervously before she spoke. "Thank you, sir."

Cassandra took her mother's arm. "Mr. Warrington knows of our situation. He's been very supportive of my search."

Mrs. Smith lifted her chin. "Well, I am glad to hear that a kind man is at the helm of Briarton Park. I lived here, I did, many years ago."

He could sense the emotion behind her words, and in effort to make her feel more comfortable, he said, "I imagine you could tell us a lot of stories about this house."

Her brows rose. "Indeed."

"Before he died, Mr. Longham said that secrets were hidden all over," he added, attempting to lighten the conversation. "Are you acquainted with them?"

Mrs. Smith nodded, but she did not seem pleased to revisit the memories. Instead, her nostrils flared slightly, and her lips tightened. "Mr. Longham was right. 'Tis an old house, with nooks and crannies e'erywhere. There's one in almost every room." She walked over to the wall between the windows and lifted a panel. "See?"

James started, and then he stepped to the perfectly hidden space that opened to a recess in the wall. He opened and closed the panel himself. "That's incredible."

"Mr. Clark was suspicious of everyone. He had a great many lies and went to extreme extents to keep 'em. He even built secret rooms. Not even his wife knew."

James exchanged a glance with Cassandra. "Mr. Longham told us about the hidden alcove in the wall in the study."

"Nah, that's naught but a storage area. I'm referrin' to secret chambers, large enough to stand in." Mrs. Smith tilted her head to the side. "Did Mr. Longham tell you 'bout the Tobacco Chamber?"

Heat was building beneath his cravat. He tugged at it in an attempt to release it. The sense that there was a secret in his own home, under his very nose, unnerved him. "No. He didn't."

She shook her head with an impatience that suggested the memory plagued her. "No one was supposed to know about it. It's a passageway, really. It goes under the ground t' the stables. When I was here, he told me 'bout it but made me swear to tell no one. I'll show you, if ye like."

With the authority that came with familiarity, Mrs. Smith led them from the parlor, through the great hall, down the corridor, and into the study. She moved toward the inner wall. "This is where most of his secrets were held, least when I was 'ere."

Mrs. Smith lifted a piece of trim work, which seemed to serve as a lock. Once it was free, the entire panel swung inward into a void.

Using the light from the fire, Mrs. Smith lit a candle, then a lantern, and then handed it to him.

Lifting the lantern, James stepped inside, illuminating several trunks and chests stacked along the narrow room.

She nodded to the chamber's far end. "If you follow this, it leads to a door in the floor of the stables."

James ran his finger along the dust atop the nearest trunk. Mrs. Smith was right. This must have been a closely held secret. And this one had been undisturbed. Undiscovered, until now.

"Thank you for sharing this with me, Mrs. Smith. I had no idea."

The mantel clock from the study struck the hour, and Mrs. Smith turned. "I must be goin'. My husband will be wonderin' where I am, and I must get supper on the table for me boys."

James bowed his farewell, and as the women exited the room, he returned his attention to the newly discovered spot. He had no doubt it held secrets, and he was about to find out what they were.

Chapter 40

James stood in the study, staring at the trunks stacked around the room.

Unbelievable.

He removed his coat, rolled up his lawn sleeves to just below his elbows, and lit several more candles. Night was falling, and he could not be happier for Cassandra. She'd appeared so joyous talking with her mother. He'd just returned from checking on Mrs. Towler, and now he was eager to dive in and see what secrets Robert Clark had left behind.

Sounds echoed in the hall, and he looked up from the trunk to see Cassandra standing in the doorway. A shawl was wrapped around her shoulders, and her chestnut hair fell gently around her face.

His motions slowed, and he straightened at the sight.

She was beautiful. If possible, she seemed to grow more alluring each time he saw her.

"Well." He put down the pile of papers he'd been reading. "This is a turn of events, isn't it?"

She shared a sweet, unguarded smile and a little laugh. "I don't believe it, really."

"What made your mother change her mind?" He veered around a trunk to get closer to her, eager to speak with her now that they were alone.

"She said she'd heard rumors about the inheritance and about Mr. Longham, and she didn't want to stand in the way of what was rightfully mine. She even told her husband about me. And look." She extended a piece of paper to him. "It's her copy of the custody agreement, signed by her, my father, and Mr. Longham."

"Well, this is extraordinary. It is what you wanted, isn't it? Answers? Family?" He reached out and set his hands on her shoulders encouragingly, but something was wrong. "So why don't you seem happy?"

"She told me something else that was alarming. I showed her the baptism record, and she told me that a vicar named Stricklin was the one who performed the baptism."

He failed to see the connection. "And?"

"According to the will, if I do not inherit the land within three years of my father's death, the land will pass to the estate of Mr. Stricklin, remember? It has to be the same man or, at the very least, the same family. She said my father and Mr. Stricklin were friends, and Mr. Longham had said something similar. But here is where it becomes concerning. Mrs. Kent told me that Mr. North's uncle was the vicar before him, and she even told me his wife's name. Alice. It makes me wonder if Mr. North really is in some way connected to either the will or even Mr. Longham's death. I can't quite put it together."

He exhaled deeply, considering everything she'd just said. Things were, in a way, starting to make sense. And this new information gave even more credence to the fact that North was somehow involved in this. The puzzle was not complete, but the pieces were there. They just had to solve it.

He studied her face to get a gauge on how she was feeling about it. "This must be disappointing to you. I know you are fond of Mr. North."

At this her eyes flashed up, and she stared at him for several seconds, as if trying to judge the meaning behind the statement. "I am fond of him, or rather, I was. He was a friend when I needed one, but now I see his motives might not have had friendship in mind. Oh, I just can't figure it out."

James needed to find out once and for all what her thoughts were on the man, without sounding like a jealous fool. "North was making his intentions quite known. Surely you saw it. I—I was afraid you might succumb to them."

"Succumb? To Vincent North?" she teased, and a hint of amusement flashed. "Perhaps I should have. I am penniless. Illegitimate. And at the center of a scandal. He'd be a fortunate man to have me."

He let out a soft, throaty laugh at her sarcasm and moved closer to her. "He's not the only man who finds you intriguing. Take me, for instance. I can barely look away from you."

At this, her smile faded. She sobered.

He took her hands in his, and she peered up at him with those wide, trusting eyes—eyes that made him forget some of the past's pain and anticipate what lay ahead. "I hope you will forget North once and for all. And think of a future with me."

She allowed him to draw her into an embrace. He rubbed his hands up and down her arms. She rested her head against his chest, and he held her for several moments, until she looked up at him. "Do you suppose one day everything will be easy? Everyone will be well and happy?"

"I don't know. I hope so." He laced his fingers through hers and kissed her hand, then pulled her even closer. "But with you here beside me, I feel happy, and I haven't felt happy like this in a long time."

He wanted her to agree, to say she felt the same way, but she stiffened. And pulled away slightly.

"What?" He flinched at the change in her demeanor. "What is it?"

"When you say things like that . . ." Her voice faded, and she averted her gaze.

"Like what?" He frowned, not sure what had upset her. "Tell me. I really don't know."

She gave a nervous little laugh. "Do you not see the similarities?"

He shook his head. "What similarities?"

She took a step backward. "I'm governess here. My mother was employed by Briarton Park too. It was messy. Complicated. And disastrous."

His eyes narrowed as the meaning of her explanation sank in. "Cassandra, I'm not like Robert Clark. I would never treat a woman the way he treated your mother. Surely you can't think—"

"No, I know that." She shook her head emphatically. "It's only that I'm frightened, I suppose. Last night . . ." Her voice faltered. "I'm frightened of what comes next. Frightened of getting hurt in a way from which I can't recover."

James could understand the fear of pain. He could also understand the vulnerability she must feel in her current situation. And the betrayals she'd felt by the headmistress, Mr. North, and also the young man Rachel told him about.

"Rachel told me that you had an experience similar to hers when you were younger. With a young man. Cassandra, I know what it is like to experience the anguish of a lost love." He closed the space that she had created. "I never want to feel that again. But I also don't want to be without love."

At the word *love*, she tensed. "But if this all goes wrong—"

"But what if it doesn't go wrong?" He brushed her hair away from her forehead. "We can't wait to see what comes next in order to be happy. Oh, Cassandra. So much time has passed. We have to find our happiness. Create it. And I want to do just that. With you."

Something akin to relief softened her expression, and she melted against him once more. He pulled her closer, feeling her softness. Her gentleness. He wanted her to trust him, really trust him, and in that moment, he believed she did. He tilted her chin up and claimed her mouth with his.

"Emotions will cloud your judgment and weaken your ability to react rationally."

The statement repeated over and over in Cassandra's mind.

Yes, there was truth to it, but it would no longer be a truth that defined her. The emotions that Mrs. Denton had so tried to steer her away from refused to be ignored. But now, instead of melancholy, she was happy. And she would allow that emotion to guide her.

Her mother wanted to know her.

James had declared his feelings for her.

And she trusted him.

She scurried about her evening duties, checking on Mrs. Towler, seeing to dinner, and getting the girls to bed, until she was free to rejoin James in his study. Candles lit the entire space, and he'd pulled out several trunks and crates. Papers were stacked around the room, covering nearly every surface.

How tempting he looked in the candlelight.

It was hard not to notice or even to focus on anything else. His coat was removed, and he wore a blue waistcoat, and his shirtsleeves were rolled up to his elbows. His fawn-colored hair was tousled and careless, and curiosity brightened his expression.

He'd not yet noticed her, so she tapped her fingers on the door. "The girls are asleep. Mrs. Helock is with Mrs. Towler." She stepped in farther. "It appears you've been busy. Have you found anything of interest?"

"Nothing as of yet, but this Clark fellow was a stickler for records." He lifted a stack of folded papers from the top of the desk. "Look at these. Letters. Ledgers. He kept everything. There are several stacks having to do with the mills, but from the looks of it, he had a propensity for cards."

She lifted a portfolio and flipped open the cover. "I do wish I could have known him. Did you know your father well?"

"I did. Very well." James straightened and lowered the paper he was holding to the stack. "But there were times we did not see eye to eye. We were quite poor when I was growing up. After my mother died, my father sold our house and we lived in the countinghouse at the mill. When he married Rachel's mother, that was when I left the family mill and relocated to Plymouth. It wasn't until then that we were able to prosper a bit."

She felt quite proud of James. Having built himself up from nothing. Maybe he was right. Maybe that was why her background did not matter to him.

The next couple of hours were spent searching through the paperwork left behind by Mr. Clark. Papers that dated as far back as his childhood were included among them, and it was like getting a glimpse into the life of the man who'd had such a profound influence on her life, even though she never knew him.

Suddenly James called to her, "Cassandra, come look at this."

She hurried to his side and looked over his arm at an open portfolio. He pointed to a number, and then she saw it.

A transaction sheet.

With *Denton School for Young Ladies* written across the top.

Excitement welled within her as they slid the entire contents of the portfolio out onto the desk. Letters and ledgers tumbled out. She recognized Mrs. Denton's handwriting immediately. Hungry to receive all the information at once, she shuffled through the papers, eager for her next discovery.

And then she saw it. Her father's copy of the custody agreement. Overwhelming relief rushed her. "Now we have both my mother's and father's copies of the paperwork."

Laughing, she turned to him. "This is wonderful! Oh, James, it is all here. Every bit of it."

She sat down with the letters, several of which were written by Mrs. Denton. The writing style was so familiar. They were full of insights on her life—on Cassandra's personality and upbringing. On how she was doing with her studies and with the other girls. It was a year-by-year account, from her earliest days.

In that glimmer of a moment she could see past Mrs. Denton's betrayal. Past the heartache. For these letters described their relationship. These letters told the story of what the woman really thought of her.

"It's like looking into my life," Cassandra exclaimed as she shuffled through the letters. "And to think she was protecting me. Her sister. Even herself. Oh, how I wish I could apologize to her."

"If she knows you as well as you think she did, then she would understand."

"I know, but it's heartbreaking. She meant so much to me, and I will never be able to tell her."

"That's the sort of thing that people who know each other well just know. She knew you loved her. And judging by these letters, the sentiment was returned."

Chapter 41

James studied Shepard's face as he picked up each individual piece of paperwork—the signed custody agreement, the ledgers of school payments, the baptism record—and read them. "Well? What do you think?"

Shepard clicked his tongue and chortled. "I don't think Peter Clark will be very happy about this."

"I don't think so either, but based on all of this documentation, Miss Hale is unquestionably the woman named in Robert Clark's will," commented James as he uncorked the decanter to pour his guest a drink. "There has to be a connection with Longham's death. There's too much overlap, and I'm guessing that whoever killed Longham knew he possessed the documents and wanted to prevent him from pursuing this in court. And that's why they were stolen from the murder site."

Shepard looked toward Cassandra and pointed a thumb in James's direction. "Do you agree with his assessment?"

Cassandra, who had been waiting quietly as James explained the situation to the magistrate, nodded eagerly. "I do."

Shepard accepted the glass from James and settled back in his chair. "Very well, Warrington. You clearly have someone in mind. It's written all over your face. Out with it then."

James licked his lips and forged ahead. "Initially I believed Peter Clark to be involved. We all know his temper. But then, when Miss Hale found the baptismal record, I realized it could not be him. He did not even know Miss Hale was his half sister until after she had begun searching for the records."

"So then, who do you think it is? Who is our murderer?"

"Vincent North."

Shepard scoffed incredulously, his already ruddy face pinkening further with amusement. "What, the vicar in Anston?"

James stood from his chair. "Miss Hale, perhaps you should tell him what Mrs. Kent told you."

Cassandra turned to face the magistrate. "Mrs. Kent confided that Mr. North's uncle was the vicar before him, and Mr. North took over the office when he died. My mother told me that the vicar who had baptized me was named Edward Stricklin—the same vicar who had once loaned my father a great sum of money and who was named in the will. These men are related, Mr. Shepard. Mr. North is Mr. Stricklin's nephew."

Shepard rubbed his chin. "Yes, I'd forgotten that the vicars had been family."

"I think Mr. North knew about the will and stands to gain if Miss Hale doesn't inherit, so he is the one who tore the page from the record but did not destroy it in case he needed it at a later date. I also think he knew that Longham had paperwork to support Miss Hale's claims and would do anything to keep it quiet."

"Even kill the man?" prompted Shepard.

James leaned forward with his fists against the desktop and fixed his gaze on Shepard. "The land in question is very valuable. It depends on how far he would go to possess it."

Shepard crossed the room and pushed the door to the Tobacco Chamber open once more and peered inside. He shuffled through some papers and opened a trunk, then turned again to James. "You do realize what you are saying, Warrington? What you're accusing him of?"

James set his lips firmly before speaking. "He knows more than he's letting on, Shepard. We need to find out what that is."

"Very well." The magistrate placed his empty glass on the table. "I think I'll go have a little chat with North."

"I'll go with you." James stepped around from behind the desk.

"And I should go as well," Cassandra chimed in.

Both men looked to her as if they had almost forgotten she was there.

"What?" She jutted her chin upward. "Why are you staring at me like that?"

Mr. Shepard guffawed. "This is no task for a woman."

"But it involved me." She skirted the chair and drew closer. "I can offer assistance. I've talked with Mr. North since the day I arrived, and I—"

"Absolutely not." Shepard jammed his beaver hat atop his auburn head. "Warrington? You coming?" Without waiting for a response from either of them, Shepard stomped out of the room, leaving them alone.

"I want to go," she whispered, rushing toward him, her golden eyes determined and pleading.

James reached forward and squeezed her hand. "It's best if you stay here. Let me do this for you. It will be easier if I know you are safe."

He squeezed her hand once more, and then he followed the magistrate outside into the night.

A heavy early winter mist cloaked the forests of Briarton Park as James and Shepard made their way to the vicarage. The hour was late—not a single soul traversed the bridge or trod the high street. Even the Green Ox Inn seemed deserted. The occasional whip of wind through the tree branches or an owl's bereft cry would pierce the eerie silence, but otherwise, all was still.

Their steps slowed as the vicarage came into view. Firelight flickered from behind drawn curtains. Even in the night's darkness, smoke ascended from the chimney.

Once at the front door, Shepard lifted his heavy gloved hand and pounded it against the wooden door.

After several seconds, no response came.

Shepard knocked again. He waited for several seconds and then jiggled the brass knob.

It was locked.

Shepard motioned for James to follow him on the path leading to the kitchen entrance. When another knock went unanswered, Shepard tried the door, and it swung open freely. Inside, a fire simmered in the grate, and candles lit the space. "North!" he bellowed. "You here?"

They waited in silence, but nothing moved until a large brown cat sauntered through the kitchen, taking no notice of them.

"Mrs. Pearson?" called James.

And again, no response.

"Come on," Shepard instructed.

James followed in through the kitchen to the parlor. Something was untoward about the state of this house. Too many candles burned. Too many items were casually scattered about in hapless abandon. It appeared that someone had been here quite recently. Or possibly was here still.

They continued through the empty parlor and through the empty dining room until they reached a space that had to be his study. It, too, was lit by candlelight, and yet there was no sign of anyone at home.

North's modest study consisted of a small desk and a narrow wardrobe chest, two crowded bookshelves, and a chest under the window. The clock on the mantel ticked away the seconds, the minutes, as the men shuffled through letters and books, drawers and chests, shelves and stacks.

They were about to give up their search when Shepard's foot caught on the rug. It slid aside, revealing a mismatched section of the wood floor. He kicked the rug aside and leaned down to touch the disparate floorboard. It lifted out, revealing a small hole brimming with letters and a few small boxes.

"Ha, ha! What have we here?" Shepard lifted the bound letters by the ribbon securing them and handed the stack to James. "Start reading."

James untied the letters and opened one.

"They're from an Alice Stricklin. Sound familiar?"

"That was his aunt, the late vicar's wife, if I recall. Here, hand me some."

Together they skimmed the letters, until something gave James reason to pause.

"Look." He held out the letter so Shepard could see it and pointed to the lines that caught his eye. "Read here."

Don't forget. You must act quickly. You must hold her at bay for the full three years. After that, the land will be yours, and it can be sold. You—we—will be very wealthy, my boy. But keep a keen eye out. Situations like this can change very quickly.

Shepard took the letter and lowered it. "I'd say your suspicion was right."

"Yes, but it doesn't tie him to Longham's murder."

"But it is suspicious enough for me to bring him in, and I'm the magistrate."

James handed the remaining letters over to Shepard. "Strange that these candles are lit and no one is home. Do you think he knows we're here?"

"Perhaps he ran off when he saw us. He's not a foolish man. No, it seems he's quite clever. Tricked us all, eh?" Shepard tucked the letters into his coat. "I'm taking these to read further, and I'm going to the Green Ox Inn. Someone there is bound to have seen him, and I'll fetch the constable to assist. You go home and let me know if you hear anything. But I'd be careful if I were you. If our suspicions are right, this man is willing to murder to keep his secrets. Best keep an eye out."

Chapter 42

In her heart Cassandra now knew that Mr. North had to
be behind this.

How gullible she'd been!

All of the signs pointed to it—all of the subtle hints he'd fed her.
He clearly did not care for her as he had projected. He was keeping
an eye on her, determined to find out what she knew and to prevent
her from learning the truth.

Yes, she'd been naive. But instead of feeling sad or embarrassed,
she felt anger brimming within her and fueling her steps.

With a candle in her hand, she made her way down to James's
study, intending to retrieve the letters Mrs. Denton had sent her
father and reread them.

But as she entered the darkened study, she froze.

Mr. North was sitting behind James's desk, his hair disheveled,
his posture slack, and his torqued expression desperate.

He lifted a pistol directly at her.

Should she scream? Cry? Run?

Shock threatened to silence her, and yet her voice squeaked out.
"What on earth are you doing?"

He eased to his feet, his pistol still steady. "I wouldn't make a
single noise if I were you. Not a peep. Close the door."

Hands trembling and without taking her eyes off him, she obeyed.

"Now that we are alone, why don't you put down that candle, sit down, and we'll have a little chat."

Resisting the urge to panic, Cassandra complied. It would not do to lose her head.

The simmering fire's light reflected orange onto his features. Stubble grew on his normally clean-shaven jaw and sweat glistened on his pallid brow. "Shepard and your beau entered my house. Why?"

She shook her head. "I—I don't know."

"I don't believe you," he spat back. "Why don't you try answering me again."

She summoned courage. "I know what you did."

"Oh, you do?" He chuckled. "And what was that?"

"You knew about me. You knew I was Robert Clark's daughter from the beginning."

"Of course I did. I've seen the will. And I was at Robert Clark's deathbed. Of course I was. I'm the vicar. Men talk on their deathbed. They talk about their regrets. And he talked about you."

Rage seethed. "Why did you try to hide it?"

"I think you know the answer to that question, don't you?"

"Your uncle is Edward Stricklin, isn't he?"

"Yes, he is. I'm Stricklin's heir." He flung his arms out, as if amused. "I'm the heir to an inheritance that is entirely dependent upon a young chit never showing up to claim it."

"So you weren't being kind to me at all. You were trying to prevent me from finding this out."

"You are the clever one." Sarcasm dripped from his tone. "To be honest, I thought you would have figured it out long before this."

"But why are you here then?"

"Because you are costing me a considerable fortune. That land is mine. Clark owed it to my family. To me. My birthright." His tone darkened. "I will get what is owed to me."

"But I have no money. You, more than anyone, know that."

"No, you don't. But your suitor does."

"James has nothing to do with this."

"*James*, is it? Well, well. It must be more serious than I thought. But believe me when I say that I'll get the money I am owed, one way or another."

She stared at him. Perspiration beaded on her brow, and her breath started to heave in ragged puffs. The reality of the situation, and the truth about how sinister this man was, sank in deeper with each second.

He lifted the pistol once again in a dramatic display, as if taking aim. "Let's just wait to see what *James* has to say about that."

James and his horse thundered back over the bridge, slicing through the fog, every hoofbeat echoing from the canopy of bare branches and midnight sky. The constable and magistrate were organizing a search for the vicar. His own pulse was racing. He intended to help them with the search. Right after he retrieved his pistol.

Once he arrived in the courtyard, he slid from his horse and jogged to the house and into the corridor toward his study to retrieve it from the chest. The memory of the horrible incident of finding Longham's body flamed anew. It was not safe while he was out there, vicar or not.

James flung open his study door, but the sight that met him stunned him into stillness.

Cassandra was seated in a chair.

And Mr. North was pointing a pistol at her.

She gazed at him, wide-eyed and pale, but said nothing.

"What are you doing?" James demanded when his words finally returned.

"Did you find what you were looking for?" North asked, his voice unnervingly calm.

James huffed. "What are you talking about?"

"In the vicarage. I saw you. And Shepard. You seemed quite intent upon finding something. So I ask, did you find it?"

"We know what's happened, North. We know you were involved in Longham's death. The best thing you can do now is stop this nonsense."

North chuckled. "That is where you and I differ, Warrington. I see this as exactly the opportunity to right what has been wronged."

At the sight of Cassandra's fear, fresh anger seared through him. He would not argue with this man. Not while he had a pistol pointed at Cassandra. "What is it you want?"

"My inheritance. *Mine*."

"That doesn't make sense."

"Oh, it makes all the sense in the world. Rest assured, I will get what I am owed. You will see to that. You're going to give me the equivalent."

"No, I'm not."

"Aren't you?" North lifted the pistol again and clicked his tongue. "A pity. I guess she'll just have to come with me until I feel compensated, one way or the other. But if we leave, you must know you will never hear from either of us again. So what will it be?"

The reality of this man's vile words sank in. "You would never get away with something like that."

North jerked Cassandra up by the arm.

Fresh fear flashed across her features.

James took a step forward, and North tightened his grip on her.

He had to think. His couldn't reach his pistol. He had some money he could give him and Elizabeth's jewelry, but it was nowhere near the amount the land was worth. He had to try. "There, there is my strongbox. Behind you. I'll open it. The contents are yours."

Suddenly a high-pitched voice cried from the chamber's entrance, "Let her go!"

They all whirled to see Rachel in the doorway, a pistol of her own pointed at North.

A flurry of activity burst forth.

Cassandra, taking advantage of the break in concentration, pushed on North's arm, shoving the pistol upward.

It discharged and a bullet hit the ceiling. Plaster rained down on them in heavy, powdery chards.

Cassandra then bit North's hand. He howled.

Seizing his opportunity, James lunged toward North and shoved him to the ground, pinning him until he could smack the gun away.

Cassandra grabbed the dropped pistol and then rushed to Rachel.

With the weapon eliminated the men continued to fight. They were physically evenly matched, until at length, James landed a punch on North's jaw and he fell back, stunned. James lunged forward again, turned North over, and pinned his arms behind him. He thrashed, but James's grip was firm.

"A rope, quickly!"

Within minutes Rachel returned with a curtain tie. With Cassandra pointing the gun at North, James secured him to the chair, and then he took control of the gun from Cassandra.

"Well," James huffed, his breath heavy from the exertion, forcing North's stare. "It seems we've had quite the turn of events."

Chapter 43

It was nearing dawn when Shepard and two constables finally quit Briarton Park with Mr. North in tow. Fog curtained the courtyard, and as Cassandra inched closer to James, she could feel his warmth.

He wrapped his arm around her shoulders, and she leaned into him.

It was over.

Mr. North—Mr. Longham's murderer—was being taken into custody by the authorities, and James Warrington—the man who now held her future—stood strong next to her.

"So Robert Clark's deathbed confession was at the root of all of this." James shook his head. "Unbelievable."

Cassandra tightened her shawl as she considered Mr. North's admission of guilt to the magistrate. His secrets had been found out, and he could not escape them or, in the end, even deny them. Among his belongings on his person at the time of arrest was some of the paperwork from Mr. Longham's satchel. The irrefutable evidence compelled Mr. North to confess.

"It's criminal how he abused his office in such a manner," she said. "Mr. North must have known about it before he even came to Anston. So many people trusted him. *I* trusted him."

"Yes, he was aware of the inheritance. He had to have been. Shepard and I found letters from his aunt—Alice Stricklin—verifying it. Vicar or not, he is still a man, susceptible to all the same manner of temptations everyone else faces."

"Yes, but he was not strong enough to resist them," she said softly before her thoughts turned to the gentleman who had been so helpful to her. "Poor Mr. Longham."

"It's a tragedy, but at least justice will be served. Shepard will see to that. North will pay for what he has done to Longham, to you, and to others." James reached his hand to her. "Come. Let's go inside."

She looked at the man who held her heart, and warmth flooded her. His cheek was already bruising from the blows he took from North, and the wind whipped his sandy hair about his face, but to her, he'd never looked more handsome. More captivating. More like home. She tucked her fingers in his outstretched hand, and together they crossed to the door.

Once inside, they turned into the study, where Rachel, whose brave actions had helped save them both, was seated.

"Is he gone?" Rachel jumped to her feet, energized.

Cassandra embraced the young woman. "Yes, he's gone. Thanks, in part, to you and your quick thinking."

"Why were you in the corridor at that hour?" asked James, hands akimbo. "And how did you know where to find the pistol?"

Rachel shrugged. "Like I told you, Mrs. Towler had awoken, and that's why I came down to find you. But then I heard your voices, and after listening for a few minutes, I figured you needed help. Mrs. Helock always keeps a pistol in the kitchen for defense. I just got it and pointed it. I have no idea how to use it."

James laughed. "Well, thankfully you were there. It was just the distraction we needed."

Cassandra removed her shawl and placed it on a chair, then turned back to Rachel. "You said Mrs. Towler is awake. How is she?"

"Yes. And she seems fine, just tired. Mrs. Helock is with her now."

"Good. We should all get some rest after such an ordeal," James said to his sister. "You'd best go to bed now. You must be exhausted."

"I am." Rachel embraced Cassandra and kissed her brother on the cheek, then she sobered. "You know, I really am sorry for the trouble I caused with Richard. I love you both, even if my actions make you question it."

James reached an arm out to hug her and kissed the top of her curly head. "Love you too."

Rachel departed from the study, leaving James and Cassandra alone in the early morning stillness. She glanced around the room at the scene where one of the most dramatic events ever to occur in her life had taken place. Plaster still covered the area from the gunshot that hit the ceiling. Candlelight illuminated an overturned chair and the stacks of paper that had been scattered during the fight. She absently rubbed her wrists where Mr. North had grabbed her.

"Does it hurt?" James asked, moving closer.

"No, not really. It's just so strange."

He took her hand and raised it, then pressed a soft kiss to her wrist. "I've never been so scared as when I came in and saw him with that pistol aimed at you."

She leaned into his embrace and rested her cheek against his shoulder, relaxing into the comfort she found there. "And what would I have done if you'd not arrived?"

He wrapped his arms around her. "I've already lost love once to death. I could not have handled it happening again."

At his mention of love, she lifted her head to meet his tender gaze.

He brushed her hair from her face and let his finger linger against her cheek. "I fear tonight has changed everything. Forever."

Her head felt light at the words. Her heart, full.

"I hope you're not too disappointed with the way everything has turned out. You came here searching for family. It was not what you expected, but I hope you still think you've found your family. With us. With me."

Cassandra set her hands on his chest and toyed with the fabric-covered button of his coat. "I did come here in search of family. And I found it, didn't I? I know my mother, my father, and even that I have half brothers. But what I now realize is that I was really looking for love and acceptance. And I found it with you. And the girls. And I hope you have found it with me."

Then he pressed his lips to her ear. "Marry me, Cassandra. Please say you will. I cannot live another day without knowing you will be part of my forever."

A tear slid down her cheek. She inched back, studying his face, the depths of his gray eyes. An earnestness and desperation that matched her own simmered there. Every emotion had registered in her over the past night, but now, as his hand caressed her cheek, she knew her heart was forever his. "Yes, James. Oh yes!"

He kissed her, and his ardent strength intoxicated her. "Can you see yourself spending your life here? With me?"

She smoothed an unruly lock of hair away from his brow. "I can see my life wherever you are."

He laughed and shook his head. "You know what everyone will say, of course. That I am marrying you for the land. Now that all of this business is settled, you will be a very important lady around here."

She returned his playful smile. "And why do you want to marry me?"

He studied her face, the fullness of her lips, the curve of her cheek, and then he sobered. "I suppose I would have to say that it's because of this charming slope of your nose, or the delightful dimple beside your mouth, or because you carry a dagger in your boot. Or because you make me feel whole after feeling empty for what seems an eternity. And why would you, an heiress, want to marry someone like me?"

Her thoughts rushed within her, and she smoothed his rumpled cravat before lifting her face to his. "That very first day when I arrived at Briarton, you were everything I thought a country gentleman would be like. Handsome, aloof, so certain. I remember wondering how it would be to have a man like that care for me. But then the more I got to know you, I found you weren't aloof after all. You trusted me in spite of all that was against me. And you protected me, even when I might not have wanted it. You, Mr. Warrington, are the dream I never thought I could have."

Fire pummeled through James's veins as Cassandra disappeared down the corridor.

She had agreed to marry him!

He hadn't expected to propose to her right there and then. But he could not resist her allure. She was inebriating, and he didn't want to part from her.

But she'd said yes. She would be his wife. Forever.

One day they would not have to part at the day's end. They would be together with the sunrise of every morning and at the close of each day.

He forced his fingers through his hair as he considered the events. It seemed every day since Cassandra arrived had brought change and growth, and he could only wonder what the next days would bring, for all of them.

He made his way up to the family chambers. He should try to catch a little sleep, for he doubted the next day would bring much rest. But there was one thing he still needed to do.

Rachel had said Mrs. Towler had gained consciousness.

And he was relieved, but as he arrived outside of Mrs. Towler's room, he paused.

The thought of Elizabeth flashed in his mind, as she did so often.

He had no doubt that Elizabeth would approve of Cassandra, but her mother was another matter. He wanted to handle this situation with respect and compassion, but he was sailing in uncharted territory. She'd been ill, and he did not want to upset her, but he also did not want her to find out from someone else about his relationship with Cassandra.

He found Mrs. Towler propped up on her pillows. She was pale, and yet she appeared healthier than she had in days, perhaps even weeks. She was dressed in her nightclothes. How strange it was to see her in the cream linen instead of the black she had worn since Elizabeth died. Even the white cap atop her wiry hair altered her appearance significantly. Mrs. Helock was sitting next to her. He cleared his throat to garner her attention.

"Ah, James." Mrs. Towler waved her hand toward Mrs. Helock. "Leave us, please. I wish to speak with my son-in-law."

He stood in silence as the housekeeper exited the room, and then he stepped closer to the bed. "You gave us quite a fright."

"A fright? Bah. It's nothing compared to hearing a pistol discharged in one's own home. Mrs. Helock told me everything. And Rachel brandishing a pistol! Why, I've never heard the like."

"It's all over now." He moved a candle closer to the bed. "Nothing to worry about."

"Nothing to worry about? I hear that North fellow broke into our home and tried to attack Miss Hale. I never did like him."

James laughed. "No, you did not."

"That's not all I heard about Miss Hale." She raised her brow. "Sit down, James. We need to talk."

"Perhaps we should wait until you are stronger. You've had an—"

"No. It cannot wait."

Bracing himself, he pulled a chair from against the wall and carried it next to the canopied bed.

"Mrs. Helock tells me that Miss Hale sat with me and helped out while I was indisposed."

He nodded. "She did. She was concerned about you. We all were. We still are."

James could see the battle warring within her. Mrs. Towler was the proudest woman he'd ever met. And yet, whether as a result of the illness or just recent events, the usual harsh lines of her face seemed softer.

"I also understand the two of you shared a very public display of affection in the courtyard. In front of the magistrate. In front of the servants."

He had not even had time to plan out the words. It was all so new still. He remained silent.

"James. I am nearing sixty years of age, and I do realize how close I was to death." She fixed her eyes on him. "I'll not wait to right wrongs. First of all, I need you to know that I am grateful to you. You did not have to allow me to stay with your family after Elizabeth's death. I recognize that it has not always been easy. You are a good father to my grandchildren."

He remained silent, knowing how hard those words were for her to say.

"Perhaps I have not made the transition as easily as I could have. I've lost my daughter, but I know things are changing. I don't want to lose my granddaughters too."

"I miss Elizabeth," he admitted. "I miss her every day. I think about her and wonder what she would think about our daughters. Our life. About me. I will always love her, but she would not want us to grieve forever. I'll not rob my daughters of having a mother figure in their lives, and I will not deny myself happiness. Elizabeth would not have wanted that. You and I both know it to be true."

He expected her to protest, to argue, but she did not. Instead, she tilted her head to the side. "I think about her every day too. I see her in the girls. And I see how happy they have been since Miss Hale's arrival. I may be stubborn, but I can admit when I've been wrong. I don't want to be sad anymore. I don't want to be angry."

"Nothing will change," he said, reading the thread of worry in her expression. "You are the girls' grandmother, and you have a home here. Always."

She stared down at her hands. "What is it that you are not telling me?"

"Miss Hale and I are to be married."

Initially she said nothing. But then she reached for his hand with her withered one. "I could tell by the way the two of you looked at each other, that very first day in the hall, that a connection was developing between you. At first it frightened me. Made me angry that you would forget Elizabeth."

He opened his mouth to protest, but she held up her hand. "But I was wrong."

She stopped short of apologizing. And at this he could almost laugh. Apologies were not in her nature.

"I will never forget Elizabeth. Ever. But Cassandra is a gift. A second chance to feel alive again. We have the opportunity for a great many fresh beginnings here. For everyone under this roof." He sniffed. "Now, the surgeon told us you will recover, but he stressed that you need rest."

"Very well. But do send the girls in once they have woken for the day. I wish to see them."

"I will."

"And, James," she said, a rare smile quirking the corner of her mouth. "I am happy for you."

Epilogue

Cassandra adjusted the reins in her gloved hands and surveyed the scene before her. Grassy land swept down to the river banks, and just beyond it stood Clark Mill, rising up in a tower of red brick and smoke.

So this was it—Linderdale. This was the portion her father had set aside for her.

James drew his horse to a halt next to her, dismounted, and turned to help her down from the sidesaddle. "So, what do you think of your first riding lesson, Mrs. Warrington?"

Mrs. Warrington.

How her heart leapt whenever he called her by that name. It still seemed like an impossible dream.

Once her booted feet were firmly on the ground, Cassandra adjusted the folds of her emerald wool riding habit around her. "It's wonderful. And not as difficult as I thought."

"See? I knew you'd enjoy it, and soon it will be second nature. You live in the countryside now, my love. Riding is an essential skill."

"It'll take practice." She laughed as she shifted her riding crop from one hand to the other and patted the horse with her gloved hand. "Maria and Rose are already both better than I am."

James took her hand in his and pivoted to survey the landscape. "Well, there it is. How does it feel to be an heiress?"

He swung his arm out wide to point out the land. "Linderdale. As far as you can see, to that stretch of trees in the distance, belongs to you."

"To *us*, you mean." She looked down to the bright green summer grass beneath her feet. This was what her father had wanted her to have. Security.

Cassandra gripped her husband's hand tighter as she turned to look down toward Clark Mill.

"I only wish Peter would consent to speak with me. I understand his anger, I do. But he is still my brother. And that was all I wanted, to know my family."

"Give him time. This is all still fairly new, and he's a proud man. Besides, he has a significant inheritance in his own right. And you have other family now too. At least your mother has consented to see you more regularly."

Cassandra wrapped her hand around his offered arm. "Yes. I never would have imagined it could turn into such a lovely relationship. And brothers! I often wonder what Mrs. Denton would have thought about how the situation played out. She tried so hard to keep this all from me. And in the end, here I am."

"I think she would be glad you have found happiness."

"But at the expense of Peter Clark? Her nephew?"

James shrugged. "I never met her, of course, but everything you say about her, the way you describe your relationship—she must have loved you. Of course she would want you to be happy."

"And I am happy," she said confidently. "When she died, I thought I would never find happiness again. Isn't it amazing to think how one man's decisions, one man's actions, have affected so many? Even in Father's death, his actions continued to affect everyone. Even Mrs. Denton's actions, for that matter."

He nodded. "Yes. But in the end everything turned out as it should. If it didn't, you and I might not be here now. We've found each other, through the twists and turns. But now we can put all of that behind us and focus on the future." He lifted her hand to his lips and kissed it. "This time last year, I had no idea what was in store for me. How you would change my life, and the girls' lives, for the better."

Maria and Rose were a part of her now. "I do love them. And Rachel. I thought I might never have a family, but now I've a full one."

"Maybe one day we'll have a child of our own."

Her heart fluttered at the mention. She'd never really allowed herself to think that thought before, but as she settled into life with James as her husband, new dreams were beginning to flourish.

The conversation of family brought Mrs. Towler to mind. "I forgot to tell you that I received a letter from Mrs. Towler earlier today."

"You did?"

"Yes. She said she is settled with her cousin. It was a short letter, of course, but it was good to hear from her."

"I sincerely hope she is able to find happiness and contentment. She has had a rough couple of years."

"She indicated that her health continues to improve and that she plans to return to Briarton at summer's end. I hope that means she is accepting of us."

"She will be. In time. Elizabeth was her life. She needs to find new adventures and carve out her own future."

The wind intensified, and Cassandra lifted her hand to still her hair whipping around her riding habit hat. "As much as I wish we could stay here forever, we should get back. Rachel will be wondering where we are. Betsy will be over soon. You know, her wedding will be here before we know it. It is so nice to have such things to anticipate, isn't it?"

"That happened fast."

Cassandra laughed. "She was never shy about it, and she always said she would jump at the first man who showed an interest. Who would have thought the interim curate would catch her eye?"

"When is the wedding again?"

"When the new vicar comes. In three weeks."

"Ah." James chuckled. "North's replacement."

"He's all Mrs. Pearson can talk about. She's still beside herself since all of that business with Mr. North, even after all these months. It will do her good to have someone else on whom to focus."

"Vincent North. Good riddance. What a fool he was. It was his loss, of course," James said with a grin, "because I think you could have fallen for him. Just a little."

"Me? Fancy Mr. North?" She turned to face him and wrap her arms around his neck. "No, no. It was you, my darling. Always you. And it always will be."

She pivoted to leave, and he playfully grabbed her by the hand and whirled her back into his arms.

She giggled at the affectionate display. "Yes?"

"I just want a few more moments alone with my wife before we return." He brushed her hair from her face, as he had done so many times. "In case I haven't told you lately, Mrs. Warrington, I adore you."

Cassandra had always wondered what it would feel like to have a home. To belong somewhere and with someone. As he drew her near and kissed her, Cassandra knew this was what she had been waiting for. And she never wanted to let go.

Acknowledgments

Writing a book is a journey, and each one is unique and special. This one was no different! It is far from a solitary endeavor, and I am thankful for the people who came alongside me to help this story take shape.

To my family—I am so grateful for your support and encouragement. Thank you!

To my agent, Rachelle Gardner—your guidance and advice is second to none. What would I do without you?

To my editor, Becky Monds, and to my line editor, Julee Schwarzburg—you two are amazing. To the rest of the team at HarperCollins Christian Publishing—thank you for all you do.

And last but not least, to KBR and KC—onward!

Discussion Questions

1. At the beginning of the novel, Cassandra learned that someone she trusted had lied to her, and it changed the course of her life. Have you ever found yourself in a similar situation? If so, how did it affect your life?

2. If you had to pick only three words to describe Cassandra's character, what would they be? What three words would you use to describe James?

3. In the story, James feels honor bound to care for his mother-in-law after his wife's death. Do his actions honor his late wife?

4. Let's chat about Mr. North. In the end, we learn that he is not who he seemed to be in the beginning of the book. Have you ever known someone like him?

5. If you could give Cassandra one piece of advice at the beginning of the story, what would it be? What advice would you give her at the end?

6. Do you have a favorite character in this book? If so, who is it, and what drew you to that person? Who is your least favorite?

7. Mrs. Denton told Cassandra the following: *"Emotions will*

only cloud your judgment and weaken your ability to react
rationally." Do you agree with this statement? Why or
why not?

8. At different points in the story, Cassandra faces rejection.
How does it shape her character? How does it affect her
decisions?

9. It's your turn! What comes next for Cassandra and James? If
you could write the sequel, what would happen?

THE CORNWALL NOVELS

Set in the same time period as *Poldark*
and *Bridgerton*, these stories are rich
with family secrets, lingering danger, and
the captivating allure of new love.

"*Northanger Abbey* meets *Poldark* against the resplendent and beautifully realized landscape of Cornwall. Ladd shines a spotlight on the limitations of women in an era where they were deprived of agency and instead were commodities in transactions of business and land. The thinking-woman's romance, *The Thief of Lanwyn Manor* is an unputdownable escape."

—RACHEL McMILLAN, AUTHOR OF *THE LONDON RESTORATION*

THOMAS NELSON
Since 1798

About the Author

Photo by Emilie Haney of EAH Creative

Sarah E. Ladd is an award-winning, bestselling author who has always loved the Regency period—the clothes, the music, the literature, and the art. A college trip to England and Scotland confirmed her interest, and she began seriously writing in 2010. Since then, she has released several novels set during the Regency era. Sarah is a graduate of Ball State University and holds degrees in public relations and marketing. She lives in Indiana with her family.

Visit Sarah online at SarahLadd.com
Instagram: @sarahladdauthor
Facebook: @SarahLaddAuthor
Twitter: @SarahLaddAuthor
Pinterest: @SarahLaddAuthor